To: Nat

Land Of The Giants

Hope you Enjoy!

Author: M. E. Nevill

Sincerely Marie Nevill

D1445740

Chapter 1

Christine Bennett walked along a slatted wood dock that separated two fingerling ponds. A noise drew her attention from the school of tiny bass that would be released into nearby Indian Creek after reaching the juvenile stage. There, they would grow to the meatier size Christine had bred them to be. It was a slapping sound. Perhaps a fish nipping at a bug hovering above the water. The frogs and crickets were ordinarily at full chorus by this late hour, but they were unusually quiet. "But it is a chilly January night," she whispered to them, as if they could hear her, and pulled her jacket and hood tighter around her tall slender figure and red hair. The Woodlands Fish Hatchery has fifty-three acres of fishponds and culture operations. It performs artificial cross breeding, hatching, and rearing through early life stages and employs two people. Christine often worked much later than her young coworker, Jeff Hudson. The forty-nine-year-old wife and mother of two, took the crossbreeding seriously. Her inventiveness had led to the creation of fifteen new species of fish, three variations of alligator and five types of snapping turtle.

"Is that you?" she whispered when she heard a louder noise. It was behind her this time, in front of the tackle shack, not far from the walkway that led to the dock. She quickly backtracked and disappeared around the corner of the metal building. There was a sudden swishing noise, a grunt and then a growl that seemed cut short. Jeff Hudson clocked out at seven p.m. that evening. That was the last time Jeff, or police detectives via security video saw Christine Bennett.

Camp Livingston is a former WWII army training post near Pineville, Louisiana that ceased full military operations after the world wars and the Korean War. It is now training grounds for the Louisiana National Guard. When someone started the rumor of a strange sighting there, Mary Lynn Bennett, who was sixteen at the time, and her squad of rowdies valiantly drove out to the post that was also part of Kisatchie National Forest to watch for the legendary hairy figure known as *Big Foot* and listen for its reported cries. Of course, there was alcohol and pot involved, and a lot of giggling and screeching at every noise coming from the dense woods and the crew soon moved on to the next dramatic adventure when nothing surfaced as drama-seeking teenagers often do.

Those carefree days of high school partying were long gone. Life took a grave turn for Mary Lynn and her family in the middle of her second semester at LSUA where she was taking classes to earn an Associate Degree in Nursing. Her mother, Christine had gone missing, presumedly on her way home from work at Woodlands Fish Hatchery, twenty miles south of Alexandria. The Bennett family subsequently went through hell because the police immediately focused on her father Al Bennett, as a person of interest while they searched the thirty-mile radius surrounding Christine Bennett's abandoned SUV that was found 10 minutes from the fish hatchery on the side of Hwy 112 near the small rural town of Lecompte. Security cameras revealed nothing. Jeff Hudson had gone straight home and stayed there according to the GPS tracking on his phone and truck. Bloodhounds and hundreds of volunteers combed every inch of ground, which included creeks and sloughs, barns and abandoned trailers. They found nothing; not a single shred of evidence or scent. Three weeks later, a bloodstained Woodlands smock with her nametag attached turned up hanging over a dumpster in Jasper, Texas. Another week went by when a man called to repair an air-conditioner found her purse on the roof of a Taco Bell in Marshall with only her driver's license inside. Al was eventually eliminated because it was deemed impossible to have dumped evidence over the combined three-hundred-mile distance while under constant scrutiny of the district attorney's office. Regrettably, all the suspicious lowlifes that detectives managed to round up for questioning had alibis. Rumors continued to flourish however, because Al was a deputy sheriff at the time and many suspected Jack Warner, the Rapides Parish Sheriff at the time, was protecting his cousin and boyhood friend.

Mary Lynn went on to earn a bachelor degree in Nursing and passed the National Council Licensure Exam, as her mother would have wanted and was now a practicing RN at Rapides General Medical Center (RRMC) in Alexandria. From the earliest years, Christine was her guiding light, her strength, the person she looked to for answers, especially when the disorder she was born with sent her into despair. Their resemblance was uncanny. Both were strikingly beautiful, tall, fair skinned, with red hair and blue eyes. Mary Lynn's appearance took on a look of defiance as she tried to mimic her mother's strong will and unnerved demeanor. The disorder allowed her to see colorful auras that surround every living being. It was frightfully distracting at times. Her mother insisted she keep the gift God gave her a secret; to straighten her back and learn to live with it, which she did.

Al Bennett retired from the department when a two-month leave of absence gave him no solace. He leased sixty acres in the Catahoula Wildlife Management Area, located in a northeast area of the state, and became a recluse, determined to spend the rest of his life alone fishing and hunting and living off the land; away from the gossip and accusing stares. Mary Lynn's brother Dale, who was seven years her senior, couldn't tolerate living amongst incompetent civic leaders. Detectives, the district attorney, even the mayor, honed in on his father. In his mind they had cast aside other possible suspects, including Jeff Hudson, who was rumored to have a record of some kind. Disgruntled, he packed up and moved to Georgia.

Harrison Foster was a lab tech at RRMC and Mary Lynn's friend since the fifth grade. He had been an active participant in all her boogieman hunts, including the one in Camp Livingston, every cemetery exploration and haunted house, abandoned or otherwise, that the party-hearty group got wind of; and there are hundreds of them in and around Rapides Parish. He was there for the weekend bonfires on the beach at Cotile Lake, trolling the Alexandria Mall until Security ran them off and drag racing on Hwy 28 east of Pineville. He was also among the hundreds of volunteers that searched for Christine Bennett. He'd sat at the Bennett supper table every evening since he was ten and was every bit as despairing over the kidnapping. Being a skinny kid, Christine gave him larger portions at the dinner table and kept one end of the kitchen table cleared during school months, designating it as his place to do homework. He might never have had the incentive to go to college if it weren't for the Bennett's kindness and taking up the slack where his own mother's supervisory skills fell short. His drunken father was killed in a bar fight when he was six leaving his under-educated mother alone to find menial work. Eventually, she ran off with a bull-rider when the Wild West Pro Rodeo, based in Silver City, New Mexico came through town. Mary Lynn's rebelliousness captivated him. He followed her everywhere hoping to absorb some of the confidence she displayed in spite of their shared desperation to fit in. Having no parents made him shy and a target for bullies. Mary Lynn's secret kept her in constant defense mode. Christine decided that Harry, and only Harry should share in the knowledge of her disorder because of their closeness, making him swear that he would look out for her, while not truly understanding why he was allowed such knowledge and not Al or Dale, or anyone else. It fascinated him, the way she could see someone's strengths or weaknesses by the color outline they projected. Harry earned a medical laboratory technician associate's degree from LSUA, completed science and liberal arts courses, and interned a year at RRMC. Not until recently had he stumbled onto Synesthesia, the medical term for Mary Lynn's unusual and most likely inherited condition according to Psychology Today. The remarkable trait kept them out of trouble when shop lifting junk food, cigarettes and beer from convenience stores. She was both perpetrator and lookout.

It seemed people forgot about Christine's abduction; at least it was rarely spoken of anymore. Robberies, shootings, drug activity, and other atrocious crimes in the central Louisiana parish had increased tenfold over the years. It had long since been pushed to somewhere at the bottom of the so-called pile of unsolved cases. A whole new generation, layered with different interests and problems had emerged that cared little about the Christine Bennett disappearance. The trauma the family endured left her with nightmares and PTSD, but Mary Lynn did her best to soldier on.

Mary Lynn had mellowed somewhat after years of living-on-the-edge but still found impulsiveness a reliable tactic when necessary to mask the anxiety her disquieting gift generated. Being a nurse seemed to calm the angst of the burdensome oddity. Caring for people soothed the menacing demon. The secret talent inadvertently made her a valued RN. Doctors and patients both referred to her as "the red-headed angel" because of her obvious red hair and because she seemed to appear from out of nowhere when they needed her the most. Blood pressure, heart rhythm, fever, even pain mysteriously improved the moment she picked up their hand. A few doctors at RRMC recognized the special empathy and were encouraging her to go for an advanced practice degree.

Dale was now married to Aria, a Georgia native, and father to a four and six-year-old boy and girl and the owner of a successful contracting business. Mary Lynn tried to visit at least once a year, usually over the holidays because her brother had sworn never to set foot in Louisiana again. Not that Georgia was devoid of its share of unsolved cases; he felt his sanity depended on separating himself from the daily reminders of what he considered an incompetent sheriff's department. She dated from time to time, even came close to getting married once until she realized it wouldn't be fair to commit anyone to her weirdness and the sadness she carried. Maybe she should have put the blame for the fruitless investigation in an anger box like Dale and blame the system. Christine would not have wanted that from her daughter, being that she was a faithful Sunday school teacher and found answers to all of life's tribulations in the white leather Bible she carried. Her mother was the most confident person she knew and someone had to hold down the home front in her place. It was a crushing burden sometimes. Nevertheless, her best friend Harry was the world's best listener.

Chapter 2

Every six weeks or so, Mary Lynn and Harrison braved the barely navigable back woods roads of the Catahoula Wildlife Management Area to check on her father.

"I don't know what I'd do without you Harry," she said on a September evening as they bounced along the washed-out tire tracks that were more suited for an ATV than Harry's Toyota Tacoma. Her ponytail flowed out the back of her purple LSUA cap reflecting slices of amber off the afternoon sunlight. "You're the only person I know that I can depend on."

"Then I guess it was a good thing for you that the Bennett's took me in." His voice quivered as the wheels ran over a patch of ground that felt like a washboard. Harry was conservative and shy, a result of being picked on by his peers most of his life. He was respectful and dependable and had a hidden audacious personality, a trait Mary Lynn helped him develop, purely for selfish reasons. A united front was required when talking their way out of trouble. Such resourcefulness had earned him a nice position in the lab at RRMC. He preferred Docker jeans to Mary Lynn's ripped Levi's, Timberland hiking boots to tennis shoes and a cap carrying a logo of current events. Today's was black with a yellow lightning bolt and *Lab Tech Wizard* stitched across the top that he pulled down over his neatly trimmed brown hair. He tried growing a mustache once while in college, but the splotches of hair were embarrassingly scant.

"Even Daddy likes you, and he doesn't like anybody anymore." Mary Lynn lowered her eyes, thinking of how more soured his disposition was becoming every year.

"Well, I learned how to call Al's bluff a long time ago," Harry joked and waited for her to look at him with her incredible blue eyes. As a result, he lost his grip on the steering wheel when it suddenly jerked to the right and the left front wheel fell into a deep rut along the rarely driven excuse for a road. "Awe, look at how thick the foliage is," he groaned after bouncing out of the hole. "We may have to machete our way in next time." Green and yellow leaves on thin limbs and gray moss flashed against the windshield as he gingerly rolled forward.

"Did you see that new hunter check-in building we passed at the turn-in?" Mary Lynn asked. "I wonder how long it's been here." She flinched when a cordon of stems abruptly appeared on the glass in front of her.

"It's one of those skidded manufactured buildings that can be unloaded off the back of a truck," Harry replied. "I hope that means someone will be maintaining the area, cut back this overgrowth and hey, maybe even check on your dad."

"That would be great; but I didn't see anyone, not even a simple glow. There's a padlock on the door and a sign; we can check for a contact number on the way out."

"Okay, we walk from here," Harry sighed after rolling the Tacoma to a stop. He scanned the woods for animal movement through the windshield before turning off the headlights. Sometimes when dusk cast its shadows, they could see sets of eyes staring back at them. Mary Lynn saw much more of course, like the subtle heat signature of an armadillo or raccoon and occasionally a deer. "There's one of my flags." He stepped out of the truck and shined a flashlight in the top of a tree."

"Don't forget the bug spray," she moaned and gingerly set her pink Nike's on the ground as if trying to keep from disturbing the pesky insects that were surely lying in wait within the vines that crept along the ground. In the humid summer months, the air and ground sparkled like glitter off the mosquitoes or moths and night crawlers.

"You should wear boots when we come up here instead of those flimsy tennis shoes." This was something Harry told her every trip. "Just wait till you step on a copperhead or rattle snake. I'll have to rush you to the nearest hospital that's in Jonesville that I doubt has a poison center."

"Harry, my God!" she groaned. "That's not gonna happen. Now let's go."

A short walk brought them to a familiar landmark, a dead pine tree lying across a barely visible trail. Mary Lynn had carved their initials in it six years ago while Harry was busy pressing one-half-inch red reflective buttons into trees with push pins to mark the trail to Al's camp. A flashlight lighted similarly pinned green reflectors on the opposite side should their stay extend past sundown.

"I'll stoke up the fire." Harry was the first to breach the thirty-foot clearing that was Al's homestead since moving out of the house on Hartwood.

"Wonder where he's off to?" Mary Lynn followed him through the shrubs. Everything looked the same as the last time they visited. The twelve-foot camper he pulled onto the site bordered the left side, a couple of tents and a twenty-by-twenty log cabin with a barricaded door formed the north and east perimeter. A neatly stacked cord of firewood completed the boundary of the estate. Four canvas chairs stood folded upright a few feet from a fire ring made of stacked flat stones. "Out hunting, I guess," she sighed, answering her own question after examining the coals in the fire pit.

Harry grabbed a stick and stoked the charred wood until a small bed of hidden red embers blinked through the white ash. "Been gone for a while, most of the coals have gone dark." He broke two small limbs abundant with pine needles and placed them over the hidden smolder creating a rush of gray and white smoke, a signal to Al they were there.

"Hope he's okay," Mary Lynn sighed. She unfolded one of the chairs and dragged it a short distance from the pit that Harry was bringing back to life.

"You're gonna want to scoot a little closer if we're still here after dark. It gets cold out here at night."

"Ha-Ha! Funny, I don't think so," she replied. "You know very well how I am about the heat."

Of course, he knew how sensitive she was to heat. He was the only person who could make light of her eccentricities and make her laugh at herself. Anyone else's remarks she took as criticisms and left her secretly mortified or openly defiant. They chatted about patients and gossiped about coworkers while shiny birds fluttered through the trees and yellow squirrels chattered around them. A sudden rustling noise just outside the camp boundary quickly silenced their conversation. A low growling sound brought them to their feet. A large black dog burst through the shrubs and trotted toward them. Harry grabbed Mary Lynn by the arm and pulled her out of the mongrel's path.

"Green and yellow," Mary Lynn whispered.

"That's good, right?" Harry asked.

Al Bennett appeared next from out of the dark into the light of the campfire. He was dressed in full camouflage hunting attire that included a hunting bow, quiver of arrows and a blood-stained pack across his back. He also held a .357 in one hand.

"Oh, it's you two," the scruffy gray-bearded man complained while holstering the gun. "How long you been here? Hush Mutt!" he bellowed at the large bushy-haired dog that was still muttering uneasiness. "Thirty-minutes or so, I guess, Daddy" Mary Lynn replied. "Who's your friend? He scared the crap out of us."

The smelly dog seemed receptive to her petting when she bent down, pushed the hair away from his eyes, and stroked the top of his thick furry head.

"I call him Mutt," he groaned.

"Hey, Mutty," she chimed affectionately.

"Mutt!" he grumbled. "His name is Mutt, not Mutty. Stop tryin' to make him all cutesy. He's a stray."

"So, how many did you bag?" Harry asked, trying to curb Al's orneriness.

"Six, lightin', he sneered, looking at Harry's "Lab Tech Wizard" logo cap. "You two want to stay for supper? You ever skin a squirrel, Harrison?"

"Uh, no sir, but I'm happy to help . . . should be interesting pathology," he said, while making a silly grimace that only Mary Lynn saw while waving his hands and mouthing, *Do you think he has any gloves?*

"Roll up your Gucci sleeves; let's go," Al gruffed and pushed his lined camo hat back revealing a thatch of gray and white chopped, self-cut hair along the back of his neck. He pitched the hat inside one of the tents as he lumbered his way toward the rear of the camper.

The cranky woodsman fried the squirrel and boiled the potatoes that he pulled from a garden just behind the two tents. The conversation around the fire was pleasant as they ate from tin plates in their laps and drank homemade tea. She told him about her patients as she usually did to make conversation. He inquired about a few she had mentioned on previous visits. In particular, he was interested in Lilly Morrison, their longtime friend from the neighborhood. The Bennetts and the Morrisons traded babysitting each other's kids back in the day. Hank was gone now. Heart failure. Ms. Lilly had been alone for nine and a half years and her health was deteriorating.

"If you like, I can bring Mutt the shots he needs." Mary Lynn was impressed with Mutt's huge hearty physique and thick hair. She had never seen a dog whose head came almost up to her shoulders. "He really should be vaccinated. I have a friend that's a vet who can give me what he needs."

"I guess that'll be okay; been wonderin' about that since he won't leave," he grumbled, looking at the large scraggly animal lying on the ground beside his chair. "I ain't seen no worms in his poop. Better bring somethin' for tics. and to bathe him with. I'll try to give him a haircut in the meantime," he said, pulling an eight-inch hunting knife out of a sheath attached to his belt.

"Don't you have any scissors?" Harry asked, but Al just leaned forward and frowned at him from across the fire.

"Daddy, we saw a check-in station when we turned off the highway. I'd like to tell whoever is working the station that you're out here. It couldn't hurt . . . right?"

Al shifted his glare to her and narrowed his eyes. "So that's who's been traipsin' around out here in my woods; thought it was a bear, except it's the wrong time a year for 'em to be passin' through from Tensas Parish. They should be makin' their dens about now, not movin' down from the northeast.

"Is that why there's a two-by-four across the door?" Harry asked, pointing with his fork to the barricaded log cabin behind him.

"I'm gonna have to put up more *Posted* signs," Al replied, shaking his head. "I hold the lease on this land," he said, raising his voice. "Nobody, not even a game warden is supposed to be out here but me. If people start comin' around here botherin' me," he warned, looking around as if the game warden was crouched somewhere in the brush listening, "I'm packin' everything up and movin' to where God Himself won't be able to find me."

"Daddy, please don't say things like that. You know how much I worry about you already, being out here by yourself. Anything can happen, an accident, and no one will know."

"Humph!" the old man groaned. "You're the one that needs to be careful. You, with your mother's O-negative blood."

"I know, Daddy," Mary Lynn moaned, hearing the reminder.

"We lost that baby boy two years after Dale was born because of that damn Rh factor," he said and snatched her empty plate from her lap while grumbling something that sounded like *At least that's what they tried to make me believe*. "She was afraid to try again," he explained to Harry while grabbing his not-yet cleaned plate from his hand. "You havin' the same blood type is the only thing that saved you." He stared down at his daughter again. "But it can also kill you." He turned to Harry again pointing the plates in his hand at him. "She can only have O-negative."

"Yes, sir." Harry looked across the fire pit at Mary Lynn. She was grinning at him. They had heard this warning hundreds of times from both her parents.

"It's time to move my chair back some," she whispered. "It's getting a little too hot over here."

"I didn't mean to stay quite so long," Mary Lynn said as she caught up to Harry after stopping to run her fingers over the initials in the log on their way out. It was a good luck ritual she liked to do, both on the way in and out. It was her way of saying a little prayer before reaching the camp to ensure a pleasant visit and then to give thanks on the way out. "It was such a nice visit; I didn't want to leave. Isn't it great that he has Mutt? All the red and orange faded after a while; he was nearly blue; like you most of the time, except for right now. What are you so flustered about?"

"Yeah," Harry whispered, shining the flashlight in the trees as he walked, lighting up the small green reflectors. "I can't hide anything from you. I just wish he would stop asking me when we're going to get married. Yes, he asked me again," he said when he heard her let out a moan and imagined the grimace on her face. "I told him 'never', like every other time. I couldn't exactly evade the question since I was holding a squirrel by the hind legs and he had that huge skinning knife. He let blood drip on my boots on purpose, I know he did."

They stopped at the hunter check-in station before turning onto the highway. The building was beige with a brown roof, constructed of sheet steel with one door and no windows.

"There's a phone number," Harry said after lowering the window. "Surely Al realizes what leasing from the wildlife department means."

There was a pen in the glove compartment and an old receipt on the floorboard. "I'll do my best to explain the kind of finesse they'll have to use on Daddy," she said as she scribbled down the information.

***

"So, Mutt," Al grumbled to his companion lying on the ground next to him by the fire while he picked his teeth with a sliver of wood. "A warden has invaded our woods . . . humph! Well, that was no warden's footprints or stench we picked up on the trail today." The large dog looked up at him through the gaps in the hair covering his eyes and whined as if acknowledging Al's remark. "I guess it's a good thing I got your ugly ass to let me know when somethin's lurkin' around." He panned the dark perimeter of the camp beyond the glow of the fire. "Guess we'll be sleepin' in the cabin tonight."

Chapter 3

"Ms. Lilly, you awake?" Mary Lynn put a hand on the elder woman's shoulder while whispering in her ear. "It's time for breakfast."

"Not hungry, honey." The pale, wrinkled woman fluttered her eyes open and followed her favorite nurse as she quietly walked around the foot of the bed in the ICU room and examined the food bag hanging on an IV pole above her head. "I think I ate too much for supper. How do I look today?"

Lilly Morrison, age 82 was spending a day or two in ICU after being admitted with chest pains that resulted in the stenting of four coronary arteries. Then, *as luck would have it,* as she liked to say, her gall bladder flared up that required another procedure call laparoscopic cholecystectomy. Her son and daughter were in the family room waiting for the next 10-minute visiting period. It seemed the Bennetts and the Morrisons were one big family when she was little. There was always a board game going or cards, hide-and-seek and kick the can. One of her fondest memories was playing I spy something (a color). She always got a stern frown from her mother when she would ask to play, *What color am I?*

Mary Lynn took a step back, cocked her head to the right and squinted one eye. "Pale yellow with a little green mixed in. That means you must be satisfied; so, I'll just hold off hanging your nourishment for now. It's no biggie." Feeling bloated could mean her pancreas was inflamed, something her doctors were monitoring.

"You're so good to me, sweetheart," the old woman chuckled while watching Mary Lynn straighten the bed sheets and blankets and fluff her pillows. "I just haven't been able to hold down anything since they took that gall bladder out."

"Sometimes it takes a few hours to tolerate food again, Ms. Lilly. You'll be up on the 4th floor soon and unhooked from all these aggravating machines," she said pointing from one IV bag to the other. "And you'll have more privacy and a window so you can see the river." Someone was always watching the patients in ICU, if not through the four windows that faced the nurse's station, then from the real time recorded image through the lens in the round black box hanging from the ceiling.

"How's Al? Is he still living up at Catahoula?"

"Yes, ma'am," Mary Lynn sighed. "But, guess what?" She sat on the edge of the bed and took Lilly's frail hands. "He has a dog; a stray that wandered up. So, he has someone to talk to now and look after."

"God sent him a friend," the white-haired woman sighed, her voice quivering. "That's wonderful."

"Yes, ma'am, I think so too." Mary Lynn squeezed her hands.

"How are you doing?" Lilly's hands were cold and crepe-paper thin.

"Oh, I guess okay," Mary Lynn sighed while rubbing Lilly's hands to warm them and putting on her best face. "Thanks for asking."

Having known Mary Lynn since she was born, she easily recognized her appeasing expression. "You can't fool me, Mary Lynn Bennett. Something's got you upset and it's not your father." Mary Lynn sighed. Ms. Lilly and her mother drank coffee in the afternoons for years when she was a child, long before Christine went to work at the Fish Hatchery in Woodworth. She suspected her mother had confided her hopes, dreams, and problems to this woman who'd kept them to herself like a good friend would. Like Harry has always done for her. She put a straw to Lilly's lips allowing her to take a much-needed drink. "You have your mother's compassion, you know. I didn't have to say a word about being thirsty. Your mother was able to sense those kinds of things. You are blessed with so much more; you make me feel better by just holding my hands."

"I've known you all my life, Ms. Lilly," Mary Lynn returned. "I know when you look thirsty."

"And I know you," Lilly said.

Mary Lynn smiled and bowed her head.

"Looking for love in all the wrong places?" Lilly giggled.

"Maybe," Mary Lynn said, smiling.

"Tell me," the elder woman asked, "is it hunting season yet? I've lost track of time since I've been in here. There are no clocks."

"In a couple of weeks," she nodded. "There's a new hunter check-in station by the highway, but no one answers the number posted on the sign."

"You gonna warn them about Al?" Lilly snickered.

"Good one, Ms. Lilly!" Mary Lynn laughed. "I'd just like someone to keep an eye on him."

"Oh honey, our poor state can somehow scrounge up the money to fund a building." Lilly whispered with a chuckle. "And then, can't pay someone to man it."

***

Al Bennett sat twenty-feet above the forest floor in his box deer stand with his big-game rifle lying across his lap. He was amusing himself by following a pair of squirrels through a set of binoculars. They were playfully chasing each other, jumping from limb to limb within the pine trees. He turned his glasses to the left when he noticed a half-dozen more squirrels leaping through the crowning foliage. The two he was watching got caught in the frenzy and joined the exodus. "What's got them all stirred up?" he whispered. Mutt's ears twitched at the sound of Al's low gravel-like voice from where he lay at the base of the tree. "Hum, birds too; you hear that?" The sound of a hundred sets of beating wings rumbled through the canopy. His new faithful friend slowly stood; his eyes fixed on the shadowy timbers to Al's left. "Steady boy," Al whispered. A large shadowy image was moving ever so slowly between the trees thirty yards away. If Mutt hadn't alerted, Al probably wouldn't have noticed. "I see it, boy; it's movin' real slow. It's huge, hairy; stay low, boy," he hissed as he patiently waited it out. "Moves like a sloth. Wait, where you goin', stupid dog?" The scraggly dog leaped away and disappeared into the brush in the direction of the unknown shadowy figure. He reappeared after a few seconds wagging his tail. A man wearing the official dark green Louisiana State Wildlife and Fisheries uniform was behind him. "Damn dog," Al's voice rumbled, "you led a trespasser right to me."

"Mr. Bennett?" The six-foot-plus warden removed his cap and ruffled his thick reddish-blonde hair as he looked up the tree. "Is that you? My sergeant told me I'd find you out in this area."

"Your sergeant, huh?" Al said and started down the ladder. "Tell your sergeant this is private property and to keep you guys away from here . . . or else." He lifted his rifle and shook it at the uninvited guest as soon as his feet touched the ground.

"Mr. Bennett," he said, replacing the cap, "I heard about, uh, I mean . . . I'm sorry about what happened to . . .," he stammered. "Well, I'm just here to remind you that hunting season is opening in a few weeks and no matter how many *posted* signs you put up, there are still plenty of idiots that think the rules don't apply to them. And I'd really like to be able to arrest them for trespassing, not you for shooting them."

"Did my daughter send you to find me?" Al asked, maintaining his distance from the intruder.

"No sir, I'm scouting the wildlife management area to familiarize myself with the territory. I trained over in Kisatchie. How about if you see someone suspicious, you give me a call; I'll give you my cell number."

"Don't have one of those. That's why I moved up here, to get away from all that and people with questions."

"Of course, Mr. Bennett." They maintained their distance, like two creatures in the wild sizing one another up on a first encounter. The game warden found the old man amusing but thought it best to stifle his urge to chuckle. "I just want to make sure hunters obey the law and not get hurt. I like to resolve things as peacefully as I can. How about I bring you a two-way that's set to the same frequency as the one in my truck. You can save the battery life by just turning it on long enough to give me a heads-up when you find someone trespassing. That way, you can remain anonymous and let me handle the situation."

"Hum," Al sighed. "I'll think about it."

"My name is Adam Reeves," he said and took a step closer to offer his hand to Al, which he didn't accept. "I'm originally from Mississippi but there weren't any openings around home so I ended up here in Catahoula Parish. I'll be back to see you when it gets closer to opening day and check your licenses and tags," he added looking up at Al's tree stand and then the high-powered rifle resting on his shoulder. "I'll have permits with me should you discover you need any."

"Humph!" Al grunted. "If you can find me."

"I see you have a friend," Adam said looking down at Mutt. "He's a very impressive dog," he added referring to his size. "Glad he's friendly. Some people might mistake him for a bear."

"Yeah, well, as you can see, he ain't no bear," Al groaned.

Chapter 4

RRMC staff rotated in and out of Red's Pub and Grill on Third Street across the courtyard from the hospital in tandem with their respective shifts. Sammy DeStefano, the silver-haired owner and chief cook, grilled, steamed, fried, and concocted whatever his creative customers asked of him, whether it was on the menu or not. Sammy, with his light-blue aura, delivered two pepperoni calzone orders to Mary Lynn and Harry's outside deck table in person and waited with his arms folded across his red apron for them to sink their forks into the steamy folded pizza and take their first bites.

"You're the world's best kept secret Sammy," Harry burbled with sauce oozing from one side of his mouth.

"Wonderful, Sammy," Mary Lynn said, shaking her head and rolling her eyes back as if she couldn't believe how great the savory pocketed delight tasted. "I'd like to order another one for a friend that's on his way," she added, picking up her cell phone and wiggling it.

"What friend?" Harry whispered when Sammy hurried away to fill the order.

"Neal," she replied in a low voice, knowing his dislike for her former fiancé. He invariably spiked a shade of red at the mention of his name but always settled back into his normal pale sky blue.

"I knew that was who you were talking about when you mentioned a vet to Al. You never told him about you and Neal Mueller?"

"No; what was the point? It was over before it had time to be official. I should have never said yes in the first place. I don't even know why he still speaks to me."

From Harry's point of view, Neal had an obnoxious air about him. Always up, seemingly having the world by the tail, believing he was better off than anyone else around him because he was from New York state and had an elite Columbia University education. Unlike the rest of the lowly souls that had to earn their diplomas from any college in Louisiana.

"Mary Lynn," Harry began, "I read an article in *Psychology Today* and been doing some research. I've been meaning to talk to you about it."

"Oh, yeah? What's that?" she said, licking mozzarella cheese off her fingers.

"Something called photism. It's a form of synesthesia. One in 2000 shows symptoms of having it and some experts suspect that as many as one in 300 have some variation of the condition. I think it might explain . . .."

"There he is," she interrupted when she saw the lime light glow of Neal's unmistakably tall physique moving toward them through the restaurant. "Sounds interesting, Harry; tell me about it later." The reddish tint in Neal's hair reflected off the bar's multicolored bottles and string of lights when he passed. He and Mary Lynn had so much in common: music, movies, food, sports, and an unbelievable physical attraction. There was that one big problem, her unwillingness to commit.

"It's fantastic out here tonight!" Neal dragged an empty chair from a nearby table, placed it between Harry and Mary Lynn, and sat down. "What is it, 40 degrees?" he asked, merely glancing at Harry because he clearly couldn't keep his eyes off his former fiancé. "It's awesome out here at night. Not as much traffic; makes all the difference in the air quality. Is this the first hint of fall I'm feeling?" He closed his eyes and inhaled. "Man, it feels great." Another thing the pair had in common, they both loved the cooler temperatures.

"It's a fluke," Harry scoffed and scooted his chair a couple of inches away from Neal. "It'll be up to 90 again next week. But I understand you're used to colder temps since you're from where . . . New York?"

"You get the stuff I asked for?" Mary Lynn leaned forward while giving Harry a perplexing look because of the sarcastic tone in his voice. A distinct array of tiny green spikes was projecting like a crown around his head.

"It's in my car. But you'll have to get a blood sample to me before injecting the heart worm prevention; I put a couple extra syringes in the bag."

"That'll be fun," she sighed. "He must be at least 200 lbs."

"I'll hog tie him for you," Harry whispered, chuckling to himself. He might as well amuse himself because neither of them seemed to remember he was at the table. What a way to act around someone you don't want to marry. "Well, your dad would get a kick out of seeing me do that. Ha!" he mumbled.

"So, your dad's still up at Catahoula?" Neal asked after turning his head briefly to look at Harry and raising an eyebrow. "He still hasn't come home, not even for a visit?" Neal put his arm over the back of her chair and leaned in closer.

"No," she whispered and cast her eyes down. "Never."

She's avoiding eye contact; she's still carrying a torch for him, Harry thought to himself.

"That's too bad. You could use a break from worrying about him."

There he goes, playing her like a fiddle.

"Well, that's never gonna happen, so, oh, here comes Sammy with your order."

"I'll take it to-go. Walk with me to my car; I don't want anyone to see me giving you the meds, particularly the rabies vax. I haven't had a chance to create a patient file in the computer yet. And don't worry about paying for anything."

"He's still crazy about you, you know," Harry said an hour later when Mary Lynn returned carrying a blue canvas zipper bag. He had moved to the bar and was now on his fourth beer; two beers past his usual limit. "I was just about to give up on you; thought maybe you two had decided to rekindle your relationship."

"He's dating someone," she snapped back. She leaned her elbows up against the bar and stared at the rectangular bag as if Neal's face was imprinted on the canvas.

"Sure, he is," Harry quipped, smiling deviously, but quickly changed his expression to a frown when he saw the wounded look on her face.

"What did you want to talk to me about earlier; you had researched something?"

"Oh, that; well . . ." Harry swayed his head back and forth.

She couldn't tell if he was shaking his head *no* or if he was weaving. "How much have you had to drink, Harry? You look a little orange."

"Yeah, maybe now's not the time to talk about diagnosis-is-is," he slurred turning the beer bottle in his hand. "I have had too much and you look upset; you look a little flushed. You know, you have telltale colors too." She paid no attention to his half-ass joke. She was staring at her reflection in the mirror behind the bar.

"Harry, did you ever say anything to Neal about Camp Livingston?" She was taking deep breaths and letting them go, like she was bracing for his answer.

"What do you mean; why would I talk to Neal about Camp Livingston?" He put the bottle down. "We used to go out there to party, but the things we did as teenagers are none of Neal's business as far as I'm concerned."

"Remember the time we went out there looking for Bigfoot?" She turned her head, looking at him dead in the eyes.

"Yeah, I remember." He returned her stare, but with a frown of concern. "Why would I talk to him about that?"

"Something happened that night." Her eyes were blinking, as if she was fighting back tears. "I never told anyone, not even you. I'll see you tomorrow." She pushed herself away from the bar and rushed out of the restaurant.

"But what . . . .." he swiveled around on the bar stool and watched her push through the front door, "what happened at Camp Livingston?"

Leaving town like Dale, had never been an option for Mary Lynn, but she did eventually move out of the house they grew up in on Hartwood Street. The new place was a two-bedroom apartment two blocks away. Countless offers were made on the house, but she turned them all down, even after a realtor warned her that the house would eventually deteriorate and lose its value. She didn't feel bad about asking the favor of Neal. They were still friends; for some reason he still dropped by the hospital every few days to say hello. His car was parked at the end of a dead-end street next to the Red River levee. After retrieving the blue bag containing the meds, they climbed the steep hill to visit the amphitheater where summer concerts were held in the spring and summer. It had been their special place while dating. They often ended their nights there, sitting on the top step and watching the street lights reflect off the river's driven current. An occasional boat would putter by, disrupting its natural rhythm. Distant music filled the air on the weekends from two restaurants on Third Street. One being The Diamond Grill, formerly a notable jewelry store in downtown Alexandria, and Finnigan's Wake, whose doors always stood open so its music would lure in the millenniums. The downtown park was behind the amphitheater, City Hall and the historic Bentley Hotel to its left.

"I see the big paddle boat is gone," he said after sitting there a few minutes reminiscing over the familiar and noting things that had changed. "Remember the night that homeless man stumbled out of the wheelhouse and fell overboard?"

"Yeah," she sighed, fighting the excitement the memory produced. "The whole police department came out and the fire department and divers. The owner sold it after the city put pressure on him. People were complaining about the illicit things that were going on in there. It was putting a black eye on the downtown revitalization effort."

"You were really freaked out over it," he chuckled, shaking his head. "You told me you hadn't been that scared since *something*," he made quotation marks with his fingers, "that happened to you when you were sixteen."

"Not about Camp Livingston?" she challenged, shocked she ever mentioned the terrifying night to him. "Well," she said after regaining her composure, "I was way too cool to admit to being afraid of anything. I was a bad-ass chick back then." *Should I tell Neal, who used to be my finance, the secret I've been carrying all these years? What the hell, who would he tell? Who would believe him?* "I was walking back to my Mustang to look for a koozie. It was dark; the concrete roads were all busted up back then because the army was trying to keep people like us from carousing around. I was trying to watch my step. I remember so vividly, the screaming crickets and frogs. The buildings had no roofs and the walls were partially knocked down, so everything looked creepy. All of a sudden, everything went silent. Then I heard this noise. I thought it was one of the guys, you know, relieving himself; but when I turned . . . .." She paused to look at him before making the big reveal, to watch his eyes when she said it.

"You saw Bigfoot," he whispered as if he had read her thoughts.

"What? How . . .," she gasped. "I never told you; I never told a soul."

"Yeah, you did." He was blinking his eyes like a classic liar, something her deputy sheriff father told her a perp always did when he was trying to get away with something, even after being caught red-handed. "Or, maybe it was Harry," he said when he saw her eyebrows pinch together. "One of you told me about the 12-foot hairy figure standing in the road and how it started walking toward you. I think you described it as swaying when it walked. I don't know; it was either you or Harry. I can't remember."

The feeling of something crawling up her spine made her cross her arms and rub them with her hands. "I get a creepy feeling every time I think about it. I can't believe I told you. Had I been drinking?" He shrugged his shoulders. "Each step I took backward, it matched by taking one towards me. Its strides were longer than mine, so I turned and ran as fast as I could back to my friends. I didn't tell them because they would've never stopped slamming me. We had all been drinking and smoking pot; we were so lame. We thought we were invincible, bulletproof. *We* were the intimidators, never afraid of anything. I was too embarrassed; I promised myself I would never tell anyone."

"It must have been Harry," he said. "You tell him everything, right?"

She was sure she'd never confided the Camp Livingston story to Neal, just as she would never share seeing colors with him. Neal rarely gave off an aura. It was a relief at first, but it made her wonder why. Like maybe he had no soul. She was afraid to tell Harry about what she saw, afraid it would be the last straw and she'd lose the one true friendship she cherished. "Sometimes I think you have some sort of hypnotic power over me, Neal, that makes me spill everything. Of course, I'll never know what terrified really means, not like . . .." She stopped, unable to finish the thought.

"Your mother," he sighed.

"Right," she said. "No matter how afraid I was that night, it must have been so much worse for her. Whoever took her destroyed our family. That's why I'm so screwed up; why I just can't commit . . . not until I can come to terms with what happened to her."

"I wasn't around when it happened," Neal whispered. "I can't even imagine what your family went through . . . is still going through. I don't get to see my parents that often with them living in Switzerland, but at least I know they're alive and going about their daily routines. I can speak to them, Skype them. I've seen firsthand how it affected you. I tried, Mary Lynn."

"I know," she sighed.

"I wish you could find someone to talk to that specializes in helping people that have been through a life-changing trauma like you have. You need to let someone else besides your friends and family give you advice."

"Neal," she groaned, "I don't want to hear this same old bullshit."

"I know," he replied. "But it was worth one last effort. There is something I need to tell you . . . in person." He bowed his head awkwardly.

Only patients struggling with death projected such a putrid purple. Although Neal's was barely visible, merely a thin line, it was vivid against the night sky. "What's wrong?"

"I'm moving to Monroe," he finally said. "I met a girl there at a seminar and I've been spending a lot of time traveling back and forth, so I found a job up there. I've given my two-week's notice and, well, I couldn't go without telling you goodbye and telling you that I hope we can always remain friends. I told Jackie all about you and she understands our friendship."

"You told her about me?" Mary Lynn grimaced.

"Of course, she, uh, knew a lot about you already, so I . . .."

"You told her how sad and pathetic I am?" she said, finishing his sentence.

"Mary Lynn," he argued, shaking his head. "That's not fair."

"You wanted to move away from here when we were together."

"Yes, I did; only because I thought a fresh start somewhere else would be good for us. I loved you, I still do," he sighed soulfully. Their eyes met; he was slightly taller and knew just how to place his hand perfectly on the back of her neck and make her anxieties drift away. "I always will, I guess," he whispered. His hand was warm as he lightly massaged her neck. "Tell me you don't feel the same?" He moved in closer.

"How can you ask me something like that?" she whimpered. "You're leaving to be with someone else."

"Kiss me," he sighed and moved his hand to her waist and pulled her closer.

As soon as their lips touched, the passion they shared easily ignited. But after a few seconds, Mary Lynn pushed him away. "I wanted to have a life with you, Neal," she said shaking her head. "I just couldn't."

"Mary Lynn, please find some help," he pleaded, "you can't go on like this."

"I hope you have a great life with Janice, or Janie." She stood up to leave.

"Jackie," Neal corrected as he watched her run down the steps and cross the front of the bandstand toward the exit.

Mary Lynn gritted her teeth, trying to subdue the sobbing as she drove carelessly through the streets leading to her apartment after exiting Red's and leaving Harry fidgeting for his wallet to pay his tab. Instead of going home to her apartment, she whipped the wheel of her blue Dodge Challenger to the right onto Hartwood and then made a quick left into the second driveway. She stood outside for a minute looking at the part brick and slate house to catch her breath. She slowly approached the front porch. The steps and porch designed with chipped red brick laid in concrete were dark with mildew. The wood trellis across the front porch that provided shade in the summer when weighted with tiny pink Rose of Montana had deteriorated down to jagged gray sticks jutting out of the ground. The key was still in the flaking carriage light on the wall next to the front door and she let herself in. There was no furniture. Dale and other relatives had claimed most of it. She gave some things to friends, others to the Salvation Army. The stained wood floors creaked when she walked across the living room to the dining room. No one had asked for the china hutch knowing how Christine cherished it. It still contained the Franciscan Rose china and crystal glassware that was set out every Sunday and on holidays; now barely visible through the mold and dust accumulated on the glass. Nothing, not the silverware, serving trays or cut-glass candy dishes had been touched since her disappearance.

Something came over Mary Lynn as she pressed her fingers around the tarnished loop handle and opened one of the glass doors. She reached for a black iron candlestick holder on the bottom shelf. It was as if a deranged person had emerged from somewhere inside her and took over her mind, body, and will, someone whose singular purpose was to destroy the last of her mother's revered possessions. She started with the glass doors and side panels. With the murky glass out of the way, the attack moved forward with vigor to the plates, bowls, coffee set, and glass goblets. When the frenzy of anger was over, she staggered through the kitchen and past the outdated built-in appliance to the back porch where she fell onto a rusty daybed that was part of a patio set that nobody had wanted. She cried uncontrollably into the weathered cushions until she fell asleep. She stirred slightly when she felt someone place a blanket over her shoulders. It was odd that it brought such comfort. Odd, because she couldn't tolerate sleeping under any kind of blanket. The solace it brought made her snuggle deeper into the eroded cushion. If she had roused the least bit, she would have been startled by the woman standing over her.

"Thanks Harry," she mumbled instead.

Chapter 5

"Hey-hey." Harry stood over Mary Lynn, gently nudging her shoulder, trying not to frighten her.

"What?" she complained sourly, looking up at Harry, groggy and confused, and wondering why his face was all up in hers. "What are you doing?"

"I barely caught sight of your car in the driveway when I passed Hartwood. Here, I went for coffee at the U-Pak after I found you asleep back here. What happened in the dining room? Someone trashed your mother's china cabinet. You weren't here when it happened were you? Should I call 911?"

"No!" Mary Lynn groaned in protest while sitting up. She clutched the cozy beige blanket while taking the cardboard cup from him. "You didn't cover me up last night . . . with this?" She held it close to her like a child would a security blanket.

"Why would I . . ." He looked at the blanket covering her legs, body, and forearms. They both knew it was something he wouldn't have done knowing how cranky she was about any heat-producing cover. "No," he replied instead of arguing. He sat down beside her and felt the blanket's texture. "Is it from the hospital? I don't think I've ever felt anything like it. Is it thermal?"

"I don't know. It's the most comfortable . . . ." She stopped herself. What was she saying? She hated blankets. "It felt so good when . . . but I thought it was you."

"What happened to the china cabinet?" Harry reached for the iron candleholder lying on its side beside the daybed.

"Please, I don't want to talk about it," she gruffed. "I was angry."

"That was you?" he couldn't help but blurt out. "Well," he said after taking a breath. "If it was me that found you here last night, I would have done more then cover you up. I would have taken you home. You need to be careful; homeless people take shelter in vacant houses like this." He drew the candlestick holder up over his head and then lowered it, play-acting the intention of crushing her skull with it but stopped and tapped her on her forehead.

"I know," she sighed while pulling the blanket over her shoulders and cuddling against him. "I was in a mood." She took the heavy trivet from him and put it down on the rusted table in front of them. "Thanks for the coffee, Harry; it's just what I needed. I feel much better now. I think I'll go home and take a shower. I'll come back later and clean up the mess."

Harry frowned when he passed the dining room while following her to the front door. He hadn't seen this kind of result from one of her fits of anger in years. Not since the summer before their high school senior year when she caught her boyfriend Tommy cheating on her at the drive-in movie. There was a tire iron in her trunk; she used it to put a hundred dents in his red Pontiac Firebird, the baddest street-racing car in north Louisiana. Tommy jumped out yelling; his date fled to the snack bar when the shattered windshield fell in their laps. The windshield, the head- and taillights looked much like the china cabinet doors and side panels.

She leaned up against the Challenger before opening the door, her eyes blinking and cast down looking at what was left of the coffee. Harry propped himself against the car and waited patiently as always, looking past the bed head hair and smudged eye makeup.

"You know, Harry," she sighed. "Neal and I had something for a minute. There was something different about him, something very easy. I guess that's why I said *yes*. I wanted to trust him, but I was fooling myself."

"I'm really sorry it didn't work out," he said, nodding his head sympathetically.

"If he just hadn't started rushing into making all those wedding plans," she continued. "I wanted to wait, let the whole idea sink in, but he was like obsessed."

"And you hate being pushed into things." Harry shrugged his shoulders, as if to say this should have been obvious to anyone that knew her, especially the man who wanted to marry her.

"Honestly, it scared me," Mary Lynn said. It seemed like a whole minute passed while she turned the cardboard cup in her hands as if she was trying to make up her mind about something.

"What was the big deal about Camp Livingston?" Harry asked.

"It was something that shook me up so much that I was afraid to say it out loud. It was like, if I said the word, it would make it real. I saw something." She flashed her burdened eyes at him and then guiltily looked away. "I thought everybody would just laugh and spread it all over school how screwed up Mary Lynn Bennett was for claiming she saw Bigfoot."

"I remember that night. But, wasn't that what we were all out there for, to find Bigfoot? I mean, we were mainly there to party but Bigfoot was the excuse we used."

"Yeah, nobody actually thought anything was really out there. But lucky me, I saw it, or something. Believe me, I've been arguing with myself over what it was or could have been ever since. This thing, it had a green aura which is normally a safe color; but it lunged at me. Aggressiveness usually emits some shade of red. To this day, I still feel like someone or something is watching me. Sometimes I think I see that same green color in my peripheral vision. But when I turn to look, there's nothing. I wish I-I wasn't so cursed with this madness."

"Why didn't you tell me what happened that night? I would never have judged you," Harry contended. "Actually, I've always thought you're seeing colors as being really cool. It certainly came in handy when we were kids; I always knew when it was time to run when you saw red. I still trust your intuition emphatically."

"You've always been my only real friend. I was afraid if I said something, you'd see right away how petrified I was, and that would be it. You would have had enough of whatever it is that's wrong with me, and I'd lose you."

"Ok, that was how sixteen-year-old Mary Lynn evaluated things. Adult Mary Lynn knows better, right?"

"So, if it wasn't you that told Neal about my seeing . . ." She couldn't say the name *Bigfoot.* "And it wasn't me, then how did he know?"

"That I can't answer, but I think you dodged a bullet by breaking up with that one."

"He used to go on and on about getting married and having kids. He wouldn't listen when I said I wanted to wait. He just didn't get me. I realized I didn't really know him either, so I called off the engagement. He was still coming around so I thought we might be able to work things out. But then last night he told me that he'd met someone, and is moving to Monroe to be with her. How could he do that so soon after asking me to marry him? It's like all he really wanted to do was marry me and have kids; and didn't really care about who I was."

Harry put an arm around her shoulder and pulled her close. "You're gonna meet some rich handsome doctor at RRMC and live happily ever after, you'll see." He blushed when she sighed and wrapped her arms around his waist. "Let me know when you're ready to clean up the dining room. I'll come over and help."

"That's okay," she replied releasing her grip on him. "I'll clean up my own mess. But I would like to ask a favor."

"Sure," he replied. They both pushed away from the car and stood facing each other. *Must be something awkward,* he thought. She took in a breath first.

"I need to borrow your truck tomorrow. I want to drive up to Daddy's and give Mutt his shots."

"Hey, you know I'd be more than happy to . . ."

"I know, I know, but I want to go by myself; driving helps me think."

"Sure, keep it as long as you like." He grinned at her and dug in his pocket for his key fob. "In fact, keep it the whole weekend. You want to swap now?"

"What's with you?" she asked suspiciously. "You want my muscle car for the weekend? What are *you* up to?"

"Yeah well, I was thinking about doing a little showing off out on 28 Saturday night."

She could see he was teasing. "Right!" she laughed mockingly. "Nobody does that anymore."

"I don't know, you still represent at stop signs," he quipped. "You've never lost that itch for going fast." He handed her the key fob. "Too bad Tommy's not still around. He'd know just the place to lay down some serious rubber."

"Yeah, he would," she sighed and placed her fob in his hand. "But he'd have to tell us from heaven."

"Thanks to a foggy night on a rain slicked highway."

"Yeah, well; remember that, and good luck with whoever it is you're trying to impress," she said, squinting playfully. "Just remember to keep it between the ditches, okay?"

"Ah! Another Al Bennett adage," he chortled. "None of us ever had him fooled." There were so many things that they surely got away with because her father was a deputy sheriff; speeding tickets, DUI's, trespassing, rowdiness, break-ins. "He was a godsend, for sure."

"I didn't realize at the time that it was him I had to thank for all that good luck," she said pursing her lips before letting out a long sigh. "That's why I need to take care of him now."

"Look at you bein' all grown up."

"Ah! Please, I don't want to hear that," she whined. "But, one thing for sure, I've been awfully lucky to have you, Harry." Her eyes widened as if she'd just remembered something. "Oh, what was it you wanted to talk about last night?"

"It can wait," Harry said opening the door to the Challenger. "There's plenty of time." He smiled at her while thinking of how the conversation about the perceptual phenomenon of synesthesia would start out. Mary Lynn would debate him at first, and then there would be hours of discussion, perhaps days. Could the stimulation of sensory or cognitive pathways really lead to involuntary experiences? A conceivable explanation for why she sees colors and possibly the strange object she mistook for Bigfoot and the feeling she was being watched.

***

As before, the metal building was unattended. A newly erected brown sign with a yellow directional arrow was now planted across from the turn-off road that read "Hunter's Check-In." There was no warden in sight when Mary Lynn rolled to a stop in front of the skidded structure. She released her seatbelt, slid out of the Tacoma and began to look around for evidence of anyone having been there. A hasp and pad-lock secured the door but she yanked on it anyway. The sign on the door with the phone number she'd been calling all week was gone. Deep-treaded boot prints in the dirt led her around the side of the building that tracked down a slope toward the tree line. A rustling noise in the thicket ahead brought her to a halt. A man suddenly rushed toward her from out of the bushes, making her step backwards. There was a dark green aura emanating off his LDWF uniform. She noticed a backpack strapped to his shoulders and a holstered gun on his duty belt. He was looking down at a cell phone in the palm of his hand, not texting or talking into it, but maybe using it more like a GPS. He looked up as if he'd reached his destination.

"Ahh! There you are, I mean, hi there!" he stuttered. He seemed oddly pleased to see her. "Um . . . can I help you?" He quickly stuffed the phone in his rear pocket.

"I was beginning to wonder if anyone actually worked here," she replied. "This is the second time I've stopped. There was a sign before."

"Oh that," he replied, shaking his head as if trying to clear his mind. "I had to take it down. It had an erroneous number on it. The department and I communicate by radio anyway." He patted a microphone also attached to the belt on the opposite side of the gun. "You've been calling the number, obviously." His thick-soled boots left the same knobby tracks she had followed as he hurried past her toward the Tacoma.

"Um . . ." Mary Lynn grunted, fearing the warden might want to check the truck for weapons or contraband, as was his job in the wildlife management area and then question her about the small, soft-sided ice chest on the passenger seat that contained the blue canvas bag with syringes and medicine vials. "My father lives out here and . . ."

"You're Mr. Bennett's daughter," he said, and abruptly stopped and turned back around. "I met him a few days ago."

There was something off about the exuberance of his nodding and grinning.

"Is he okay?" The thought occurred to her that something might have happened to her daddy and the warden was stalling, trying figure out how to break the news to her.

"Oh yes," he said, slipping the pack from his shoulders and resting it on the ground. "In fact, I requisitioned this radio for him. I've been meaning to get back out there to give it to him." He pulled the top flap away and removed a small box containing the radio. "He agreed, well sort of agreed, to let me know if he saw something I should check on."

"I can't believe he would even entertain the idea," she countered, frowning "I guess you must have made a good impression."

"That remains to be seen," he chuckled.

Mary Lynn was still getting a strange vibe from him even though he was trying his best to be friendly. A thin red line had developed around him.

"My name is Adam Reeves." He touched the bill of his cap and nodded. "I'd be happy to give you a ride to his camp in my quad." He looked back toward the thicket he had just popped out of. "It's pretty rough-going in these woods."

"No, that's okay, I know the way in." Every warning sign she had ever sensed was going off in her head, telling her not to let him come near her.

"Do you mind if I follow?" he asked when she started toward the truck.

"Sorry, I'd really like to visit him privately." He had already started toward the woods to retrieve the quad.

He stopped, hesitating before answering as if embarrassed, or maybe disappointed. "Of course. Tell Mr. Al I'll be out soon with the radio and show him how to . . . oh, that's right." He looked at the box in his hand. "He was a deputy; he already knows how to use one of these." His lips formed what she perceived as an eerie grin.

"Sure, well, it was nice meeting you, Adam. I'll be on my way now." She quickly walked around the truck to the driver's door, got in, and pressed the door lock button. She watched him through the rear-view mirror while she drove away. She saw the radio spring cord stretched across his forearm, the microphone up to his mouth.

Adam Reeves pushed the button while watching the Tacoma slowly maneuver down the uneven dirt road. "I need a license registration check," he said into the microphone. The device made a high-pitched tone when he let off the speak-button and then settled to a constant static. "So, she comes up here alone sometimes," the warden whispered.

Scant wafts of smoke flittered from the ashes in Al's fire pit and meandered across the camp. Mary Lynn buried two medium-sized green limbs into the remnants that quickly produced a defined smolder. She strolled around the camp, glancing inside the two tents, and opening and closing the door to the second or third-owner camper. It took two hands and some straining to lift the heavy two-by-four barricade that secured the entrance to the small cabin. Inside, she was surprised to find a bounty of food supplies: rice, potatoes, flour, sugar, coffee, canned goods, powdered milk, and a 5-foot army green footlocker full of MREs.

"Ok," she whispered, while sitting the soft sided ice chest down on a table in the middle of the room. "I'll no longer worry about you having enough to eat."

"Come on out of there!" she heard Al bellow from outside. Mutt pranced in ahead of him wagging his tail. "Stupid dog!" Al grumbled from outside.

"Daddy, it's me," she yelled out and then squatted down to pet the large black dog. "How are you Mutty? I have a bag of food for you in the truck and some medicine over there that you're not gonna like so much." Mutt reciprocated the cuddling by scooting closer, ignoring the sound of Al's boots lumbering up the three wooden steps and scuffling over the door jam.

"I knew I shoulda padlocked that damn door," he grumbled, planting his boots firmly on the wood floor.

"Hey, Daddy." Mary Lynn jumped up and threw her arms around the musky-smelling man wearing a camouflage jumpsuit. He reciprocated by patting her on the shoulder. "I brought some things for Mutty."

"Mutt!" he quickly corrected.

"I had no idea you were so well stocked."

"Yeah, well, don't you go and blab to people that I got this stuff," he said glancing around the small room at his inventory. "Some idiot 'll try 'n steal it."

"Who else is out here besides you and that creepy wildlife dude I met up by the highway? He called you by name and showed me this radio he got for you."

"Why didn't you bring it with you?" he grumbled.

"I don't know." She shrugged her shoulders. "Something bugged me about him. I just wanted to get as far away from him as I could." She frowned and shook her head. "Maybe it was the way he just popped out of the woods in front of me. I didn't even want to tell him about the bag of dog food in the truck bed much less Mutt's vaccinations."

"You and those weird feelings," he grumbled. "You shouldn't be comin' up here by yourself anyway. Where's Harrison?" Her father could pile on the gripes when he was in one of his moods. He was in one now judging by his orange aura.

"Somethin' else is livin' out here in these woods," he groaned. "I'm not quite sure what, but it leaves tracks like I ain't never seen before."

"A bear?" she gasped. "Daddy, a bear?" she crooned louder.

"Bigger," he said sternly; "and smart. It's figured out how to trip my traps without getting' caught. When Mutt starts actin nervous, I lock us up in here."

"Daddy, my God," she panted. "Now I wish I would have brought you that radio."

"Don't worry, there's nothin' out here I can't handle. Let's get this chore over with."

She unzipped the ice chest and the blue canvas bag and laid out the meds and syringes. Al lifted Mutt's massive body up on the table and held him while she dispensed the injections and drew two small vials of blood.

"Daddy, I really need to talk to you about something," she said after the inoculations were over with and Mutt had been freed to shake off the stings. The small cabin fell uncomfortably silent. "I'm sorry to bring this up because I know what being out here means to you." She took a deep breath because his temperament was too sour to suggest what she was about to say, but she took him by the hand anyway. "Daddy, I really need you to come home; I don't think I can keep pretending everything is normal anymore."

"Can't do that," he said starkly and quickly pulled his hand away. "There's no way I can go back there." He rushed outside leaving her standing alone in the cabin with her arm hanging in the air. He went straight to the woodpile and busied himself stacking pieces of split wood in one arm.

She watched him from the doorway. His aura projected red while he stooped on one knee to place the wood next to the squatty stones that surrounded the pit. "Most everything is gone, given away," she said, tip toeing warily down the steps toward the pit. "And last night, well, I went stupid insane and completely destroyed Mama's china cabinet and everything in it."

It took him a few seconds to stand with the help of a piece of split wood and a couple of grunts. "You did what? You know what that china means to her?"

"Meant to her," Mary Lynn corrected. "It's like I was trying to destroy her memory; get her out of my head, my life. It's time we stop waiting for her to come home." His eyes were pink, almost glowing against the white and gray hair around his face. His whole essence transformed into a distressing fiery orange. "Please, Daddy." She followed his steps as he paced back and forth in front of the fire pit as if trying to shake her. "We could remodel the house, get new furniture. It would be a great project for us to do together. Please Daddy, work, friends; nothing is enough anymore. I even tried to have a relationship, but . . ."

He stopped, sliding his boots and kicking up dust. "So, this is about some man?" he blurted out.

"No!" Her voice broke as if the powder he kicked up had suppressed her vocal cords. It was evident by the fluctuating orange to red that he was ready to lash out more. "It's just that sometimes I feel so paralyzed."

Al's distressed expression slowly calmed; his color lightened. "Come with me," he said. To her surprise, he put an arm around her shoulders and led her to a trail behind the two supply tents. "Mutt, you comin'?" he hollered. They had walked about 100 yards when the path sloped and then dropped drastically. Luckily, it was abundant with large roots that served as stair steps to the bottom where there was a sandy creek bank. The threesome walked along the bank until they came upon a wide aluminum boat tied to a tree. There was a tarp under a large bush covering a tackle box and three fishing poles. "Put these in the boat and let's go catch supper."

"Are you serious?" Her mouth gaped open as he handed her the poles.

"You bet," he replied. "I've got a worm bed just over here. Come on," he said, grinning at her grimace. "What's with the face? You used to love this when you were little." He slid a cinder block off the lid of a buried ice chest and they sifted through the loose black dirt. After collecting the bait and settling in the boat, Al pushed away from the bank and trolled a short way to a bend. "You remember the last time we went fishin' together?" He said as he pushed a fat brown earthworm onto her hook.

"I guess I was thirteen, maybe?" she said from her bucket seat in the rear of the boat, just in front of the motor. "You and Dale went most of the time."

"Yeah, I used to let him sit up here in the casting seat and operate the trolling motor. It was hard to get you to do anything like this once you got interested in boys and started drivin', but we had some good times wettin' our hooks on the Red and Lake Buhlow. After that, most of our communication was over all those speedin' tickets I had to pull." He cast out his baited hook and it made a small splash in the middle of the creek. "Go ahead, let's see what you remember."

She whipped her pole in the air and the line flew across the water. "Ha! Mine went further than yours," she said and gave him a competitive smirk. "Oh my God, I think I got one already!" she shouted and jerked the rod back.

"Okay, good set. You remembered what I taught you." He sat up and leaned close to the edge of the boat. "Reel it in and keep pullin' your pole back, keep tension in the line; don't lose him."

"I got him, I got him," she shrieked. She flung it into the boat where it flopped around on the bottom unsettling Mutt.

Fish were always mint green, maybe because they were cold-blooded. "What now?" Mary Lynn asked.

"Swing your hook over here so I can bait it again."

"I'll do it," she said and grabbed the worm can. "I remember how."

Al cackled in delight as he watched her wind the worm through the hook, but his expression changed quickly when his pole suddenly vibrated. "Damn, I got a hit!"

"I think . . . oh, me too!" Mary Lynn wailed. Her line was in the water ten seconds. "This is freakin' awesome!"

Later that evening they sat near the fire pit balancing their tin plates of fish, fried potatoes, and ketchup in their laps. "I love livin' here," Al said, stirring the ketchup in his plate with a potato. "It's peaceful. I don't like bein' around people anymore."

"What about that bear, or whatever, that's out here?" she asked, gazing around the outer limits of the campfire. There were no peering eyes from foraging rodents, just sparkles emitting from a few insects. Not all insects gave off an aura.

"Well, it doesn't seem to be hurtin' anything. To be honest, when Mutt goes out lookin' for it he always comes back waggin' his tail. Maybe it's like me and wants to be left alone. Look," he said, putting his plate with several leftover fries on the ground for Mutt. "Don't worry about what you did to your mother's china. I suppose I'm okay with it. You're right, she's never comin' back."

"I know Mama couldn't help what happened to her," she sighed. "Everybody's moved on, you've moved on. So should I."

"Well," he sighed deeply. "It's about time I told you somethin'." He nervously wiped his hands across his camo pant legs three times, leaned forward, and clasped his hands. "Your mother and I . . . well, we weren't gettin' along so good back then. I'm pretty sure she was cheatin', you know, seein' somebody, another man."

"What? That's crazy Daddy!" she gasped. "Mama would never do that!"

"We kept all that hidden from the two of you," he continued and bowed his head. "The baby she miscarried before you were born . . . it wasn't mine. I had taken a month off and was up at the huntin' camp at the time she would have conceived. I never told anybody, never even confronted her about it. Everybody thought she was such a good Christian and all. I forgave her and then we had you. Things got better, but it was never the same. I think she had started seein' whoever it was again just before she, well, you know."

"Daddy, you should have said something," she gasped. "He might have been the one that killed her."

"Honestly, part of me thinks she ran off with him and staged the car and the purse. I didn't want you and Dale to . . . you know, hate her. You two shouldn't hate your mother. She loved you."

"Oh, Daddy!" He was projecting honesty, truth. She stood up, without thinking about the plate in her lap. Potatoes, bits of fish and ketchup scattered in the dirt that Mutt quickly attended to.

Al reached out to her but she was already pacing and crying. She shouted and kicked the ground; picked up pieces of firewood and threw them wildly into the woods while calling her mother names. The rant went on for over five minutes.

Al waited patiently while she reminded him that back then he was never around; if his wife had turned to someone else, then it was his fault. "Well," he said when she finally flopped down in the canvas chair to wipe the tears from her face. "You're right about half-a that stuff." Everything fell quiet long enough for the crickets and frogs to brave their songs. "How 'bout if I come in for a weekend every now and then?" he finally conceded. It had the desired effect. Her face seemed to relax. "To help you with that redecoratin'. You're off on the weekends, aren't you?"

"Yes," she gushed. She lunged toward him and grabbed him around the neck. She landed on him so hard that the chair started to fold, nearly knocking them both over. "I'm so sorry. I didn't mean any of that stuff I said."

"Maybe just a little," he whispered in her ear while he held her close. "But that's okay. It's nothin' I ain't said to myself before." Later, he walked her to the Tacoma and gave her another long hug before she stepped inside.

"I'm actually glad you told me, Daddy," she said somberly. "I'm really sorry about the tantrum. Thank you for telling me the truth. I'm gonna try and build the rest of my life on it." She sighed. "Maybe I'll even forgive her, someday. You know, she was the only person that truly understood me and all my quirks."

"Except for the kid," he said with an affectionate smirk.

"Harry's always been a loyal friend. But Mama seemed to understand my quirks; she made me feel normal when I was at my worst. Daddy, you should tell Dale what you just told me. Who knows, maybe it'll bring us all back together; we could be a family again."

"Let's don't get ahead of ourselves here," he sighed. "We'll talk some more when I get down there." He pulled the bag of dog food out from the bed and threw it over his shoulder. "Next time you bring somethin like this with you, make sure to lock it in the cab." He patted the bag with his free hand and looked around the surrounding tree line. "This here's a temptation for all sorts of critters, big and small."

She slowed as she drove past the empty metal building after battling the arduous substandard road and breathed a sigh of relief because there was no sign of creepy Adam.

Chapter 6

Harry was perched on a stool in the hospital lab, leaning over a digital microscope with his eyes fixed on a murky slide. He didn't notice Neal at first when he pushed through the door carrying Mary Lynn's soft-side ice chest.

"Mueller, how did you get in here?" He was surprised Neal made it so far into the lab without been stopped, ID-ed, tagged, and suited up. "It's mandatory in the bio lab, dude," he reprimanded, pointing to his own protective gloves, white vinyl coveralls, and cap. "How did you know I was in here?"

"I sweet-talked the desk nurse into telling me where to find you and she let me back," he said with a grin.

"Please don't make me report that nice woman for not following protocol," Harry rebutted. Neal Mueller was one of those lucky guys who could easily charm women into anything by just looking at them a certain way with his sea-blue eyes. And there was that reddish beach-boy hair and general good looks that made them feel giddy and weak.

"Don't get anyone in trouble over me, man. I promised her I wouldn't take long. So, it took me about 15 seconds to determine that Al's dog doesn't have heart worms," he sighed. "I guess Mary Lynn didn't want to wait; she left this on the receptionist counter with instructions to give you the results." He laid the cooler on the counter next to the microscope.

"Well, actually, it was me that left the cooler at Mary Lynn's request." Harry purposely closed the laptop on the counter beside him displaying the image from the microscope.

"You didn't find anything unusual, oh, like mange or rabies," Harry added. "I was sort of expecting something, because he's a stray."

"No, nothing," he said, shrugging his shoulders. "If she'd drawn blood into the second vial, I could have checked for a number of things," Neal said. "You didn't see a second one, did you?"

"No, man, I didn't," Harry replied. "She drove up to the camp by herself. Maybe she didn't fill the second one or disposed of it with the syringes and med bottles."

"I suppose." Neal seemed to be stalling. "I guess she told you I'm moving. I wish, I wish . . .," he stuttered, frowning pitifully as if still grieving over their break up. "God, I wish things could have turned out differently. I wanted to marry her so much and have a house full of kids. I think the kids idea may have scared her a little."

"But obviously you know her blood type would make that difficult," Harry said.

"That's the thing," Neal replied. "We both have the Rh factor, so we could've had as many as we wanted. I hope she wasn't too upset the other night after I told her I was moving and about my new girlfriend."

"Well, you know Mary Lynn," Harry said, picturing the china cabinet in his mind. "She's a complicated woman.

"I'm glad she has you for a friend, Harry. You seem to understand her. She needs someone like you to talk to."

"We've known each other all our lives." *He knows we're good friends, why is he wasting my time with this idle chatter.* Then, as if on cue . . . .

"I'm sorry, man. I didn't come here to plead my case; it just kind of spilled out and. . . .

"Believe me, man, I understand what you're trying to say." Was Neal angling for something? Information would be his guess. "Best of luck, okay?"

"Yeah, thanks for everything, Harry." They shook hands and Neal took his leave.

Harry leaned into the lenses after Neal left, not really focusing on the object pressed between the slides. He didn't know Neal carried the same Rh factor as Mary Lynn. That would have been a big plus for their relationship. He never really liked the dude; he had an untrustworthy vibe, and he never was as sympathetic about her mother's disappearance as he should have been. Granted, he wasn't close to his own parents since they lived in Switzerland and they had boarded him in schools up until Columbia. How could he not notice how she interpreted things by using colors? "And how could you have missed something so obvious?" he whispered, glancing from the lenses to the vial labeled "Mutty" standing upright in a carrousel rack behind the microscope. "I'm no geneticist, but I'm pretty sure this dog's not from around here." He focused intently on the swab of blood in the microscope. "You have very different markers, Mutt. So, guess what? You're going to the state lab in Shreveport."

***

Al followed the fourteen-by-ten-inch footprints in the soft mud along the edge of the meandering creek for a quarter mile after picking them up while following a game trail. The creature had padded around back and forth at the bank's edge and then veered up a slope into denser woods very near where Al had one of his two big game traps set. He climbed the steep hill following the deep gouging impressions, reminding himself to be careful. A bear, or whatever made the large prints, might be caught in the trap's forty-pound jaws and mad as hell. He found the end of the chain on the ground, minus the trap. The heavy-duty Master Lock, and what was left of the chain, was still wrapped around the significantly besieged tree. He searched the area, moving vines, fallen leaves, and tree limbs with the butt of his rifle. He found the trap after widening his search thirty feet. Like the other big-game trap, it was tripped, and the five-inch spikes clamped. Mutt had fallen behind and trotted up beside him.

"Take a whiff of this Mutt," Al grumbled. "Freed itself again. Only this time it left some blood and hair behind." Al turned the forceful trap back and forth in front of the dog's nose. "You got any bloodhound in you?" Mutt looked up at him and wagged his tail. "I didn't think so," he grumbled and then stuffed the trap into his game bag where he had stowed the snapped chain and lock. He hung the strap over his shoulder and followed a blood trail that disappeared after another thirty feet. Bewildered, he pulled off his hunting cap to scratch his head before starting the long trek back to camp. Just as he slipped the cap back on, Adam Reeves appeared from out of the trees.

"Mr. Bennett!" He greeted Al with a handshake. "What's in the bag?"

"Collecting my last traps," Al said starkly as if not wanting to hear any dispute of his word. "Don't want any of them squirrel hunters to get hurt while they're trespassin' on my land. What happened to you; you hurt? Where'd all that blood come from?"

Reeves had blood smeared all over the arms and front of his shirt, plus down around the cuffs and lower part of one of his right pant legs. "I just got back from carrying a doe up to the check-in station that I had to put down. Its right front leg was nearly severed. You don't suppose it got caught in your trap before you collected it?" The game warden looked curiously at the game bag and then at Al. "I see bloodstains on your pack."

"That's from the squirrels I shot early this mornin'. Somethin' got caught in the trap though, but it released itself. I doubt your doe did that. I'd like to take a look at it though."

"Someone already picked it up. It's going to a halfway house in Jonesville. I came back down here to see if I could figure out what happened to it."

"Humph! Well, somethin' snapped my trap from its chain. I lost its blood trail right around here. Doesn't seem likely it was your deer."

"That's a little worrisome; I'll have to report this to my supervisor." Reeves pointed to Al's game bag. "Mr. Al, you know it's illegal to set those kinds of traps out here. I've been giving you a lot of leeway because people like you are a valuable asset to wildlife management areas. You don't destroy things or do anything illicit; you take care of the forest. And, because I kind of like you."

Al inhaled and made a grumbling sound to blow off the warden's sucking-up and nodded to the blood on the warden's clothes. "When you tell your supervisor about that deer, tell him he's gonna need somethin' bigger than any trap I know of to catch whatever's out here."

"But what do you think it is? No bears have been reported for months."

"Come on, lemme show you somethin'." Al led the way to the creek bank where the set of enormous wrinkled pads was imprinted in the soggy mud. Mutt trailed behind with his nose to the ground. Al couldn't help but notice Adam's limp every time he looked back to make sure he was keeping up. "They almost look human except . . .."

"It's a prank, Al," Adam interrupted. "I've seen these in other areas of the management area. Kids with nothing else better to do press forms into the ground with homemade stencils. My boss in Kisatchie caught 'em last year on their trail cams. They sneak out here ahead of hunting season to prank the hunters."

"Trail-what?" Al groused.

"Trail cameras; I'll requisition a couple. We can put 'em up around here and catch them in the act. It'll be fun."

"Humph!" Al grunted, not willing to accept the warden's explanation. There definitely was something larger than a bear moving in the shadows of the forest. "Can it tell us why the thing smells like a corpse?"

"You were close enough to pick up a scent?" Reeves asked, watching Al as he abruptly turned and whistled for Mutt who had wondered further down the bank. Reeves followed Al back up the trail until they came to a fork. "Just a reminder, Mr. Al," he said. "One more week until the shooting starts."

"You sure you're okay?" Al asked. "That limp seems to be getting worse, especially when we were climbing up the hill.

"I think I must have twisted my ankle when I lifted that deer onto the quad," he said with a grimace. "I'll have it looked at when I get off work."

"Put some ice on it; wrap it up tight." Al frowned and shook his head. "But I guess you don't need my first aid advice."

"Oh, I almost forgot, I left that radio and some batteries for you on top of your wood pile. Remember your orange vest this weekend; bow hunters will be out here hunting deer along with the squirrel hunters."

"Yeah, yeah," Al mumbled and then stepped into the thick timberland with Mutt at his heels.

Mary Lynn stuffed the syringe and small bottle of heartworm prevention in her pocket before they approached the check-in station. "There's that creepy warden; don't stop, Harry. Just keep driving."

"But he's waving at me to stop," Harry replied when the notably tall LWFD agent waved his arm up and down and then walked directly into their path.

"Hey there, Ms. Bennett," Adam greeted when Harry put the driver's window down. "You must be Harrison Foster. Your friend was up here in your truck a few days ago," he added nodding a hello to Mary Lynn.

Harry grinned at Mary Lynn. His smile changed to a frown as if agreeing with her opinion of the ominous warden. "Yes, and now we are both here to visit her father."

"Sorry, I check all vehicle plates that enter the management area," he explained. "That's so we know who's in here. You two live down in Alexandria, right? I'd be glad to give you my cell number, Ms. Bennett, if you need to get a message to your father. Might save you the long trip." He took a business card out of the pocket of what looked like a freshly pressed shirt and scribbled a number on the back.

"That's actually a good idea, Adam, uh, Mr. Reeves," Mary Lynn replied and took the card he put in Harry's hand. "Thanks."

"I was just with him down by the creek; he should be back at his camp by now. Y'all have a good visit," he said, lifting his cap slightly.

They both laughed at Harry's suggestion that the warden had a thing for Mary Lynn while he maneuvered down the dirt road as far as the thicket would allow.

"I don't trust him," she whispered, as if he might hear her. "His colors are like a kaleidoscope."

"Man, wish I would've brought a hedge trimmer," he sighed and plowed his truck through a patch of low hanging branches. "Huh!" He grunted with surprise when the trail opened up to a newly graveled road. "Someone cleared this and filled in the ruts.

They looked at each other and spoke at the same time: "Creepy Adam."

"Daddy won't like this," she sighed.

"So, don't tell him; let's just give the dog his heart worm shot and get the heck out of here." He opened the door, slammed it closed, and locked it.

"What's with the attitude you've had all afternoon?" she asked as they started their walk toward the campsite. "I told you, me and Daddy had a good visit. He took me fishing. I think we're a little closer now. He might come for a visit." She wasn't ready to tell Harry that her father told her about her mother's cheating. She hadn't quite come to terms with it herself just yet. "So, don't spoil it by making him mad." Harry's colors had been all over the place all afternoon but she purposely decided not to mention it, suspecting it would make matters worse.

"Mutt's blood-work was odd, that's all," he said in response to the frown on her face that meant she was analyzing him with her celestial vision. "I kept one of the vials. I'm not a biochemist, but there's something strange about his DNA markers. I hope he's not predisposed to going mad."

"Wow, really Harry? He didn't even fuss when I inoculated him and took some blood. Sure that's all that's bothering you?"

Harry frowned. "Let's just give him the shot."

"No, not until you tell me," she balked and planted a fist on her hip.

"I-I'm glad you're so happy about your father," he sighed and moved toward her. He put his hands on her arms as if trying to make himself perfectly clear. "I just hope he meant what he said about coming to see you. That he doesn't disappoint you . . . again."

"He meant it," she said defensively. "I know he did. Let's go."

"What are you two doin' back here again so soon?" Al suddenly stepped out of the bushes behind them, startling them. "And where's your orange?" His own orange canvas vest clashed loudly against his green camouflage overalls.

"You two sounded like a family of buffalo trampin' through here. You stirred up every animal within a mile."

"Daddy, I told you I'd be right back with Mutt's heart-worm shot." Mary Lynn gave him a hug. "It has to be given right away after a negative blood test."

"You're gonna stick that poor dog again? You're gonna make him run off."

"Ohh, I see you gave him a haircut; wow!" Mary Lynn said when Mutt sauntered up with his head lowered as if embarrassed. Her eyes met Harry's and judging by his yellow aura and expression, he was doing his best to suppress *butchered,* the description she almost used.

"Much easier to bathe now," Al replied, and pulled his long hunting knife from its sheath. "His hair's so coarse I had to sharpen this afterwards."

After Mutt's shot and a brief visit because Harry kept hinting that he had to be at work early the next morning, Al walked them back to the truck. Mary Lynn realized how right her father was about the noise they made walking through the woods. Brightly colored birds took flight from the canopy above them as they passed underneath. Only one crow stood its ground and squawked its protest. Mutt followed on Al's heals, sniffing the black trash bag his master carried low to the ground in one hand until they reached Harry's truck and he put it behind the driver's seat.

"Since you're into pathology and all," he said as if challenging the young lab tech. "See if you can tell me what snagged my trap. That pain-in-the-butt warden tried to convince me it was a deer, but I know better."

"I can't seem to get away from animal genetics," Harry said and winced from the rancid odor escaping from the plastic bag when he peeked inside.

"Put it in the back once you've left the management area. It's best the game warden not know about this."

"Mr. Al," Harry said, catching his arm before he turned away. "Mary Lynn seems different since her last visit; happier actually. If you two worked something out, that's great; but you and Dale went your own way, left her alone, and deserted her. She's had to deal with the gossip and the daily reminders of what happened to Christine by herself. Please, don't disappoint her."

Al frowned at him and then nodded. It was rare that Harry spoke so bluntly to the intimidating man. Out of respect for his honesty, he walked around the truck to the passenger side and put an arm around his daughter. "I'll be down to see you as soon as I can, I promise."

"Oh Daddy," Mary Lynn gushed and threw both arms around his waist.

"Love you, baby girl." The gruff woodsman's eyes found Harry's just as he was settling behind the wheel. He felt a lump in his throat, like his airway was constricted, making him swallow hard. Guilt was pulling at his conscience. He didn't know if he could make himself go back to the house on Hartwood.

***

It was late. Mary Lynn paused in the dining room to lean against the broom in her hands. All that remained of her mother's china and glass cabinets lay out by the curb for the city refuse department to pick up, and in the gray thirty-three-gallon trash can in front of her. When she was a teen, she used to daydream about modernizing the interior of their out dated house. Most of the kids she knew had brick homes and split-level contemporary style houses with modern built-in appliances. *All it needs is a little updating, fancier trim, paint, maybe the wall knocked down between the kitchen and dining room,* she thought as she waltzed around the room with the broom. *And it should happen sooner rather than later.* "I'll have the utilities turned back on first," she whispered out loud to the faded paneling. "I can live here, maybe hire someone to help with the heavy work until Daddy . . .." She paused, remembering Harry's warning on the way home. *Don't count your chickens*. "It's time I got my shit together," she argued and carried the broom to the kitchen where she paused to look at the outdated appliances. "Nothing of yours will be saved," she sighed. "Turns out, I didn't know you at all. Why should I hang onto anything of yours?" She turned to look at the living room where the family used to watch TV together and play parlor games. "Yeah well, how many kids really know their parents?" She'd have to break the news to Dale someday . . . and Harry. She could hear Harry's response, *why didn't he tell you before now*? "This house wasn't the happy little home we all thought it was; but neither is it going to be 'the poor Bennett house' any more. I'm claiming you," she addressed the house. "And my life. Everything's going to be better. Better than ever."

Three nights later, Mary Lynn was busy stripping wallpaper in Dale's old room when she heard a ringtone. At first, she thought it was Harry's ringtone, Disney's *Lab Rats* theme song. She had been waiting for an apology after he had been such a butt about her daddy promising to visit. It was Reeves, concerned because he hadn't seen or heard from Al in days.

"I was hoping you had," he said, "or better, that he was with you . . . like the two of you talked about. I know how self-reliant he is, but I'm getting a little worried."

"No, I haven't heard from him," she gasped. "How do you know what we talked about?"

"Oh-uh," he paused. "He told me."

She could feel her pulse rise. "What about Mutt, his dog?" she asked in a panic. "There was something out there, a bear, or something. Were you aware of that? Wait, how did you get my number?"

"My sergeant got it from the State Police."

"Oh," she sighed. "Did you check the fire pit?"

"It was cold when I was there two days ago and again today. I tried building a fire using green wood, but it didn't bring him in. I haven't seen the dog either."

"How did you know to do that?" she quizzed.

"I know the habits of every living creature in my management area, Miss Bennett. Let me know if you hear from him and I'll do the same.

Chapter 7

An early five-car accident on a high-rise section of I-49 that cuts through downtown Alexandria kept Mary Lynn busy running between the OR and ICU the entire Monday. It was late evening before the last of the critically injured was stabilized. She passed by the lab at lunch but Harry waved her off because he was deep in conversation with a man in a dark suit and then he was nowhere to be found when she signed out at 7:30. How dare he wave her off like she was nobody, and now he was ignoring her calls. "Dammit, Harry!" she said and threw the phone down on the seat of the Challenger. "Don't you know, I have things to tell you?" She picked up a sandwich to-go from Red's and tried Harry again while she sat at the rusted table on the back porch on Hartwood. Again, it went to voice mail.

The next day she left work early. It had been hard to concentrate on anything for worrying about her father. She drove to Catahoula alone, without Harry . . . his payback for not returning her calls. She was very pleased that her lead foot got her and the Challenger to the turn off fifteen minutes sooner than Harry would have. Another shortcoming she'd throw in his face. She parked in the new gravel and hurried through the thicket. She stooped and rubbed her fingers over the initials in the log and laughed to herself, "Who am I fooling, I can't stay mad at Harry." A group of birds fled the canopy above her all at once, making her freeze in place on top of the log. A raccoon suddenly waddled across the path, startling her. They all projected red: fear. An overwhelming rancid smell filled the air, a skunk perhaps. She slowly stood, carefully stepping over the log, trying not to cause another disturbance. She moved forward, looking up to find one of the red tags to point her in the right direction, but the odor was strong and dizzying. *I must be right on top of it.* She pulled the collar of her tee shirt up over her nose. Something suddenly grabbed her around the waist from behind and yanked her backwards. It happened so fast she barely had time to expel the short squeak that came out with the force. A large hairy hand that smelled like cow shit covered her face. Her captor swung her around like a sack of potatoes and pinned her to its side. She pried two of its fingers apart with her one free hand and saw glimpses of ape like legs and large hairy bare feet that were flattening the tall grass and overgrowth. The thing pushed over small trees in its way as it tramped through the woods. She kicked and wiggled her body in a desperate attempt to slip free and nearly succeeded when she hooked her legs around a young tree. The tree skinned her legs and caught on her jeans, ripping them more than they already were. In the few seconds it took the creature to tighten its grip on her, she was able to drag her feet along the ground, creating ruts and losing her tennis shoes in the process. The stench and the jostling made her so nauseous that she blacked out.

Mary Lynn awoke lying on a thick layer of pine straw and brown vines that were lightly dusted with snow. She scrambled to her knees and frantically looked in all directions for the monster that grabbed her. She looked up and realized snow flurries were touching her forehead and dampening her hair. The sky was gray and the woods were cloudy. Tree limbs were bare of foliage like they get in winter. It was cold. She stood and was quickly reminded of her bare feet after taking a first fleeting step that landed on a prickly ball from a sweet gum tree. Parts of broken limbs had been left in the wake of the abduction. While backtracking, she came upon a white deteriorating hollow log. She brushed the frost from its slick surface and found a set of shrunken distorted initials so curled within itself she could hardly make out the *MLB* and *HF* she had scribed there only five years ago. The trek brought her to a glade where her father's camp was supposed to be, but there was nothing. Just a stand of brittle frostbitten weeds.

"Daddy!" Her voice batted against the silent precipitation. A black crow, somewhere in the grayness responded as if complaining about the outburst. Then she heard its wings flapping as it took flight. Daylight was gone and the sleet was turning to snow. As it accumulated, the wood's appearance changed even more dramatically. She thought she could backtrack and find the Challenger in spite of the lack of light to illuminate the markers. She found the log. Its wrinkled remains pointed her in the direction she needed to go, but there was no new gravel or the Challenger. She actually wished Creepy Adam would pop out of the woods as she stumbled down the rutted road toward the highway. A cloud of white steam expelled from her mouth when she paused to rest where the check-in station was supposed to be. Ten minutes of trotting south along the highway gradually became a brisk walk. It must have been thirty minutes before a car approached from behind. A white SUV with a University of Louisiana Monroe sticker on a side window stopped alongside.

"Thank you so much." Mary Lynn anxiously bellowed fog in the young woman's face when she rolled down the window. The young woman leaned across the seat and asked her if she needed a ride. Her eyes matched her blue/green aura.

"Well, I had to stop for my red-headed sister. I know you're not out here for a jog . . . barefooted." The woman smiled generously at Mary Lynn when she got in. "I'm Diana. Are you broke-down somewhere? I didn't see a car on the side of the road." Diana was wearing a maroon University of Louisiana Monroe sweatshirt and baseball cap. Her auburn hair was braided into a single pigtail swept over one shoulder.

"My car is in the woods . . . somewhere," Mary Lynn sighed. "Are you going as far as Alexandria?"

"Sure am," she said. "I'm on my way to Mansura for the weekend; just dropped a friend off in Jena. Are you sure you're okay? You look a little, I don't know, upset. Lose your shoes in the woods too?"

"I just want to go home." Who would believe her story about being attacked by . . . what was it . . . not a bear? That wasn't a bear. She needed time to sort out what happened. Had she fell and hit her head and dreamed she was grabbed and dragged through the woods? Diana was staring at her ripped jeans and bare feet. "What kind of car is this?" she asked, trying to divert the college student's attention and give herself time to think. "I've never seen a digital display quite like this before; is it electric?"

"Yes," Diana replied proudly. "It has all the bells and whistles."

"Guess that's why I didn't hear you until you pulled alongside."

"It pretty much drives itself. I still like the feel of the steering wheel though." She massaged the leather wheel with one hand and with the other made several strokes across the touch screen on the dash with her fingers. "I'm majoring in physics at ULM. Ah, I see that look," she said melodiously. "I've always loved math and my world needs mathematicians."

"Your world?" Mary Lynn asked, but decided it must be some sort of urban college reference. "What's going on with the weather? It never snows this early . . . if ever."

"It's worse further north. I'm trying to beat the cold front home."

It was very generous of the young woman to stop for a total stranger and not press her as to why her clothes were torn and smudged and why she was missing her shoes. It was 9:15 on the digital clock display in the SUV's windshield when Diana pulled up next to the ramp that led to the ER at RRMC. Her light blue glow meant she was happy about dropping Mary Lynn off "so a friend could take her home." She watched the SUV silently drive away and then turned to look at the familiar eight-story hospital where she was hoping to find Harry playing catch-up in the lab. "Wait . . . what?" A small cloud of moisture appeared with her gasp. The lettering on the hospital was lighted in green instead of the usual red; in fact, the whole façade looked modernized with multi-tone beige and white panels and rounded contoured corners. She looked around for someone to ask how this happened, but there was no one, not a single person. The hospital was always busy, even outside. A canopy stood fifty-feet from the door where at least one person would be standing under to grab a quick smoke . . . the canopy was no longer there. Hospital personnel usually took walks on their breaks, and relatives sporadically came and went through the automatic doors. Maybe someone at Red's could explain. She looked across the courtyard, then squeezed her eyes closed to clear her vision, to make sure what she saw was real . . . Red's was a Pizza Hut. A bright yellow SUV pulled up. A man stepped out of the electric vehicle wearing a yellow cap that read, *TAXI.* He had the same peaceful sea green aura as Diana. "Can you take me to Hartwood Sreet?" she asked. The cabbie nodded and she climbed into the back seat when the door opened, seemingly by itself. The cab's dash was digitized like Diana's with the instrument readings in the windshield. There was no steering wheel. The driver had a computer monitor positioned at an angle next to him. She exited quickly when the cab pulled up in front of the house on Hartwood in spite of the driver's repeated reminders of the fare. Every light in the house was on and through the windows she could see shadows moving around inside. The lit carriage lights revealed a bright red front door and a landscaped yard with trees and shrubs and a flowered-bordered walkway. The cab driver had exited his vehicle by now and was standing next to her at the edge of the sidewalk. She looked up at him. Snow was rapidly accumulating on his shoulders and she realized for the first time how very tall he was. His voice sounded far away, like an echo when he asked if she was okay. He had no aura. "No," she mumbled, shaking her head slowly. "Something feels very wrong." Her knees buckled; she felt herself falling.

She woke feeling somewhat relieved to find she was in what looked like a hospital room at RRMC. That gave her comfort for about a second. An intravenous infusion tube was attached to her arm; she could hear the drip rate monitor tapping softly behind her to the left. A two-pronged nasal cannula was set under her nostrils dispensing supplemental oxygen. As her focus became clearer, she realized the room actually had the appearance of a hotel suite more than a hospital room. The furniture was Victorian and very large; there were old-fashioned paintings with antique frames hanging on the walls in both the bedroom and the living area beyond the door. The ceilings were extremely high. The lighting was dim and she had an eerie sense that she was being watched.

"You're awake." The familiar voice startled her. It came from somewhere in the shadows behind her and to the right. Neal quickly appeared, parking himself on the edge of the bed. He picked up her hand and caressed it to his cheek. The first thing she noticed was he had no aura, not even a thin one.

"Neal, am I dead?" Her voice sputtered because of the phlegm caught in her throat. "I feel like I'm in some kind of limbo."

"You're not dead." His face was beaming, like a kid that just opened the present he wanted from Santa. "You're perfectly fine; you just need time to adjust."

"Adjust to what?" she asked. "I-I," she stuttered. "Why am I so disoriented? What happened to me? How did you find me? I think I-I was hallucinating or . . ."

"Shh . . . slow down," he said and patted her hand. "I'll explain everything, a little at a time, of course. I don't want to overwhelm you."

"Let's start with where am I?" she asked pointedly because of his patronizing tone. "What is it you don't want to overwhelm me about?" she continued when he bowed his head. "Is this your place? Am I in Monroe?"

"No," he sighed and shook his head. "You fainted because, well, I'm sure it's because of the thin air; high altitude makes people light-headed when you're not used to it. Your body needs time to acclimate. Don't worry, you're perfectly safe."

"High altitude; acclimate?" She pressed her fingers to her forehead to try and evoke her memory. *Something happened to me in the woods*, she thought; *a young woman picked me up on the side of the road and that's when everything got weird.*

"Mary Lynn, you're going to have to trust me," he begged.

"I was going to see Daddy." She suddenly looked up at him with fear in her eyes. "Is Daddy okay?" Maybe they had both been in an accident that she couldn't remember.

"He's fine," Neal insisted and rubbed her arm to reassure her.

"But I couldn't find him . . ."

"He's at his camp, safe and sound."

"No, he's not; everything was gone." Her voice trailed off as she rubbed her forehead again. "Nothing makes sense."

"Please, be patient," he implored. "I can get you something to help you sleep," he said and kissed her forehead and then tried to kiss her on the lips. She almost allowed her lips to meet his, but stopped. "You'll feel better soon, I promise," he whispered.

"Promise?" she sighed as he brushed his hand on her cheek. She suddenly felt woozy like she did after stepping out of the cab.

"Yes, I promise," he said in a very low voice. He leaned in and kissed her on the lips. She felt very sleepy and laid her head back on the pillow. Neal left when the monitors showed she was asleep.

Something woke Mary Lynn. Maybe it was the door closing, maybe it was a dream. Whatever it was, it made her sit up. She tried to pull the IV needle from her arm, only to be snagged by a set of monitor leads attached to her torso that she hadn't noticed before. After ripping off the sticky patches, she grabbed a thick white robe hanging over one of the bed's corner spindles. She slipped it on over a blue nightgown she didn't remember putting on. The next room had more light, allowing her to see just how tall the ceilings really were. Another door across the room looked like it might lead outside. It had an upper and lower component much like a Dutch door. When she pulled on the oversized handle, only the eight-foot lower section opened. A man at least twelve feet tall with human features stood against the wall across the hall with his hands folded behind his back. He was dressed in loose dark-brown pants, sandals, and a maroon tunic trimmed with gold squares. His reddish hair was long and bundled behind his head; his expression was quite menacing. He seemed as startled to see her standing in the doorway as she was to see someone of his enormity guarding the door. *None of this can be real; I see no auras.* She quickly ducked back inside and pushed the door closed. She leaned up against it, as if her insignificant stature would somehow stop the humongous man. She desperately looked for a place to hide from the gargantuan that she feared would burst through the door at any second. She ducked behind an oversized sofa, crawled along the floor and slipped behind a heavy floor-length drape. There was a window seat behind the drape with gold velvet cushions. She scrambled onto them. She listened from within the bay window shelter for the door to open. The scenery outside, that she had merely glanced at, started to register; she slowly turned to look again.

"Where, wha . . ." she gasped and crawled closer, pressing her hands against the thick glass panes that separated her from the outside and a snow-covered mountainous landscape. Blusterous white clouds hovered above and below the limited view. Neal's reference to high altitude echoed in her head.

"Beautiful, isn't it?" It was Neal's voice again. "So majestic," he sighed and let go of the drape he was holding and sat down behind her.

"I'm in Switzerland." He had told her many times that his parents lived in Switzerland.

"We were meant to be together," he whispered.

"No," she scowled. "We broke up." She turned around to face him, frowning, trying to be brave in spite of realizing that he had somehow arranged to have her kidnapped and brought to his childhood home. "Was the girlfriend story supposed to make me jealous? How on earth did you get me here?" It must have taken fifteen hours to fly from Louisiana to the Swiss Alps.

"I think I fell in love with you the first time I saw you," he reminisced. He wanted to take her hand again, but knew enough about her moods to sense she might shove him off the window seat. "Remember, it was at the blood drive in the parking lot of St. Francis Elementary." He smiled as the memory made his heart beat faster. "I couldn't take my eyes off you while you tended to the donors. It was amazing how you could take on what they were feeling; your compassion is truly the most remarkable part of your care. I was so grateful to be the one . . . I mean . . ." he corrected, "Grateful I finally worked up the nerve to talk to you a few days later at the Christmas parade."

"So, you were stalking me?" She glared at him as if daring him to lie or make another enticing attempt toward her.

"I wasn't expecting to fall so deeply in love," he said.

The reverie made her turn away and close her eyes, hoping that when she opened them again the nightmare would dissolve. There would be no snowy mountain peaks, no bay window, no Neal. The colors would reappear and she'd find herself safe at home on the air mattress in her old bedroom on Hartwood. "Why is there a giant man outside my door?" she whispered, after opening her eyes and seeing that nothing had changed.

"He's there to protect you," he replied. "Mostly from yourself."

Mary Lynn shook her head. He was patronizing her again, not listening, as always.

"He's a Nephilim." He slid the drape to one side on its rings as if presenting the interior of the great room to her. The reason for the high ceilings and oversized furniture was starting to make sense when she saw the portraits on the walls of proud giants dressed in tunics of thick animal skins and holding spears and shields. Simple scenes that seem to symbolize events from an ancient era were displayed around the room. A gold statue of Buddha stood in one corner on a stone plinth. A gold-fringed maroon pillow lay on top of an eight-foot blue rug on the floor in front of it. "The Nephilim fought on the front lines for the Romans in ancient times," he sighed after walking her to one of the oil paintings of a gritty battle scene. "They are the offspring of The Fallen, the angels banished from heaven by the gods millions of years ago."

"You mean by God, don't you?" she countered. She remembered the story from one of the many Bible stories her mother read to her and Harry.

"I know this is unsettling, but it's important." He tried to touch her shoulder but she pulled away. "The Nephilim were renowned warriors in the days of old and feared by everyone. Evil warmongers used them as shields and battering rams. He directed her to another painting of a giant Nephilim that was dressed in full metal armor running toward a charging army of human-sized infantrymen whose arms were cocked and ready to launch their inconsequential spears. "A few thousand live within these mountains, away from the modern world and The Fallen who they fear are still looking for them."

This would be an incredibly unbelievable tale except for the twelve-foot man standing outside in the hall. She picked up a dark-colored sculpture from an end table. It was a black angel with drooping wings. "Is this what The Fallen look like? Its face was grotesque and evil-looking."

"Yes, this is what they looked like when the gods banished them from heaven," he replied. "They roamed the earth, god's prized creation, out of retaliation. They mated with the women they found here. Earth became so corrupt that the gods sent a great flood to destroy the giants as well as every living creature. They stripped The Fallen of their powers for seventy generations. Some of the giants survived and migrated to Scandinavia and others made their way here to Bhutan."

"Bhutan?" she gasped and looked back toward the window. "In the Himalayas?" That's where we are? The highest peaks of the world."

"Yes," he said. "They choose to live as far away from earth's chaotic societies as possible, knowing they will never be anything but feared oddities. An order of monks has held claim to these mountains for as long as anyone can remember. From the time they settled here, the monks helped the giants develop their inherited powers for the use of good instead of evil."

"Neal, I hear what you're saying." She walked toward the large sofa and pulled one of the cushions onto the floor to sit on. "You're right; I need time to think about this. You have to tell me, please, why am *I* in Bhutan? Are you going to take me back home?"

"Mary Lynn." His face erupted into a prideful smile. "You carry the Nephilim gene; as do I," he boasted. "We were supposed to be together." He cast his eyes down. "I know I messed up. I'm still trying to figure out where I went wrong; I'm sorry for whatever I did that made you reject me. You deserve to know who you are. You shouldn't spend your whole life looking for the answers as to why you feel the way you do and why you see the things you see. No one you know will ever be able to give you those answers."

"See things?" she repeated barely above a whisper, wondering how he could possibly know her secret. Mary Lynn looked around the walls covered in part by tapestries and dotted with battlefield paintings and portraits of distinguished-looking leaders. "I'm related to . . . these . . . creatures?" she sighed.

"You look tired; I've told you a lot more than I intended. You should rest." He offered her a hand; she slid off the cushion and followed him to the bedroom. "Tomorrow, I'll take you to observe the giants as they go about their daily routine. Please don't leave your room," he said after tucking her in. "And keep this in place." He put the oxygen nodules under her nose. "You could become light-headed again, fall and possibly hurt yourself."

"What else do I need to know, Neal?"

"We'll talk more tomorrow." He patted her on the shoulder.

"Neal, did I imagine the young woman that gave me a ride and the cab driver and my house?"

"You're suffering from acute mountain sickness," he said. His voice had the appeasing tone again, renewing her distrust of him. Five minutes after he left, she pulled the oxygen tube over her head and threw the covers back. She rushed across the living room and pulled the handle of the heavy door. She had to see if the freakish man was still there or if it was a hallucination. There he was, still standing against the wall. She motioned for him to come inside the suite. "You'd still be on duty," she argued when he frowned and shook his head; "just not in the hallway." She coaxed him again, pushing the lower half of the door open wider.

"No, ma'am," he said politely. "And, there is no *duty*; I chose to be here."

She dragged two cushions from inside the suite out into the hall, climbed onto them, and signaled him to sit on the floor. "What's your name?" she asked when they were both settled.

"James." He took up most of the width of the hall. He sat up straight with his back to the wall and his legs folded Indian style. His hands were propped on his knees, similar to the posture of the Buddha statue in her room.

"How old are you, James?" she asked, examining his seemingly young facial features.

"Twenty-eight," he replied. "I have fathered six children and have as many siblings." He stated these statistics with great pride. "We are trying to deter extinction. Your culture takes life for granted. Some of you throw it away; it's precious to us."

"Your children, are they like you?"

"You are referring to my size. Yes, I have three sons that are like me, two that are your size and live with the monks, and a daughter like you. Very much like you, in fact. She lives and studies here."

"James, is it true? Am I Nephilim?"

"Yes," he replied. "Women of your size living outside the mountains have been giving birth to our offspring for thousands of years. It's not my place to tell you how this is done or convince you of its ethicality. Our endeavor is to cultivate the earth with our lineage, as pure a lineage as possible. The world will never accept us as we are, but our DNA is necessary for humans to access the gods."

"Hum," she said, frowning. "You know I believe in one God, right? So, why am I here?" she asked when he nodded.

"You are the daughter of hierarchy. You must be given the opportunity to unlock the gifts you inherited. The monks will help you with that."

"Is that why I see colors or used to until I woke up here, and why I feel things?" she asked. "Did I inherit that from . . . the Nephilim?" Her mother always hushed the issue of her seeing colors and never brought it up to any doctor.

"So many questions," he said shyly, smiling and shaking his head. "I'm afraid I can't give you an explanation for everything. I can tell you that we live by the teachings of Gautama Buddha, the ancient and wise Sage who taught that the mind is very powerful and that we become what we believe. I suspect you developed gifts on your own as a coping mechanism, but I cannot be sure of how many. Buddha teaches, if our minds are pure then joy will follow us like a shadow and never leave. We are fortunate to live in a country where its people strive to live peaceful lives. We are safe because the Kingdom of Bhutan forbids people to travel these mountains without permission from the monks. We live simply; we spend our days farming, tending our flock, and in prayer. Climbers attempt to scale our slopes, but we can sense their presence and relocate them. Don't frown," he said when he felt her questioning the civility of the practice. "They are never harmed. They wake up in their base village with a fear of the mountains and no recollection of the climb. The Nephilim have many such abilities. For example, I can sense your questions." He felt the doubt in her mind. "The monks taught our forefathers these arts through meditation. Meditation has allowed us to atone for the sins of our predecessors who were responsible for the deaths of thousands in the early wars. Yes, like the paintings on the walls," he said when he saw her eyes dance back and forth as she recalled the anger and determination depicted in the faces on the canvases. "Meditation is all-consuming and enables us to tap into our extraordinary skills. Our children are taught these exercises from the moment they are born. Our masteries are as second nature to us as walking and talking are to you." He leaned in closer as if to make sure she could hear him clearly. "The Fallen are responsible for all the prevailing evil in the world. They are responsible for the egregious sin that one of our gods martyred Himself to rectify. He became one of you in order to do this. In days of old, the land was abounded with the gargantuan offspring of The Fallen. The early Nephilim were misused by the wicked warriors."

"Then came the flood," she said softly. She had been able to see everything he described. It appeared in her head like an idea, as if she were watching a movie. It was as if James had projected through her eyes the scene of what he believed they had experienced. "Noah and the great flood," she added.

"Yes." He nodded.

"But there was no mention of a land of giants in the Bible," she whispered, mesmerized by the story that somehow was making so much sense to her. She was on her knees now, unafraid of the huge man whose face was but inches away from hers. The story was the same as Neal's, but the way James presented it left little doubt in her mind. Besides, Neal had lied to her; it was hard to take him seriously when he always seemed to be looking out for himself.

"It was decided by every church hierarchy in existence that our story be left out of the Holy Scriptures," he continued. "The only works permitted were those promoting Christianity and the god called Jesus Christ who, as it is told, came to earth not only to die in atonement for the sins of our forefathers but to teach humanity how to go forward and overcome the evil that had spread so vastly. I often think," he said, leaning against the wall, "if people could only understand how devastating evil truly is . . ." He paused as if to quell an emerging emotion before continuing. "They would do everything they could to stop it; perhaps learn to meditate as all good Buddhists do. The Christian Bible mentions only one giant, Goliath, who was defeated by David. It was only mentioned because it was a precursor to the story of David's greatness as a warrior, civil adjudicator, righteous King of Israel and ancestor of the future Messiah."

"James, explain to me how I'm . . ." she began, but he cut her off.

"I'm not allowed to explain your bloodline," he replied before she could finish. "But it is important for our future."

She exhaled with a groan. *Is it impossible to hide my thoughts from him?*

"It is our hope that you accept who you are," he continued. "I was the one that brought you here," he said, answering her next unasked question. "I was by your side throughout your journey. I allowed you to meet Diana and experience your home as it will look in the future," he said and then shook his head. "I apologize; I'm not giving you a chance to verbalize.

I forgive you, she jibbed silently and then they smiled at each other. She was feeling a connection with him that seemed more like kinship. "If you promise to always be honest with me," she said aloud.

"You will learn the art of meditation," he said. "It may take some time."

"I guess you really do know me," she replied with a slip of a smile. "I never liked going to church."

"I know. I've been watching you since the day I was told you existed. I failed horribly on my first attempt to bring you here; I was an adolescent with little experience. I planned it better this time."

"You don't mean Camp Livingston?" Mary Lynn winced. He nodded. "You were Bigfoot?"

"We often use folklore to our advantage; we're the reason the rumors persist. We have a wide range of wardrobe." He moved his enormous hand up to the side of her head but didn't touch her. It was a gesture of affection that he didn't intend to make. "I'm not here to guard you but to make sure you are safe."

"Will I be allowed to go home?" she sighed. "Will I remember this place, and you, James?" she asked, thinking about the climbers. "I want to remember."

"It is our hope."

"You look nothing like the paintings on the walls inside," she whispered. "You're just like me except . . ." She suddenly felt tired. "I should go back to bed now."

"Sleep well." James smiled, stood, and took his post against the wall. "I will be right here."

Chapter 8

Harry's shift had been every bit as hectic for Mary Lynn on the day of the *Horrific Interstate Pileup* as was the headline on the front page of the Alexandria Daily Town Talk. An article below the fold, five pages in, reported that a mobile home had gone up in flames two hours prior to the accident. Two brothers, ages four and six, playing with matches, accidentally set their bunk beds on fire. Detectives suspected chemicals commonly used in meth labs were the reason for the home going up so quickly. The RRMC chem and path labs received over 250 heat-sealed nylon and paper evidence bags from the mobile home that contained samples marked urgent by ATF. This was on top of the normal daily samples of blood, tumor, and cist biopsies, some of which came down during surgeries and awaited diagnosis. The children's bodies were in the morgue waiting on tissue analysis. The police were awaiting results from the surviving parents after having tested positive in a field test for suspicious substances. There was no time for the man dressed in black, wearing sunglasses, and brandishing a badge who entered the lab in the middle of the hubbub. He opened his wallet and identified himself as FBI Agent John Greenfield, Special Division. Harry, drained from overwork, began to school him in the lab's sterile protocol. The agent took the opportunity to suggest they move to the more suitable consult room outside the germ-free lab. The agent was asking about a blood sample he sent to Shreveport. Harry was barely paying attention because Mary Lynn was standing in the hallway on the other side of a glass door, signaling him to join her outside. He shook his head and nodded toward the agent who'd put the sunglasses away and was now unfolding a leather-cased notepad he produced from an inside jacket pocket.

"One of the nerds at Langley," the agent said, while scrolling up the screen, "was scooped up by the big wigs at the FBI Quantico lab in DC several years ago. Quantico put him in charge of creating a team to expand a project he initiated."

Harry was scarcely paying attention to the agent as he watched Mary Lynn wave a *never mind* at him and then dart away.

"Take a look." The agent nudged Harry's arm with the notepad forcing his attention away from the door. "So, the nerd is in charge of a four-man team tasked to collect data from around the world. They take reports from the thousands of mysterious disappearances that are reported every year and compare them to various phenomena such as UFO reports, alien abductions, and other strange incidences." Harry turned the device towards him with one hand and looked at the meaningless map pocked with clusters of small glowing red dots. "I know it sounds a little strange, but the team has compiled and collated an incredible amount of data in support of the theory that they're all connected. The Virginia headquarters formed a division charged with connecting the dots to something, well, hum . . . I'll use the word *ominous* for now. So, that gets me to why I'm here." He flipped the case closed and returned the notepad to his inside coat pocket. "The blood sample you sent to Shreveport contains DNA markers similar to some present at a few sites where those incidents took place."

"I send dozens of samples to Shreveport every week," Harry countered. "Can you be more specific?" *Was the agent here to question his proficiency? Had he made an interpretation error from a sample involving a government case?* He tried to search his memory for recent cases that might have involved the U.S. Marshal's Office or one of the local army installations. Nothing came to mind that would have involved the FBI.

"The one labeled *Mutt.*"

Harry frowned. "Mutt?" What could be so interesting about the DNA of a stray dog that would send the FBI knocking? The agent was now shadowing his every move in the lab in spite of his turning the second vile of Mutt's blood over to him and sharing as much as he knew about the large bushy-haired dog that wandered into Al's camp. The agent insisted on looking at files, computer records, coolers, slides, anything having to do with the dog's blood. It took Harry the weekend and all of Monday to catch up on the backlog of accumulated work because of the two tragedies and the agent's phone calls, drop-ins, and hovering.

On Tuesday, the agent appeared in the lab, frowning. He wanted to interview Al Bennett and his daughter. "I understand you and the girl are friends."

Harry quickly led him to the consult room. "What's wrong?"

"She didn't report for her shift Monday morning and her cell phone is going to voice mail. Phone records show she tried to call you several times until mid-day Sunday when the phone was turned off or . . ." He blew out a sigh instead of finishing the sentence. "I obtained a court order and searched her apartment after getting no answer at the door. A team from the U.S. Marshall's office assigned to help me, found no indication of foul play inside. Three days' worth of letters and junk mail had accumulated in her mailbox. The house on Hartwood is vacant, although it's possible, she has been living in both places. "I understand you two are close friends," he said holding up his notepad. I issued a 'be on the lookout' on her car, a Blue 2015 Challenger."

Harry suddenly realized four days had gone by since he last saw Mary Lynn. He was swamped, tied up with catch-up work, and of course, dealing with Greenfield's questions. "She's missing? Wait, we exchanged vehicles," he said thinking aloud as if in a daze. "But that was a week ago on a Saturday. She drove up to give Mutt his heartworm shot. We switched back Sunday night. There was something she wanted to tell me, but she was too tired; we never got around to . . ." The realization that his best friend might be in trouble was sinking in. "She was outside that door," he said, turning to the glass window and imagining her looking at him from the other side. "Standing at the window, the first day you were here." He rushed to the door, and turned around. "I ignored her. This is your fault. I would have gone to the door if it weren't for you."

"Tell me what you know about the fiancé," Greenfield said bluntly, ignoring Harry's distress. "Neal Mueller."

"Former fiancé," Harry corrected. *How did he know about Neal?* Less than a handful of people knew about the short-lived engagement. How did he find this out so quickly? "What about him; do you think she's with him?" Harry sat down in one of the consult chairs and got up again. His mind was racing. Obviously, the FBI has information on everything and everybody: Mary Lynn, her family, himself. Moreover, all of it readily available on that notebook he treasures. "Neal is a veterinarian," he said thinking this information was probably redundant. "He gave Mary Lynn the inoculations for Mutt. He dropped by the lab, giving me the okay to give Mutt the heartworm shot. I had dropped the blood sample off to his work earlier in the day. It's the reason she went to Al's camp Saturday. I offered to drive her, but she wanted to go alone, to talk to Al about something. She said she would tell me about it later . . . she was tired

"I went to the ex-fiancé's supposed work place. There was a Neal there." He tapped a photo icon and turned the pad around.

"That's not Neal," Harry said after looking at the photo of a man wearing glasses and with speckled gray hair. He looked up from the pad and frowned at Greenfield.

"This is Neal Miller," the agent grunted. "They have no idea who Neal Mueller is. You wouldn't have any photos of him, would you?"

Greenfield departed to re-interview coworkers. Harry rushed to the sixth floor where the elderly Ms. Morrison had been transferred from the ICU. She too had been wondering why Mary Lynn had not been to see her.

"She always comes by at breakfast to check on me when she's on duty," she reported. "I was afraid something had happened to Al. He has a dog now, you know; she was very pleased about that."

"Did she ever mention a man by the name of Neal, Neal Mueller?"

"No honey, she didn't. Please tell me she's okay."

The floor supervisor said she requested a day off, but that day had passed and no one had been able to reach her. He decided to check the house on Hartwood for himself. He found an air mattress, stripped wallpaper lying on the floor, and wadded up carry-out bags from Red's in the trash. If he had only talked to her the day that she waved to him at the door. The guilt was ripping him apart. A real friend would have said *excuse me,* and met her outside in the hallway.

Greenfield started the next day lurking around the lab, taking notes, and conversing over the ever-present notepad, making it hard for Harry to concentrate on work.

"Don't you think it's time we drove up to Al's camp?" Harry blurted out just as the agent reached for a sample tray in one of the refrigerators. The stern man let the door go and looked at him curiously. "That's the only place I can think of that she might be since her car is missing. She took my truck the last time, but . . ." His eyes pleaded hope. "That must be what she wanted that day; to borrow my truck again. So that's where she is; she drove up in her car."

"I've been thinking the same thing, Mr. Foster," Greenfield said, snapping the notepad closed and shoving it in the large side pocket of his black field jacket. "That's where the dog is, right?"

"Yes, but promise me you won't take the dog," Harry said, grabbing hold of the agent's sleeve as he walked past.

"Examine him, take blood, tissue, whatever; just don't take him away from Al. Mary Lynn wants him to have someone . . . a companion."

"Sure," he replied brusquely as if someone's feelings were the last of his concerns. "Meet me at that place across the square at 6:00 am, Red's. She was getting takeout there up until Sunday. We'll eat breakfast and leave from there."

Harry convinced the agent in the parking lot of Red's that his Tacoma was better suited than the government-issued SUV for the back roads leading to Al's camp. The agent had traded his black suit for a pair of jeans and a black sweatshirt with *FBI* printed in small yellow letters on the left front. He was wearing a pair of well-worn hiking boots. Apparently, this was not his first time going hiking.

"How long have the two of you been friends?" Greenfield asked, breaking twenty minutes of silence, only after catching up on notes from the ever-visible notepad.

"For as long as I can remember," Harry replied. "We went to the same schools: elementary, high school, college. I grew up in the Bennett house. My father died when I was little and my mother left me with the Bennett's after hooking up with a bull rider."

"Nothing romantic between the two of you?" he grunted, smirking ever so slightly. Harry could see the trip outlined in yellow on the notepad in his lap. He should have been enjoying the view outside his windows. He was missing some of the state's finest views. Luscious magnolias and tall pines lined the roadway that gave way to the occasional farmhouse and barn that housed tractors and hay. Fields of cows and horses grazed in its perimeter. There were tilled rows that went on for as far as the eye could see where cotton, corn, and soybeans would be planted in the spring. It was hard to tell what Greenfield was thinking behind the sunglasses and expressionless face.

"I guess I do love Mary Lynn," Harry said. "But it's a brotherly kind of love. We've never kissed, well, not in a passionate way." He thought about when they were kids and how they would sneak out at night and run the neighborhoods while her parents slept. "We went from catching fireflies at night to looking into windows, sneaking into houses, and taking whatever snacks we could find. We progressed to borrowing bicycles," he said, making the two-fingered quotation sign with one hand. "We rode them around town and then put them back when we were done. As teens, we graduated to walking out of diners without paying, driving off without paying for gas, and buying things at a department store and returning them for a refund when we were done with them, if we hadn't destroyed them first, that is. We broke into empty camps at Kinkaid Lake and threw parties. I remember dancing on the docks and on top of cars. I don't know how we got away with some of the shit we pulled." Harry smiled, blushing from the reminiscences.

Greenfield nodded slowly. The hardened agent produced a slip of a smile that lifted one corner of his mouth. "Well, maybe it had something to do with her daddy being a cop," he finally said, with an ill-natured slur.

"Yeah," Harry sighed. "Maybe we weren't as smart or as lucky as we thought we were. My life didn't start out that great, but after the Bennetts took me in it was better than I could have hoped for." He pointed to the notebook and shook his head; his whole life story was probably right there in a file. "I felt safe with the Bennetts; not just because her father was a deputy and her mother a devout Christian. There was structure there, peace and security . . . until . . ."

"Christine Bennett disappeared," the agent exhaled, interrupting as if his story was a boring tale to a man who had heard it all.

"Yeah, so what don't you know?"

"How you felt about the Bennett's until just now," he replied distantly. "Did Mary Lynn have any other boyfriends other than this Neal?"

Harry told Greenfield about a few insignificant boys she made fools of over the years including Tommy, the cheater. "She was never serious about anyone until Neal. He was different, not from around here, New York State. He never pushed her to talk about Christine or her past boyfriends; none of it seemed to matter to him. Everybody gave up on her," he recounted. "Her brother, Al, they just picked up and moved away." There was a resentful tone in Harry's voice. "They left her here alone to deal with the detectives, the sorrow, the memories, and the everyday reminders of what happened. Are you even listening?" he sneered with disgust when he noticed the agent concentrating on the notepad in his lap. "Am I boring you? Why do you stare at that thing so much? Does your existence depend on it? Tell me, is Christine Bennett one of the dots on the map you showed me?"

"Yes, as a matter of fact she is," the agent replied without looking up. "I'm as familiar with her case as I am with all of them."

"All of them?" Harry repeated.

"The numbers are staggering; far too many will never be solved."

"Please don't talk about Christine like she's a statistic," Harry scolded. "Her disappearance was a tragedy for us."

The agent ignored Harry's burst of frustration. "Fortunately, advances in technology and new DNA testing have tied a good many of the dots together. Christine Bennett is among them. Hair and blood samples from suspected sites are being retested. The results are encouraging, according to the Quantico Nerd and his team. Your Mutt sample contains indicators matching other blood evidence found at some sights."

"Maybe your technology is flawed," Harry snarled. "What does a dog have to do with Christine's disappearance?"

"I don't expect this to make sense to you. I just need to study the dog and interview Mr. Bennett and his daughter, if she's with him."

"Al will never let you take Mutt if that's what you have in mind; neither will Mary Lynn." Harry waved his hand, pointing to the blacktop road in front of them as if she and Al were standing there on either side of the yellow line with fists on their hips daring anyone to try to take Mutt.

"The people that claim they were abducted and the ones still missing have a commonality," the agent said, looking at Harry over the top of his glasses. "Their blood contains the negative Rh factor."

Harry's brow fell, his mouth dropped. His heart felt as if it had stopped even though he could feel the veins in his neck pulsating. "R-Rh," he stuttered and gripped the wheel stiff-armed. "Al always reminds me of Mary Lynn's O- . . . in case . . ." The tighter he squeezed the wheel, the harder his foot pressed the accelerator.

"Slow down," Greenfield grumbled, "didn't you see the speed trap at both ends of that little town we just went through?"

"Shut up! You can flash them your ID."

Greenfield crept through the dense trail as if a suspect lurked behind every tree and under every vine. He listened carefully, turned over suspicious-looking leaves, and carefully examined every broken branch with his flashlight. He found a set of footprints. "Too large to be a woman," he mumbled but marked them with a yellow post-it that he anchored with a twig from a tree limb.

"She's here, she's here," Harry kept repeating to himself. "She was expecting him to come home. He must have called her to come get him. That makes sense, doesn't it?"

"There was a call made from this area the night before she failed to report to work."

"He could have borrowed the game warden's cell phone!" Harry gushed with renewed confidence. *Okay, that's it, Al called her.*

As soon as they entered the camp Harry hurried to stir the coals; a warm glow appeared. "They can't be far. If we call out, they might hear us."

The agent ignored the suggestion and walked around the camp pointing his flashlight as he turned things over. He flipped the switch to the radio that was sitting on the floor just inside one of the tents. Faint voices and static filled the tent; he turned it off. When he pushed back the tent flap to step back outside, Al was standing across the camp next to the woodpile with his rifle pointed at him.

"Mr. Bennett, put down the rifle," Greenfield said calmly while placing his palm over the Smith & Wesson attached to his waist.

"Al," Harry cried out, stretching his arms out between them as if trying to hold the two men in place. "Please tell me Mary Lynn is here, *please.*"

"What are you talking about?" he growled, putting the rifle down by his side.

"No one's seen her in three days." Harry's voice cracked as he lowered his arms.

"Don't you see her every day?" Al demanded.

"I got busy at work," Harry replied accusingly. "I lost track of time," he added, looking at Greenfield.

"You have a dog, Mr. Bennett," Greenfield said. "Where is it?"

"Who cares?" Al growled and then marched toward Harry as if he intended to tackle him. "I depend on you to keep an eye on her."

"There's, there's something different about Mutt's blood." Harry's voice quivered nervously. He could feel Al's angry heat as they stood nose to nose. "Remember the blood she took?" he managed to whisper.

"Where's your dog, sir?" Greenfield repeated.

Al pointed the rifle in the air and pulled the trigger twice. "Hopefully, as far away from here as he can run." The blasts from the rifle sent Harry to his knees as he covered his head with his arms. When he looked up, Al was glaring at Greenfield, his boots planted in the dirt.

"Mr. Bennett," Greenfield said with well-trained patience. "Put the rifle down. I only want to examine the dog."

"Aren't you concerned about my daughter?" Al moved slowly toward the agent, dragging his boots in such a way that called instinct into play; he quickly removed the S&W from its holster.

"Put the rifle down, Mr. Bennett, please," the agent growled loudly. The agent held the gun steady with both hands, arms straight out, elbows locked. "We'll get to her in a minute."

"Wait!" Harry called out while scrambling to his feet. "What about Dale? She could be at Dale's."

"She's not there." Greenfield still had his eyes fixed on Al. "We have people watching that house."

"I suppose you're here to accuse me of somethin' like before," Al grumbled. The agent put the S&W away and produced his wallet. Al cradled the rifle in one arm to examine the credentials and then leaned the weapon against the woodpile. He uncharacteristically exhaled as if weakened by the realization that his daughter was missing.

"Can you think of anything that might help us find her?" the agent asked, sounding almost sympathetic. "Did you notice anything unusual about her when she came to visit?"

"What's that?" Harry turned toward the woods behind him.

"Sounds like a motorcycle in low gear," Al said.

Whatever it was went silent. For one anxious moment and out of options, Harry thought it might be Mary Lynn. A few tense seconds passed before Adam Reeves limped into camp.

"Creepy Adam," Harry whispered under his breath.

"Al, everything okay?" Adam still had the limp as he walked toward them. "I heard your rifle."

"Go away," grumbled the old man. "Get off my property; I can't deal with you right now, unless you've seen my daughter."

"Well, technically, Mr. Bennett," Greenfield interjected, "you're on US Forestry land which is government property." He examined the wildlife agent's ID that he'd quickly produced.

"My lease is paid. I have every right to be here and demand that every one of you get off my land."

"Al, just let him ask his questions," Harry begged. "Mary Lynn got a phone call from this area. Was it you?"

"It wasn't from me," Al growled and looked to Adam. "I don't have a phone; what about you?"

"No sir." Reeves quickly reached in his shirt pocket and pulled out a phone. "Here, check it out."

Greenfield took the phone and immediately pressed the *recent calls* icon. "You mind if I plug this into my device? Not waiting for a response, he carried the phone to the woodpile, laid the two devices on top of the split wood, and connected them. In a matter of seconds, the Quantico team had the cell's information.

Is she supposed to be here?" Adam asked as he and Al huddled together out of earshot of the FBI agent. "There's been no mention of her on the radio."

"She's not here," Al grumbled. "I would know."

"I'll contact my boss, Al," Adam whispered. "He'll get the word out. If she's in the area, we'll find her."

"People are on their way to set up a grid search," Greenfield said, interrupting their hushed discussion. "Let your people know that we have a missing person," he addressed Adam. "Tell them that this could be a crime scene and to keep the public out. Mr. Bennett, pack whatever you need, you're coming back to field headquarters with me."

Al felt like giving him an argument but Harry touched him on the arm. The pleading eyes of the young man he helped raise were begging him to cooperate.

Chapter 9

Harry tried to keep his eyes on the road on the drive home, but he could sense Al glaring at him from the passenger seat making it hard to shake the urge to look over at him. Greenfield sat behind them in the backseat, sending messages, making requests, receiving reports, and observing his two most important witnesses.

The agent broke the awkward silence. "What is it you want to say to him, Mr. Bennett?" He looked up from the notebook. "Your eyes have been drilling holes in the side of his head since we got in the truck. Go ahead." He wiggled a finger back and forth between them. "Say what you want to say."

"I ain't got nothin to say!" Al barked and turned his head to look out the window.

"What you're not saying could very well hinder us in finding your daughter." The agent leaned forward. "Mr. Bennett, I understand you don't like me and what I represent, but my team can't do its job unless we know everything you know. There are a hundred nerd-heads on the other end of this." He held the notebook up so Al could see it if he chose to turn his head, that is. "They know how to take the slightest detail and turn it into a lead. So, whatever it is please spit it out."

"She had her hopes up so high." Harry jerked his head back and forth between Al and the road. "You were taking too long. Why couldn't you just have that creepy warden bring you home?"

"You were supposed to be watchin' out for her!" Al blared at Harry.

"That's better," the agent interjected. "Mr. Bennett, Al, what can you tell me about Adam Reeves?"

"Nothin'!" Al barked, still staring contemptuously at Harry. "Says he's from Mississippi, worked in Kisatchie for a while." He shook his head in disbelief of the situation and turned to stare at the road ahead. "He gets on my nerves when he just shows up outta nowhere when I'm in the middle of somethin', like just now."

"Okay, better," Greenfield nodded. "Do you know how he got the limp?"

"Yeah," Al said. "Hurt it carryin' a deer up a hill. That's what he said, anyways."

"Is that all you want to say to Harry?"

The two men in the front seat looked at each other. Al narrowed his eyes and turned his head to look out the passenger window again, propping his elbow on top of the door panel. Greenfield sat back in the seat and reported the conversation.

"We should be at my apartment in about ten minutes," Harry said when they passed a city limits sign. He saw the agent nodding through the rearview mirror, his eyes not moving from the notepad.

The agent suddenly came to life and slapped the case closed. "I'll pick up my vehicle and head over to the US Marshall's office at Beauregard. I'll be coordinating the search operation from there. You two can go home; I'll be in touch in the morning."

"I thought you were bringin' us in for questioning?" Al complained. "You dragged me down here for nothin'," he grumbled defiantly. "I ain't goin' to Mary Lynn's and definitely not to the house."

"You can stay at my place, Al," Harry conceded. He looked over at Al for his reaction. "I have an extra bedroom."

"Don't wanna do that either," Al complained. "I'd rather sleep in the park."

"Come on, Al, I'll pick up some food on the way. How about your favorite, Church's Chicken? Bet you haven't had that in a while."

"I'd take him up on that Mr. Bennett," Greenfield encouraged.

There was that suspicious half-smile again, the one that barely raised one corner of his mouth. *His manipulating asshole smile*, Harry decided.

"You'll be dealing with me again in the morning," the agent continued. "A good night's sleep sometimes helps people remember things."

John Greenfield drove away in his black SUV with a three-piece meal from Church's, leaving Al and Harry standing beside the Tacoma in the parking lot outside Harry's apartment complex.

"Al, why didn't you say anything about the trap?" Harry asked when they headed to the stairs, Al with a duffle slung over his shoulder and Harry carrying their white plastic food bags.

"I don't trust him," Al grumbled. "So, what'd ya do with it, anyway?" He wearily grabbed hold of the iron hand railing to pull himself up the steps.

"I'll show you." Harry tucked the bag of food under his arm and unlocked the door. "You okay?" Al was breathing heavily.

"I'm fine; just a lot to take in." Al threw the duffle on a chair and followed Harry to the kitchen. "Humph!" the old man grunted, staring at the garbage bag containing Al's trap in the upper freezer compartment. "I sure wanted to hunt that thing down. Not so much as to shoot it, as to watch it and learn its habits. Find out what it eats, where it beds down. I never had the feelin' it was harmful."

"We're going to show this to Greenfield in the morning." Harry placed a comforting hand on the old man's shoulder. "Full disclosure, okay? For Mary Lynn."

Al's exhale was long and loud as if he'd been defeated "I know."

***

Agent Greenfield stared at the notebook screen in front of him while sitting on the edge of a cot in one of the US Marshall's dormitory rooms at Camp Beauregard. He was the only occupant of the six-bed barrack. He watched as the two men stared into the top section of Harry's refrigerator from the wireless camera his team placed next to a hurricane lamp on Harry's faux mantle. Wireless cameras were in other strategic places throughout the apartment. "How did our guys miss this?" he whispered to himself. *I could give them the opportunity to bring me whatever's in that bag*, he argued to himself. *I really don't want to threaten them with obstruction. They are not the bad guys; they're victims, like all the others.* His training, experience, and gut feeling told him he should have the bag seized immediately. He lay back in the cot to weigh the options; should he go alone or send a team? Too many officers with weapons could turn the old man even more hostile. The next thing the agent heard was a piercing recording of a reveille bugle. A speaker, purposely loud enough to wake the entire camp in time for daylight muster must have been right outside the barrack. It made him think of Quantico, Virginia, the "West Point for Law Enforcement" that occupied 547 acres on a Marine Corps base forty miles from DC. The ingrained training brought him swiftly to the side of the cot, sitting up "attention-straight." Not as straight as the twenty-two-year-old that trained with the Green Berets at Fort Bragg, when he first joined the army, but he did manage to stomp-plant his boots to the floor. He scooped up the snoozing notebook from the floor and reversed the video of Harry's six-room apartment to the point where the two men closed the freezer door and then took their boxed meals to a dining nook, then retired to their respective bedrooms. He fast-forwarded through the uneventful hours of darkness until he caught up to the live feed in the kitchen. Al was looking through cabinets for a coffee cup. Harry entered and grabbed two K-cups and other coffee-making ingredients. Greenfield put his cell to his ear and speed-dialed the waiting evidence team. "Meet me in the parking lot of Foster's apartment ASAP."

Harry answered the door. A three-man team dressed in army greens quickly pushed him aside. "What the hell," Harry said to Greenfield when he crossed the threshold. Al, a veteran lawman, calmly watched the familiar procedure from the table while sipping a cup of coffee. One soldier jerked the freezer door open: a second stood next to him at the ready with a large brown evidence bag; the third trained a flashlight inside the freezer. Then all three dutifully turned and looked at Greenfield.

"Nothing here, sir," said the one holding the flashlight.

Greenfield rushed in, pushing the men aside. He threw four ice trays and a gallon container of Blue Bell ice cream onto the kitchen floor. He turned to Al who seemed to be the least troubled person in the room. "Where is it?" he demanded. "The bag, what did you do with it?"

"It was there when we went to bed," Al grumbled. "You obviously saw it at the same time we did. Check your video. You won't see me takin' nothin' outta there, not unless I walk in my sleep."

"Get dressed, both of you!" the agent ordered. "You're coming with me."

"I guess the kid told you all about the trap I gave him," Al said when Greenfield finally entered what was likely his interrogation room. He had been waiting for an hour and a half. Normal procedure when sweating a suspect. The chair was required to be uncomfortable. His was a worn-out, thinly padded, wooden folding chair. There was a long, intimidating conference table. He didn't see a rectangular two-way mirror, but these days it wasn't necessary when electronic surveillance was everywhere. At least the walls had some interesting things to look at. An impressive aerial view and a map of the army training facility from back in the forties held his attention for a while, as well as portraits of the various captains and colonels that headed Camp Beauregard throughout its many transformations since the World Wars. He was examining a remarkable miniature model collection of armed vehicles encased in a glass cabinet when the agent thrust open the door.

The two men stared at one another in silence at first, as if waiting for the other to make the first daunting remark.

Greenfield reached out to shake Al's hand. "The two of you weren't talking to one another in my presence." The elder reacted by slipping his hands inside the front pockets of his jeans. "I thought you might open up when you were alone," he tried to explain further. "Tell me, what you were trying to trap up there?"

"I never got close enough to get a good look," Al reluctantly answered. "It was upright, moved different, slow. Not like a bear, not like any animal." He shook his head and walked to one of the second-level windows. He could see a small group of soldiers marching in cadence in a field a few blocks away. "You'd o' thought it was human, but it was too big. I know how nuts it sounds," he sighed. "But, years ago, there were rumors . . . silly rumors."

"What rumors, Mr. Bennett?" The agent folded his arms across his chest and waited. It would be hard for the retired deputy to admit seeing something that would label him certifiably insane.

"I showed the warden the big footprints I found. He said it was kids hoaxin' the hunters."

"What do you think?" Greenfield waited patiently for Al to tell him what he was waiting to hear, but Al just turned and stared at him in silence. He couldn't make himself say it.

Greenfield slid the notebook across the long table. It stopped at the edge in front of Al. He looked down at the photo.

"Hundreds of people have seen this creature. You're not alone in this, Al."

"Nonsense! What does that have to do with Mary Lynn?"

"That's what I'm trying to figure out." He picked up the device with the photo of a fuzzy ape-like creature standing within a densely wooded forest. He took the silence to mean the skeptical father was not ready to be sucked up in such a ridiculous scheme. "I understand how conflicting this is for someone like you. But fifty-two women have gone missing in Louisiana alone over the past five years under similar circumstances." He moved closer and flipped the screen to a map of the US "The blue dots denote sightings like yours," he said, pointing out sporadic clusters across the map. "The red dots represent abductions. Most of them mysteriously returned, but the rest are still missing. All of them have the Rh blood factor."

"Rh?" Al grabbed the edge of the pad and pulled it closer.

"The dog's blood matches DNA discovered at several of the abduction sites," the agent continued. "He could be its companion."

"You're tryin' to tell me . . ." Al's voice rattled like it was about to erupt. "You're proposin' that thing, whatever it is, took my daughter and that Mutt's its pet?"

Greenfield had seen and heard the disbelief in the voices of victims and family members countless times. Panic and anger usually followed. There would be crying and then silent despair. The theory was no easier to tell than it was for someone to comprehend. Procedures called for waiting out the initial shock and then continue with the assigned job. "There's more, Adam Reeves is in the wind. We checked with Wildlife and Fisheries; they have no record of him and there is no record of him in Mississippi. There is no Adam Reeves. A grid search has been underway since daylight. Foster is down the

hall with a US Marshall facial rec artist trying to get the
fiancé's face down on paper. We can't find a single video
clean enough to get a clear picture. Foster described him as
tall with reddish-blonde hair."

"I never met him," Al sighed, still trying to wrap his mind
around the fact that a Bigfoot-like creature had taken his
daughter. He wasn't ready to buy it.

"Mr. Bennett, I've been chasing foot prints and blurred
photos all over the world for five years. The sample your
friend sent the state lab was viable DNA of a conspirator's
companion. I don't think of it as a coincidence that it was
wandering around your camp and that your daughter is
missing. We need to find the dog, the fiancé, and the man that
led you to believe he was Adam Reeves. I provided a
description of him as best I can remember from when I met
him yesterday, including the limp; but I'm thinking you got to
know him somewhat."

Al nodded in affirmation. "I don't believe this theory of
yours, but I'll tell you anything you need to know. I'll show
you where I found my trap, somethin' worthwhile might still
be there," Al said, feeling embarrassment and regret for not
opening up sooner. "Surely you have an image of who took
the trap from the freezer."

Greenfield slowly shook his head. "We gave it to our
experts to figure out why thirty-minutes after you and Foster
went to bed, there was thirty-seconds of pixilation. There's no
explanation for that happening to one camera out of eight that
we hid in the kid's apartment."

"You know about my wife?" Al sighed.

"Oh, yes," the agent said. He picked up the notepad and
pointed to a red dot over Lecompte, Louisiana. "There was
evidence she was killed, but there was no body, therefore it's
considered an active/open case in my division."

"Christine's Rh-negative blood was always a curse," Al
sighed as if conceding. "It made her life difficult . . . our life
difficult. Dale's and Mary Lynn's too. Now someone may

have taken them both because of it. Alright, Agent Greenfield." Al heaved a sigh. "Let me help, I know every inch of Catahoula."

Al noticed the agent's eyebrows knit together over his sunglasses when they turned off the highway and passed the check-in station. "You guys search that place?"

"Yeah," the agent grunted. "It's empty, no fingerprints. LWFD had a man scheduled to work here opening weekend."

"That's this weekend," Al said.

"No one will be manning it this weekend," the agent sighed. "Or any weekend. The area is closed until further notice."

They passed dozens of government search teams combing the management area wearing white coveralls, gloves, and facemasks, carrying grabbers and a supply of markers and evidence bags as Al led Greenfield to the creek bank where he found the footprints. The prints were eroded to unrecognizable dents in the muddy bank. Al found the tree where the second trap was chained. The sterile team meticulously combed the area and found what they believed to be small smudges of blood and strands of wiry animal hair. They searched Al's cabin when he recalled leaving a piece of the broken chain there.

"Did anything stand out to you about the blood and the hair on the trap?" Greenfield asked Al while the old man snatched open one of the folding chairs and collapsed into the canvas to catch his breath. "Anything at all?"

"Hair coulda been from a bear," he replied shaking his head. "But bears that come through here are smaller than what I saw. And the footprints, they looked human . . . just bigger."

The agent felt the notepad in his coat pocket vibrate; it was an alert from one of the search teams. "Al, they found something in Section C. A pair of pink tennis shoes and drag marks in the dirt."

Al pressed a hand across his eyes, fighting the tears that were fast forming. You think that that thing . . ." His other hand was pounding his knee, "grabbed . . ." His speech was broken to the point he was incoherent and hard to understand.

"I wish I could be more reassuring, Mr. Bennett." Greenfield knelt down on one knee in front of him. "Al, the geeks and nerds I work with in DC have their theories, but hypotheses are never taken seriously unless substantial physical evidence can be produced." He put his hand on the older man's shoulder and squeezed. "You helped us find some good stuff here today that could turn out to be very helpful. Don't give up on us . . . on me. I promise I'm going to do everything I can to find your daughter."

"Show me where your people found the drag marks . . . and the shoes."

"Sure, you'll need to verify they're hers." He held his arms out, ready to catch Al if necessary, as he staggered toward the door.

Chapter 10

Mary Lynn begged James to stay; to share the huge breakfast he rolled up to her door on a four-foot hand-etched wooden serving trolley. He respectfully declined and took his place against the wall while she walked around the cart admiring its vivid carvings of the sun with expansive rays that presented flowers, birds, and other small wildlife within the deeply polished surface. Its wheels were smooth with ornamentally carved spokes.

"The elders may not understand my borrowing their cart," he explained, smiling. "I wanted to show you an example of the Nephilim wood smith's remarkable work," he added when she made a face that started out as a frown and ended with a smile.

"It's beautiful, James. I used to borrow things; sometimes I returned them, sometimes not.

"I know," he said with a slight laugh.

"These are wicked wheels. The street-smart holla-back cruisers on Jackson Street would be envious."

When Neal stepped off the elevator pulling a telescoping suitcase behind him, he found Mary Lynn sitting on the stacked cushions outside the door next to the cart. James was sitting on the floor with a napkin on one knee and a coffee cup in his hand that looked like a doll's teacup between his large thumb and forefinger. He pulled the scissor door closed, feeling the slow burn of anxiety rise inside him. Jealously was his nemesis. He had never quite learned what to do with it. Her playful eyes suggested she had made an emotional connection with her attendant. The giant was reciprocating with gestures unbecoming a security guard on duty.

"You're supposed to be watching out for her," Neal scolded as he neared them, bouncing the bag behind him on its tiny wheels, "not having a picnic."

"Neal," Mary Lynn interrupted before James could respond. "I didn't want to eat alone. There was more than enough and James wouldn't come inside, so I . . ."

"James?" Neal huffed. "You're calling him James?" Neal turned his disapproving scowl to the giant.

"No worries," gentle James replied, unaffected by Neal's tantrum. "I would never let anything happen to Mary Lynn. I have a personal interest in her safety." He looked across the cart at her and grinned.

Mary Lynn frowned at Neal; he was glaring at the giant. His colors had always been confusing, his moods hard to read. She no longer had the crutch to rely on; not since she woke up in the Himalayas, but she didn't need them to know he was acting like an ass. He set the case upright on its wheels, put his fists on his hips, and poked out his chest. What reason could Neal have for taking such a defensive stance? Ignoring Neal's adversarial posture, James unfolded his legs and stood. Even though he towered over both of them by 5 feet, a confrontation was never going to be initiated or settled by the peaceful giant.

"I brought you some clothes," Neal said, turning to Mary Lynn when James returned to his position against the wall, rationalizing he had won the argument. "I'll be taking you on a short tour today." He opened the door and strutted through it ahead of her. "You're not supposed to interact with the Nephilim," he said in a calmer tone once he was inside. "Not yet. It's too soon."

She looked back over her shoulder at James standing against the wall before she closed the door. He nodded at her. His lips formed a line and then a trace of a grin; she couldn't help but brandish a smile.

Neal took several loose-fitting garments from the suitcase and laid them over the cushions of the large sofa.

"But they're all different shades of gray," Mary Lynn complained with a whine. "You're changing too?" she said when she realized he had already removed his North Face jacket and was tying a black corded belt around a dark gray toga.

"It's important we be inconspicuous," he said.

"Well, you shouldn't have been so mean to James," she scowled. She chose a light gray wrap and slipped it around her shoulders. "You're not resentful of our friendship, are you? He feels responsible for me because he's the one who brought me here."

"I thought . . ."

"Thought what?" Neal had dropped the jacket on the floor and was looking at her strangely.

He picked it up and laid it over the suitcase. "Nothing," he sighed. "James can tell you himself." Neal knew he had ruined his chance for a life with her by rushing things. If he'd only been born and raised American, he'd be accustomed to the freedoms she enjoyed her entire life. If only he had biological American parents, a sibling and a best friend. He spent his formative years in a small village in Switzerland and was brought up by adoptive parents. They shuffled him off to the monks in Bhutan when he was seven, where he studied Buddhism. It was there that he learned of his Nephilim bloodline. He received his high school educated at a monastery and then was sent to Columbia University in New York City where he graduated with honors and received a crash course in American culture. The whole purpose of his existence was to meet the daughter of Nephilim royalty and have Nephilim children. He had failed this endeavor and was counting on the monks to help Mary Lynn understand the value of their relationship.

The elevator was a cage lift with a hand-operated sliding scissor door. The thick wood- slatted box swayed inside the slick mud walls as it rose. Mary Lynn thought she could hear its motor somewhere, but could not be sure if it was above or below. Neal yanked on a dangling rope next to the door and the cage came to a trembling stop. He pushed aside the door and they stepped into a foyer of flat smooth mountain stone. Red and yellow hand-painted hides dressed the otherwise bleak gray walls.

"The generator power ends here." Neal guided her onto a mezzanine that encircled a large oval area. Across the expanse, beyond the hand-carved baluster railing were large cathedral-like archways and columns that led to dark, who-knows-where places within the mountain. Thirty feet below was a group of men and women kneeling on pillows and folded rugs. Some were the size of James, others larger. None had an aura; no matter how hard she concentrated; she couldn't see one single twinge of light around them. All were dressed in tunics of varying colors and were bent over chanting, some rocking in total submission. Hundreds of flickering candles lighted the dim chamber. Two glowing hearths heated the hallowed room. All congregants were facing in one direction toward a golden statue of Buddha that sat atop a flat polished stone.

"These are our people," Neal whispered reverently. "We were born with their genes to carry their sequence forward should something happen to them."

"Are they in some sort of danger?" Mary Lynn asked in an equally respectful voice.

"They're always in danger, but they live without fear. It's remarkable that they haven't been discovered for all these thousands of years."

A waft of air lifted her hair when she leaned over the guardrail. "Where is that coming from?"

"Isn't it amazing?" he sighed, stepping closer to the railing to feel the uplifting draft against his face. "Their mantra produces an energy that flows directly to the gods. You can measure its intensity by the flickering candles and the pace of the prayer wheels."

"Are their prayers always so forceful?" There were scores of glimmering candles tiered along the spherical wall. The wood prayer wheels looked like empty canisters embossed with raised symbols.

"What are they praying for?" she asked as the tiny flames bent over and the prayer wheels spun.

"Enlightenment, peace." He guided her away from the edge toward a carved-out passageway to keep their voices from disturbing the ambiance below. "They pray for forgiveness because of the actions of their forefathers in the early years. The Fallen have regained their power, as foretold, and are looking for evidence of the Nephilim as they go about the world spreading chaos. The need for prayer is greater than ever." He placed both hands on her arms as if to comfort her, but she got the feeling he was really trying to comfort himself. "The monks provide them protection but it may not always be enough. A young king rules Bhutan now. He has allowed solar power into the remotest of villages. People everywhere will soon have access to the entire world and its evil influence."

The prayerful whispers were hypnotic, as was the bobbing flicker of the candles along the wall cavity.

"Peace is all they know or desire. It is difficult to achieve; I struggle with it daily. I picked up some bad habits while in New York." The muffled chants were making him realize how badly he acted when he saw Mary Lynn and James in the hallway. "Nephilim choices are simple. They live ready to give their bodies back to the earth and their spirits to the gods. Our belief is that everyone is reborn and continually cycles through birth, life, death, and rebirth. The monks will impart these things to you. You will learn the four noble truths of Buddhism, and how to use the gifts you inherited. And the importance of passing the knowledge onto your children and to everyone you come in contact with."

Maybe it was the worshipful whisperings or the tears that had welled up in Neal's eyes that made the mantra seem to fill the cavity of the enormous cave, penetrating every part of

Mary Lynn's being. "Neal, I'm so sorry we didn't work out," she whispered. "I'm just not capable of . . .." His eyes suddenly shifted to look over her shoulder. "What?" she asked. He placed his hands on her shoulders to keep her from turning around.

Someone was standing in the shadows inside one of the archways on the opposite side of the mezzanine. It was someone, a human like themselves, dressed in light-colored garments; but they vanished into the niche after realizing they were seen. "Someone else is here," he whispered. "We may have overstayed our time; we should move on."

"Can we please stay?" she sighed. "I feel so weirdly sublime."

"No one is ever the same once they experience this place." He quickly escorted her out of the mezzanine and across two more carved-out passageways until they reached a ladder that led to a wooden catwalk. The walkway was braced against the wall by large tree trunks, and secured with thick marine-type ropes. "This is built specifically for humans like us," he informed her. "To observe the mighty inhabitants and not disturb them." From the lofty vantage point, she watched what could have just as easily been ordinary humans going about their daily routine. Not like a modern era, but those of 150 years ago. Tools, buckets, every utensil appeared handmade. They were tending large gardens; moving about with the strength, agility, and ease of toned athletes. She would have thought their massive size would cause them to struggle. Neal led her past a group of women sewing and weaving with great dexterity and then to a hide tanning room where men were meticulously skinning and scraping the hides of large species of goat known as a takin. There was a kitchen where women and girls were preparing and preserving food. Cooking was on fireplace hearths where they also melted snow for fresh water and cleaning.

A dog trotted across a midway of workers, guiding a small number of goats. "That dog," she gasped; "I've seen one like that."

"It's a mastiff," he said, patting her on the shoulders indicating it was time to move along. "They're intelligent herders and exclusive to this part of the world."

There was that patronizing tone again, but she let the petty annoyance go because it paled in comparison to what she was witnessing. He led her from the work area to another large cavern where she found it impossible to quell her panting amazement over the huge walls etched with hieroglyphics from their base to as far up as she could see until they disappeared in the shadows. She placed her hands against some of the carvings and followed the markings with her fingers. She looked at Neal, wondering if he knew their symbolism or how to interpret them.

"The Nephilim's evolution is recorded here. The scribes started with the day of their conception. Here," he said, moving to the left side of the entryway to place his hand over a symbol of the sun with pointed crowns. "These first three symbols are words taken from the first-ever recording of our history. *In the beginning was the Word*," he said translating the first three symbols.

"John 1, verse 1," she whispered. "It's from the Bible, every Bible."

"The history of mankind started the same." He reached his hand across the storyboard, stopping three rows above. But it was a different beginning for the Nephilim." His hand uncovered a wild evil-looking face that looked like the devil with deformed animal horns protruding from the top of its head.

She heard a scurrying noise. "What's that?" The towering walls made it seem to come from every direction. She ran to Neal and grabbed his tunic. "Footsteps."

Neal listened but shook his head as if he heard nothing.

"They're getting closer. There are two of them."

"How do you know that?" He did not wait for an answer and motioned to a large boulder that the scribes might have used for scaffolding when carving their artwork at the higher level. They rushed behind the protruding rock wall. Seconds later, two giant men dressed in thick animal hide and holding picks and shovels walked by. They were involved in a conversation that echoed loudly throughout the lofty passageway along with their heavy footsteps.

"They're talking about work," she whispered to Neal.

"How could you hear them?" Neal asked.

"I don't know," she said, reasoning that losing the sense of seeing colors, could have enhanced another. "I put all the sounds together and came up with a conversation about their work being almost finished."

Neal led her out of the cavern into a narrow cave that ended at a large stone. He pressed his hands against the massive rock. It had wooden rollers underneath that aided him in gliding it to one side. He opened it just enough so they could squeeze through one at a time. The slight path beyond the rock was a winding cleft that gave way to a snow-covered deck. He brushed the powdery flakes off the bench that nature carved out of the icy mountainside.

"Here, please take my tunic." He was already shedding the cloak.

"No," she said, looking out over the cascade of snow-covered peaks and valleys. "I'm hot-natured, don't you remember?" He should have remembered this. He offered her his coat every time they sat atop the amphitheater and she had turned him down saying, *don't you remember, I'm hot-natured?*

"I do," Neal replied. "I just like to hear you say it. Because it's part of the uniqueness we share. We have extra layers of collagen, richer blood."

She had no idea what that meant, but he could be exhaustingly melodramatic when in pursuit of her affection. All she knew for sure at this moment was how very small and insignificant she felt sitting in the stillness of the world's tallest mountains and its vast endless pinnacles and crowns. The subzero chill was actually exhilarating; the thin air refreshing and as uplifting as being on some sort of drug-induced high. The wind suddenly changed direction creating a whistling sound from the rock's icy edges. It brought her back to reality with a startling thud.

"Neal, is Neal Mueller your real name? Do your parents really live in Switzerland? I always thought something was off about that."

"Yes, it's true; they're my step-parents. There's a lot I didn't tell you."

"I can't help thinking that this is all some kind of dream," she sighed. "That maybe I was in an accident on the way to Daddy's camp." Like in the Wizard of Oz where Dorothy's dream swept her off to a different world after being hit on the head during a tornado.

"You're tired and overwhelmed." He gently wrapped an arm around her and coaxed her to her feet. "I should take you back to your room now. It's difficult to legitimize our relationship with the Nephilim under the best conditions. You'll feel better tomorrow after you've slept and given your mind time to process today."

She nodded in agreement. There was no pretense in his voice this time. "Neal, are you ever going to tell me the whole truth about yourself?" she asked after they squeezed through the door's small opening and he secured the rock back in place.

"Someday I won't have to."

"What does that mean? I hate it when you talk to me like this." The serious expression on his face seemed to counter the accusation.

"What I'm saying is, after you've spent some time with the monks, you'll understand everything."

***

Harry went to the house on Hartwood after walking through Mary Lynn's ransacked apartment. The FBI did a great job of combing through the apartment's cabinets and drawers and throwing their contents everywhere looking for evidence. How would they know if anything was missing? Like her blue toothbrush and ULTA hair products and her purple and gold LSU travel bag. Evidence of what she was doing the few days before she went missing was clearer in the house. The remains of stripped wallpaper were on the bedroom floors, and the coffee pot from her apartment was in the kitchen and used towels on the bathroom floor. Her toiletries lined the edge of the bathtub and her blue toothbrush was in the ceramic holder attached to the wall above the sink. He picked up a hair dryer lying on an air mattress pushed into a corner of her old bedroom. *I was with you the day you bought this at Walgreens.* The LSU travel bag was on a shelf in a closet. "I guess I was expecting to find some sort of sign, something that would tell me where you are, what happened," he whispered to the empty bedroom. Other than there being no cell phone, wallet, or keys, everything looked normal, as if she just threw the sheets back and jumped out of bed. He reached down and picked up the thermal blanket on the floor next to the mattress. "I can just see you kicking this thing off," he reminisced, running his fingers across the plush pile. "You thought it was me that covered you with this that night, but it wasn't . . . it wasn't me," he gasped.

Chapter 11

"How long does it take your people to get results from blood and hair samples these days?" Al asked the agent before opening the door of the blacked-out SUV. He hesitated to pull the handle. They were in the Hartwood driveway, parked behind Harry's Tacoma. "It took us weeks to get anything important back from the Shreveport lab. Even with the daily badgerin old Jack Warner gave em."

"Preliminary, four hours," Greenfield replied after killing the engine. "A little longer when it's a difficult analysis. How can I reach you?"

Al shook his head and expelled a sigh. "I don't know. through the kid I guess."

"I'll send someone over with a phone. You really should have one." The agent reached for the notepad that was on the back seat and logged on. "I can get you a truck from the US Marshall Pool as well."

"That's okay; I got a friend that can fix me up." AL wrapped his fingers around the door handle but stopped mid-pull.

"Something else, Mr. Bennett?" Greenfield asked, looking up from the small screen and noticing the hesitation.

"I'm gonna tell you somethin' I promised myself I'd never tell anyone," the old man said solemnly. "I made a pact with myself to take it to my grave. I told Mary Lynn the last time I saw her. Maybe I shouldn't have."

Greenfield stared at Al in silence, trying to be patient as the seconds passed. He was starting to grow fond of the testy old man but protocol took precedence over likeability when an uncharacteristic behavior presented itself. He was definitely not acting like himself right now.

"My wife's car was found abandoned, as you already know," Al finally said. "Not one speck of blood or evidence of any kind was found inside or out. Her bloody smock was discovered hangin' over the front of a dumpster in Texas, and then her purse with nothing in it except her driver's license, a hundred miles away. My experience with the department shouted this was just too convenient. No one leaves evidence like that out in the open unless they want it to be found."

"What are you getting at, Al?" Greenfield asked. It was clear the old man was wrestling with something.

"Christine and I," he began but stopped as if having second thoughts about continuing. "Christine got pregnant a couple of years after we had Dale. She miscarried at three months; nurses said it was a little boy." He bowed his head sorrowfully. "It wasn't mine." His voice cracked with bitterness. "I suspected she was seein' someone else and . . . well, we weren't havin' those kinds of relations at the time. This wasn't a happy house," he added, glancing up at the green-crusted vinyl siding he put up over the wood frame house twenty years ago. "Not for the two of us." The once snow-white fluted columns along the front porch were stained with mildew. "We reconciled after the miscarriage, had Mary Lynn a few years later and were doin' pretty good. Then she started actin' suspicious again as if she was hidin' somethin' from me . . . right before she disappeared. I couldn't help but think she was havin' another affair and ran off with whoever it was and they tried to make it look like she was dead. I couldn't tell Dale or Mary Lynn what I suspected. It was hard enough on them as it was; I couldn't tell them their mother just didn't want them anymore."

"Al, you realize these suspicions gave you motive," the agent sighed.

"Yeah, I was already the number one suspect. I didn't need to give them a better excuse to haul me off to jail. I didn't want anyone to know what I suspected for Dale and Mary Lynn's sake. I knew I didn't do it."

"I know you didn't kill your wife, Al," Greenfield said and gave him a reassuring pat on the shoulder.

"Jack Warner, the Sheriff back then, was also my cousin. We spent hours lookin' over security videos from the place she worked down in Forest Hill. She worked in a genetics lab at the fish hatchery. They were experimentin' with cross breedin', tryin' to create a meatier species of fish and some other kind of algae-eatin' breed to protect the environment. At least that's what she told me. She loved that kind of stuff. Jack did me a favor and let me look at the evidence before the FBI packed it up and took it with them. There was only one other employee working there, Jeff something. They both clocked in and out on time. Security video recorded no secret meetings inside or outside of the buildin'. No sign of her lover in the parkin' lot, no ridin' off together."

"FBI found nothing unusual about either one of your financials or her vehicle's ONSTAR. If your suspicions are correct, they hid it extremely well."

"Another thing I never told anybody: her car wasn't on 112 when me and Jack first went lookin' for her. We drove right by that spot twice. Someone found it there the next mornin'. Jack left it up to me whether to say anything about it."

"Interesting," the agent mumbled. "Where's Jack now?"

"He's in a hospice facility up in Pollock. Mary Lynn told me he had a stroke a year ago."

Al looked as if he was wrestling with another memory. Agent Greenfield waited out the old man's struggle.

"You shoulda seen Mary Lynn when I told her what I suspected about her mother." Al's voice was low, as if he was ashamed. "I swear I wouldn't a said a word if I'd a known she was gonna take it that bad. She blew up, said things she didn't mean. I guess that's why I went and told her I'd start comin' down to visit because she was so tore up." He rubbed his hand across his eyes as if trying to massage away the burn. "I just thought all this was somethin' you might oughta know," he sighed.

"Al, did you know your daughter was engaged for a short time to a man named Neal Mueller?"

"She said somethin' about havin' a boyfriend but they had broke up."

"He was using a false name, just like Adam Reeves. We can't find either one of them. It's like they never existed."

"Maybe she just ran away with her mysterious lover, like her mother did. Maybe their dots don't even belong on your screen," he said waving his hand at the notepad in Greenfield's hand. "Your crazy sasquatch theory may not have anything to do with what's goin' on here."

Greenfield sighed and then opened the map up again. "It just adds to the mystery," he said, staring at the multicolored clusters. "There are a few, like your wife, that have never been heard from again. The majority returned, but with no memory of what happened. Some have recurring nightmares." He tilted the screen so Al could see it, but the older man turned and looked out the side window while grunting something inaudible. "I'm sure you've heard about people that claim they were abducted by aliens." Al had nothing to say; he only shook his head. "Some women think they were artificially impregnated. Every woman on this grid has a bizarre story. And they all have the Rh factor."

"I'm gonna be sick," Al muttered. His throat felt hot and secreted phlegm. "Don't wanna hear anymore. Yep, I'm gonna throw up." He pushed the door open while swinging his legs outside. He cradled his head with both hands while he hurled onto the busted concrete driveway. Greenfield opened the glove compartment, pulled out a handful of MacDonald's napkins, and handed them to him. There were a few minutes of muttering while he wiped his mouth and chin. "This is absurd," he warbled, trying to clear the chunky liquid up from his esophagus. "You expect me to buy this crap; you people are crazy. Ain't no aliens or no Sasquatch abducted my wife and my daughter. My God, the government actually pays you idiots to shovel this load of horseshit. You don't know what the hell you're doin'," he whaled.

Greenfield cleared his throat. "Al, I don't think people are being abducted by aliens or Sasquatch. I do think something terrifying happened to them, so terrifying that their brains blocked it out of their memories and came up with its own interpretation, something familiar, something they heard of before. I know how this sounds. But every theory is being considered. I've been chasing leads down all over the world: Russia, India, Tibet, Alaska, Canada, South America, and Africa.

"Russia?" Al grunted.

"Yes. I was in Siberia two years ago. In the frozen Arctic prior to that looking for a creature the locals call Almasti. It means "Wildman". An old man claimed he killed one and kept some of its hair. It turned out to be a brown bear. In the Tibetan Himalayan forest, someone saw another large being. Fourteen-inch footprints were found nearby. Hair samples came back to be an ancient polar bear which was, in itself, impossible at 16,000 ft. where they can't possibly survive. The team is committed to getting to the truth, Al. Results from samples have come back all over the chart, from a black, or brown bear, to deer, antelope, even raccoons. Witnesses pass lie detector tests."

"Yeah, well, I know how reliable those are," Al muttered. "Did you ever find any blood?"

"You can count the number of times blood was found on one hand, and I'm talking samples so small only a bloodhound could find it."

"And, you checked the DNA obviously."

"In recent years, labs have been given permission to use a new method of amplifying DNA in small samples. Test results came back as a Bhutan mastiff. The sample from your dog was the initial reason I came here." The notepad suddenly alerted. "Al," Greenfield sighed after reading the message.

"What now?" the old man grunted.

"The team's been using sonar to search the creeks and lakes in Catahoula. We turned up her car in Dempsey Lake." Al's back was to him. He could see his chest rise. He didn't exhale. He was holding his breath, waiting for the dreaded words. "She wasn't in it," Greenfield said quickly. Someone definitely tried to cover this up."

"Sounds like somethin' a human would do, a stupid one. I can't do this again Agent Greenfield." He still had his back to him, his head down. "I can't go through losin' my daughter like this . . . not like I lost Christine."

"Come on, I'll walk you in," Greenfield said after giving Al what he thought was sufficient time to compose himself. "I should update Foster."

They found Harry sitting in the rusted glider on the back porch, the thermal blanket folded on the seat next to him.

"There's coffee," he said in a low voice, looking soberly at the dregs in the bottom of the cup in his hands. "Cups are in the cabinet. Mary Lynn brought them over from her apartment; there's sugar, milk." He couldn't seem to make himself look up at either of them. "She was staying here; I didn't know she was staying here." He sounded remorseful. "What kind of friend . . ."

"While you're sittin' there feelin' sorry for yourself," Al interrupted after exchanging glances with the agent, "I'm gonna get me some of that coffee." He tramped into the kitchen not wanting to be within hearing distance when the agent told the kid about the car.

Harry picked up the blanket and held it out to Greenfield. His eyes were red and glassy from crying.

"Someone covered Mary Lynn with this one night last week when she fell asleep out here. I found her the next morning right here, sleeping, covered with this blanket. I should have remembered it before now," he moaned. "It didn't suffocate her like most blankets do."

"Are there any paper bags in the house?" the agent asked, snatching it from him. "Find one, now! I need to send this to our lab."

***

When Mary Lynn walked into the living area the next morning, someone had parked a breakfast cart, a simple unremarkable cart, just inside the door. She found the hallway empty. *Have I gained their trust?* She wondered. *Or, they know I've realized there's no escaping this place.* She took two sips of coffee, picked at the scrambled eggs and nibbled on a piece of bacon. Boredom lured her to the bay window. Neal could help himself to the leftovers when he arrived to take her on the next excursion. She pulled back the drape. Once again, the scenery took her in. Snow flurries fancifully danced about on the other side of the thick panes. It almost seemed they were putting on a show just for her. The tiny flakes swirled as if being stirred with a swizzle stick every time the corners of her mouth lifted. She had just made herself comfortable on the velvet cushions when she heard a thump in the hallway. She slowly opened the door. The hallway was empty except for a large white leather-bound book lying on the floor at her feet. She heard a noise down the hall that compelled her to trot toward the elevator to investigate. To the left of the closed scissor door was an opening to a small alcove that she'd paid little attention to before. It led to a rectangular stairwell that disappeared into infinite darkness above and below, like many of the caverns Neal led her through the day before. Someone below was carrying a small torch that lighted the endless squares of orange-tinted posts and handrails. She caught glimpses of a beige skirt swishing between the rungs, and a hand, a small woman's hand, not Nephilim, grab the corner post caps as she rounded the staircases and made leaping strides in order to negotiate the large landings that accommodated the giant's long gait.

"Wait!" she hollered; *wait, wait,* her voice echoed all the way up and down the well-like structure but she had ducked into a door somewhere in the dark limitlessness below.

The book was heavy, weighted by thick binding and a thousand gold-edged pages. She caressed the burdensome volume against her chest that seemed to demand respect because of its lavish imprinted patterns, and of course its title, *Bible.* She laid it on the velvet cushion in the bay window, sat down, and carefully lifted the cover. There was one word written in ornamental calligraphy on the first page, "Nephilim." Hieroglyphic etchings like those on many of the walls she'd seen in the caves bordered the page. She turned to the first chapter, Genesis, 1.1 where, as in every Bible she'd ever read, related God's creation of heaven and the earth. There were highlighted chapters containing text she had never read before that lamented the insufferable treatment of the Nephilim from the time they were born into the world as offspring of the cast-out gods. Subsequent verses chronicled the wars they fought and the pain they suffered at the hands of their cruel and daunting masters. They vanished into obscurity after only thirty survived the great flood. The authors wrote of how the gods rewarded the Nephilim with hope because of their righteousness and gave them even greater strength than they already had, bestowing great spiritual capabilities upon them. Further verses spoke of how holy men took them in, offered refuge and taught them the value of meditation. Their all-consuming petitions pleased the gods so they rewarded and protected them, allowing them to flourish. The last pages contained ancestry brackets, chronicled by the surviving elders throughout the generations. Her mind was whirling by the time Neal arrived.

"How-who-where did you get this?" he stuttered when he saw the book open against her chest when she answered the door. He immediately took it from her and fanned through the pages. "It's a reproduction of the original," he said, after examining the front and back covers. "The original is so large that . . . how much have you read?"

"Some," she panted, "mostly the highlighted pages. Whoever left it at my door obviously wanted me to read them first. Why is there no mention of the Nephilim in the Christian Bible?"

"They were purposely left out." Neal walked to one of the battlefield paintings. He was visibly upset and addressed the giant warriors standing their ground as living barriers, facing soldiers with arched arms with spears pointed up at them. "You suffered outrageous atrocities at the hands of ancient enemies," he bemoaned. "They thought you were inferior beings, monsters. They treated you like animals, refused to feed you, threatened to kill your children unless you followed orders. The monks treated you kindly and taught you to embrace the gods." He turned away from the portrait and addressed Mary Lynn. "They understand very well why they must remain hidden."

"I would think their family tree would be larger after all these thousands of years," she said, taking the book from him and turning to the last section of a hand written list of names.

"Our forefathers wisely split the Nephilim into three colonies in sufficient time before The Fallen regained their power in the 1900's."

Mary Lynn watched Neal walk slowly from artifact to artifact, staring sadly at each portrayal and gently touching the small statuettes and busts. The normally confident former fiancé was noticeably sad; she had never seen him act so woeful. "Each settlements agreed to record its own separate lineage with no mention of the others. That way, if anything happens to one, the other two will be spared."

"Is Switzerland one of those colonies?"

"No." He looked past her at the tall and mighty structures outside the bay window that were the keepers of Nephilim secrets. "But I'm sure the other colonies are in places just like this, uninhabitable and inaccessible."

"You said your parents live in Switzerland, that you grew up there." She walked to him and put her hand on his arm. He seemed to be lost in the sorrow of his own narrative.

"I wasn't totally honest with you about that." He cast his eyes around the vaulted room as if trying to avoid making eye contact with her and then slowly walked to the small statue of Buddha. "I was told my mother was from Switzerland, but all I remember is being raised by a family in one of the villages in the lower mountains and then boarding at one of the monasteries." He touched the corner of the statue's base as he recounted his upbringing. "The monks told me my biological father is Nephilim and that I was to marry a woman whose father was also Nephilim. After finishing my education with the monks, Cornell University in New York accepted me. The plan was to sweep you off your feet and bring you here voluntarily, but that didn't work out . . . I failed. You're very special, you know." He moved from the statue to another portrait of a proud-looking Nephilim dressed in hides and armor. He wore a helmet like a medieval knight, shin guards, and boots with thick straps and held a spear in his right hand. "He's the reason you're here and why someone left the book at your door."

Mary Lynn moved to stand next to Neal. "Who is he?"

Neal looked at her and then back at the portrait. "This is one of your ancestors going back 120 generations. That's why it's hanging in your quarters. I have a similar one in mine, but my bloodline is not as renowned as yours."

"I'm so sorry you were taken from your parents," she sighed after studying the stern face in the canvas. "You must have been so lonely. It makes sense to me now, why you seemed so anxious all the time."

"It's okay," he chuckled as if blowing it off. "You're here now and I suppose that's what matters."

"No." She looked around at the treasured objects that Neal revered. "It's not okay. You had far too much pressure put on you. I would have much rather met the real Neal, the one standing in front of me now. Instead of that other Neal that was trying to impress me. You know, my daddy just told me a few days ago that he believes my mother left him . . . all of us, for someone else. I was so angry."

Neal smiled. "Your passion will always be one of my fondest memories."

"At least I got to know my real parents; you didn't."

"I doubt my parents ever knew I existed; that's how it's done. The Nephilim have the ability to control what humans remember. No one is ever the wiser."

Mary Lynn's gasp was shallow and inaudible. "They take people's babies without their knowing?" she asked, wanting to make sure she understood what he was saying. Neal nodded. "But that's against the law; against the law in every civilized country in the world."

"The Nephilim future depends on it," he sighed. "That wouldn't have happened to us if . . . if we would have worked out."

"Our children would have strong Nephilim DNA markers," she whispered.

Neal gave a short quick nod. "Not all civilizations believe in marrying for love, but for the good of . . ." He suddenly looked pale and sickly; he weaved forward but caught himself.

"Neal, what's wrong?" She reached out to steady him.

"The gods have given me a warning. Only the monks are to introduce you to your heritage. I don't know what came over me; I'm sure it's because of my feelings for you. I told you too much. I need to spend more time in meditation, to regain my spirituality and ask for forgiveness."

"Neal," she whispered gently. "It's okay. No harm has been done."

He straightened his back and lifted his chin with renewed resolve; his stiff demeanor returned. "I have nothing to figure out. I shouldn't have allowed myself to indulge in weakness. I acquired this weakness in America; it won't happen again. Please get ready; it's time to go."

"Neal, what's going on with you?" Mary Lynn asked, totally confused by the sudden transition.

***

"I don't understand, mother; why did you give her your Bible?" James asked the woman standing in front of an arched balcony-like opening in her private quarters. It overlooked a large dining room where colossal women were scurrying around cooking eggs and serving bread and milk to nearly twenty Nephilim children. Her red hair was streaked with white and gray. She was not one of the giant women. The furnishings in her carved-out residence reflected her smaller size with a few exceptional chairs for visitors like James. "You cherish that book; it never leaves your quarters . . . why?" His arms were stretched up to the domed rock ceiling as if reaching to the gods for the answer. Dark maroon rugs with fanciful animal designs dyed in to its fibers decorated the upper walls.

She wore a green tunic over a tan, ankle-length skirt. A dark brown head wrap was loose around her shoulders. Her cheeks were damp under her blue eyes. "She must understand the evolution of her ancestors," she sighed. "Seeing our history in print will give it validation. It's imperative she be aware of our history if she is ever going to consider becoming one of us."

"Well, Neal is up there giving her a broken man's interpretation," he contended. "Exposure to the American university and lifestyle has made him arrogant and selfish. My father will not be pleased, nor will the rest of the elders."

"I'll speak to Kokabiel." She looked up at him as if his gigantic physique didn't exist as any mother would her child. "You should take her to the monks right away," she added while twisting and tying her long locks on top of her head. "There's a reason I insisted you bring her here now. She had reached a critical breaking point. Your father and the other six elders are preoccupied. Rightfully so, the border disputes and the U.S. military encroachments are keeping him busy. You and I must attend to this personal matter ourselves. Kokabiel and I have discussed the options where she is concerned. He agreed to allow her to grow up as human first; in turn, I gave him my word, I would let her learn from the monks. The monks will open her eyes, teach her how to access her inherent abilities. Neal's faith wasn't strong enough. They threw him into a society he wasn't ready for. The modern world is too fast- moving, complex. You observed it for yourself on your excursions. Not everyone is suited for it."

"I will take her to Kunchen myself, mother, right after I get my crew lined up for the day. The army post is deploying small objects called drones in the sky that are taking pictures of the valley and our mountains. The elders have ordered all escape routes to be readied sooner rather than later."

She went to a bookshelf where framed photos and cherished nick-knacks were on display. Memorabilia she periodically gathered and tucked away in the trunk of her car before the time came for her to leave with Kokabiel. Not obvious things that would be missed, just memorabilia with special meaning only to her and duplicate photos. "I suppose everyone is looking for Mary Lynn like they did me," she sighed. "Al shouldn't be a suspect this time," she nodded, assuring herself. Her face broke into a smile as if suddenly remembering something. She hurried through an arched doorway that led to a chiseled-out closet where a wardrobe of printed dark red, blue, and green robes and assorted scarves hung over a rod. She returned carrying a folded tunic the size of a king-size bed spread in her arms. "I made you something, sweetheart. Please, try it on." She draped it over the arms of a large chair. "Do you think the elders will approve of the color?" She looked up at him, proud of the handmade creation. "The blue is from berries I grew myself."

"It's beautiful, mother," he said. "The color is not like any berry I've ever picked. You are crossbreeding plants again;

and pressing your luck with my father." He smiled and picked up the cloak-like garment and pulled it over his head.

Kokabiel brought Christine to the Himalayas when their son was displaying risky emotional upheavals that made the elders question whether he could ever become a leader. Their son had been going through the normal growing pains of an adolescent. She found James to have a sensitive soul and they developed a close friendship. The hormones eventually settled down.

He held out his colossal arms to admire the soft goat hair. "Your weaving has reached near perfection, mother."

"Your father likes the subtle changes I make. Men and women down in the villages wear much brighter colors. His eyes light up when I wear them; it adds a little spark to our relationship."

"Mother, please don't explain what you mean by that," he moaned. "I'm just going to keep on thinking of you as the lovely grandmother that teaches our children history and the science of botany."

"How is my granddaughter, Alisha?" Christine asked.

"She is fine," James replied. "Curious, best in her class, I'm told. Understands Buddhism well. She wants to travel the world with her father. I suppose that's the human in her."

"She is beautiful. She's not in any of my classes. I tend to put a Christian twist to my lessons since I was brought up with the teachings of Jesus Christ. It wouldn't be appropriate. Your father and I have many intense discussions on that subject too. You know, the Nephilim were not always Buddhist. It was only after the monks promised them protection and opened the door to their spirituality that they embraced it. I have no objection to Buddhism. The principal beliefs are basically the same as Christianity, except Christians believe in one God and that we only die once."

"Yes, mother, there are those two small exceptions," James jested. "I'm not arguing with you about that either."

"It's not that important," she said, smiling. "Although," she added, squinting, "the Nephilim have six elders with one supreme leader. Having a supreme leader is a necessity to prevent chaos."

"Sorry, Mother" he said, looking into her challenging eyes. "I'll not spar with you like my father. How did you manage to soften the goat hair?" he asked to change the subject when she pouted. "This will keep me very warm on my night hunts."

"It's just another one of my secret concoctions. I was tempted to sew a yellow cross on the hood so I could pick you out in a crowd." She looked up at him, smiling.

"And why would you do that, Mother?" he laughed.

"I'm kidding. "It's a memory that just popped into my head from a lifetime ago," she sighed. "I actually used to do that so I could find Mary Lynn and Dale in the park or the grocery store. I even sewed my name, Christine Bennett, along with our telephone number into their clothes."

"I'm feeling your regret," he said tenderly. A slight frown pierced his smile. "It's always there, isn't it? You miss those days. I'm grateful that my father loves you. I'm grateful you convinced him to give me another chance and bring my sister here after botching it so badly the first time. And I know it was you that persuaded him to let me observe the complicated humans." He shook his head. "It's so tragic how these people live their lives with blinders, just like the yaks that carry supplies to and from the villages."

"Kokabiel predicted your frustration, but a future leader must see the human complexities and understand the dangers the Nephilim face outside these mountains."

He walked to the viewing deck and looked down at the five-foot children sitting on long straight benches eating their breakfasts. They were destined to live within the mountain walls; and never walk among the villages beyond the valley or anywhere else. He moved away from the balcony and sat down in a large chair.

"Don't be sad, my beautiful son."

"I'm not sad, Mother. I've been having feelings of dread."

She crawled onto the arm of the large chair and snuggled up to his shoulder. "Yes, I've been feeling it too. Kokabiel will take care of us. I remember how I used to look forward to your father's visits. I was afraid he might forget about me after you were taken from me before you were even born. But he didn't. I remember feeling his presence when I was at work, then I would sneak out to meet him behind the hatchery ponds. He brought me here to hold you when no one could stop you from crying. It was in total disregard of the decree that forbids personal contact. It was heartbreaking having to leave you and go back home." She curled her arms around his hefty bicep and smoothed the new garment. "I feel sad that people in other lands will never know how kind and gentle the Nephilim are."

"Father says evil has laid its groundwork too well for that to ever happen," James sighed.

"All the more reason to have a strong spirit like your sister's on our side."

They suddenly looked at each other, realizing something at the same time.

"You should hurry," she said, sliding off the arm of the chair as he stood. "Your crew is wondering where you are."

"Yes, I am aware."

"You look very handsome in your new tunic," she said, smiling at her magnificent son.

"Thank you, Mother; I'll have to come back for it." He shed the new garment and draped it over the chair. "I can't wear my best clothing while working in the tunnel." He shifted his broad shoulders to straighten his yak hide work clothes. "A captain must set a good example."

"And I have a class to teach," she said, following him to the door. "Have a blessed day, my son."

"May the gods be with you, mother," he replied.

Chapter 12

Harry's full attention was on the matted, pink web-like splotches of a viral pneumonia sample that was safely secured in an airtight slide, unaware that Agent Greenfield had entered the lab until he slapped a brown folder down on the counter next to the microscope.

"Tell me if you recognize any of these." His voice was as gruff as ever.

"Crap!" the lab tech moaned, wishing the annoying investigator would give him a warning phone call or text before the unorthodox visits. "You know, we could meet in the conference room or at Red's." It had been two weeks since his first unannounced visit and many of the other techs were beginning to lose their patience over his frequent contaminating bursts into the lab. The guilt of letting the blanket slip his mind was the only reason he held his tongue. Greenfield laid the folder open, revealing a small stack of 8x10 color photos of large dogs.

"Your blood sample was this breed," the agent said. "They come from different parts of Tibet, India, Bhutan, and Nepal. So, which one of these mastiffs would you say looks like the one Al found in the woods?"

"Why don't you ask him?" Harry sighed as he flipped the photos over one by one with his gloved hand.

"I did; I just need you to confirm. You saw how he reacted when I asked him to produce the dog up at his camp. He might try to steer me in the wrong direction."

"Here," Harry said, pointing to one particular glossy photo. "See this black hairy one with the brown spots over its eyes?"

"Okay, good. This one is from Bhutan. They're used for goat herding in the Himalayas. I suppose someone could have smuggled one in, but . . ."

"But what?" Harry sighed as if weary of his theories.

"Hair and blood samples have put them at a few sightings. And there's the blanket," the agent added, "it's woven with goat hair. Takin to be exact, also found in the Himalayas. So, I'm leaving for an army base in Bhutan in an hour."

"You'll need to pack warm clothes." Harry swung out of his chair and carefully put the pneumonia slide away in one of the refrigerators and pulled off his gloves.

"What are you doing?" Greenfield asked, straightening the photos in the file.

"I'm going with you."

Greenfield frowned while watching Harry swipe the cap off his head and unbutton his lab coat.

"I'll just need to run by my apartment and get a few things."

"No time," Greenfield grumbled. "The necessary gear will be waiting for us by the time we get there. I guess you could be useful, if by some miracle we find something."

"What about Al?" Harry asked.

"I've had someone watching him since we started combing Catahoula. I'll keep them in place until we get back."

"Is that a hopeful ring I hear in the pessimistic voice of Agent Greenfield?"

"Ah!" he sighed. "Take heart; this is probably another one of the hundreds of dead-end roads I've been down."

Other than checking his notebook from time to time and a few spurts of chitchat, the agent slept for most of the eleven-hour flight to the U.S. Army Garrison Baumholder in the German federal state of Rheinland-Pfalz.

Harry tried to pass the time, as well as settle his nerves by walking around the huge belly of the military cargo plane. It was loaded with sand-colored containers stamped "US Army" in dark brown letters, along with three military

Humvees and cargo trucks. When he became somewhat acclimated to the constant rumbling of the huge airbus, he sat down in a webbed sling next to the snoring Greenfield. Somewhere over the eastern Atlantic, turbulence shook the agent awake. He asked something unexpected.

"Did you and Mary Lynn ever have a romantic relationship?"

"Where did that come from?" was Harry's reaction. "I told you already, we're friends. And, she never hinted that she felt that way about me," he conceded. "We were both just happy to have each other. What does that have to do with anything?" Greenfield was staring at him as if expecting more details. "I didn't want to lose her friendship."

"So, tell me what she liked about this Neal fellow? She must have confided that to her best friend."

"He was tall, handsome, outgoing, responsible, I suppose. They had things in common. They both like cold weather, if that means anything; I don't know much else."

"Were you upset because she was in love with this guy?" Greenfield persisted. "You seem a little upset right now, just talking about him."

"No, 'cold weather' just reminded me of something. Christine and Al used to argue over the thermostat," he said, smiling. "Al wanted to put a fireplace in the living room one fall and Christine wouldn't have it. She was hot-natured like Mary Lynn. I think about that sometimes, when I watch Al stoke the campfire. Sometimes he gets a faraway look in his eyes as if he's remembering stuff like that too. The Bennett family is responsible for most of my good memories," he reminisced. "I'd give anything to turn the clock back to those days. If I could just do that day over when I saw Mary Lynn standing at the window."

"The boyfriend, Neal?" he asked. "What else do you remember?"

"Oh, yeah," Harry sighed wearily. "He was from the Netherlands or Switzerland . . . Switzerland, that's it. He was educated in New York. Maybe that's why he never seemed to fit in. You know, being from up north and not used to our laid-back ways. I think Mary Lynn only agreed to marry him because she wanted to see what it felt like to be engaged."

Greenfield actually grunted a chuckle, although it was hard to tell over the engines. "And she broke it off?"

"Yeah, after two or three days," he said, shrugging his shoulders as if he was still surprised over the engagement. "I knew she wasn't ready." Harry thought he heard the agent remark *you're a good friend* over the deafening noise level. "Your people still haven't found him?"

"They're working on it," the agent sighed.

"How about sharing a little of your back story? Tell me a little something about John Greenfield?" Harry asked.

"I'm from a family of cops," he replied. "Been divorced three times; no kids, thank God. That's all you need to know." He looked at his notebook to check for updates.

"Now wait a minute," Harry said. "Three women couldn't stay married to you?"

"You've known me long enough to figure out why."

"I'm not trained to recognize the little nuances in people's expressions, so just tell me."

"I tried to warn each one of them that an FBI agent wasn't good husband material: the lonely nights, interrupted dinners, secrecy, moodiness, and insensitivity. They were all okay with the pitfalls, in the beginning. They thought they could change me. Ha! None of them lasted very long."

"So, they proposed to you?

"Yeah, I guess they did," he chuckled. "Maybe I was like your friend; I just wanted to see if it would work. There was no harm, no foul, and there was always a pre-nup."

"Wow, what a romantic story. Should I believe any of it?"

One corner of the agent's mouth turned up slightly and then he reached for the notepad.

"Tell me about the people that went missing," Harry said, looking at the ever-present notepad.

"Not much to tell," Greenfield replied trying to skirt an answer. "They were ordinary people going about their ordinary lives, until something happened that changed all that. You've seen the documentaries about people who claim to have been abducted by aliens. Sixty percent of those stories took on a new dimension after being overlaid with evidence of a different kind." He held the edge of the notepad and waved it back and forth.

"What kind of evidence?" Harry asked.

"That's classified, kid."

Rheinland-Pfalz was affectionately known as "The Rock" because it was set in the rocky wooded hills of the Western Palatinate. Harry received inoculations there and then outfitted with desert-sand camouflage attire. They took a smaller cargo flight to the Central Industrial Security Force Camp, Area Support Group at Indira Gandhi International Airport near New Delhi. They touched down in the wee hours of the morning. Another cargo plane took them to the international airport in Paro, Bhutan, and from there to a classified army post called Yangphula located near Laya. It was a temporary dark facility with one purpose, to search for ISIS militant sympathizers hiding in the mountains for the winter. Harry crashed as soon as his body hit the cot inside a small tent the army grunts set up for him. He didn't crawl out of the sleeping bag until voices outside the canvas walls woke him. He stepped outside into the late-morning sun wearing sweatpants and a tee shirt expecting the temperature to be as warm as the inviting sunshine. Rows of identical sand colored camouflage imprinted shelters surrounded his tent. The post was located in a rocky barren valley bordered by mountains of endless summits, some of which were in the clouds. A Velcro sign was stuck next to his door flap with "Foster" printed on it. A round thermometer attached to a tent pole registered 15 degrees.

"Burr!" he gasped as the stinging temperature hit him. He hurried back inside to search for more clothes that he hoped were inside a footlocker that mysteriously appeared during the night and also had his name stenciled on the outside.

A young corporal suddenly stepped inside. "Mr. Foster, I see you're up. I'm here to escort you to the mess tent. Agent Greenfield is waiting for you there."

"Right," Harry answered.

"Thermal wear is in the locker." The corporal raised the lid. "Here," he said, handing him two pieces of underwear and a set of coveralls with "*Foster*" printed on the front pocket. "Boots, socks, a thermal hat, yes, it's all here. I'll wait for you outside."

It had been a long 24 hours and Harry was starving. Greenfield gave him a challenging five minutes to scarf down the eggs and bacon he piled on his plate.

"Grab your juice, let's go," he gruffed from across the table in the noisy mess tent after an intolerable three minutes passed. The corporal was waiting for them outside behind the wheel of a Humvee. He drove them to a large village fifteen miles from the camp where other personnel were already quizzing shopkeepers, showing them photos representative of Al's dog and Mary Lynn. Boemena was crowded with buildings of various sizes and very populated. Not exactly modern, and the streets were narrow, making driving difficult for the limited number of compact cars that rambled through them. Vespas seemed to be the vehicle of choice. Most of the men had on knee-length robe-like skirts tied at the waist with a gho and wore leather shoes. After three hours of interviews, Greenfield took to his notebook. "Lots of dogs, just not this one," he grumbled. He looked up at the higher levels where grassy hills spread just below the snowy backdrop of the tallest mountain range in the world. "Let's keep moving. Villages are scattered all over in these mountains." He was right. They worked about ten more and headed back to camp after a long, unproductive day.

"You said this is a rare breed," Harry reminded himself as they sat across from Greenfield in the mess tent. It was late so the cooks were gone. Packaged food and snacks were the only things available, along with coffee and canned drinks from a refrigerator. Seven or so army personnel sat sparsely around the large dining room. "Maybe Mutt was just a stray after all. And he just happened to have the same genes as the ones we're looking for," Harry sighed, propping his head up on the table with one arm.

"We've been given permission to travel farther up the mountain," the agent said, ignoring Harry's fatigue. "Takin graze up in the high valleys. I'll advise the post commander that we'll be starting early in the morning. There are a few more villages I want to hit along the way."

"Like how much farther?"

"The higher peaks are managed by an order of monks that live in monasteries. They've been here literally forever. Rumor has it, some live to over 100. They must have seen these mastiffs."

"If only finding this breed would lead us to Mary Lynn," Harry sighed.

"Patience my boy; be patient. I've been to this area before chasing down hair samples and footprints. The people of Bhutan are friendly, polite, very accommodating, like today . . . well, most of them are."

"What does that mean?" It wouldn't surprise Harry to hear the agent had upset a few of the locals on his previous trips. "Anyone in particular we should avoid?"

"No," he barked, "no one."

"Wait a second," the younger man interjected. Greenfield's reply had been suspiciously loud. He'd ducked his head as if embarrassed, making his reaction that more suspicious. "Come on, fill me in. Something went down; what was it?" The agent became unusually fidgety. He pressed his coat pockets, looking for the notepad that was clearly lying in front of him on the table next to his coffee. How uncharacteristic.

"Keep your fingers crossed that the weather's suitable in the morning," the agent replied. His normal gruffness was back. "It can be unpredictable. We'll be taking a bird up to one of the monasteries. An ISR sent coordinates for a suitable landing site."

"ISR, you mean a drone? Exactly what is the army doing up here?"

"You know that we're practically next door to one of the hottest spots in the world?"

***

Mary Lynn sat on the icy bench outside the wall fissure beyond the sliding stone watching Neal solemnly stare into the wintry distance. "We've been here for a while," she said. "Are you sure someone's coming?" Neal didn't respond. She looked across the ribbon-like clouds for some sort of vehicle to emerge from them. "I'm starting to sweat inside this garment." She lifted the hood of the white goat hair robe and looked out at the lofty peaks and endless crowns that seemed more alluring every time she stared at them.

"Someone will be here soon," Neal replied, barely turning his head. "You'll go first; I'll follow."

There was no denying a serious and dark change had come over him. It started the second he saw the Bible in her arms. "Neal, what's wrong? Talk to me!" She left the bench to join him at what seemed like the edge of the world. He turned around with a jerk when she touched his shoulder. The charismatic Neal whose eyes used to light up at the sight of her had no spark whatsoever.

"I'm sorry, Mary Lynn," he sighed, expelling a long breath of frost. "I can't be that person you used to know any more. I was caught up in the mission. I know what I must do now. Start over; go back to the beginning. Those of us with a human side can do that, you know. We're not failures if we can acknowledge where we went wrong and then do what's necessary to correct our mistakes."

"That's true, but . . ." she began.

"I'm going to live with the monks, relearn the doctrine of Buddha for the sole purpose of enlightenment. When I saw you clutching the Bible to your chest, I realized we were never going to work. Maybe we were never intended to work. Maybe I was just supposed to get you here. You were right to break it off. You were being honest; I wasn't." His gaze shifted from her to something behind her, over her head.

Mary Lynn turned when she felt a whooshing gust of wind against her back. A giant was standing behind her on the land shelf. He wore a similar white hooded robe. It was speckled, making him blend well into the frozen rocky surroundings and nearly transparent. "Don't be afraid," she heard Neal whisper. "You'll be fine." The wind picked up, lifting their robes. "You're going to learn many exciting new things. You'll learn to read thoughts, which I can only do when my mind is just right, and make weather. Thus far, I can only stir up a little wind. Take it all in; you'll be an excellent student." The giant raised his cloaked arm and wrapped the soft fur around her.

Neal watched her melt away. Only a tiny whirlwind of flurries remained where she had stood. A second giant appeared and another handful of snow lifted and fell, leaving only the sound of the mountain whispers to blow their goodbyes.

"Don't worry, you are perfectly safe here."

Mary Lynn recognized the familiar voice when the giant released her from the crook in his arm. "James, it's you," she said.

He pushed the hood away from his head. "Your spiritual guide, Kunchen, will be here shortly," he said. "I'll stay with you until he arrives."

"Where are we?" she whimpered, looking up at the plastered walls painted from top to bottom with religious symbols. Narrow banners with Tibetan writing hung twenty-feet apart from gold-colored ropes just under continuous rows of small windows.

"You have nothing to fear," he said, sensing her anxiety. From nowhere it seemed, a short elderly man dressed in dark red robes trimmed in gold appeared beside them. "Mary Lynn Bennett," James said, bowing his head reverently. "This is Kunchen, your lama and spiritual guide. I'll return for you when I am summoned."

"How long will that be?" she sighed, breathless with apprehension.

James turned his head toward the windows ten feet above his head that lined the lofty ceiling. His brow furrowed; alarm contorted his face. He rushed closer to the wall, never taking his eyes off the windows. His stance was rigid as he glared toward the belt of mountains on the other side of the wall. Every muscle in his face bulged like hardened stones. "I just sent the warning," he said and then turned to them. "You should move to the internal rooms now."

"What's happening?" Mary Lynn gasped. She looked back and forth between the enormous giant and the monk who was two inches shorter than her.

"Please, come, we must move along quickly," Kunchen said and extended an arm directing her to a doorway that led to a hall. James nodded his approval to her and then vanished before her eyes.

***

"We'll be landing in two," the voice in Harry's headset dictated. He looked at Greenfield sitting in the front seat ahead of him, who had heard the same report from the Augusta pilot seated across from him, and he nodded. Two army corporals seated behind Harry tightened their gear, readying for the impending landing. He glanced out the side door window. An alarmingly huge gray cloud about 100 yards billowed out, curling and swelling. It reminded Harry of the steam plumes that flow out the stacks of the P&G soap plant in Pineville, across the river from Alexandria. This was no plume and it was spiraling towards them.

"Hey, you see that?" Harry queried, holding the mic in his headset close to his mouth to make sure everyone heard him clearly. "Over there to the right?" He pounded Greenfield on the shoulder. The helicopter suddenly tilted and jerked to the left as the pilot made a sharp turn, throwing his passengers forward and then backward when he increased speed and altitude. Harry pressed his shield against the side window to see where the maneuver had put them. "It's overtaking us," he gasped. The Augusta started to shake.

"Hang on kid," Greenfield bellowed. "We might land a little hard."

The storm freakishly kept up with every tactical move the pilot made. Its tentacles seemed to lay waiting behind every mountain he sought refuge behind and then jolt to life at the sight of them. The pursuit ceased only after the pilot dipped the aircraft down to a lower than preferred altitude, giving villagers, goats, cows and mules a start as the craft blew by only a few feet above their heads. The Augusta's tailwind shifted skirts, snatched scarves, and scattered baskets; some people fell to the ground in fear. The pilot guided the limping aircraft back to the Yangphula army post after he gained control.

"What was that?" Harry asked with a sigh of relief after what seemed like a fifteen-minute roller coaster ride.

"The weather is always tricky up here," Greenfield grumbled. "Forecasting is impossible when you're up where weather is born." The pilot gently set the plane down. "We'll try again tomorrow after I do a maintenance check."

***

Mary Lynn periodically looked behind her as the monk, Kunchen, led her through one mundane corridor after another. She tried to memorize the number of lefts and rights, but gave up after the sixth or maybe seventh set of turns. It made her think of the October cornfield mazes she loved to get lost in with her high-school posse. They would play Marco Polo; it was a must-do at Halloween. The ceilings got lower and more claustrophobic the further they traversed the network of hallways.

"How does James do that, just instantly go where he wants?" she asked. "I felt nothing."

"By way of teleportation," Kunchen replied as if it was a familiar mode of transportation. "It is one of the many gifts the gods bestowed upon the Nephilim."

"And he had to leave so abruptly because . . .?"

"A storm of high-velocity winds is passing over our complex; a blizzard, if you will," Kunchen said in a soft instructional voice that carried no excitement whatsoever in spite of the apparent emergency. "Our windows are strong, but it's best to move away from the exterior."

There was no indication of a storm, no rattling or sound of pounding rain. The small corridor gave her a claustrophobic, sweaty feeling that made her shed the coat, wad it up and clutched it nervously.

"This section of the Dzong was built to house Asian monks like myself," he said as if realizing her concern over the mere inches between her head and the ceiling. "The outer galleries were fortresses in the early wars and used as lookouts. Because of its limited accessibility, our monastery is used to accommodate the Nephilim. It's where they can study and pray. In turn, the Nephilim protect all our dzongs, monastery schools, as well as the people of Bhutan. You are here because I have been asked for assistance in introducing you to the teachings of Siddhartha Guatama, also called the

Guatama Buddha. Together, we will find and unlock the abilities you have inherited."

"Abilities?" she whispered. She wondered if he meant the colors.

"Yes, you have experienced a change to this particular gift," he replied calmly.

How did he know that . . .?

"But first, I must teach you the basics of Buddhism." They paused outside a large door carved with squares of Buddhist symbols. "Buddhist monks follow a hierarchy."

He looked at her instructively with the same demeanor as one of the first semester no-nonsense LSUA professors that she detested. Her work was never good enough, always in need of extra effort.

"There are five masters in charge of teaching the following subjects: religious tradition, liturgy, logic, and university. I am privileged to be among the five. Our days are consumed with teaching, study, meditation, and performing rituals, such as monastic singing and chanting in group prayer which you will participate in right away." He separated the two large doors and led her inside. "Many great monuments have been built to honor the dead heroes of Buddhism; each wall covering speaks to their honor." He made a slight turn and guided her attention to the walls in the temple where eight large gong-like metal discs hung from the ceiling. Each had a different face imprinted on it. "We paint prayer flags of dyed fabric; blue, white, red, green, and yellow." There was a strand of the colored fabric folded neatly over a pillow. "You already have interpretive knowledge of these colors. We paint, and sometimes sew prayers into the flags and then drape them around the compounds and villages in order to ward off evil and demons. They keep our holy ground holy and bless the surroundings. Flags primarily represent the different elements that create health and harmony through balance. There are five dzongs; each has its own temple, which we will visit while you are here learning Buddhist philosophy. Only vetted visitors visit our temple. They come here expecting miracles, but many leave disappointed."

Mary Lynn scanned the interior walls that were painted in brilliant reds, gold's, blues and greens. Colorful layered sashes hung from the ceiling on one side. Lotus butter lamps sat atop handcrafted holders as well as colorfully beaded Ghee-lamps. Some were short and stocky; others were tall and skinny. There were far too many to count. Prayer wheels lined the temple on two sides. They had similar markings as the ones in the large cavern where the Nephilim were praying. The ceilings were blocks of painted frames containing depictions of ancient oriental faces, their importance a mystery. There was an altar at one end, graced with large jars, ribbons, and candles. Behind it was a large gold statue of Buddha. Wall-to-wall red carpet covered the floor; large yellow kneeling cushions were stacked in a row beside the door. Three pews lined the back wall that she presumed were for the visitors he mentioned.

"Meditation has begun," he said, lifting his head as if hearing something. "My brothers have gathered in smaller groups today because of the impending danger."

She could hear nothing, no storm, or serene songs, only his monotonic voice.

"You will join my group today. Chanting releases the barriers people spend their lives building around themselves. And," he added, almost as an afterthought, "you will be relieved to know all danger is passed."

I never heard the storm. I don't hear any chanting. How can he hear these things? I wonder if he can read my thoughts, like James.

"James has always been a good student," he said. "Your friend Neal on the other hand, has more to learn. Please save your questions. Sometimes you realize the answers you seek during meditation." He pointed to another door that led to yet another hallway. "Come, we will join our brothers in prayer."

Chapter 13

"Second Lieutenant, right?" Harry called out to the approaching uniformed soldier with the single gold bar on his jacket sleeve. "Have you seen FBI agent John Greenfield this morning?"

The Second Lieutenant politely slowed just long enough to answer the barefoot civilian standing in front of the tent wearing gray sweatpants and a sand-colored hoodie. "Command tent," he shouted. "Next row over, nearly all the way down," he clarified because Harry was squinting as if he had just woken or was lost. "Next to the satellite truck," he shouted temporarily slowing. "It's covered in netting." He continued on his way, even after Harry gave him an unconvincing nod.

Harry dressed, grabbed a coffee and an omelet burrito from the mess tent, and left in search of the unmarked command tent. Two MP's were guarding the entrance. They wouldn't allow him entry before verification from inside and confiscation of his coffee and the half-eaten egg wrap. Inside were rows of tables crowded with electronic equipment and cables. Nearly all personnel were wearing earpiece/microphone sets. They were busily conversing in low voices while monitoring data from various screens. He found Greenfield in the utmost rear of the pavilion dressed in sand-colored camouflage fatigues and staring at one of the larger screens.

"This is the storm that chased us out of the mountains yesterday," the agent said when he saw Harry approaching.

"Good morning to you, Agent Greenfield," Harry sighed.

"Four hours ago, it was a good morning," the older man grumbled.

"Looks like an animation," Harry said after watching the video loop three times. "That can't be real. It looks like the storm was chasing us."

Greenfield blew out a heavy sigh. "The post commander's not happy about the evasive moves our pilot was forced to make. Apparently he took some heat over it from His Majesty, King Wangluck."

"Well, I'd like to shake our pilot's hand. I don't know how he flew us out of that," Harry said as he watched the video loop again. "So, this was taken by a drone?"

"Oh yeah," Greenfield replied. "Post Commander Hanna has access to some pretty fancy high-tech surveillance platforms. This image was recorded twenty minutes before our incident." The agent clicked the remote in his hand that switched the screen to a frozen video frame showing the side of a snow-covered mountain. "See it, right there?" He zoomed in. "Something is standing there, something that could be a man. A very large man. It's there for less than thirty-seconds, and then it just melts away."

"Could be a shadow that disappeared with the sun," Harry countered, shrugging his shoulders and frowning at the image on the screen.

"No. Something or someone is standing there," rebutted Greenfield. He tapped a key on the pad below the screen twice, adding, "and then it's not. And look at this . . . a second one," he said after keying up the next frame. It has broader shoulders. We're getting ready to go back up. Post commander Hanna is out arranging an M134 operator to ride along. He's of the opinion that they're ISIS enemy combatants and possibly armed."

"What do you think, a monk?" His comment produced an impatient frown from the agent. "The villagers told us the monks live in the mountains."

"That's no monk," Greenfield snarled. "Nothing lives that far up. I don't have any more time to wait. Cdr. Hanna said he'd have an Augusta ready in five out by the hangers. That was fifteen minutes ago. You don't want to get this hard-nosed commander on your bad side. Are you coming?"

"After yesterday's cool ride, you bet!"

"Kids!" Greenfield grumbled under his breath.

FBI Agent John Greenfield, Special Division came from similar beginnings as Commander Robert Hanna. His interest in the FBI spawned from the hard-core training he received alongside the Green Berets at Fort Bragg, North Carolina prior to being deployed to Iran. He carried the impressive discipline with him throughout his career. Cdr. Hanna received similar training at the same facility only months apart from Greenfield. Hanna made a career in the army; Greenfield became a police officer, then a detective, and trained at Quantico. He could see a little of himself in Hanna. Their intense training had taught them to be forceful and committed and had molded them into good soldiers. Greenfield went on to relentlessly hunt public enemies as an FBI agent, while Hanna became a hardheaded, hard-core soldier. An order from the buzz-cut, stone-faced commander meant there would be no discussion. The FBI went forward only after examining clues from inside out. Granted, Hanna didn't have the luxury of time in some cases. But he demanded perfection out of every exercise. Greenfield gave him the benefit of the doubt, because he might have turned out just as uncompromising had he made the military his career.

"Hanna said not to expose the M134 unless it's necessary," Greenfield dictated through the mouthpiece of the oxygenated helmet after they were in the air and headed to the coordinates where the ISR platform had recorded images of two shadowy figures.

"You're not concerned about stability at this altitude?" Harry asked, noticing frost forming on the windows.

"Hanna says the Augusta can handle 25K," Greenfield grunted. "We'll be fine; just keep your helmet and oxygen mask on."

"We'll position a Recog UAV first to take a look around," the pilot dictated over his headset. A few minutes later, he gave the two corporals sitting in the rear the order to deploy.

Harry watched them uncover a small fixed winged drone. A bulky notebook linked up the two devices. A door was slid open just wide enough to quickly deploy the drone.

"We're right over the coordinates; maintain your position as best you can, sir," Harry heard one of the corporals dictate to the pilot over the flight helmet. "Looks good," the voice narrated. "Nothing but snow so far . . . rocks . . . still panning." The two identical monotone voices sounded a mile away instead of right behind him staring at the laptop screen. After seven minutes of meaningless observations, one said, "I see a cave, sir." Both Harry and Greenfield unstrapped themselves and huddled around the real-time video. "Going in; lights on." The second corporal in control of the joystick narrated the video: "rock, rock, more rock; dead-end, exiting."

"Wait, turn it back around," Greenfield shouted so loud it created static. He pointed a finger at the screen. "That rock looks like it's been moved. It has scrape marks. Ready the hoist; we're going down. Not you, Foster; I might need someone with muscles to help me move that stone."

Harry wasn't about to argue. The helicopter seemed a much safer place than dangling from a harness and walking around on what could be an unstable ice shelf. The UAV recorded Greenfield and the second soldier as they were lowered. The Augusta hovered over the icy ledge. Their boots sank two feet into snowdrift before finding solid ground. The drone followed behind them, recording them and their trenched paths through the snow until they entered the cave. "They're coming out already," Harry whispered and leaned in closer as if that would help him discern why they were stumbling backward.

"What the hell is that?" the corporal's voice screeched. He squeezed the joystick with both hands. "Holy crap, it's a Neanderthal!" The humongous humanoid stood at least six feet taller than both men.

The huge creature shook its head and threw back its white tunic exposing its bare bulging brown shoulders and arms. The mammoth anthropoid clutched a huge club-like object in its hand. The UAV produced the bird's-eye view of its grotesque angry face when it looked directly up at the Augusta.

"It sees us," Harry whaled. A second creature appeared at the cave's entrance and stood beside its comrade. Greenfield and the soldier were now attempting to conceal themselves behind a large rock near the rim, but the gigantic brutes spotted them quickly. Their only hope of escape was the hoist, but it was swinging wildly in the air too far out from the edge for either of them to grab hold.

The corporal operating the UAV had already repositioned himself behind the M134D. "I'll take them out. Open the door!" He looked at Harry and nodded vigorously, signaling him to slide the door open. The soldier rotated the gun around and aimed the killing machine down at the two creatures.

Harry sat down after sliding the door open and threw his arms over his helmet, bracing himself for a torrent of thunderous blasts. The laptop rested on the floor, having lost its connection to the drone that was drifting away with the downdraft of the aircraft's rotor blades. An overwhelming wave of nausea suddenly came over him at the same instant he heard the pilot's voice in his headset say, "Hold on." The aircraft weaved and then accelerated forward. He felt himself being tossed violently from one side of the cabin to the other. Instead of smashing into things, breaking ribs and limbs, he seemed to float. He rolled in the air and bounced off the inside walls, as his air tank ripped away from his chest. He flailed his arms uselessly as if trying to hold onto consciousness and perhaps life itself because the light of day was closing like a camera shutter.

He awoke dazed and confused, and with no idea why he was lying across a random seat inside a helicopter, or why a soldier was moaning on the floor behind him. The pilot was strapped in his seat, his arms limp by his side and his head moving slowly. Harry tried to focus, to make sense of things in spite of the searing pain emanating from every muscle in his body. He lifted his head to look out a missing side door. A dozen army personnel were running toward the craft. Four stopped to tend Agent Greenfield and a soldier lying on the ground fifty feet away. Although he was able to recognize the FBI agent, he had no memory of what had happened.

Harry woke up the second time in the army field-hospital tent. A nurse rushed over when she noticed his head moving from side to side. She closed the curtains around him and adjusted his bed to an upright position.

"What happened to me?" he muttered groggily, looking at the IV needle taped to his arm.

"You were in an accident, sir," the nurse replied dutifully. She wore gray hospital scrubs and her hair was in a tight bun. Her movements were a testament to strict training. "Don't try to move; I'll get the doctor, sir."

Less than a minute later the military doctor whipped the curtain open and closed. He held a plastic drawstring bag that he tossed on top of the bed. "I'm Dr. Rush," he said and began removing the IV needle from Harry's arm and the oxygen tubes from his nose. "Well, your team has managed to get the attention of the commander of Middle East operations," he said sarcastically. "I don't know how you landed back on post unscathed and without radar detection, but you'll be able to tell your story to Col. Jackson in about five minutes. You're lucky you're only suffering from acute altitude sickness. Get dressed," the doctor ordered, nodding at the plastic bag that evidently contained his patient's clothes. "I'll get word to the colonel that you're conscious. There's a lieutenant waiting outside to escort you to him."

"John Greenfield. Where is Agent Greenfield?"

"Confined to quarters, like you are for now," the doctor replied. "He's already given his statement. You're the last one to wake up. You've been out for a week."

It was hard to answer the questions that the roundtable of military hierarchy was throwing at him. They constantly cut into his vague responses, demanding more details, including details about Afghan soldiers that he had no recollection of. A frowning Col. Jackson sat opposite him at the head of a twelve-foot table. Two lieutenants and four sergeants sat on either side taking notes even though there was a bank of microphones on the table recording everything. Harry started at the beginning, when John Greenfield showed up at his lab after the blood work of a friend's dog caught the intention of his FBI team investigating certain missing persons around the world. Coincidentally or not, his best friend went missing along with the dog, a game warden, and his friend's ex-fiancé. "I'm here with Agent Greenfield. We're following a lead on the dog while investigators back home continue to look for the missing," he continued. "Apparently, this is the only place in the world where the Bhutan mastiff is found. And there was a blanket that someone left at my friend's house woven with the hair of a takin." He rubbed his head as flashes from the past few days started to come back to him. "We interviewed villagers, but that's still fuzzy. There was a cave in the side of a mountain, but I don't know if I'm remembering a real cave or a video." After an hour of testimony, sometimes repeating the same answers over again, Col. Jackson slapped his notebook closed and shook his head as if dissatisfied. The rest of the inquisitors gathered their notes and agreed it was time for a break. One made the appeasing remark, "maybe you'll remember more tomorrow." One of the lieutenants escorted him to his tent where he found a guard posted outside. It felt good to lie down on the normally uncomfortable lumpy sleeping bag spread across the cot. He closed his eyes, hoping the flashes of memories might meld together and make sense, and the missing hours before he woke up in the hissing downed helicopter would come back to him. His interrogators had pressed him hard to remember someone shooting at them. They wanted to bend his account while trying to make sense of why they mysteriously fell out of the sky, landing intact with crew and passengers unconscious, yet uninjured and with no recall of the ordeal. He didn't realize he'd fallen asleep until something bumping his cot awakened him.

"Foster wake up!" Greenfield's voice was gruff even when he was whispering. He felt another jolt.

Harry opened his eyes to see the agent was standing over him. "They didn't put a guard outside your tent?" Harry asked sluggishly, slurring his words.

"I cut a hole in the bottom of the tent behind my locker," he whispered and pushed Harry's feet to one side so he could sit down. "How are you feeling kid?"

"My whole body is sore," Harry groaned. "I can't remember what happened."

"The last thing I remember with any clarity is being in the command tent," the agent recalled. "After that . . . everything is spotty. I see flashes of things that don't make sense."

"Yeah, me too," Harry said, pushing himself up. "How long were you out?"

"Five days." The agent frowned at him. "You were out so long that you sprouted facial hair."

"The command tent . . ." Harry paused to clear the phlegm from his throat. "I remember standing in front of a monitor looking at a video . . . of a ledge," he said, rubbing the side of his prickly face. "The video was taken by a drone, I think. Oh, God; I feel dizzy again . . . Ohh." He put his feet over the side of the cot and held his swimming head in his hands. "I'm never getting on another helicopter."

"Yeah, I'm having those same feelings. Air sickness, the doctor said. It hits every time I try to remember what happened. I lost my notepad so I thought you might help me fill in the blanks. The colonel sent the pilot and crew back to Paro, so they're not gonna be any help . . . not to us anyway.

Hanna's narrative is we were attacked by rogue Afghan militants hiding in a cave."

"I wonder if he'd let us see the video I'm remembering? You know, to help us piece things together."

"Were we together when you saw this video?" the agent asked.

"I think I walked in on you and Hanna or maybe some techs, I think. Wait, I asked directions from someone . . . a lieutenant. I'm confused; he directed me to a camo net covering a satellite truck."

"Satellite truck?" the agent asked, slapping him on the hip. "Come on, kid; I know where that is." Greenfield got up and headed for the opening he had cut in the back of Harry's tent.

They slipped through the dark camp, ducking within shadows of bivouacs and vehicles until they found the large utility truck parked between two tents and covered with camouflage netting. The lift was fully extended. "This must be it," Greenfield whispered from their hiding place between two box trucks. "Uh!" he suddenly grunted. "Are you having trouble breathing? Let's go then," he whispered when Harry shook his head.

"A lot of personnel are in here," Harry whispered nervously after circling around the back and finding a way inside through an opening that facilitated a mass of cables. "See those four bulky laptops?" he said as they crouched between two tables. "There was one in the helicopter behind the pilot . . . whoa," Harry gasped and grabbed his head. "I'm starting to feel really queasy."

"Strange how that happens every time something starts coming back." Greenfield reached up and slid one of the laptops off the table. "We must have been drugged." He opened it and they looked at the blank screen and then at each other. "Something's wrong," Greenfield whispered. "My mind just went blank; How do I turn this on?"

"Put it back!" Harry gasped. "I'm feeling weird. It's like we're not supposed to see what's on here."

Greenfield suddenly felt tightness in his chest. "Oh God, I-I feel like I'm having a heart attack!" He grabbed his left shoulder. "My neck, my arm!" he whispered.

"Let's get out of here," Harry bleated quietly.

Greenfield refused to go to the medical tent, no matter how many times Harry tried to steer him in that direction on the way back to his tent.

The next morning, an annoyed Cdr. Hanna summoned them. When Hanna produced a security video of them sneaking into the command tent, they expected to be escorted to the stockade. They learned Col. Jackson was on his way back to Germany after verifying Greenfield's mission with Quantico. To their surprise, Hanna gave them permission to move about the camp again, but with a warning not to go off-post without his knowledge and to report to him upon their return. The agent quickly asked for a Humvee and permission to continue interviewing villagers, which Hanna agreed to with some reluctance. There was a stare-down over a new notepad and Harry's request for a cell phone. It was granted, but with a repugnant grimace.

The Humvee came with a driver, a sergeant assigned to keep an eye on them. Greenfield sat in the front passenger seat and retrieved files while the sergeant drove them up a winding dirt road toward the smaller villages that dotted the higher levels. "You can by-pass this one," he told the sergeant when they approached the outskirts of a village called Mondar.

"What's the deal with this village?" Harry asked from the back seat. The agent didn't answer but he noticed him scanning the crowds until his eyes seized on one particular group of merchants. A woman, standing in a crowd in front of a butcher stand, stopped to stare back at him in much the same challenging way. She wore a green wrap-around printed cloth for a skirt and a white blouse, covered with a light-burnt orange jacket. The butcher behind the counter also stopped his conversation with a customer to look at him. A boy in the small group of children she was apparently in charge of held something in his hand that caught Harry's eye. He slapped Greenfield on the back to get his attention. "See that kid over there by the butcher stand? He's holding a Surface Pro. Where do you suppose he got that?" The agent reluctantly directed the driver to stop. The woman Greenfield recognized rushed toward them when they exited the vehicle; Harry suspected it was to head them off after seeing their interest in the boy. The butcher walked around the front of the stand and folded his arms. She wrapped a yellow Rachu (a wrap worn by women to cover their shoulders) around her face and head, exposing only her dark brown eyes that she fixed on Greenfield.

"Her name is Karma," Greenfield whispered to Harry under his breath.

"What?" Harry choked out, thinking his companion was joking.

"Agent," Karma said cynically. Her eyes expressed distrust.

"Karma, how have you been? And you, Bidhan?" He nodded to the butcher.

"We are doing very well, thank you." She folded her arms in front of her. "And you?"

"We're just fine," he said, glancing back at Harry to see if he had noticed their familiarity.

"Are you here searching for the Almasti again?"

"Actually, I'm looking for a missing woman and a Bhutan mastiff that might be with her. We noticed the Surface Pro the boy is carrying." The boy had curiously followed Karma and eagerly stepped forward when he realized the stranger was talking about him. "Does he speak English?"

"You deal with me, not the boy." Karma's eyes squinted suspiciously when the agent looked past her.

"Where did you get that?" Greenfield asked the boy.

The boy stared up at him in silence after recognizing Karma's indifference and then ducked behind her kira.

Harry snatched Greenfield's notebook from under his arm and stepped forward. "Look, I have one too," he announced and quickly squatted to his knees in front of the boy who giggled when Harry opened it to the round FBI symbol with a plain blue wallpaper. "Not a very imaginative screen, I know, but I just got it this morning." The boy opened his laptop to show off the home screen picture of his classmates. Harry put his hand up, and to his surprise, the boy slapped it with his bare hand. "Alright," Harry crooned. "Hey, how 'bout taking a picture with me?" he asked the boy, who eagerly agreed. "Can you send it to me? I just got this new phone; I'll take one of you and we can share."

While Harry and the boy exchanged email addresses, Karma turned to Greenfield. "The children are issued these at school."

"You're English has improved." Greenfield smiled at her, turning his back to Harry and the boy to block her from seeing their interaction, and to keep Harry from seeing the way he was looking at Karma.

"These devices teach many languages. How many have you learned from yours?" she asked sarcastically.

"I don't have time to study languages."

"You're not looking for the Almasti again?"

"Primarily, I'm looking for a few people who are missing. We believe the dog I mentioned originated from here. There could be a connection to the Almasti, or Sasquatch, as we call it; I'm not sure. Right now, we're interviewing people to see if anyone has seen them."

"That's what you are doing, interviewing children?" she challenged. "Your first priority is your job, I see . . . as always."

"It seems my job has brought me back here, to you. Maybe I'm meant to be here." A rare smile spread across his face. She tried to resist blushing, but her olive-brown skin was already glowing with a tinge of pink.

"The King gave computers to every child that attends a monastic school," she said after collecting herself, straightening her back, and tightening the rachu. "Soon everyone will own one.

"Where does this boy go to school?" Greenfield followed her amazing brown eyes as they steered him to the mountains north of the village. A wave of nausea suddenly fell over him. "I don't think I'm ready to go back up there." He rubbed his chest with one hand, digging a path with his fingers toward his shoulder.

"That was you?" she gasped. Rumors had spread throughout the villages about the two helicopters that were hurtled out of the sky. One had flown dangerously close to rooftops during its descent and the other had plowed to the ground in a cloud of dust after rolling end over end. "Then you are a threat," she snapped back when he nodded.

"To who, the monks?"

"The gods, the monks, to us all," she said, with knitted brows. Her eyes were piercing. The passion she felt for her country, its children, and their gods were as evident as ever in those amazing chestnut eyes. That look was something that excited him the most about her. "The gods do not want you in their mountains."

"Do you suppose it would be okay with the gods if the monks gave us permission?" Greenfield asked.

"You mock us, but you cannot go. . .never!" she fretted. "Just here, no further."

"Karma. . .why?" he whispered. "Please, tell me."

She held the yellow rachu tightly around her head and face. "The mountains are sacred. Only students of the monks are allowed."

"Why is it so off-limits? What are they hiding?"

"You are just as hard headed as ever, Agent John Greenfield."

Her eyes were like magnets; they pulled at his soul. "It's been a pleasure seeing you again, Karma, as always." He wasn't usually so polite around women, not after being burned three times. Something was spellbinding about the woman he met two years ago while tracking down a reported Almasti sighting. She could tear down his walls with a look, like the one she was giving him now.

"They believe their gods hold some kind of power over the mountains," Greenfield told Harry when they were settled back in the Humvee. "The monks supposedly intercede between the gods and the people. Whatever the monks decree, it's protected by the King who holds tightly to the Buddhist faith that's woven into the fabric of every Bhutanese citizen. It's part of their national identity."

"And you know Karma from when you were here before? When you were investigating a sighting?" John had led Harry to believe his relationship with Karma was casual, but it certainly seemed like they knew each other better than that. It wasn't just their animated discussion; it was how their eyes lingered on one another. "Well, Bassui speaks pretty good English," he said, looking curiously through the side window at a sprinkling of distant structures built into the sides of the mountains. "He goes to a boarding school at one of the monasteries up there. They were sent home because of the weather. Might have been what we got caught up in, except . . . something else happened to *us*. Damn, I wish I could remember. Anyway, we exchanged info." Harry held up the Android. "Can your people access files from his emails and phone number?"

"Well, Foster," Greenfield growled, "look at you acting like an FBI agent. Must be the new facial hair."

"Well, I might not have seen Bassui holding the Surface if you hadn't been staring at Karma and she hadn't been throwin' all that shade back at you."

"Go to hell, Foster!" John snarled.

A technician in the command tent prepared Harry's phone to link with Bassui's before sending the photo. The capable tech created a link enabling him to access the boy's internal files. By the time the boy looked at the photo an hour later the tech had copied everything from the Surface.

"I carried books and paper to school," Greenfield grumbled as he watched the technician work. "Kids today use their thumbs to press icons and send buttons."

"Transfer his photo folders to my phone," Harry said anxiously. "He may have taken a picture of Mutt without knowing it," he added. "Or, maybe by some miracle, Mary Lynn in a crowd. I'd recognize her no matter what the setting. I've seen her at her best and worst, from dressed to the nines to coveralls wading through the mud, frog hunting." He smiled as he reminisced. "From eating filet mignon to sucking crawfish heads. Thank God, I didn't lose those memories."

"I knew you two were more than best friends," John couldn't resist saying when he saw the deep sentiment on Harry's face. "I'll requisition you a notepad and an extra drive. You know how kids are, there's no telling how many pictures he's taken."

When the photos from Bassui's Surface were uploaded to the external drive, Harry took it and the government issued notepad to his tent to study them in private. There were far too many observers with agendas milling around in the busy command tent. He rolled up the sleeping bag, propped himself up against it, and connected the two devices. He let the cursor rest on the gallery box. Were his expectations too high? Would a mastiff photo come up right away, or one of Mary Lynn? *Not very likely,* he warned himself. He wondered how people like Greenfield did this every day: the searching, traveling, the unsettling questioning, upsetting people's lives, breaching their internet. He took a breath to quell the built-up anxiety and tapped the gallery box. The first pictures that came up were of Bassui's schoolmates. The boys appeared studious and disciplined in the array of twelve pictures, working in silence, heads down, taking notes using pencil and paper and communicating to their monk instructors over their personal Microsoft Surface Pro's. There were ten more photos depicting somber well-behaved students. Their expressions were nothing like the friendly, smiling kid he befriended. It wasn't until the boys had removed their gho to play soccer and basketball in the next twenty or so photos that the smiles appeared. Harry noticed that not all the boys were native to this part of the world. Most had dark hair and olive skin, but a few had red hair and fair skin . . . *like Mary Lynn*, he thought. Their height is what drew his attention to them. They were three to four inches taller than their classmates.

Bassui had a good eye for nature's beauty. His album contained many shots of flowering fields against towering snow-tipped mountains that he must have taken while on school fieldtrips. He was also organized. Every file was identified by field trip, event, and location. The file called *Rainbow Valley* held pics of budding hillsides with meandering grazing herds of goats. *Prayer Bridge* contained shots of beautiful temples that could only be reached by walking across suspension bridges that stretched across rivers or deep valleys that divided steep hills. Bright-colored flags were strung between buildings, across roads, and along bridges. Many magnificent Buddhist symbols were displayed on building walls and pedestals, doors, gates, and windows. *Markets* had photos of streets lined with tables loaded with produce, rugs, plates, trinkets, clothing and home goods, all decorated brilliantly in honor of the nation's religious beliefs. *Misc* depicted fellow students and village dwellers as they went about their daily lives in and around their familiar surroundings. *Home* contained candid shots of Karma sweeping the floor inside their modest home, cooking, hanging colorful cloths on a line behind their simple hut, and sitting on the edge of a fountain while reading to a group of children on the ground around her. Harry dozed off for twenty minutes. When he woke, a goat's face was staring back at him through the twelve-inch screen. Its wide yellowish eyes were looking directly into the lenses of the Surface; the tip of its tongue was curled outside its open mouth as if bleating something to the photographer. He swiped the screen to the next photo. It was a close up of another animal's face . . . a Bhutan mastiff with brown spots over its eyes. There were seven pictures of the dog. In four, he was trotting beside a small group of goats. The rest were of him sitting in lush green grass as if guarding the four yaks in the background.

"Mutt!" Harry gasped, jolting upright and straddling the cot. "John!" he yelled, surprised at himself for calling the agent by his first name. He had been thinking of him as *John* lately as he was growing more comfortable around him. Maybe it was because of how vulnerable he appeared around Karma. He ran from the tent in his socks and sweat suit after fumbling with the Velcro door flap, carrying the notepad under his arm. He ripped through the agent's door in the same manner and feverishly rushed back outside after finding the tent empty. He'd been running on adrenalin and was now feeling the cold. He grabbed a blanket that had been thrown over a nearby four-wheeler and sprinted through the rows of tents to the command center.

"How can you be so sure this is Al's dog?" Greenfield asked after scrutinizing the photo of the scruffy black animal.

"Compare it to the stock photos," Harry insisted.

"Similar markings," Greenfield mumbled as he considered the possibility. "Except the hair looks different in the one he took, it's shorter, and all chopped up."

"That's because Al gave him a haircut with his hunting knife." Harry could hardly contain his excitement. "Mutt looked just like those bushy-haired dogs beforehand," he said. "But this is how he looks now."

"Text your little friend. Send him copies of the stock photos. Ask him again if he has seen these dogs. It might encourage him to tell you where he saw this one. Didn't he deny seeing them before?"

"What'd you expect? You're girlfr-uh, he was too scared to say anything in front of Karma. I just hope it doesn't dawn on him, or her, how we're using him. I really like this kid. Well, here goes." Harry tapped the touch screen, composed a letter to Bassui, and attached the stock photos. "I noticed something about a few of his classmates," he said after the *email sent* notice appeared. "They're not from here."

"I know," John replied. "I asked Karma about them when I was here before. Orphans from all over Europe are taken in by the monks and then distributed amongst families. They come from desperate conditions. Their parents have either abandoned them or can't afford to feed them. The monks allow certain households to adopt them. No one knows for sure where the tall, light-complexioned children originate from."

Chapter 14

A boy of about thirteen, wearing a dark green shirt, orange gho and brown cut offs led Mary Lynn to the entryway of a twelve-by-twelve room that had no door. She stood within the frame and looked inside at the bare plastered walls inside. A single bed was against the wall in one corner. A dim whispering lantern hung from the ceiling; a straight-back chair sat against the opposite wall. The floor was stone.

"Distractions impair meditation," he said timidly. "Elaborate interpretative offerings are only found near the temples."

She looked at him, "Thank you, I was wondering why it's so plain in here."

"The corridors visitors pass through are more decorative," he continued. "The artists hope their work will convey meaningful interpretations to those who visit. This will be your room during your stay with us." She gingerly stepped inside at his direction. "A lavatory is just down the hall. You can bathe if you wish. Heated stones keep the water warm and a robe is hanging on a peg. Sleep well," he said after a few seconds of awkward silence. He bowed at the waist and left her standing alone in the room. A single lantern in the hallway led her to the lavatory. When she returned there was a wooden lap-tray on the seat of the chair containing a third of a loaf of bread on a wooden plate and a cup of milk.

The next morning, boredom had her trying to find patterns in the plaster. She sat up in the bed with her legs crossed in front of her like Kunchen taught her the day before, but meditation just wasn't coming. There was no rhyme or reason to the bumps and short strokes. With so much artistry in other parts of the monastery, she wondered how the mudders and painters had resisted making at least a few creative swirls. Her eyes were drawn to the doorway and she was startled to see Kunchen standing there. She had seen no one since the boy the night before. The thin olive-skinned man spoke only after she stood.

"My name means 'all-knowing.'"

She wondered why he began with an interpretation of his name, instead of "good morning, did you sleep well?"

"You will be called Prana, 'the healer,' from this day forth." He stepped out into the hall and then paused.

At first, she thought something was wrong, but then realized he was waiting for her to follow him. "I'm sorry, this is all I have to wear," she said, referring to the robes she wore from the day before.

He ignored her apology and immediately started in with the first lesson of the day. "Buddhism is a spiritual approach to living a fulfilled peaceful life," he said in a low calm voice. "It began in the first century BC," he continued, taking it for granted that she was following him within listening distance. "It takes discipline and much concentration to become one with the environment, to pull energy from the air and all things in it. The Nephilim carry an extra sense. They are blessed with the ability to see and feel everything going on around them. Every monk meditates and strives to become one with the gods, but Nephilim are of the gods. You are Prana, the healer, descendant of the gods and Nephilim hierarchy."

"Prana, the healer," she repeated. *It's no secret that I'm a nurse.*

He stopped and turned to her. "Yes, you received a proper education in preparation for your standing in the Nephilim community. You already experienced your healing abilities."

There was no denying her empathy with patients. The dormant seeds of nursing sprang to life when she was seven years old. A neighbor's dog was hit by a car. She heard the motorist's screeching tires, saw the dog roll out from under the wheel and yelp. To her it sounded like "help." The driver sped away leaving the dog panting on the asphalt, its tongue hanging limp from its mouth and white from shock. It whined when she gently placed her hand on its side. She closed her eyes and prayed the "Hail Mary," a prayer her mother taught her and the first one that came to mind. When she opened her eyes, the dog was alert, staring at her with bright brown eyes and beating its tail against the pavement. It scrambled to its feet, licked her on the face, as if to say thank you, and ran home.

Kunchen seemed to be waiting for her to finish her thoughts before continuing. "Buddhism," he said and shuffled onward, "has been traced to the teachings of Siddhartha Gautama, an enlightened teacher who is referred to as the Buddha. Buddhism involves elements of belief, faith and . . ." he slowed and gave her a meaningful look as if he was about to say something that she needed to pay attention to, "self-transformation." They stopped outside a large meditation room; it seemed to be their destination. "Our credence does not mandate worship or the belief in one God or a superhuman controlling power. Our guidelines help those who desire to achieve peace."

Peace, such a complicated word, she thought to herself. *So elusive, something I will never be able to find or hold onto.* It was impossible, considering her oddities. Worry, self-doubt and embarrassment were the basis of her existence. Nothing was as it was supposed to be in her family. Present circumstances added to the certainty. *Will I ever see home again?*

"You worry about trivial things," he said as if answering her thoughts.

Trivial to you, maybe, she thought.

"Buddha's teachings state the purpose of life is to do away with such worry and suffering. You must put an end to your desire to seek happiness through material pleasures." He led her to the center of the large room and then pointed to the maroon rug they were standing on; he signaled her with his eyes to sit down. "I will show you how to explore your own consciousness and teach you the means to control your thoughts." She followed his lead and crossed her legs, then rested her hands, palms up on the side of her knees. "Close your eyes," he whispered.

At some point within the hour of listening to the monk's nonstop mind-numbing philosophy, her body started to feel weightless. It was a pleasing feeling; she gave in to it and allowed the peace to wash over her. She felt nothing, not her body, nor the ground, not even the hunger that had been gnawing in the pit of her stomach all morning. Kunchen's gentle litany continued.

The beliefs of Buddhism: reincarnation, the four noble truths, and the five precepts infiltrated her mind with ease. It was more like a realization than a lecture: *There are three trainings or practices in Buddhism: Sila, the practice of virtue, morality and good conduct is compared to the classic golden rule of Christianity; do unto others as you would have them to do unto you; Samadhi, the mental development of concentration and meditation. The development of one's mind is the best way to lead to personal freedom. Prajna, the third, is the discernment of enlightenment where wisdom emerges into a person's calm and pure mind.* She found herself completely absorbed in the homily. That night, after the daylong orientation and a meal of rice and vegetables she slept wonderfully for the first time in a long time, perhaps ever.

Upon returning from her bath the next morning, Mary Lynn found a folded brown garment and a pair of sandals lying on her bed. A wooden bowl containing fruit was on the chair. She dressed quickly while scarfing down the grapes, pears and mangos. She sat on the side of the bed and waited for Kunchen to appear in the doorway again. Weariness set in after an hour. She lay down and thoughts of home flashed through her mind like a slide show. She thought about the last time she saw her father and his suspicions about her mother. Then Neal, who tried too hard at everything and ended up disappointed in himself. She yearned to hear Harry's reassuring words, or anyone's voice other than Kunchen's or her own voice inside her head. She got up and paced around and around the twelve-by-twelve small room until she was dizzy from the circling and plopped down in the chair. Her eyes fixed on the drab pasty wall three feet in front of her. Harry's face slowly formed from out of the bumps and obscure lines in the plaster. His was squinting as if the sun was in his eyes. He was wearing a purple and gold striped knit skullcap pulled down and covering his forehead. He had facial hair and he was smiling. The corners of her mouth rose; relief bloomed within her cheeks. She wanted so much for him to be there, but the vision faded and he was gone.

"Harry?" She leaped at the wall and pressed her palms against it as if trying to find his face.

"No, Prana," someone answered from behind her. "It's only me."

Mary Lynn quickly turned. Neal was standing in the doorway. His whole appearance was changed: head shaven, small gold rings hanging from both earlobes. He was wearing a traditional dark red toga trimmed in yellow over tan pants. "Thank God!" she gushed. "I was just thinking about you." She rushed toward him, but stopped abruptly when she saw a boy standing off to the side in the hall. A monk was standing beside him. He appeared to be about ten-years-old, human, like herself, and cradling his left arm with his right hand. "Oh," she sighed. "Who is this?"

"Daiji," the monk replied. "It means 'Great Compassion.'"

"What happened to your arm, Daiji?" she asked and knelt down in front of him. She reached for his arm, but he tensed up and pulled it closer to his chest. "It's okay. I might be able to help."

"He was playing, sliding down a stair railing. He fell and landed on top of his arm," the monk explained.

"I was instructed to bring the boy to you," Neal added. "Because of your nursing skills."

"It's okay, Daiji, this is Prana," the monk said, trying to encourage the boy, who stepped forward and cautiously held out his arm.

Mary Lynn took his hand first, closed her eyes, and then began to feel his arm from the wrist to the elbow. "There's a hair-line fracture," she whispered. "And slight swelling."

"Prana?" Neal said after a minute passed. "Prana," he repeated and leaned forward to touch her shoulder.

"Don't interrupt," the monk said, blocking his hand. "She's praying."

Neal frowned at the monk, but stepped back.

Mary Lynn breathed in deeply, opened her eyes, and looked at the boy. She smiled and made one last pass over his forearm. "How does it feel?"

"Good," Daiji said. "Good as new. Thank you, Prana."

"It would be a good idea to keep it stabilized for a day or two." She looked up at Neal. "Get my rachu on the bed please, Neal." She made a sling with the rachu, tied it around Daiji's neck and gently placed his arm inside. "That should do it," she said, smiling.

The monk bowed at the waist and took the boy by the hand and led him away.

"What did you just do?" Neal asked.

"I think I might have mended the fracture," she whispered and moved closer to him, but he backed away.

"We need to go," he said. "You'll be late for meditation."

"Neal, I feel confused," she said as they walked. "Please, can we go somewhere, somewhere outside, like before? I don't even know if it's day or night anymore."

"Who did you see?" Neal asked. "Before, when you were staring at the wall."

"What?" she asked, puzzled by what sounded like jealously. "I'm going stir crazy, Neal. I thought I saw Harry's face. Something's happening to me."

"I'm to escort you as far as the prayer room. Please discuss your concerns with Kunchen."

"Neal?" she whimpered, but he didn't respond. She stared at him as they pressed on in silence through the maze of hallways, wondering why he was acting so distant.

"I'm not being distant," he said when they stopped outside the prayer room.

How did he hear me?

"I've decided to dedicate my life to the teachings of Buddha. I don't regret my time at the university in America or our time together. I am returning to my roots. I'm not jealous; it's alright that it wasn't my face you saw in the wall."

Her mouth fell open as Neal left her standing at the door to the prayer room. Then she heard Kunchen's soft voice behind her.

"It's time for morning prayer."

Morning...it's morning, she said to herself.

***

"You truly have never played soccer before, Mr. Foster." There was laughter in Bassui's voice as he watched the awkward man from America stumble after the worn checkered ball. The boy literally stopped breathing when Harry's kick sent it sailing in the wrong direction. A quick-thinking vendor leaned across her table crammed with trinkets and novelties to bat the profoundly out-of-bounds ball down with one arm just in time.

"I've never been good at any sport, I'm afraid," Harry huffed, kicking up dust when he slid to change directions and chase after the deflected ball. Bassui jumped to his feet and reached the ball first, bumping it straight up with one knee. "Look at you," Harry panted and shrugged his arms. "This is why I'm always picked last when it comes to choosing teams. I have zero agility. Do you think you could teach someone like me how to control a ball like you do?" Harry pulled the purple and gold knit cap off his head and wiped his sweaty forehead with his shirtsleeve while watching Bassui bump the ball back and forth from one knee to the other.

"Okay," the young boy said and clamped the ball between his hands. "But I'm not sure I have enough time."

"Come on," Harry laughed at what sounded like a jab. "Am I that bad?"

"Yes, but I can teach you, no problem," he said, grinning. "It will have to be another time. We are going back to school tomorrow, to a monastery near the valley. The weather emergency has passed; we must leave early to get there by dusk."

"Okay. Is there like, a school bus?" Harry remembered seeing small wagons pulled by yaks and mules in the small village, but nothing motorized like in the larger villages at the lower elevations. He hadn't given much thought as to how people traveled the mountainous terrain up to the monasteries or how they crossed the lush valley basins.

"I know what a school bus is. But no, we take turns riding in a wagon; mostly we walk."

"What if I get my friend John over there to requisition a truck big enough to carry . . . how many?"

"Seven from this village; we pick up twelve along the way. Will you come with us, Mr. Foster?"

"Yeah," Harry said nodding and then looked around for Greenfield, realizing the awkward position he might be putting him in with Cdr. Hanna. He spotted him sitting next to Karma on a log bench in front of her earth and plaster hut. He assumed the agent was keeping her busy while he spent time with Bassui. "Bassui, I'm really hoping to find the dog in the picture I showed you. In your email, you said some of these dogs were near your school. Do you think if we saved you some travel time, you could show me exactly where you saw them?"

"I don't understand." Bassui looked up at him frowning, squinting one eye against the bright sky. "There are many dogs such as that in the valley."

"I'm trying to find just one; the one that belongs to my friend." Harry couldn't hide his somber tone. "I'm hoping that if I find this dog . . ." his voice cracked, "I'll find her." Harry took his phone out of his pocket and showed Bassui a photo of Mary Lynn. "She's my best friend."

"Indeed, your face says she is someone very special." The boy took a moment to consider Harry's offer to provide a truck and help him find the dog. "Families gather in front of my house before dawn."

"Thank you, Bassui." Harry handed the boy the knit hat in appreciation.

"I'm not sure the colors are appropriate," the boy said, stretching the cap in his fingers. "The monks may not approve. The color purple means many things. Peace after death, or it can also be a warning." Bassui handed the cap back to him.

"Purple and gold are the school colors of Louisiana State University in the United States. I found it on one of the tables in the market. I was so surprised that I had to buy it." He turned the hat inside out. "See the tag? That's the LSU tiger, the school mascot."

"The King allows students that earn the highest marks to go to universities in the United States. But sponsor families are hard to find." The boy sounded resigned to accept the lesser fate. "My grades would have to be perfect."

"Then we should keep in touch. I'll find someone in Louisiana to sponsor you if you'd like to go to LSU. Heck, I'll sponsor you myself. You hang onto this as a reminder." Harry handed the cap back to him.

"Thank you, Mr. Foster." The boy seemed touched that he would consider helping him in such a big way.

"Call me Harry. Where I come from, friends call each other by their first names."

"So do friends in Bhutan, Mr. Harry." With excitement in his eyes, Bassui pulled the skullcap on his head. Harry tucked and rolled the edges up and gave him thumbs up approval. Bassui scanned the area looking for Karma to see if she noticed the cap exchange. She was standing beside Harry's friend, agent Greenfield, in the fruit section of the market eating a fresh pear. No matter where Bassui played in the village, Karma always positioned herself where she could keep an eye on him. "I think it will take some time for Karma to get used to the LSU colors."

***

Later in the afternoon, Harry found John in the command tent standing next to Cdr. Hanna. They were both studying, with great concentration, the video that had compelled them to take the initial helicopter ride into the upper elevations of the Himalayas.

"There, see that?" he heard John say. "There it is again."

"Yes," Hanna replied gruffly from the side of his mouth because a cigar was clamped between his teeth on the opposite side. "I see two rebel soldiers," he grumbled, pointing to the screen.

"I'm not so sure about that," John said, shaking his head. He was taller than Hanna, but the soldier's brawny build and overbearing personality made up for the difference.

Nearly all data pertaining to the tumultuous second trip was corrupted, making it impossible for technicians to construe what happened on the three-hour ill-fated flight. This included ISR information of the flight path and conversations of the crew on board. Only a few snippets of drone images survived, and they were mostly of rock and snow. A short spurt of five-second pieces of video had been put together and interpreted to be Greenfield and one soldier, as they were being lowered by cable to an ice ledge. It skipped to a frozen image of them hunkered behind some large icy rocks. Hanna was convinced they were taking cover from Afghani rebel snipers that were shooting at them from a position somewhere off- camera.

Harry walked to the coffee station and motioned to Greenfield. When the commander overheard Harry's appeal to ask for a truck to transport students to a monastery school in a part of the country where the military was never allowed, the commander seized the opportunity to get eyes and ears into that area. He quickly put together a small intelligence gathering detail to accompany them.

***

Greenfield had been debating whether to call Al since Harry ran into his tent to show him the pictures of the dog in the boy's digital photo album. Karma inspired him to make the call when they were sitting together on the log bench watching Harry make a fool of himself at soccer. He confided to her about the older man from Louisiana who lost his wife and now his daughter under similar suspicious circumstances. "Al is a proud man," he said, "and rather than let people see how broken he was over his wife's disappearance or how angry he was over being suspected of killing her, he chose to live alone in the woods. Now that his daughter is missing, he has nowhere to run to. I'd like to bring his daughter home and give him some peace." She gently placed her arm around his forearm to comfort him and once again, her eyes said it all as she nodded her approval.

It was against protocol to disclose details of an FBI investigation, and he was finding it difficult to hide things from her. She could prompt his feelings to the surface whether she was flashing him a critical look or a glowing smile. As they sat there, surrounded by the bustle of the busy market and courtyard, she shared some of her own story, how Bassui and his sisters had been left to squander in the slums of India and brought to her when they were mere toddlers. On Greenfield's prior trip, he learned how families living in Mondar entrusted her to care for their children while they worked in the markets and fields; it was how she bartered for food and other necessitates. She had never married, a woman obviously independent and a loner. John's innate talent for hunting down criminals had made him a terrible life partner. Maybe it was her inaccessibility that made him want to be closer to her: her non-interest in him; her ridiculous belief that a variety of gods controlled specific facets of life. Her indifference toward him made it easier to open up because he knew he had no chance with her.

"John, everyone has difficulties; some have experiences that are worse than others. Some are so devastating they are never the same or choose not to survive at all. The gods directed someone to bring Bassui and his sisters to me. I, too, was displaced as a young girl after losing my parents to disease. They directed me here to this land of the gods where helping hands awaited me. Yes, you should call your friend, if for no other reason than to let him know you care about him. It will give him hope and strength."

Simple, heartfelt advice. He was careful not to tell her the army had hacked into Bassui's files and viewed his photos. Instead, he told her he learned through interviewing villagers that not all boys living with the monks were native to this part of the world; some were tall with light skin and red hair.

With much reverence, she bowed her head and said, "It is believed that these children come directly from the gods." She lifted her head; her eyes found his. "However, I find it hard to believe anyone from any of our villages would have told you this."

There she was, challenging him again; too smart to let a half-truth slip by. He only blinked and nodded, careful not to mention the boys in Bassui's photos that shared distinct similarities, none of which included Eastern descent. "Karma," he said. "Remember I told you something else brought me here? Not to look for the Almasti but in search of three people who are missing. I think the children you are calling "children of the gods" could be another clue to my finding them. I remember seeing them when I was here before. Al's missing daughter is like them. She has red hair and is tall."

"Turn to the gods; they will give you the answers you seek."

That seemed to be her answer for everything, John thought, as he followed Karma to the fruit stand. He couldn't tell her there were victims that described being taken and then returned after being poked and prodded; some insisted it was in a sexual way. There was no physical evidence of it and no resulting pregnancies. Perhaps these were just dreams, but something about these particular orphans was gnawing at his subconscious.

***

Later that night, under the cover of darkness, he scrolled through his contacts list while taking a walk through the army's tent city. "Hello, Al, how are you?" He was near the satellite truck when Al answered. Its generators made a low rumbling noise that was just loud enough to neutralize the conversation.

"I'm doin' fine." The old man sighed as if expecting bad news. He laid the paintbrush in his hand down over a gallon can of yellow paint and retreated from the kitchen to the back porch. "Looks like I'm gonna be here at the house for a while since your people locked down the entire Catahoula Wildlife Management area. Everybody's still scratchin' their heads over how Mary Lynn's Challenger got out in the middle of Dempsey Lake without leavin' any tracks. Can't get any of my stuff outta there either."

"Sorry." Greenfield let out a long breath that expressed his fatigue. "They're about to wrap things up. I'll see what I can do about allowing you back in there. I don't really have a whole lot of news," he continued. "I just wanted to touch base and let you know we're gonna be over here a little while longer. We've run into a few problems that I won't go into now, but the kid saw a dog in a photo that he swears is Mutt. I never saw the dog, but he recognized it from the haircut you gave it. A student took the picture and he's supposed to show him where. As it turns out, Foster has better instincts than I gave him credit for. It might have something to do with how he feels about your daughter."

"Well, don't tell him that. Believe me, all you'll get is an eye roll." Al expelled a grumbling noise as he paced back and forth across the porch that had recently received its own fresh coat of paint. "I don't get how Mary Lynn or Mutt could be where you are."

"I don't understand a lot of things I've been chasing for the past five years," John said, rubbing his tired eyes. "Al, I don't suppose you ever heard of a place in Alaska by the name of Nenana?"

"Hell, no," he grunted. "Why would I?"

"I was up there last year doing a follow-up on an old report. Nenana is a borough of about 378 people. It's about sixty-eight miles south of the North Pole. There's a place called the Grisly Bar in the middle of a row of weathered wooden buildings where patrons go to drink tequila shots and wash them down with pints of beer and tell embellished tales of their adventures out in the wild. Examples of their kills are mounted on the walls: moose heads, full-bodied Dall sheep, caribou and bear hides. I kind of liked the atmosphere, myself. I think you'd like it too. There are thousands of decal stickers and photos taped to the walls. Each photo or souvenir comes with its own story. The bartender only allows prized memorabilia on the mirror behind the bar. Two blurred Instamatic's of a hairy upright creature are taped back there. They were taken by a man with shaky hands, thirty or so years ago. They call the creature Yeti in Alaska. A hunter was checking his traps when he walked up on it pulling fur off of a marten, a weasel-like creature that was caught in one of his box traps. The bartender said there was a black dog with him, but it wasn't captured in the photo. The creature turned its head and looked directly at the hunter with its large yellow eyes when it heard the Instamatic eject the prints. The hunter, who was wearing a hooded, heavy fur coat, feared it might mistake him for its next meal and ran."

"Yeah," Al sighed. "I've heard stories, too. I know a guy that keeps a picture of one in his wallet. He took it down in the Atchafalaya Basin. I couldn't make anything out but shadows. But he's convinced those shadows between the trees is Sasquatch. He said I had to be there and see it with my naked eye."

"There are hundreds of Bigfoot videos on YouTube that experts determined are staged."

"You-what?"

"It's a social media thing, Al. All those reports have been investigated and debunked. Some sound similar to what you told me you saw in Catahoula. I scanned the photos from the bar. You know what an evidence board is, don't you?"

"Yeah," the old man grunted. "We used a cork-board back in the day when I was a deputy."

"I've got one in my head that has a picture of your daughter, your dog Mutt, and a memorized sketch of the boyfriend and the game warden. I just added a new one . . . orphans. There are orphans here." John heard Al blow a sigh that sounded like impatient confusion. "They have red hair Al, and are taller than the kids their age."

"Red hair . . . tall," Al sighed. "Like Mary Lynn."

"I'm not leaving here, Al, until I find your daughter and the answers to the questions I have rolling around in my head. Quantico finished analyzing the samples we collected. The blood's human but not of anyone on record. However, the hair is takin, which is a large goat, native to this part of the world. That's another puzzle piece pointing to Bhutan on the board in my head."

"Hum, that is interesting," Al sighed. "That so-called game warden was limpin' and had blood on his clothes. Mighta been his blood on the trap. He claimed it was from an injured deer. There sure ain't no takin in Catahoula."

"Or, a Bhutan mastiff," John added. "Animal hair found near abductions and sightings have been native to the respective areas they were found in, up until now. I'm considering it a break that I was there when your daughter went missing. Reeves or someone didn't have time to clean up the evidence. I'm having my people recheck the hospitals and urgent care. Reeves had to have gone somewhere if he was injured."

"Wish I could be there to help," Al said and looked up at the clear blue morning sky. A hymn he remembered the church choir sing came to mind. *Pass Me Not, O Gentle Savior.* Why he thought of it, he didn't know. He only heard it once, and it had stuck with him. Sometimes he found himself whistling it when he was cutting the grass or cleaning fish. He didn't go to church that often, just on holidays, or for a wedding or a funeral. "I guess I wouldn't be much help; I can't seem to keep up the pace like I used to. It's a beautiful day here. Fall ain't ready to give it up to winter just yet. Maybe it's waitin' on Mary Lynn to come home."

"If it's winter you're looking for, you should be here. It's below freezing most of the time, and believe it or not, solar power and the internet have reached the most isolated place in the world. I think about you a lot, Al, when I look around at these happy people living their simple lives. Like you, they keep to themselves and enjoy being self-sufficient. Yeah, I think you'd like them. They depend on their gods to provide for their needs, like you depend on nature."

"Yeah, well, their world is fixin' to change really fast now that the internet has invaded. Their gods should be worried; they're about to be replaced. Besides, I ain't religious; that's probably one reason why Christine left me. I'm not crazy about livin' in cold weather all year round. I kinda like experiencin' all four seasons. Let me know when those jokers have vacated my land. Dale and me are gonna put up some of those cameras the game warden told me about. You and the kid be careful over there. And John, thanks for the update; it means a lot."

"You're welcome, my friend. Thanks for listening to my rambling."

Chapter 15

The wide wheel-based army transport truck was in no way suited for the narrow path carved along the hillside by foot traffic and small rickshaws pulled by mules. Lt. Cara Fisher, the driver of the awkward vehicle draped in desert sand canvas, threatened to turn around several times when the trail narrowed and the left side wheels caused small rock slides. She precariously crawled along the slope, tilting passengers and cargo. Some spans even required excavation with picks and shovels so the truck wouldn't turn over. They caught up to fifteen locals walking single file carrying large packs on their backs. Lt. Ron White and two other soldiers that were riding in the back with Harry, Bassui, and twelve of his schoolmates, jumped out the rear and ordered them to step aside while the truck passed. Bassui explained to Harry that there was little gas available for motorized vehicles and this was how supplies got to the villages and monasteries in the higher areas. The students bailed out the back as soon as the truck pulled to a stop inside the compound. They were eagerly greeted by classmates who had already arrived or who had never left because they had nowhere to go. Harry thought he recognized a few of them from Bassui's photo files; the taller ones were the easiest to pick out.

Greenfield rode in the passenger seat next to Lt. Fisher and spent most of the time reading the notepad. Bhutanese tradition had sparked his interest, probably because of the look of warning Karma gave him from behind the rachu that morning as she watched her children climb into the back of the overbearing truck. He was hoping for an update from the Quantico team, but thus far, there was nothing new on the whereabouts of Adam Reeves or the other mystery character, Neal Mueller.

Bassui led Harry to his favorite place to meditate; a hillside outside the monastery walls where he confided with much sincerity how the panoramic views of lush green valleys surrounded by sculpted verandas and countless mountain peaks is where he felt closest to the gods. They sat for a long time in the grass scanning the tiered landscape through binoculars that Harry confiscated from a supply tent before leaving the post.

"Thank you, Mr. Harry," Bassui finally sighed. "These glasses are allowing me to better see the glory of our land. If I had the means I would purchase one of these from Amazon."

"They're called binoculars . . . binos for short," Harry replied. "You can keep them; the army won't miss them."

"Oh, thank you Mr. Harry!" Bassui gushed.

"Bassui," Harry said with a vexing exhale. "I know you have access to technology, yet when I look around, I see your country is very underdeveloped."

"Karma says change is coming," he replied, continuing to press the binos against his eyes. "It used to be that only the merchants bought from Amazon and eBay. But now everyone with internet access can buy from everywhere in the world." Harry put the binos up to his eyes and they both silently scanned from left to right, up and down.

"Ah! I think I see a vulture," Harry gasped. "Look, flying over there to the right, just off the edge of the cliff that sticks out.

Bassui turned his glasses in the direction Harry was looking. "Yes, I see. It's a griffon; it's looking for small animals. There's a nest; see, it's slightly back from the edge?"

"Bassui, is that a tiger?" Harry gasped. He hadn't thought about tigers as being part of Bhutan's natural wildlife.

Bassui immediately refocused his binoculars a few yards to the left that was actually several miles away. "Yes!" he sighed admiringly. "Tigers are excellent climbers and revered in Bhutan; it is good luck to see one. They live off the wild takin in the valley; shepherds must keep close watch over their herds. It's important to protect the goats; they provide food and clothing for . . . um." Bassui paused and looked at Harry sheepishly as if he said something he wasn't supposed to. "Um, everyone," he finally said. "Including the small settlements in the mountains," he continued quickly. "If you look carefully, you can see the oldest subsidiary of the Gasa Dzong built into the side of the mountain. Gasa was built in the 17th century as a bulwark against attacks from the north; the subsidiary was built a short time later for the gods to . . .." He paused.

"For the gods to what?" Harry asked, his eyes still focused on the view.

"I meant to say, in honor of the gods," Bassui replied.

The view was so commanding, he had missed the five multi-level buildings inlaid within the greenery and jutting rocks in the cliffs.

"Bassui, I couldn't help but notice that not all children in the compound are native to this part of the world and there are no girls."

"Many orphans are sent to the monks. Girls are not allowed to stay in the monasteries. They are sent to the villages along with most of the boys. Only the enlightened remain. Native children, like myself, work very hard to reach enlightenment. After that, we can decide if we want to become monks. The enlightened are destined to become holy men."

"Have you thought about it, becoming a monk?" Harry lowered the glasses when Bassui sighed. He was frowning as if considering his answer.

"I know it will disappoint Karma, but what I would really like to do, is to go to a university somewhere, perhaps in the US, maybe even Louisiana, where I could spread the teachings of Buddha."

"Well, LSU's mascot is a tiger. Could be a good omen, right?"

Bassui partially pulled the purple and gold knit cap from his jacket pocket and crammed it back inside. "Perhaps this hat will keep me in good favor with the gods."

They affectionately bumped shoulders and laughed. The shoves grew harder and so did their laughter. Harry picked up a small rock, pitched it into the air, and listened for it to land below. Bassui followed suit and another game ensued.

"How can you tell if an orphan child is an actual descendant of the gods?" Harry asked when their laughter turned into ridiculous moans. "Outside of their appearance, that is? In America, everyone is different: short, tall, dark, white."

"They seem to act no different than any other child who attends school here," he replied. He leaned in close and lowered his voice. "It's their gifts. I once saw a boy called Sangay raise a plate off a table in the dining room by just looking at it. He got in trouble for doing it in front of us. Please do not tell anyone I told you this, not even your friend John Greenfield, or Karma; she will be very disappointed in me."

"I won't," Harry whispered.

"Down there," he said pointing his glasses toward the valley below, "that is where I took the picture of the dog. There is a foot trail once you clear the rocks."

"How long does it take to walk there?"

"One hour," he replied. "You should not go alone. I'll be restricted to the school compound after today and unable to guide you."

"John and I will figure something out."

The boy's eyebrows knitted deeply together as he looked at him. "You must be careful." There was a deeper tone to his voice; his eyes narrowed. "There are other dangers beside tigers; there are large bears and snow leopards, wolves and . . ." He paused and swallowed as if his throat had gone dry.

Harry touched the boy's arm, trying to reassure him. He was holding something back, something he really wanted to say, but couldn't. "Bassui, it's okay, you can tell me. What other animals?"

"All creatures are guided by the gods. If you are perceived as a danger, the gods will allow them to attack you." He seemed to be afraid to let his eyes meet Harry's as he spoke.

"What animals, Bassui?"

"Please, whatever you do, don't get caught in the valley at night. That's when they hunt."

"It's okay, Bassui," Harry said and pulled the boy close to him. "We'll be careful."

***

"So, did you get anything out of the boy?" Greenfield asked.

Darkness had beat Harry to the mini bivouac site. Bassui's warning about the local wildlife had him expecting to see something hiding in every ominous shadow. Greenfield was sitting on the ground between two tents the soldiers erected.

"I know where he took the picture of Mutt." Harry looked down at the binos in his hand as if the view of the panoramic valley was still on the lenses. "It's an hour's walk to the valley floor. Starts out pretty rugged, so we'll have to hike down through some rocks first. What did you do all afternoon?"

"I tagged along with them," he said, motioning to the second tent eight feet away. "Apparently they were ordered to take pictures of everything, and use mountain goats and anything else that moved, for target practice."

"Bassui told me there are predators that roam freely in the valley. I might be able to scare off a wolf but I'm not so sure about a bear or a leopard. I actually saw a tiger!" He held up the binoculars.

"We'll have them with us," the agent said, looking at the neighboring tent. "What else?" There was a lingering frown on Harry's face. His lips were pursed and he was looking around nervously. He bowed his head and shuffled one foot, a classic stalling tactic while one gets up his nerve.

"Well," he exhaled. "He says there are *creatures* out there that are guided by the gods. Who refers to wildlife as creatures? He was trying to warn me about something that terrifies him but he was afraid to say it out loud, as if the gods might hear him."

"The legendary Almasti, perhaps," Greenfield scoffed.

Harry continued to stare at the ground.

"Come on; what else did he say? Spit it out Foster!"

"Why was she brought here? You saw the children in the compound and the pictures of Bassui's classmates, the tall ones with red hair."

"I saw them," Greenfield said. "What's your point?"

"He said they come from the gods. He saw one of them lift a plate by just looking at it and then begged me not to tell."

"Karma described them the same way: *from the gods*. I've been trying to figure out what the hell she meant by that."

"Mary Lynn is special," Harry blurted out. "There's something I didn't tell you about her; it was our secret. She can see colors, auras. She sometimes sees colors in words and letters. There's a name for it, *synesthesia*. Look it up on your notepad."

The agent looked at him disgustingly; his mouth was turned down, his eyebrows drawn together. He slowly pushed himself off the ground.

"She can feel what other people feel. It's called *mirror touch synesthesia*. It's what compelled her to become a nurse. She doesn't even know there's a name for it," he sighed, sounding regretful. "I read an article about it in a medical journal. I was going to tell her that night . . . he night Neal told her about his new girlfriend and that he was moving to Monroe." Harry looked up into the clear cold night sky in an attempt to sooth his stinging eyes. "And then Al told her something that upset her. She never told me what it was. Then

you showed up. The right time to discuss it just never came."
Harry took Greenfield's silence to mean he was appreciative
of the emotional testimony.

"I want to know something: why am I just now hearing
about this synesthesia?" The agent shoved his hand so hard
against Harry's chest that the binos flew from his hand and
struck the transport truck parked in front of the four-man tent.
He stumbled backward but was able to stay on his feet.

"It was our secret," Harry said and rushed toward
Greenfield with closed fists. "We trusted each other."

"Does Al know about this synesthesia?" Greenfield asked,
stepping closer.

"No one does. Not Al, not Dale, just me and, and
Christine." He took a breath, thinking about how demanding
Christine always was about keeping it secret. "Christine told
us not to discuss it with anyone. And uh, I guess I should tell
you something else."

John was pacing now, stopping every few seconds as if
trying to put what Harry told him in its proper place within the
plethora of evidence and interviews the team had collected
over the past five years. He stopped and glared at Harry.
"What?"

"Mary Lynn thought she saw Bigfoot. It happened when
we were like, sixteen."

"Unbelievable! Dammit, Foster," Greenfield exploded
and punched at the air instead of Harry's face.

"I didn't believe her," Harry said, dipping from side to
side in case the agent decided to land one of the air-punches
on his body. "I didn't think she really saw it; I just went along.
We'd been drinking."

"Don't you know information like this, no matter how
insignificant or preposterous . . .?" He turned and walked
away, hands on his hips and shaking his head. "Didn't you
think this was important enough to tell me? After all the
absurd statements you know I've taken on this very subject
and you kept this from me?" He paused as if trying to choose

the right words or maybe to control his temper. "Ahhhh!" he bellowed and then rushed at Harry and shoved him. Harry stumbled backward and fell to the ground. It took him a couple of seconds to get back on his feet. He lunged at Greenfield. The agent went down on his back with Harry on top of him, punching him on the head and shoulder. Greenfield kneed Harry in the stomach hard enough to make him roll off, bent at the waist in pain. Greenfield stood up with his arm cocked, ready to push him back down if he came at him again. Harry crawled to his feet holding his gut.

The door flap of the second tent suddenly flew open; Lt. White appeared. "We heard a ruckus," he whispered loudly. "Everything alright out here?"

Harry straightened his posture after dusting himself off. Greenfield stomped to the small tent they were to share and ripped open the flap, mumbling profanities.

Harry apologized to the dutiful Lt. White and then looked around for the binoculars. He found them on the ground about twenty feet away. The lenses were shattered; as shattered as he felt.

It was pitch dark inside the tent except for the tiny green light on Greenfield's notepad lying on the floor next to his sleeping bag. He felt the gut punch when he bent over to reach for it, and again when burrowing inside his bedroll. The tent was small with little standing room, just big enough for two sleeping bags and not much more. He zipped the bag up all the way in order to read in private a PDF file Bassui sent to his phone after they parted ways. The file was a complete dissertation on the beliefs of Buddhism, much too large to upload to his phone so he forwarded it to Greenfield's notepad. The next morning, he was awakened by the sudden jolt of Greenfield kicking him.

"Where is it, Foster!" he hollered loudly and kicked him again, harder.

Harry unzipped the sleeping bag just far enough to launch his arm outside with the device in his hand.

"You better not have used up all the power," the agent grumbled, snatching it from him. "Look at this," he mumbled, looking at the low battery warning light. "It'll take my solar panel an hour to bring it back to full power. You thinking about converting?" he asked, after looking at the text on the screen.

"No." Harry nudged his head through the opening. "Bassui sent that to me. I guess he's trying to share some of himself with me. Thought I'd do him the courtesy of reading it." Harry unzipped the bag further in order to sit up. He scratched the growing stubble to disguise the grimace from the lingering soreness in his stomach. "Actually, Buddhism is not so bad, not really so different." A grunt slipped out when he reached for his army-issued camo jacket.

"Yeah, right, except they believe in reincarnation and more than one god," Greenfield replied mockingly.

"Did you know Buddha lived 500 years before Christ? Jesus could have been a reincarnation of Buddha."

"Don't forget about the secluded life those monks commit to," Greenfield sneered while shoving the notepad into his backpack and attaching the flat charging pad to the outside of his vest. "Don't get sucked into that mumbo-jumbo; there are as many religious beliefs as there are countries and tribes. Each one tweaks their divas to suit themselves. They romanticize their monsters to suck people in." He'd been to scores of countries, heard of numerous gods while on his quest to chase down videos, stories, hair samples, and footprints. "These monks . . ." he nodded toward the outside, "they pray and chant for hours, days, and rarely see the light of day. Yeah, I've been doing a little research of my own; it's always best to know one's adversary."

"Adversary?" Harry pulled on his army-issued hiking boots. "Monks are peaceful, harmless."

"You left out fanatics," John complained. "Something's definitely not right about this orphan situation. Stop frowning," he growled.

"Did Karma tell you something about them? I mean, you two seem to have developed a pretty close relationship."

"My friendship with Karma is none of your damn business," the agent snapped back.

Harry raised himself to his knees so they were face to face. "I'm sorry I didn't tell you about the colors," he sighed. "Or her seeing Bigfoot. Mary Lynn and I have been friends for all our lives. The oath of secrecy I took is second nature to me . . . engrained in my brain. My duty has always been to protect her from gossip and bullies, just like she protected me."

"The Quantico team says that only one percent of our abductees reported having this synesthesia and it never was considered significant. They're giving it another look. Thinking she saw Bigfoot is significant. So is the fact that she has the same physique as the orphans. There's something going on here and I think the monks are involved."

"She's a girl," Harry said. "Women aren't allowed to live with the monks."

"What's the worst reason you can think of for her being here?" the agent asked. "Why are women usually kidnapped? Come on," he groaned when Harry wouldn't answer. "Because they are women. You've heard of human trafficking. You're a lab tech; you work in a hospital. You've seen the unthinkable things people do to each other . . . to women."

"No, the monks wouldn't do that; they're holy men, revered by . . . everyone."

"You need to think about something. You might have a new role to play in her life if we find her, helping her recover from whatever she's been put through." A wave of compassion came over him when he saw the look on Harry's face, the look of disintegrating hope. He must not have considered or wouldn't let himself consider that something so horrible could be going on. "Look, I have to consider every possible motive for her being taken. Prepare for the worst, hope for the best, right?" Harry shook his head. "Okay then, gather your stuff," he said and shuffled toward the door with his gear. "Our detail is waiting for us outside."

Harry had been riding high with hope from the time Greenfield told him the DNA collected from Al's camp was from the local breed of mastiff and takin and then showed him photos of dogs that looked like Mutt. It's what drove him to board the military plane out of Camp Beauregard. The agent's queries churned in his head. *Is Mary Lynn an orphan? If not, why is she here?*

"What if it's something else?" Harry blurted out. "Something bigger than anything you or the Quantico team has thought of?" Greenfield was halfway out the door.

"What are you talking about now, Foster?" The irritation had returned to Greenfield's voice. "Did the boy say something else?"

"What about the orphan boy that levitated a dinner plate?" Harry persisted.

Greenfield glared at Harry. "This is the result of reading that bullshit," he contended. "When I see that happen for myself, I'll believe it."

"No. Think about what happened to us; we were forced out of the air-twice. By what? Was that bullshit?"

Greenfield took in a compromising breath and blew it out. "I don't have the answer, Foster. My advice is to stop reading about Buddhism. Look, Hanna gave us this detail because ISIS is resurging and he thinks cells might be hiding up here. What better place could they find to blend in than with a bunch of enigmatic, religious zealots like themselves? Let's use this opportunity to gather as much intel as we can and leave it at that."

John was right; there was no point in arguing. They were here to find Mutt and if they were lucky, interview a monk or two.

***

The four-man detail found the foot trail much more bearable than the slippery jagged rocks that formed the foundation of the monastery compound. A defined animal path took Greenfield, Harry, and two lieutenants, Ron White and Cara Fisher, through a dense forest with permanent patches of icy snow in shaded areas that never saw the sun. It took them forty minutes to clear the trees. They were now standing at the edge of the green lush valley Harry observed through the binos the evening before. There were no shadows in the valley; only full sun and warmth, prompting the group to rip their Velcro, open their jackets, and push back their fur-lined camo caps that they were grateful for while in the silhouette of the mountain. The grass was waist high at the tree line but tapered gradually as they approached a loose horde of grazing takin that turned out to be more sizeable up close than expected with their massive shoulders and long hair. Halfway across the valley Lt. White suddenly put up his hand signaling the group to halt after observing a shepherd standing within the herd. The hooded overseer stood motionless, leaning to one side on a staff, wearing a hooded dark brown ankle length robe that was tied at the waste with a green gho. The lieutenant slowly pulsed his fingers forward, meaning they should move cautiously. The shepherd's head was bent forward slightly as if he was napping.

"Looks like a scarecrow," Lt. Fisher jested as they slowly skulked through the four-foot tall bulky takin. Greenfield had allowed only one rifle on the expedition; Lt. Fisher was carrying it. She went down on one knee and took aim when the shepherd turned his head when one of his droves cried out. A significant limp explained his dependence on the staff.

Harry extended an arm as a gesture of friendship that he quickly withdrew after the man's trembling hand pushed the hood back from his head. He was bald, pale, and sickly gaunt, but recognizable. It was Adam Reeves.

"Do you see who this is?" Harry gasped, addressing Greenfield without taking his eyes off Reeves.

"One of the walking dead?" the confused agent countered.

"Where's Mary Lynn?" Harry shouted, pushing bovines to one side until he was within inches of the shepherd. Reeves's jaw quivered as he struggled to speak.

"The game warden?" Greenfield uttered and stepped closer. "I only saw him the one time, but . . . damn!"

"Don't move," the postured Lt. Fisher warned Reeves when he managed a step; it seemed like a painful one.

"Does he speak English?" Lt. White demanded.

"Oh, he understands," Harry growled. "Where is she? What did you do with her?" Harry reached out with both hands for Reeves intending to shake the truth out of him. Reeves weaved to one side, lost his grip on the support, and collapsed to the ground, scattering the nervous takin.

"Where is she, you bastard?" Harry knelt down, grabbed the semi-conscious shepherd by his robe, and shook him until his eyes fluttered open.

"Foster!" Greenfield yelled. "Stop, let me call for a . . ." He couldn't finish the sentence; the thought of riding in a helicopter again made his head swoon.

"Harrison Foster?" Reeves was barely coherent. Liquid had collected in his esophagus and dribbled from one side of his receded jaw. He reached out for Harry but had trouble finding him. His trembling hand finally touched the side of his unshaven face. "I almost didn't recognize you," was all he managed to say before closing his eyes again.

Greenfield's fingers were frozen in place on the notepad. The man lying on the ground could very well be the break the team back in Virginia had been waiting for. To Harry, it meant they were closer to finding Mary Lynn.

"Sir, his leg is severely injured." Lt. Fisher had removed his leather boots and ripped open his bloody right pant leg. Several deep gashes were oozing with dark blood and green puss. "And possibly fractured," she added.

Greenfield finished his request for transportation and knelt down to examine Reeves while Harry tried to pace away his anger a few feet away. His forehead was hot with fever, his leg black from the knee down and burning hot.

Harry squatted down beside the agent. "That smell," he panted, covering his nose and mouth with his collar. "I don't need a lab to tell me it's gangrened."

"Yeah, his only chance to survive will be to lose the leg ASAP," Greenfield sighed. "Help me tie it off with his gho. It might slow the poison; pray we can get him to the infirmary in time.

"Mary Lynn can't be far from here," Harry lamented. "You go; I'm not leaving."

Greenfield assigned Lt. White to Harry; he and Lt. Fisher would make the trek back to the monastery. "I'm leaving you the rifle and my backpack," he shouted over the noisy helicopter lifting off behind them. "It's got water, MREs, and my solar panel. I'm going to fast-pace it out and take the truck back to the post to question him; I still can't make myself board one of those things." The agent had tried to push through the nausea but felt his chest constrict the moment his boot hit the craft's side rail; normal breathing didn't return until he had cleared the blades.

Harry's concentration had been on the hills on the far side of the valley while Greenfield dictated the plans. "There's a Dzong up there, in the hillside," he said after the rotors were mere whispers. "I saw it yesterday when Bassui and I were scanning the mountains. There are other buildings up there too. Reeves must be from one of them. If Lt. White and I hurry, we can make it to the Dzong before dark."

"I'll catch up to you tomorrow," John said. "Be careful."

"You be careful," Harry countered. "One of those predators Bassui warned me about might be what attacked Reeves."

Chapter 16

"It is apparent that meditation has opened your insight, Prana. You are progressing; your mind is becoming uncluttered of its former worldly distractions." They were walking along a foot trail lined with purple poppies that led back to the Dzong. The gusts had calmed, except for the swaying rhododendrons they passed and the sand that noticeably stirred under her sandals. "Your true inner-most self is immerging and will take precedence if you allow it."

"You saw what happened, didn't you?" Of course, he had been aware of what happened with the boy's cap, even with his back turned. He didn't seem alarmed. In fact, he seemed pleased. "The knit hat," she attempted to explain. "The colors represent my home state college."

"Unfortunately, the boy took your photograph, several in fact. This is why we remain secluded. The outside world has no respect for our beliefs or our privacy. We will continue the incantations to enable your full capabilities and pray for a flawless transition as they continue to emerge. Starting and ending the day with prayer, along with meditation, will give you the wisdom to know how and when to use your inherent abilities. These are gifts from the gods, Prana. Like artistry, genius, and strength, they must be practiced, honed, and understood. Your parents will be pleased to hear of your accomplishments." He suddenly stopped walking, clasped his hands together, and without warning stretched them upward as if reaching for a deity in the white cotton-like clouds above them.

"But my mother is . . ." She couldn't make herself say the word *dead*, not again. "And my father . . ." Like most introductions to one of his lessons, (that were more like riddles) she didn't understand what he was trying to demonstrate. "I appreciate your efforts, Kunchen. You have truly helped me renew my perspective of life, but you must be mistaken. My mother is gone, dead, and my father is a hurt and angry man that chooses to live alone in the woods to forget her."

Kunchen slowly pulled his arms down and looked sheepishly from side to side as if trying to hide his embarrassment. "Of course, no one has properly told you," he whispered resolutely and then dropped to his knees. "May the gods forgive me; I have allowed my own self-indulgence to overcome propriety." The gravity of his shame was apparent as he bent over allowing his lips to touch the sandy ground. After a moment of silent prayer, he stood upright, cupped his hands, and faced her. "I have been given permission from the gods to tell you that your father's name is Kokabiel. He is the highest-ranking Nephilim elder. His name means 'star of God.' His word is revered; his mightiness protects us. He allowed you into our community to be educated in our beliefs with your mother's approval."

"My mother, in heaven with the gods?" she asked, confused.

"Your mother lives there." He raised his hand, pointing to a hazy mountain peak.

"You're wrong. My mother is-my mother is," she stuttered. She suddenly had a strange, out-of-sorts feeling. It reminded her of when she woke up in the woods and the mountain quarters for the first time. Kunchen's voice was in her head.

She takes care of Nephilim children until they are old enough to enter school. She is a teacher, a caregiver, but not the healer that you are, Prana.

"My mother is . . .?" Mary Lynn's chest heaved with anxiety. She felt the wind brush against her cheeks again and pull at her robes. It came up quickly and more forcefully than before. It bended the rhododendrons and the Spartan junipers that lined the path and dotted the hillside. The dirt under their feet exploded, creating dust clouds.

Not wavered by the commotion, Kunchen rested his hands on her shoulders. "Take control of this!" he said sternly.

"That's me?" she panted, looking around.

"It's imperative that you learn how to control what has awakened in you," he said aloud and then led her to a space behind two whipping alpine firs. He directed her to sit on the ground; he sat down facing her. The winds calmed as soon as his voice captured her attention. "You were misled and now you are hurt and confused. But it was for a good cause." The steely look in his eyes meant he was telling her something important. "But you must use restraint; redirect the emotions you're feeling because of this revelation. Otherwise, evil will always have its way with you. We will pray here, right now, and you will give your fury to the gods." He closed his eyes, held his arms out in front of him, and turned up his palms, a practice performed regularly to give and receive favor from the gods. She assumed the familiar pose and prayed with him. "Jehi Vidhi Hoi Naath Hit Moraa Karahu So Vegi Daas Main Toraa." The winds settled.

***

Lt. Fisher radioed the two remaining members of the detail ahead of time, so they could break camp, load the truck, and be ready for immediate departure. She climbed behind the wheel of the transport truck and carefully maneuvered down the tedious mountainside trail. The medical tent was her first stop after the guard gate. Greenfield nodded a 'thank you' to her when he got out.

Reeves was still alive, but barely, according to Dr. Rush who was standing over the one and only patient in the dimly lit infirmary. The only overhead lights were the two above his bed. Red and green digits from the bedside monitor reported his vitals and rate of IV flow. Everything had been done for

Adam Reeves to save his life. His life now depended on the blood and powerful antibiotics pumping through his veins, and whatever strength he might have left.

"Blood and prints are on the way to Quantico as you requested," Rush reported. "Cdr. Hanna thought you would come here first; he wants you to report to the command tent ASAP."

"Yeah, okay," Greenfield gruffed. Reeves' color was deathbed ash.

"We had to take the leg at the quad." Rush lifted the sheet so the agent could see the heavily bandaged thigh. "I'm sorry, Agent. I doubt he'll make it through the night."

"Send the leg off, too," Greenfield barked. "Put it on ice; call FedEx or whatever, but send it. If he dies, send his body. I want to know everything there is to know about this man."

***

"You left one of my men out there alone?" Hanna ripped into Greenfield when he appeared through the door flap. "ISIS sympathizers are everywhere. They'll pick off a US soldier in a heartbeat."

The angry greeting didn't faze Greenfield. Right now, his only interest was in satisfying his desire for a cup of coffee, get what he could out of Reeves, and then rush back for Foster.

"Just imagine how much pleasure they would get out of capturing, torturing, and killing a US soldier and an American citizen? Well," he paused his rant long enough to rumble a sarcastic laugh. "They'd really get off on torturing a US citizen. They'd tag him with some sort of anti-American poster," the commander was spitting as he yelled at the agent. "Get him to recite some kind of propaganda and flood YouTube with it." A large monitor behind him looked like infrared surveillance in real time. "Yeah!" Hanna barked, "You see that?" Greenfield stepped in front of the large screen after finding the coffee pot empty. "Remember when our birds picked up that suspicious activity in the hills? Remember?" he growled impatiently. "Well," he said after getting no response from the FBI agent, "they've moved to the higher elevations. I've got orders to snuff out the bastards," he snarled. "The man you medivaced here is most likely one of the pricks that attacked you and my man on that ledge."

"Where is this?" Greenfield asked, pointing to a cloudy aerial view of a jagged icy peak that was somehow jogging a memory.

"Our techs were finally able to retrieve the last recorded position of the Augusta before it was shot out of the air. We've picked up heat signatures. I've got men up there now searching for the hostiles that attacked you."

"Reeves isn't a hostile." The agent shook his head trying to comb through his scattered memory of that day. "I just wish everything would come back at once instead of in pieces.

"It's the concussion," Hanna gruffed; "happens all the time. Well, this guy, sympathizer or not, ain't gonna live long enough to tell us anything."

"I know the guy," Greenfield countered. "He's one of the missing I've been looking for. He went by Adam Reeves. He was in Louisiana only a few weeks ago." He pulled out his phone and tapped the photo gallery. "I want to show you something; Foster found the dog we've been looking for."

"Humph!" Hanna grunted after looking at the photo.

"Lt. White and Foster are headed to one of the dzongs to see if Reeves was staying there. The woman we're looking for could be there. I'm going back up in the morning. I was hoping to question Reeves but the doc doubts he's gonna wake up."

"Humph!" Hanna groaned. "Get some sleep. Lt. White has a tracking locator on him. I'll turn the ISR platform in their direction."

"I'll be in the infirmary in the bed next to Reeves." Greenfield felt somewhat relieved. The tracker would make it easier to find Foster in the morning. Thank goodness for technology.

***

Lt. White spotted a large white building with a tiered, burnt-orange pagoda roof through his field glasses. It took them thirty minutes to reach the white forty-foot wall structure that had a row of inaccessible windows set just under the eaves. There was one very solid wooden door. They bedded down for the night a short distance from the fortress within a stand of trees after their knocking produced no one. Dark set in and a light snow began to fall along with the temperature. Mutt kept them warm inside the lean-to they constructed out of a tarp and brushy juniper branches. It must have been his imagination, but Harry thought he could smell a faint fragrance of shampoo in his thick coat as he lay between them. Could it be the shampoo Mary Lynn gave Al? Mutt restlessly lifted his head from time to time. Harry suspected he worried about his herd that was miles away and unprotected, or maybe, as Bassui warned, he detected the scent of a wolf pack, a tiger, or a bear or whatever was out here the boy feared so much he couldn't say its name. Harry closed his eyes. When he opened them, after what seemed like a mere second, Mutt was gone and so was the lieutenant. He crawled out of the lean-to with his eyes opened wide hoping to hasten the adjustment to the dark. He heard a crackle and looked toward the sound. Lt. White was crouched behind two hemlocks looking at him with a broken stick in one hand and a pair of binos in the other.

"You see something?" Harry whispered, after shuffling through an inch of snow to join him behind the trees. Lt. White grabbed him by the arm and pulled him down to his level. "Where's Mutt?" Harry peered over the non-responsive soldier's shoulder and saw nothing but an open field. He rummaged through the backpack Greenfield gave him until he found the field glasses.

"He's gone; a strange smell woke me," the lieutenant whispered. He had his red lenses trained on the open field below. "I decided to do a little recon."

"Are these infrareds?" Harry asked, imitating the lieutenant's low whisper.

"Yes," he replied. "Slide the lever under the center stem. These have extra-low dispersion HD lenses and give optimal contrast in poor light. The resolution is awesome at extreme long range." Harry had never heard someone speak so clear when they were whispering.

Harry tried to do the same but his words came out too loud. "Awesome." Apparently, there was training involved to speak distinctly in a whisper. He moved to an adjacent birch and pressed the glasses to his eyes. "Yeah," he whispered, smiling like a kid with a new toy. "I can see the goats in the valley, amazing! I don't see Mutt, though." It was hard to distinguish the individual goats until they moved. Harry almost lost his grip on the glasses when he saw a strange creature suddenly rise up from out of the herd. It stood upright at least six feet above the four-legged takin. "What the hell?"

"Shush!" the lieutenant whispered, hearing the alarm in Harry's voice. "I've been observing them for ten minutes. There are two of them; they appear to be harvesting those big-ass goats."

"They're bipedal." Harry was trying to remain calm even though the pulse in his neck was pounding so hard it hurt.

"You ever hear of Bigfoot?" Lt. White replied.

Did the lieutenant overhear his argument with Greenfield? Was he being facetious? "I need to capture this on my phone, but we're too far away and it's too dark."

"Enlarge the focus on your binos and then push the button between the barrels at the top." Lt. White quickly joined Harry behind the birch. "I've been taking videos to send to the commander. He's gonna go ape-shit when he sees this." He pulled a cord from a side pocket on his backpack and connected the field glasses to a notepad while Harry snapped his own shots. "I'd swear those things are human except for the size and all the hair. Well, that's for someone else to figure out. Okay, it's sent; we should fall back now."

"What about Mutt?" Harry whispered. "We can't leave him out there with those things."

"Mutt will be fine." He put the notepad away and zipped up the backpack. "In fact, he's probably the reason they didn't know we were here. They were close enough that their stench woke me. Mutt jumped out, distracted them, and steered them away. They interacted like they were familiar with one other."

"Interacted?" Harry repeated. "How do you mean?"

"Like you or me would with one of our pets. Your Mutt acted as if he was happy to see them, and vice versa. So, I figure they must come through here often."

Harry looked through the glasses one last time, hoping to see Mutt. "Hey, they're on the move with their kill across their shoulders."

"Away from us, that's good." The lieutenant moved to a cluster of waist-high Kashmir shrubs to watch them. "They're at least two clicks out from the herd." He adjusted his binos to 15x peak magnification. "Look at 'em. I've never seen anything that big move so fast. Damn, lost 'em; they must have…I don't know, disappeared in the tall grass maybe."

Harry slumped to the ground and stared at the field glasses in his trembling hands. "John's never gonna believe this; no one will; just like I didn't believe Mary Lynn."

"We both saw them, remember," White said, "and, there's the video I just sent to Hanna. Gather your gear; we can't afford to spend more than thirty seconds scouting for the dog. There could be more of them."

***

Greenfield heard a swishing and rustling noise. Helicopter blades came to mind . . . no; someone is running towards me . . . no. He saw himself clinging to a cable dropping him into a white void. Someone called his name. "Rush?" he scowled, when he opened his eyes and saw the doctor looking down at him. "What?" He sat up quickly and then turned to look at the stripped-down bed next to him. "Was he airlifted? Did he say anything?"

"I'm sorry, sir," Dr. Rush sighed. "He didn't make it; his body is being prepped for transport to Germany. You still want it sent to Virginia?"

"Good, God!" Greenfield sighed, expressing his disappointment. "Yeah, yeah; send it to Quantico."

Rush nodded to the door behind him. "Lt. Fisher is waiting for you outside to escort you to the commander. I'll be glad to walk you over to the morgue on the way if you want to take a look at him before we box him up."

"Yeah, I'd like that," he growled and slid off the bed. He finger-combed his hair, grabbed his field jacket hanging over the end of the bed, and followed Rush out the door.

"Lt. Fisher tells me you have a problem flying?" Cdr. Hanna lashed out as soon as he saw the agent entering the command tent. "How the hell did you get here if it wasn't by air?" It was as if he'd been waiting to hit him with the jab. He didn't know if the commander's ill will towards him was because his presence was interrupting his mission, or if he was suspicious the FBI had sent him to look over his shoulder, or if he just didn't like him personally.

"Coffee first," Greenfield gruffed and walked to the large brewing station. Hanna waved him off as if annoyed and returned to the large monitor he had been studying before he walked in.

"Reeves is dead." Greenfield reported as he gingerly sipped the hot bitter coffee and walked up behind the commander.

"I know," Hanna returned curtly as if uninterested. "Tell me what you think this is." His tone was provocatively challenging.

An ISR's view of another icy mountain filled the sixty-five-inch screen. Its ghostly image reminded the agent of something, something he'd seen before, and then a wrenching knot formed in his stomach.

"Now, I want you to look at what Lt. White sent me a little while ago."

The agent wasn't listening. His hand was shaking; the black liquid in his cup rippled over the rim. His eyes began to puff. "What's in this coffee?" Greenfield dropped the cup; he watched it hit the floor and splatter and then grabbed hold of a nearby chair and sat down hard.

"What the hell's wrong with you?" Hanna howled as if aggravated.

Greenfield was grateful to hear the commander's dictatorial voice order someone to get the doctor. He pressed both palms against his eyes. It was a useless attempt; he couldn't stop the apparitions from coming. The first image was of him trembling on an icy ledge like the one on the monitor. He was acutely aware of being afraid of something. Next, he saw one of Hanna's men standing next to him inside a narrow cave; he had a look of horror on his face. Two gigantic figures stood in front of them blocking the way. It was too dark to make out their faces. They had no place to go except for the way they had entered and back out onto the ledge. The monitor's image must have triggered the vivid recollection. The reverie ended with him seeing the creatures get smaller after being blown off the snowy shelf by a tremendous blast of air. He felt Hanna grab his shoulder and shake it. He looked up; Lt. White's video of the two creatures walking across the valley appeared on the screen. The loop of terror resumed; he dove off the chair and attempted to crawl away but Hanna caught hold of him. The visions didn't stop until Dr. Rush arrived with a syringe of diazepam. "You'll feel better in a minute," he heard Rush say through the murk of confusion. The debilitated agent felt the warm solution rush up his arm, and then he drifted into unconsciousness.

He awoke with a pounding headache, but thankful to be in the med tent and see Dr. Rush standing over him. "Where's Hanna?" Greenfield asked.

Dr. Rush hesitated, fearing it might trigger another episode. "He left in search of insurgents after receiving a report from the field."

Greenfield sat up in the dimly lit room. The memories that put him the infirmary returned, but this time without the intensity thanks to Dr. Rush's injection. "From the field? Did he go after Foster and Lt. White?"

"I think so," the doctor said, nodding.

"You said insurgents?" Greenfield remembered the two images on the screen. "The video Lt. White sent; those aren't rebel insurgents." *They're Almasti,* he dared not say aloud.

Harry and Lt. White relocated their shelter to just outside the fortress door with a better appreciation for its massiveness and thick walls. Harry held close the meaning of Bassui's warning. The lean-to wasn't as warm without Mutt, but the dog apparently had an inbred allegiance to his herd. They managed to get someone's attention shortly after dawn, after the lieutenant's relentless beating on the door and clanking the round metal doorknocker against its lion-head base.

"Finally!" Lt. White sighed after the peephole's rusty steel grate slid to one side.

"This is a place of seclusion, please stop your pounding," said a faceless hoarse voice through the hole in the thick timber.

"My friend and I are looking for someone we believe is lost. Can you help us?" the lieutenant shouted. "I have a photo. We just want you to look at the photo."

The door handle vibrated; the deadbolt made two hard clunks. The door popped and cracked as if it hadn't opened in a long time. A five-foot-tall tall monk dressed in a pale-yellow toga cautiously stepped through the doorway. "You failed to mention you are military," he reprimanded after looking them up and down.

The lieutenant already had his phone out and a picture of Adam Reeves on the screen. "This guy; do you know this guy?"

"This is the lost person you are looking for?" The monk looked up at the soldier, frowning as if confused. "This is one of our shepherds. He is in the valley tending the goats. He asked for the work so he could meditate and ask the gods to heal him. Is he sleeping; why are his eyes closed?"

Harry peeled back his jacket pocket because his phone was vibrating. It was Bassui sending a text with an attachment. *"This lady recognized the cap you gave me,"* was the text above the photo. It was Mary Lynn dressed in a pale maroon robe with an olive green rachu draped under her chin. A monk was standing behind her. Before he had a chance to react, his phone vibrated again; it was Greenfield. Harry answered, but the agent was talking very fast, trying to tell him many things at once. "You remembered the crash? Yes, I know about the video Lt. White sent to Hanna. Hanna's on his way?" He said, repeating everything for Lt. White's benefit. "Slow down, we're at the door to the Dzong." The photo of Mary Lynn with the monk on the bridge was still on the screen when he lost Greenfield's connection. A monk was standing behind her. *Surely, they all know each other.* He pushed past Lt. White and shoved the phone in front of the monk's face. "Have you seen this woman?" he blurted out. "Have you seen this woman?" he repeated louder when all he got from the monk was a wide-eyed frightened expression. "What about the monk in the background?" he shrieked. "Do you know the monk standing behind her?"

"I, can't," his voice quivered.

"Don't try to shade the truth, father, brother, whatever you call yourself. It's the same as a lie."

"Please, we are supposed to be left alone." The monk backed toward the open door, steadied himself with one hand against the wall after stumbling and losing one of his sandals.

"That's not going to happen," Harry said, grabbing the monk's forearm. "You're about to get a whole lot of company. The army's on its way; do you know what that means?"

"Please, no," the monk begged, seeing the wild look in Harry's eyes and feeling the pain in the arm he was now twisting.

"They're after those things we saw in the valley last night; you know what I'm talking about don't you, those two-legged huge creatures?"

"No," the monk gasped while trying to pry Harry's hand off his arm. "You must allow me to go warn my brothers so we can pray for this danger to pass."

"Let him go." Lt. White put his hand on Harry's shoulder, effectively defusing his rage. "We'll regroup when Cdr. Hanna gets here."

"He's seen her, he knows where she is; I can see it in his eyes," Harry shrieked after releasing the monk who immediately scurried through the door and slammed it hard behind him. They heard the deadbolt clunk twice back into place. Harry picked up the sandal and threw it against the door.

"Problem is, he's right," Lt. White said and took the phone from Harry. "We're not supposed to be here. They have the King's ear and control pretty much everything that goes on in these mountains. So, this is the girl; not bad," he said, nodding his head. "I've seen this bridge before on video aerial recon; it's not far from here."

"Then we're definitely in the right place." Harry's eyes scaled the wall. "Those windows are at least four stories high but we could cut one of those trees." He pointed to a stand of birch near the wall. "We only need to lean one against the wall and crawl up."

"Hear that?" Lt. White interrupted, putting a finger to his lips. "We have to go; Cdr. Hanna's here." He motioned for Harry to follow. "That's his bird landing in the valley; he'll give us our orders."

"I'm not leaving." Harry shook his head resolutely.

"I have to report to my commander, man," White argued. He opened a pocket on the side of his pack. "Do what you can with this," he said and tossed him a tightly bound nylon strap. He reached into another Velcro side pocket. "Take this; it's my personal weapon." He handed him a Glock 9 and looked up at the windows. "You can use it to blow out one of those windows or protect yourself if need be. I'll advise the commander of your whereabouts. Good luck."

Harry didn't waste time trying to dissuade the lieutenant. He stuffed the Glock into Greenfield's backpack, grabbed the rolled-up strap and loped away in search of a way into the fortified building.

Chapter 17

"Prana, today we will explore the four noble truths of human suffering."

Kunchen's low monotone voice, that would have required great concentration a few weeks ago, took far less effort now. The deeper the lesson the more benevolent was his tone. It made quick immersion of her mind, body, and soul. They were in the main temple sitting on a plush yellow prayer cushion in front of the large golden statue of Buddha. Two monks were crouched on kneeling pads chanting somewhere outside the light of the candles. They were facing each other, legs folded Indian-style, elbows bent at their sides, palms up. Mary Lynn closed her eyes and centered her thoughts on Kunchen's lesson of the day.

"*Dukkha* teaches us that suffering exists," he whispered slowly. "It states that suffering is universal and everyone feels it. *Samudaya* states there is always a cause for the suffering that everyone experiences. It's the desire to have and control things that leads to suffering." He paused as if to give the insight some time to soak in, as if to allow the hypnotic mantra to penetrate the deepest crevasses in her brain. "*Nirodha* tells us there is an end to suffering. You can only reach Nirvana when you allow your mind to experience complete freedom and non-attachment."

She felt light, weightless; wishing with all her heart for the freedom and non-attachment the spellbinding words described. Her eyelids involuntarily opened to slits. Through them, she saw that Kunchen was not moving his lips, yet she could hear the lesson clearly.

"*Magga* is when you understand . . ." Kunchen stopped abruptly, as if something had interrupted him.

Mary Lynn's eyelids fluttered, but she remained calm, even with the realization that she and Kunchen were four feet above the pillow. He slowly locked his hands over her forearms and left them there until they were safely resting on the cushion again. His eyes moved slowly toward the temple door. Without turning around, she could see through his eyes . . . Neal standing in the doorway with his mouth ajar. She could feel his surprise.

"Something has happened," Neal said. "The military is outside the compound. I'm here to escort Prana to safety."

Kunchen took her hand and gently helped her to her feet. "My apologies, we were in deep meditation," he explained to Neal. "I failed to hear the alarm." He turned to his student and bowed. *"Take what you have learned here Prana into your next life."* His unspoken words sounded as if he was telling her good-bye for the last time.

Neal was looking at her as if he'd seen a ghost. "What's wrong?" she asked.

"Nothing," he whispered, but continued to look at her strangely. "Have you reached Nirvana?"

"I don't think so." She turned to Kunchen for his reaction to Neal's question, but he was gone. "Where . . .?"

"We must hurry, James is on the way," Neal said while he guided her through the labyrinth of corridors. "I've studied with the monks for most of my life, but I have yet to experience transference."

"Can we slow down?" She had to raise the hem of her robes to keep up with his pace. "Neal, what is so urgent?"

"You can't be here when the Army arrives."

"Are you coming with me?" she panted. "I'm sensing that you're not?"

Neal didn't say anything else until they reached the large room with high ceilings. "I'm staying, Prana," he said solemnly. "I didn't fully realize until just now how truly amazing you are. I'll work very hard to make you proud of me."

"Neal, this can't be good-bye forever." She moved closer. "I understand now; how important our relationship was to you, to everyone. I'm sorry I was such a ridiculously spoiled child."

They heard a popping noise and glass shattering above them. Jagged pieces of window glass fell and bounced on the hard floor.

"What's that?" she gasped. A green strap dropped from the broken window.

"The army has breached our walls," he warned. He grabbed her arm to guide her back to the hallway and out of harm's way when James suddenly appeared in the large room. He was postured between her and the helmeted intruder that was now stepping his way down the wall while holding onto the strap. The soldier looked over his shoulder and lost his rhythm when he saw James and then his footing. His body banged against the wall and the lifeline spun him in circles. He managed to hold on long enough to clamber down and leap to the ground. There was nowhere to go and the gargantuan was closing in on him.

"James, don't!" Mary Lynn peeled herself away from Neal's grasp.

The giant's long strides quickly had Harry pinned against the wall. There was no doubting its capability to crush him with a swipe of its huge hand. Harry removed the helmet and slowly set it on the ground, hoping the giant would interpret it as a peace gesture. Removing the helmet enabled him to see the creature's face more clearly. It was more humanlike than monster in contrast to the animal-hide clothing it wore beneath a dark-blue tunic. Something that resembled a hood rested on his shoulders. It had the features of an animal complete with snout and ears. It curiously resembled the creatures he and Lt. White observed the night before.

"Harry?" Mary Lynn whimpered, wondering if she was having another vision. His eyes shifted to her; it *was* Harry.

James shifted his left foot, planting it between them as if daring Harry to move.

"James, no!" she screamed and darted between his legs. She flung her arms around Harry's neck when she reached him. "Harry, I can't believe it!" She sensed his endearment when he encased her in his arms. He was holding her tighter than he ever had. "Harry, Harry," she sobbed into his shoulder. She heard his thoughts in her head, repeating: *thank God, I found you.*

James squatted to his knees in front of them, patiently waiting for the reunion to quell. "I cannot allow him to remember me," he said when Mary Lynn finally turned to face him.

"He won't tell anyone; he's always kept my secrets." She didn't see Harry pull his phone from his back pocket and snap three pictures while she was pleading with James to spare him. "I trust him with my life."

He attempted to send the snapshots to Greenfield, but got a "failed" message. He quickly scrolled to *Bassui* and tried again while Mary Lynn debated with the ferocious-looking creature that she seemed to know very well. Unfortunately, the send circle spun continuously, forcing him to put the phone away when he heard someone else speak. "You brought her to this place?" Harry asked Neal through clenched jaws when Neal stepped into view behind the giant.

"You look different than the last time I saw you in the lab," Neal replied, as he stepped closer, ignoring Harry's anger. "No white coat and sterile gloves. When did you join the army?"

"When did you become a monk?" Harry complained, putting himself between Neal and Mary Lynn while examining him up and down.

James arched his enormous arms to cover all three with his tunic, but Neal stepped back before the giant could encircle him.

"Prana," he said, bowing respectfully at the waist to his former fiancé. "I'm staying here to study; I have so much more to learn. I wasted too much time in America. Harry, my friend," he said smiling. "In all seriousness, it is good to see you again. I wish you both well."

"More uniforms are approaching," James announced and beckoned them with his opened arms to hurry.

"I'll see if I can buy you some time." Neal stepped backward while James enclosed the two inside the dark blue tunic.

"What's happening?" Harry asked.

"It's okay," Mary Lynn assured him. "James is taking us somewhere safe."

"How?" he asked confused. There wasn't a quiver of movement inside James' arms.

"The giants have their own unique way of traveling," she said.

"Because of my sister's request not to harm you," Harry heard James say in a milder tone, "your fate will be decided by the elders." Harry wondered why James had referred to Mary Lynn as his *sister,* and who the *elders* were, and how many more giants there were?

It wasn't long, perhaps thirty-seconds, before Neal heard a loud thud against the thick wood door. He managed to take a step toward the door before it shuddered and exploded. The ruptured door fell flat on the floor making a loud thud; the splintered framework and disintegrated pieces of mortar spewed in every direction. Two soldiers leaped through the breach. One held a battering ram in both hands by its straps, the other a rifle. Three more men in full tactical gear rushed in behind them with rifles pointed at every wall ready to engage whatever they deemed a threat. All four turned and took aim at Neal after clearing the periphery. "Please, don't shoot." Neal raised his hands above his head. "Are-are we under attack?"

"We have one individual, looks like a monk," one of them reported through an undefined communication device. By now three more had entered. Hand signals were thrown back and forth and they split into groups to search every corner of the large room. Harry's rope was discovered and the silent communications continued. "Where's the man that came down the strap?" demanded the soldier standing closest to Neal with his rifle trained on his chest. He poked him with the muzzle when he didn't answer right away.

"I was investigating the noise, the breaking glass," Neal replied, looking up at the window with the missing glass and the strap draped over the sill. "Then you-you busted through the door."

"We have video of two insurgents walking in the valley before dawn today. "Video!" Neal gasped. "I saw no one."

"We'll see for ourselves." The man on point jerked his head forward, signaling the detail to search the hallway.

"No one is allowed to enter any sacred Dzong in Bhutan without first obtaining permission from the King," Neal insisted to the point man. "And only when an appointment is coordinated with our lama. Your army is in our country by special permission. If you upset the lama the King will ask you to leave."

Agent Greenfield and Lt. Fisher recognized there was a standoff as soon as they stepped through the breached doorway. They quickly rushed to the wall to examine the strap. "It belongs to Lt. White, sir," Lt. Fisher said, holding the strap between her fingers. "And look, there." Lt. White's Glock lay a few feet away.

"The kid did this?" Greenfield muttered while looking at the rock tied to the end of the strap. "Hum," he muttered after picking up a piece of thick glass from the floor and smelling it. "Gun powder," he whispered. "Better not let the monks see the gun." He turned to the small troop of infantrymen. "Why are you pointing your rifles at this unarmed monk?"

A distinct softer-spoken voice suddenly replaced the agent's. "Bless you, Brother Neal." The meek voice came from a small man in red robes standing in a large open space behind Neal. He was standing under three streams of light that were shining on him like spotlights through three windows along the edge of the ceiling. Neal bowed his head and stepped aside, yielding to his superior. Three members of the small troop moved toward the man standing within the dusty luster and aimed their rifles at him. "One of you is here looking for someone in particular." He stepped forward, raised his hand, and pointed as he looked over the group as if searching for that individual. "You will be given the guidance you seek." His finger stopped on Greenfield. "The rest of you will not find what you are looking for inside these walls; you will have to conduct your search elsewhere."

"I'll see to it that your door and window are replaced," Greenfield said. The soldiers reluctantly left the large room after a back and forth with Cdr. Hanna who was waiting at an Augusta in the valley.

"Your help is not necessary," Kunchen replied. "We have our own skilled carpenters."

"Brother, brethren," the agent stammered. "May I ask a question of this man?"

Kunchen looked at Neal and then back at the agent. "You may ask me your question."

"I'm looking for three missing persons from the US. I found one of them, Adam Reeves."

"Yes, he is one our shepherds," Kunchen interrupted and nodded out of respect for his passing. "He now dwells with the gods."

Greenfield quickly deduced someone, perhaps another shepherd in the valley, must have seen them approach Reeves and then airlift him out. But, how could he have known he died; it had only been a few hours ago?

"Our brother chose to leave his fate in the hands of the gods," the monk said, answering Greenfield's unspoken query.

"Followers of Buddhism do not fear death. Death simply leads to rebirth."

Greenfield looked at Lt. Fisher standing beside him. She raised an eyebrow but maintained a neutral posture. "I'm also looking for Mary Lynn Bennett," he continued, and Neal Mueller, her ex-boyfriend." He looked at Neal. "I suspect Mueller is this man. I'm not clairvoyant, brethren, but I'm trained to know when someone recognizes their own name like he just did."

Yes," Kunchen said lowly, looking at Neal. "The girl you seek was here, but no longer. She was sent away because we sensed danger was near, and it seems to have arrived."

"Sent away where?"

"Home," Kunchen replied softly.

"Home, do you mean to the United States?" Greenfield asked. "Was someone with her, someone by the name of Harrison Foster?"

"Someone else was here," he said looking at the strap dangling from the window. "He wore a uniform, like yours and the men who broke down our door. He left with her. That is all I can say. What you are about to ask, I cannot answer because you will be treading on sacred topics."

Greenfield moved closer to Neal who had been avoiding eye contact with him. "Where'd they go?" he growled. "Her family is worried sick and counting on me to bring her home."

"She is at home where she belongs," Kunchen whispered after stepping between them. "There will be no further guidance; it's time for you to leave now."

"That monk's an expert at answering questions without telling you anything," Greenfield grumbled when he and Lt. Fisher were outside. The rest of the detail was already on its way back to the valley to report to Cdr. Hanna. "At least everyone's accounted for now. Somehow that monk already knew Reeves was dead."

"They just let him go off and die?" she sighed. "And Mueller is who, sir?

"The girl's ex-boyfriend," he said ardently.

"That's incredible," the lieutenant said.

"Yeah." He looked at the open space in the wall. "The girl was here; Foster is with her . . . somewhere," he said. "The older monk said she went home, whatever the hell that means." He looked at the lieutenant as if the answer was hers to supply. "He said she *went home*." He was pacing now, arguing with her even though she hadn't uttered a word. "Where is home?"

"I don't know, sir. Perhaps you should contact your people on the ground in Louisiana," she said to the perplexed agent. "This is all very strange to me, too, how all these people ended up here. How the monk knew Reeves was dead. In fact, it's remarkable. If she's not in Louisiana or on her way back there, then you need to find out what *going home* means to the monks. If the Quantico team is no help, perhaps the locals can shed some light; it might be a familiar term for them."

"You're right, Fisher," he sighed and pulled a small white plastic prescription bottle from his shirt pocket.

"Are you having chest pains again, sir?" She watched him fish two pills from the bottle, throw his head back, and slap the palm of his hand against his mouth.

"Dr. Rush gave me these for anxiety. I can't seem to board that damn helo without them."

"Yes, sir, we should head back before the commander, you know, gets impatient," she said.

"You don't think he'd leave us, do you?"

"He does seem to enjoy teaching lessons, sir."

Chapter 18

The first thing Harry saw when he pushed aside the tunic's folds blocking his view of Mary Lynn, was her amazing blue eyes staring back at him. Her smile always melted his heart even though he was afraid to show it . . . until now. An unbridled grin erupted across his face when she touched his hand. All the hardships he'd endured to get to this unforgiving place had evaporated. He was breathing freely for the first time since she went missing. The freezing temperatures, the pissed-off FBI agent, the arrogant commander, two near-death helicopter crashes. None of that mattered; not even the gigantic creature that had them pinned up in his arms. Whatever was next, they would get through it together. Her eyes seemed to hold more depth than before. Maybe she had undergone some intolerable trials of her own these past weeks. The tunic suddenly parted like a curtain. Even though there had been no sensation of movement, they were in a large cavern that looked like someone's quaint living quarters. Deep red, blue, yellow, and green carpets hung from the walls and covered the stone floor. There was furniture, some large enough to accommodate the giant, but mostly suited for someone the size of himself and Mary Lynn. All were arranged in defined living areas for sitting, dining and sleeping. He wondered, as he looked around at the sculpted walls, if they were in another part of the Dzong or in a cave within the vast range of mountains that could be seen from every village.

"Harry, I've missed you so much." Tears rolled down Mary Lynn's cheeks. She leaned forward, burying her face in his camo shirt as she sobbed.

"Thank God you're okay." He eagerly slipped his arms around her waist and pulled her close.

The giant quietly stared down at them as if waiting for the reunion to quell.

What in God's name are you? Harry thought to himself as he scanned the giant figure from his leather boots, hide pants and woven tunic, all the way up to his human-like face.

"I am Nephilim," the colossal man answered and dropped to one knee. "Prana and I are half brother and sister. Nephilim are unknown outside of our world; it is our desire to keep it that way." James straightened his back and spread his arms to their farthest lengths to display his mighty posture. "You can see why."

"I do," Harry replied. "But, how is it possible for you to be her half-brother?" Harry tried to hold on to Mary Lynn, but she pushed herself free when she spotted a table with photographs propped up within a small rock garden. She picked them up one by one by their wood-carved frames and then carefully placed them back. Harry followed her, repeating the motion. They were old studio portraits of the Bennett family, extra copies from package deals that no one would miss. He was in two of them standing to the left of Christine; Al, Dale, and Mary Lynn were on the right. When he looked up Mary Lynn was staring at a wall portrait of a Nephilim giant. She was studying the man dressed in animal fur and holding a long staff. Her expression was endearing, suggesting she might know him. Then she turned her back to it and walked to a stone balcony that overlooked a common area thirty feet below, as if she was trying to gather her thoughts, her emotions. The photographs, the half-brother; Mary Lynn was coming to the same conclusion as he was. This is where Christine has been living all these years. Was it by choice or was she taken like Mary Lynn?

Women below in the common area were scurrying around gathering cookware and utensils and packing them in wooden boxes. Mary Lynn's eyes drifted to the vastness above them; flashes of life on Hartwood appeared. She never paid much attention to what went on between her parents. There were contentious stares that hung in the air without words to explain their meaning. The uncomfortable silence that prevailed at times, particularly when her mother worked late which seemed to be every night in the latter years before she went missing. She took this to be their normal marital relationship that she took for granted. After all, she was busy with her own struggles navigating through a world of colors and trying to fit in with intimidating peers that inevitably turned her into a desperate, rebellious adolescent. Her father was the image of a Louisiana man living in a sportsman's paradise and a rough, gruff deputy sheriff. Her mother was a dedicated research technician at a fish hatchery who read the Bible and taught Sunday school. The differences between them were obvious, but they loved each other, at least, that's what she thought. The miscarriage two years before she was born had thrown her mother into a deep depression. "James!" she gasped and turned to look at him. It was as if someone had suddenly jerked a veil away and freed her from servitude. "It was you!"

"It would have been impossible to carry me to term," he said as if he had been waiting for her to ask him that very question. "One of the healers removed me from her womb and placed me inside one of our surrogates. This practice has been used for generations, but can only work with certain women. Women who carry a particular blood type and are also blessed by the gods with a certain awareness."

Hours of meditation with Kunchen had taught her to pray through upsetting circumstances. According to Buddha, *everyone experiences shock, sadness, and fear. Recognizing it is half the battle to understanding and peace.* Her mind was certainly reeling. Where did she fit in this scenario? She had a rare blood-type. Was seeing colors the awareness he was talking about? She turned away from him and laid her hands across the flat cool guardrail to find composure. She took in a cleansing breath, closed her eyes, and searched her memory for one of Kunchen's curative chants.

Harry rushed to her, repeating: "Are you alright?" But it was as if she couldn't hear him.

Whispers from the women below had flooded her mind. A vision appeared within the veins of her eyelids. The women were huddled around a child lying on his side; his knee was bent and he was clutching his leg up close to his chest. They had been cleaning the large hearth filled with glowing coals when the boy tripped and fell into them searing his leg. When Mary Lynn opened her eyes, she saw that the vision was real. The women were gathered around the boy, praying. She turned and locked eyes with James. He nodded and then evaporated before their eyes.

Harry's mouth fell ajar. Before he could ask what was happening, the giant reappeared holding a child in his arms.

James laid the five-foot, seven-year-old down on a sofa. A woman dressed in colorful flowing garments slipped into the room behind James. At first, Harry thought it was a curious monk checking on the boy's condition. But it was a woman with graying hair, dragging an animal hide duffle bag behind her. She made every effort to be inconspicuous; edging along the wall, ducking behind furniture. He recognized her when their eyes met. They were the eyes of the kindest woman he had ever known. Christine, the woman who saw to his every need after his mother abandoned him.

The child's legs took up most of the human-sized Victorian sofa. He leaned his body against James and the rolled armrest for support while bravely enduring the severest pain known to man. *No blisters*, Mary Lynn observed while placing both hands inches above the traumatic injury. *The burn is radiating too much heat*. The wound was black around the perimeter, dark red along the oblong inside edges, and blood-red in the center. Experience told her it was much worse than third degree. Nature's healing blisters would not form in such a deep burn and could ultimately be fatal in a place where nothing is available for pain or antibiotics to fight the infection that will surely set in.

"Prana is one with the healing gods," James whispered to Harry when he moved closer to peer over the hand-carved cherry wood trim. Her eyes were fixed on the injury that had burned through flesh, muscle, and vessels; her lips were moving as if she were talking to herself.

Mary Lynn didn't know the prayer that effortlessly came to her. The words were loud and clear in her head. James bowed his head respectfully, caressing the boy and joining her in a silent prayer of his own. Harry watched and waited. His eyes were drawn to the alcove when he saw Christine emerge with the bag that was now filled with robes and scarves. She removed the portrait of the giant, stuffed it in the duffle, and then moved on to the rock garden of small photos. His attention went back to the boy when Mary Lynn spread her palms across his lower right shin. She was rocking and whispering the indiscernible incantation over and over. When she withdrew her hands, the oblong wound was the color of new pink skin.

James broke the silence when he saw the disbelief on Harry's face. "My sister is no longer a child that requires coddling. It would be wise to not stand in her way." His voice was as intent as Cdr. Hanna's. "She must be allowed to follow her calling, as our mother has." James gathered up the boy and transported him back to the women below. Harry moved around the sofa and placed a hand on Mary Lynn's shoulder. She was still kneeling, staring blindly at the cushions where the boy had been. "That was unbelievable," he whispered. "But, how?"

"I used to see what people are thinking in the form of auras," she whispered in as clear a voice as Lt. White when they were outside the Dzong trying to be as quiet as possible. "Now I see it in my head." She looked up at him. "The colors have been replaced by something else."

Harry helped her off her knees to the sofa. "You don't see the colors anymore? Okay, explain to me what you mean."

"Remember Mama telling us how education can make a person grow? No, I think the word she used was *evolve*. I believe that's what happened. Please, Harry, you've been through so much because of me. I need you to understand the transformation I'm going through."

"I do; I will," he said shaking his head as if confused. He took her hands. "You know you've always been the most exciting person I've ever known. I don't expect a little evolution to change that."

"I saw your face in a vision, Harry," she said tracing the thin line of his beard down the side of his face with her fingers. "I never saw you with a beard before, but there you were, and wearing a purple and gold skull cap."

"You did see me," he nodded as he watched her eyes move slowly across his face, as if examining every pore, every hair, and every line. It was exhilarating not having to pretend how he felt about her anymore. He was free to be more than her friend.

"I saw the cap in a boy's school bag."

"Bassui," Harry replied, and took his phone from his pocket to show her the photo Bassui sent him. "I can't tell you what a relief it was to see this."

"I saw you at other times too, while I was meditating. I saw you sleeping on a cot in a tent." She slid a hand down the sleeve of his camouflage shirt while recalling the clothes he wore in the vision. "Another time you were in the valley with Mutt. Your head was resting on a backpack. Someone else was there with you. I've been thinking about you a lot."

"Mary Lynn, I'm so sorry I didn't pay more attention when you waved to me from the lab window that day. An FBI agent was asking me questions and . . ." he paused . . ." that was the last time I saw you."

"I remember that day," she said, smiling and frowning at the same time. "It seems like years since that day. I was on my way to see Daddy."

"He was questioning me about Mutt's blood sample."

"He's here with you," she said intuitively.

"Yes, looking for you. I wouldn't be here if it weren't for John Greenfield. I'd never have found you." She looked at him strangely, seriously, with a hint of a frown.

"He's asking questions about things he must never know the answers to."

Harry forgot about Christine. She had disappeared into the alcove again, probably to look for something else to put in the duffle. He was consumed with Mary Lynn. She was touching his newly weathered skin and embedded creases of concern. He touched her lips with his fingers; her eyes were as relaxed as her demeanor. There was nothing to hide anymore or to talk around, or excuse; she was free. It looked good on her. The moment was broken when something distracted her. Mary Lynn's eyes shifted to where the pictures were once propped in the small rock display. Harry looked up. Christine was standing behind her.

"You're responsible for my being here," Mary Lynn whispered. She seemed to be staring into space.

Harry stood up, ready to confront Christine because of the pain she caused her family, but his love and respect for her silenced him.

"Yes," Christine sighed, submitting to her daughter's allegation.

"You know, Mother." Mary Lynn slowly rose and then turned to look at her. It was if she had completely overlooked Christine's aged face and silvering hair. "It's perfectly clear to me why you took me to Kunchen first." Her voice was emotionless as she slowly stepped toward her. "You wanted me in this frame of mind before I learned you were still alive and that my father is . . ." She took a deep, calming breath. "That was wise, I suppose; I do have a better perspective. But it doesn't excuse how you manipulated Daddy, Dale, and Harry and . . . whoever my father is."

"Kokabiel," Christine replied calmly.

Harry decided not to interfere, to let them say what they needed to say to each other, even though he was in an emotional upheaval of his own.

"Kunchen taught me how useless anger is," Mary Lynn said, ignoring the tears that were slowly trickling down Christine's matured face.

"It's okay to be angry with me," Christine said in a low voice and wiped her face. "But there's no need to be so formal. I've missed hearing you call me 'Mama'."

"You're not her anymore," Mary Lynn replied. "I don't think I ever knew her."

"I wish we had more time, sweetheart," Christine said. "We'll have to talk about this as we go." She grabbed hold of the bulging duffle bag. "The colony is preparing to leave . . . evacuate. The army is on its way to destroy our home. Kokabiel and the elders predicted this day would come and have wisely prepared for it."

"It was you that left the book at my door."

"Yes. I'll tell you everything, but we must hurry." The ground trembled as soon as she turned toward the doorway.

"Did you feel that?" Harry gasped.

"The military has arrived," Christine replied. "We don't have much time." She lifted the bag over her shoulder. "Follow me; we'll get the Bible and then James can take us to safety."

A mournful sound that Harry compared to a whale call filled the peaks of the vast hallway just as they entered it.

James abruptly appeared in the hallway. "The alarm is sounding. I will take all of you to one of the escape tunnels; then I must go help with the diversion."

Mary Lynn turned to Harry. "Your friend, John, is not part of this wave of attacks. He won't get here until it's too late."

"The army is looking for ISIS militants." Harry stared into her eyes, as if doing so might allow him to see what she could see.

"I must take you to the tunnels now, before it's too late," James urged, motioning them to move closer to his opened arms. "Transporters are working non-stop carrying everyone to the new homesite."

"No," Christine insisted. "Go help your father."

Harry snapped a picture of James while Christine was convincing her giant son that she knew the way to the tunnels. As before, the circle continuously spun against the solid gray background when he pressed send.

***

Agent Greenfield entered the command tent pulling an egg burrito from his pocket. It had a single bite taken out of one corner and made a thump when it hit the bottom of the trashcan next to the coffee station. It tasted just like his body felt . . . stiff as cardboard. He had slept like a rock and he needed a strong cup of coffee. His mind wasn't up to an analytical recap of events from the previous day. He needed to get his head straight before confronting Cdr. Hanna who was hovering over a radar screen while spouting short iron-fisted commands to a couple of technicians seated across from him. The notepad tucked under the agent's arm vibrated, making his finger slip off the coffee dispenser knob. Hanna turned his head upon hearing the sharp snap.

"There you are," he snarled. "Come take a look at this," he bellowed as if giving him an order and ignoring the agent's lethargic appearance. Greenfield sat down at the nearest mess table and opened the overnight message he received from Harry. The *non-response* struck the commander as blatant, so he visited the coffee pot and sat down across from him. "What the hell happened to you?" he grunted, observing the puffy dark circles under the agent's eyes.

"It's these damn pills the doctor gave me," he moaned, pulling the white medicine bottle from his jacket pocket and slapping it down on the table between them. "Just give me a minute."

"You hear from Quantico?" Hanna nodded at the notepad cradled in his hand.

"They're checking inbound flights, but . . ." Greenfield shook his head wearily, meaning the answer was obvious. Mary Lynn had not been spotted.

"What about Foster?"

There was something suspicious in Hanna's tone. He was fishing. "Appears he took infrareds of two guys walking across the valley. I just got them." He pressed his finger to the screen and enlarged the two figures. "I'm thinking a couple of night hunters. There's been nothing else from him. He's the one that slipped down the strap we found in the monastery. That monk just wouldn't tell me where he and the girl went."

"That monk is keeping things from us alright," Hanna grumbled. "You sure those are hunters in the photos?" His eyebrows were raised. "Lt. White's observations tell a different story."

"They're not ISIS militants," Greenfield moaned.

"No, they're not." He gulped down his coffee and set the cup on the table. "You know what FBI, we're both dedicated military men." He was now tapping the bottom of the cardboard cup on the table. "We both believe in our missions." (Tap-tap.) "I hunt evil terrorists in some of the scariest places in the world." (Tap-tap.) "You waste your time searching for missing people you'll never find. Ha," he grunted, and gave the cup one last tap, "you could never survive the battles I've fought or stand up to the monsters I've faced. Look at you," he sneered, looking up at his uncombed hair and down at the wrinkled uniform. He gave the cup one hard last tap. "My men come in from hand-to-hand looking better than you do right now."

"Is that so?" The agent took a sip of his coffee.

"You couldn't handle the conditions we face every day. You're soft."

The agent's face warped into a stern frown. "They're here. The three missing people I've been looking for." He pounded the table with his fist. "They're all here."

Hanna equaled Greenfield's coiled glare from across the table. He stood and shoved back the folding chair he was sitting in. "You need to stay out of my way FBI; I can't be held responsible for what happens to you and Foster if you get in the way of my operation. My men have finished combing the valley. I've given them orders to advance to the upper levels."

"You can't just force your way into the mountains. You'll create an international incident."

"Eyes in the sky, remember? Anyone . . ." he shifted his eyes to the notepad, as if referencing the objects on Greenfield's screen ". . . or anything moving around up there will show up on our screens."

Greenfield slowly stood. "Yeah, well, I'm pretty good at what I do. One of my jobs is reading people. You have the look of someone addicted to the adrenalin rush that comes from attacking and destroying. That uncontrollable desire has taken over your reasoning. Have you ever had a round table with your commander general about what Lt. White reported or what you're planning?" He picked up the prescription bottle, popped off the top, and poured the remaining pills into what remained of the black liquid.

Hanna knitted his brows thinking the agent was about to turn the cup up and drink what surely was a fatal mixture. He would reach across the table and knock it from his hand if he lifted it to his lips, and then get back to the more important task at hand of gunning down ISIS hold-ups. Instead, the agent dropped the cardboard cup into the trashcan next to the burrito. "I need Fisher to take me into Mondar.

"Good idea," the commander countered. "Go to Mondar. You'll be out of my hair. Make sure my soldier comes back in one piece."

***

A merchant rushed up to Greenfield and Lt. Fisher when they climbed out of the Humvee. The agent shrugged his shoulders but returned the man's bow when he gifted him with a banana and the lieutenant with an orange from his fruit stand. His reason, "The gods spoke to me and said you were in need of these particular fresh fruits this wonderful morning."

"I've been deployed to many foreign countries," Lt. Fisher said while she peeled the skin from the orange as they continued through the narrow walkways of the crowded marketplace. "The locals in Bhutan are the kindest and most caring. They seem to go out of their way to please; there's something innocent about them."

"And, they're hiding something," Greenfield slurred, his cheeks bulging with his first bite of the banana.

"I don't think they care that ISIS terrorists are hiding in their mountains or that a war is raging in a country on the other side of their peaks. All they seem to want is the inner peace they offer to everyone," she added when he shook his head in disagreement. "They even accept that we don't get it."

"You're mistaking that for deceit."

"Boy, you're in a mood today," she retorted.

"Look, there she is," he said and handed Fisher the rest of his banana. Karma was standing within a group of tourists near a table loaded with polished multi-colored wooden bowls. The green rachu that usually covered her head was around her shoulders exposing her dark sweptback hair and brown face. "She's not so gracious with me, but she's honest." *Her beauty always stops me in my tracks.* The thought brought a smile to his face.

"You come to see Bassui again?" Karma barked when she saw the pair approaching. "Are you responsible for the schools closing?" she ranted before either could answer. "People are evacuating the mountains." Her piercing eyes were focused on Lt. Fisher and her full military gear.

Greenfield grinned at Lt. Fisher because not more than two minutes ago she was raving about how gentile the Bhutanese were. "The army is making a nuisance of itself searching for terrorists, isn't it?" he said. "Unfortunately, these sympathizers make a habit of hiding among the innocent and use them as human shields."

"Your army has increased its presence above the monasteries. Now our streets and homes are overcrowded with people who are fleeing their homes."

Lt. Fisher sympathetically rested a hand on Karma's shoulder. "I'm sorry this is happening, but it's necessary. If you see anything or anyone that looks suspiciously like . . ."

Karma quickly pulled away from her and covered her head with the rachu. Then she wrapped it around her face, lifted her chin in defiance, and turned away.

The agent nudged the lieutenant by the elbow when Karma carried her insolence further by pretending to help a customer. "Come on, I think I know where the boy might be."

The courtyard was crowded with children playing or waiting to join a never-ending soccer game. They found Bassui sitting on the ground in the shade next to a building with the blue Surface in his lap.

"Bassui, you're not playing?" Greenfield queried, trying to sound cordial.

"I played earlier," he replied, "before the yard was so crowded. Have you heard from Harry?"

"I was hoping you had," the agent sighed. "I spoke to him on the phone; he was outside a Dzong on the other side of the valley. Thanks to you, he found the dog we've been looking for. But I haven't been able to reach him since then."

"Neither have I; I pray for his safety."

The boy seemed troubled so Greenfield bent down on one knee next to him. "Thank you, Bassui," he whispered. "Your prayers will certainly help. I could use your help with something that has me a little confused. One of the monks told me that Mary Lynn, the lady we're looking for, 'went home.'"

The boy bowed his head, as if ashamed. "I saw her, the lady. I took her photo and sent it to Harry."

"I know, thank you for that, it was extremely helpful. I just don't understand what 'went home' means. I'm sure Harry is with her, but they're not in Louisiana or on any inbound flight that would take them home. Please, do you have any idea what that means to the monks?"

Bassui touched the tablet screen a few times and then turned it around to face Greenfield. Three ice-covered mountains were on the screen. The summits were high and blocked by clouds. "Home is here, where the gods reside."

Greenfield thought the image looked familiar. He looked up past the bowing gables that surrounded the courtyard and there they were, the identical peaks as on the screen.

"That's where they are?" Lt. Fisher gasped.

The boy looked up at her and frowned. "Your army has been sending helicopters there since dawn. The gods will fight back . . ." His chest heaved as if he was about to cry. "And then nothing will ever be the same."

"What are you saying, kid?" the agent pressed, putting an arm around his shoulder to comfort him.

"He is saying the mountains are sacred!" It was Karma's voice sounding as if she was stating a decree. When Greenfield stood, she quickly positioned herself between the pair and Bassui. "Your army will suffer greatly." She squeezed the green rachu tightly across her face with her fist. "What is worse, if they persist, the gods, who have protected us for thousands of years, will leave for someplace safer."

Lt. Fisher, the well-trained soldier that she was, propped one hand on her belt where a stun gun was holstered. "Gods . . . are you referring to the monks?" There was no reply except for a cold stare.

"I'm sorry, Karma," Greenfield said. He tried to project sincerity by pressing his hands together in a praying fashion. "Please, I didn't mean to upset Bassui, or you. I'm worried about my friend Harry. I think he's up there." He looked up over her head at the mountains. "I think everyone I'm looking for is there."

"You must leave our village." Her voice was calmer now that Bassui was safely standing behind her ankle-length kira. "And never come back!"

"Of course." Greenfield nodded to her. "Again, I'm sorry." He saw Bassui peek from around the skirt. "Please-please, pray that we find Harry and the girl," he stuttered. He couldn't keep from looking back at Karma as they walked back to the Humvee. He wanted so much to make amends with her, but it would have to be another time.

"Well, that went well," sighed Lt. Fisher.

"I just hope she doesn't find out Harry and Bassui have been emailing each other," he grumbled as they hurried through the village to their vehicle. "It's best that we keep their friendship on the down low. What?" he asked when he saw her reaction to the urban slang. "Stop laughing!"

"I can't help it," she snickered. "You know, I don't think I've ever seen you smile before today," she remarked.

"Stop talking, Fisher!" he barked.

"Before, in the market, you smiled at the man who gave us the fruit. You smiled at me when you got in the Humvee earlier and look at how compassionate you were with Bassui just now, and of course, with Karma. You have the look of a sick cow when you're around her."

"Don't get any ideas, Fisher," he complained.

"Oh, you're still an ass; I just didn't know you had feelings or could smile before today." He put an arm around her shoulder and pulled her close so she could see the exaggerated grin on his face. She shook loose and pushed him away. "I'm not so sure I like this John Greenfield," she said and walked ahead, maintaining a three-step gap in front of him. They both stopped when they heard a thundering roar. It was the rhythmic rumble of two H60 Black Hawk helicopters flying at max speed overhead in the direction of the sacred mountains.

***

Greenfield paid no attention to how alive with activity the command center was. He stormed in and went straight to Hanna and screamed in his ear. "You couldn't wait until after I retrieved Foster and the Bennett girl?" The twenty or so uniformed men and women shuffling around from station to station and conversing over headsets stopped, turned, or looked up. Hanna remained steely-eyed with his arms folded across his chest, his eyes fixed on the monitor in front of him. "Is that real-time?" Greenfield asked.

A violent explosion had erupted on the screen. Rock and powdered dirt jutted from the side of a mountain. Debris jettisoned for miles in every direction.

"While you and Fisher were interviewing villagers, the ISR recorded this." Hanna pressed half a dozen keys on the pad below him. "See that cave and the trail leading up to it?" His eyes never left the real-time action even as he split the screen and initiated a slide show. A montage of still shots of the large opening prior to its being pounded scrolled by. Several individuals in robes and turbans were moving in and out of the entrance as the shuttered action pulsed across the screen. Each was carrying high-powered automatic rifles strapped around their necks and shoulders. Two of them had their weapons held upright as if guarding the entrance.

"I'll be damned!" Greenfield blurted out in disbelief. "ISIS militants. How many?"

"Eight," he replied, his eyes were fixed in one position on the screen. "There's another entrance on the backside." The view quickly changed to the opposite side of the hill. "This has been a principal point of action for the past few days; lots of in-and-out activity." The screen separated and quadrupled the view. "They're like moles; you can never eradicate them all. We're panning for survivors now. If any happen to stick their heads out, front or back, we'll destroy what's left of that hill." He diverted his attention to look at Greenfield. "And before you start, we have the government's okay where the ISIS is concerned."

"Just don't aim any higher. I have reason to believe Foster and the Bennett girl are somewhere near the summit." He pointed to the hazy distant mountains on one of the screens that were nowhere near Hanna's interest. He wasn't sure if Hanna was listening because he was reaching for a SAT phone while staring at the current activity on one of the quartered screens. Hanna gave a "Go 2" order and a second later a flash erupted drawing his eyes to the top left view. Rock and sand spewed into the air. When the dust cleared, the side of the hill had been obliterated.

"Hold 2," the commander said through the mouthpiece. "One, move to Beta."

"Is Beta another target?" Greenfield looked around the busy room when Hanna ignored his question. Every eye was focused and dedicated to make Hanna's missions a success.

"You're getting on my nerves, FBI," Hanna grumbled. "You're becoming a distraction to my personnel. If you think you know where they are, pitch me a plan to extract them; otherwise, stop interrupting."

A portable spotlight was trained on a four-by-eight-foot scaled-down layout of Bhutan. Stacks of foam represented the Himalayas. Small, tan-colored plastic toy soldiers marked the locations where suspected ISIS activity was recorded. Most were knocked on their sides.

"Someone's been messing with your markers," the agent said, noticing two planted at an elevation far too high for any human to climb.

"Don't tell me you still can't remember what happened there?" Hanna barked.

Of course, he did. In a most unsettling way, making him feel like he could go into another spiral at any given moment.

Hanna stepped away from the monitors and thumped over a group of eight miniature figures that were standing on a lower set of blocks. Other small groups of figures lay on their sides in three areas representing the chain of mountains. "When I'm finished with these rag heads, I'm gonna find out who or what attacked you and my guys on that ledge." He pointed to a monitor above the layout. An ISR was steaming live video of the infamous mountain ledge. "I trust Lt. White's assessment of what he saw in the valley." Four plastic soldier figures were lined up along the edge of the prototypical table. They were covered with the cut-off fingers of a black glove. Hanna placed two of them in a replicated valley made of pieces of green construction paper where Lt. White took the video. "Judging by what I witnessed when you finally remembered what happened to you on that ledge . . ." He picked up the two figures planted in the higher foam blocks and replaced them with the two remaining dark models. "I'd say I've got something more interesting to investigate than ISIS."

"Make sure you take this up the chain of command before taking action," Greenfield said, glaring at Hanna from across the crude diorama.

"Like I said," Hanna growled, "pitch me a plan." Hanna sneered and snorted with contempt while he watched the agent exit the tent.

***

"How much further?" Harry asked Christine after sneaking a selfie in front of a tremendous wall scribed with row after row of endless hieroglyphics. He lagged behind, positioning his phone beside his hip, taking as many shots as he dared of the incredibly carved outlying rooms Christine led them past. Christine didn't answer; her attention was on the daughter she hadn't seen in seven years. It allowed him to turn a shoulder, to hide his efforts to attach the snapshots to emails intended for John and Bassui. Whether or not they would ever receive them was questionable, because there had been no verification that anything sent so far had gone anywhere.

Something was going on between the two women Harry couldn't quite make out from the distance he had fallen back to. They were walking side by side. Mary Lynn's arms were folded in front of her; Christine was holding onto the strap and balancing the duffle on her shoulder and waving one arm. They were talking quietly, yet looking at each another intensely. It was giving him the opportunity to take and attempt to send more photos.

"Daddy told me he thought you ran away with someone," Mary Lynn said, blatantly interrupting Christine's animated explanation of her deep feelings for the giants. Her mother had a faraway look in her eyes and the same excitement in her voice as when she used to talk about the genetic experiments at the fish hatchery. A subject her daddy often turned a deaf ear to. "He's smarter than you gave him credit for, you know. Did you know they suspected him of killing you?" she quickly continued, not waiting to hear her excuses. "Did you know that he's been living in Catahoula for the past six and a half years? Did you know Dale left home because everything reminded him of what happened to you? Do you know that he's married and that you have two grandchildren?"

Christine nodded in response to each charge. "I put all of you through much pain and sadness, my daughter. I am sorry for that, but I had no doubt you would survive. Al is in his element living in the woods. Dale matured, found love, and started his own business. You followed your instincts and now you are a great healer."

"Nothing about any of this bothers you?" Mary Lynn asked.

"I raised you and Dale to fight your own battles, to be strong, and you are," Christine replied earnestly. "I released Al to become who he wanted to be, and he did."

"That sounds like something Kunchen would say," Mary Lynn said as they came to the end of the stone passageway. "I know this place," she said when they reached an area with a stone guardrail and circular walkway surrounding a large open space. "This is the mezzanine where Neal brought me." She rushed to the paling and looked over the edge. The great room was vacated and hazy with dust. There were no rugs, kneeling pillows, smoldering hearths, burning candles, or prayer wheels.

"Everything has been packed and moved," Christine said.

"We need to hurry," Harry complained nervously. Dirt was falling fast in many areas of the mezzanine. A layer of crumbled rock covered the entire floor.

Christine hurried to the lift door. "It won't take us long to get the Bible."

"Why didn't you just have James retrieve it for you?" Harry asked. "He does things much faster."

"He's busy helping his father right now," Christine replied. "Please, Harry, help me slide the door open." She stepped inside first and shoved a lever to the right of the door. They heard a motor. "Thank goodness the generator still works."

Mary Lynn felt deception in her mother's words. The mountain was deteriorating around them, they should have gone with James, yet she was insisting they follow her. Christine could feel her daughter's distrust.

Harry held his hand out to Mary Lynn after opening the door and stepping inside. She took it, but with reservation. The whole idea of going back to get the Bible felt wrong.

***

Agent Greenfield never drove the crude dirt road to Mondar. He always rode shotgun beside someone who was well trained in operating the fortified mine-resistant, ambush-protected Humvee. It was wider and taller than the usual government-issued SUVs he was accustomed to, and quite unnerving to operate. He idled to a stop, parking six feet off the road near Karma's mud and mortar hut. He exited quietly, not wanting to wake anyone in the quaint village that was completely buttoned down for the night. The narrow streets were abundant in shadows. Tables were covered with tarps along the storefronts and shops were secured with chain-link fencing blacked out with plastic. The backside of the hut had a single window covered with a piece of animal hide. He carefully moved it to one side. Eight children were sleeping on mats on top of several layers of rugs.

"I told you to never come back here!" Karma's stern whisper startled him, making him stumble when he turned around. "What do you want from Bassui?" She was standing against the wall in the shadows cast by the protruding curved eves.

"Karma . . ." he whispered, moving closer so he could see her face. The face he had grown to crave. Her intense eyes blazed back at him through the narrow opening of the rachu. "I didn't come here to see Bassui. I'm here to see you, to apologize, again. Karma, I know what your children mean to you. I know you're trying to protect them."

"Okay, you have apologized," she said impatiently. "Now go back to the post."

Greenfield led her away from the back of the house into a cluster of hemlock conifers, away from any curious ears they might have awakened. He started by reminding her of his five-year quest to find Sasquatch, the creature she knew as Almasti, and the odd disappearances that coincided with the sightings. "You know I've been chasing these reports all over the world, the latest being the girl from Louisiana, Harry's friend. Her mother Christine Bennett went missing seven years ago and now it looks as if my friend Harry has too. Most victims have no memory of their abduction or what happened to them. Some recall bits and pieces weeks or months later. There were sightings of a tall hairy creature before the abductions. Mary Lynn's father had been tracking something very similar in the woods she was taken from. It was larger than a human or any species native to Louisiana or anywhere." Karma was avoiding looking him in the eye; in fact, she was looking everywhere else, the hut, the trees, and the shrubs beyond them. He found himself comparing her reaction to suspects he'd questioned before that lied by omission. Hers was the classic look of someone holding back. "You're in a losing battle, Karma. The world has discovered your unique and beautiful country. Tourists are coming here by the busloads. Your King is inviting modernization."

"I don't like it," she whispered. "I want things to be as they were. I wish your army would leave, and you with your questions."

"Karma, something strange is going on here. Inevitably, more people like me are going to notice. I'd like to get out in front of this if I can. There are people, families waiting for answers. Their lives are forever changed because of something that happened to them or because they lost someone dear to them. I feel like I'm closer than I've ever been to solving this mystery. Do you know anything that might help me give these people closure? Help me find out what's going on before a saber-rattling commander like Hanna does something stupid."

She took a deep breath and once again cast her eyes downward, this time as if beseeching spiritual guidance. "We are taught from birth not to talk about these things," she whispered. "We are profoundly indebted to the gods for choosing our mountains for their home and bestowing so many blessings on us. We are indebted to the monks who protect them." She secured the rachu with one hand and grabbed his arm with the other and pulled him deeper into the group of hemlocks. "They live within the highest peaks," she continued while darting her expressively fearful eyes back and forth to make sure no one was within hearing distance. "They are capable of miraculous deeds. It is said they can travel the world in an instant and can see the future. They could be here, listening right now. Legend states they are descendants of the Fallen, the gods that were cast out of heaven. They are known as the Nephilim. Monks living in the mountains gave them refuge thousands of years ago after they fled seeking isolation. The monks helped them reach enlightenment and become one with the gods again. I do not know exactly where, but it is said they live where no human can survive. No one I know has ever seen them; I had never seen them . . ." She quickly covered her mouth, holding her hand in place, over the rachu as if trying to resist a great temptation. ". . . until now," she whimpered as if her breath had been taken away. Tears filled her eyes as she took Bassui's blue Surface tablet out from under her kira and handed it to him. "It alerted when he was sleeping; I was coming outside to destroy it until I saw you crossing the road."

"What is it?" he asked, but she only shook her head as if ashamed.

"The gods might see . . . hear us," she finally whispered. She swayed back and forth fretfully and gripped her clothing nervously. "Please, don't look until you are far away from here; we never spoke...I must go. Good bye, John Greenfield."

"Karma, wait," he whispered and grabbed hold of her arm before she could escape the privacy of the trees. Her eyes expressed unbelievable fear. "What's wrong? Please, don't go until we can talk about this." He gently pulled the rachu from her face and wiped the stream of tears away with his fingers. He held her close to comfort her, but couldn't resist kissing her on the lips. She lingered and he felt her kiss him back. She started crying harder; he tightened his arms around her while she sobbed. A minute passed. John felt like he was in heaven, but the moment was cut short when she pushed herself away and covered her face and head with the rachu. He watched her trot back toward the hut, holding her head down and hiding her face. He was sure it was out of shame for what she told him, for giving him the Surface, for giving in to her passion. The hemline of her bulky ankle-length rectangular wrap, flit back and forth in rhythm with her steps. He watched until he lost sight of her when she turned the corner in front of the hut. He made his way back to the Humvee, trying to be as inconspicuous as when he sneaked in. He was anxious to see what Karma was so afraid to show him. The low battery warning in the upper right-hand corner of the screen flashed in red when he opened the cover. He tapped the email symbol anyway and found an email from Harry. In spite of the risk of losing power, he opened it. There was a photo attachment, a snapshot of Mary Lynn. "Proof of life," he whispered aloud inside the cold metal armored vehicle. She was looking over her shoulder at Harry. Apprehension, anxiety, or fear. He wasn't sure how to interpret her expression; her mouth was open that formed a half-smile, her arms swung out away from her sides. "What the hell?" he gasped under his breath when he realized there was a large hairy upright creature standing in the background. "My God!" he gasped after scrolling through the second and third attachment shots of the Bennett girl that included the unbelievable beast, although its entire physique was too large to fit the frames. It had on clothing made of animal hide and a thick cloak made of…*animal hair, takin hide*. "No!" he gasped, slamming the notebook closed. He stared into the darkness through the dusty bulletproof windshield, breathing as hard as if he'd been running. *Hanna can never see this*, was his first clear thought. The irrational commander would hunt it down and destroy it. *Nor Quantico*, at least not yet. He barely remembered the drive back to the post for trying to wrap his mind around the creature in the photos. He compared its large hairy appearance to every description, tearful interview, unbelievable statement, oversized footprint, and DNA analysis he'd studied and restudied for the past five years. *Could whatever-the-hell that is be the answer to one of the world's most elusive mysteries?* He thought about Karma, his beautiful Karma. Was this monstrous upright animal the basis of her deep religious fervor; was it worthy of her devotion and the monk's protection? How many are there? Why do they abduct people? Are the orphans their offspring, what if they are? Victims had dreams of being prodded; did that mean their eggs were being harvested? Investigators concluded they were mere dreams; because they showed no physical signs of what they described. He thought about the crew of the Augusta, himself and Harry. Everyone returned intact and alive in spite of being tossed violently from the sky and suffering from some sort of post-traumatic stress. Quantico had put the team together after one of their geeks gave a compelling PowerPoint presentation suggesting an eighty percent possibility that a small number of missing and outlandish accounts coincided with Sasquatch sightings. Another thread tying this together was the Rh factor the abductees carried. Cdr. Hanna couldn't care less about research and would shoot whatever he considered an adversary first and leave the glossing over of the facts to someone else. Greenfield wore the same blinders for most of his career. Answers to why a perpetrator would rob, rape, or kill came after their capture, unless the suspect decided they'd rather die than face the truth. Experience taught him the most complicated cases came down to the simplest of truths; someone had cheated or lied, stolen or disrespected. Perhaps it was the near-death experience in the out-of-control helicopter or, as Fisher put it, the people of Bhutan had rubbed off on him. It was more likely his attraction to Karma and his desire to please her that kept him thinking about getting back to that fateful ledge, to find a reasonable explanation for the orphans and to make sure no harm came to her gods.

***

The threesome found James waiting for them inside Mary Lynn's apartment. All the paintings and sculpted artwork were gone. Furniture from the two rooms was shoved to the middle of the main living room. An easy chore for any Nephilim. "I understand your confusion, Mother." James stood in front of the pile of furniture with the white Bible resting in his palm. It looked like a novel-sized book in comparison. His voice touched on sadness for having to deny his mother. "You are conflicted. You want to go with Prana, wherever that might be, and yet you want to stay with us. But whatever you decide, it will be without this."

"James." Christine looked up at him with imploring eyes because she knew he was considering placing the book she labored over for years deep within the pile that was to be left behind and burned. She had hoped to teach from it someday, to pass it on to her daughter so she could do the same.

"I'm considering destroying it," James said, confirming her fear.

Harry placed a protective hand on Mary Lynn's shoulder, afraid for her safety when Christine rushed closer to James to plead her case.

"It could be reproduced, circulated," Christine argued, "planting a seed in the mind of each person that reads about the Nephilim. The suggestion that you have existed since the beginning of time will prepare people for the day when the actual discovery is made. James, the foreboding we've both been feeling is a warning."

Her gargantuan son was silent, but his thoughts told her that he was considering the case she had presented.

"The day is nearing," she continued. "Look at what's happening right now. It's foolish to think you can remain hidden forever. Eventually there will be nowhere to hide. The book will help introduce you to the world."

"Mother." Mary Lynn took a step toward the arguing pair. Harry tried to hold her back but she shook free. "Not all people can be trusted to do the right thing; you'll be labeled a fanatic."

"Yes, I would be ridiculed, scorned, maybe even killed. That's the reason for the indecision you sense, James. I've prayed about it. It's my burden to bear. I am not afraid. I've learned a lot about bravery from you and your father."

"And what did my father have to say about this idea? That's what I thought," he said when she hesitated. "He disagrees. It's decided, you and the book will stay." He pulled his arm in close to his chest, folding the book within his hefty hand. Then he turned his head and looked suspiciously at Harry. "You have brought an item into our home that is not permitted. Give me the device."

"Device?" Harry whispered nervously.

"The cell phone, please." James bent down, lowering his free hand to within an inch of Harry's chest. "Just because we don't use them doesn't mean we don't know about them and how they are used."

Harry quickly pulled the slender phone from his back pocket and placed it across the broad rough palm. James curled his fingers around the phone, tightened his fist, and crushed it, leaving little doubt in Harry's mind what could happen to his own insignificant frame if the gentle but mighty giant chose to do so. He watched as broken pieces protruded between his fingers and then fell to the floor. James threw the remains still in his hand into the pile of furniture and then raised his chin; he seemed to be eyeing Harry's backpack. "Do you want this too?" He slid a strap down one arm.

"No," James replied. "There's nothing in it that can harm us."

Christine fell to her knees in disappointment. Her hair came loose; its gray and crimson streaks spread across her back and shoulders. At least he hadn't thrown the book into the pile.

Harry turned away to catch his breath, grateful to have been spared the same fate as the phone. There was no way of knowing if the pictures he took went anywhere. They were up too high for normal cell reception and deep within mountain walls. He headed to the bay window; Mary Lynn followed him.

"Amazing, isn't it?" Mary Lynn whispered over his shoulder when she saw him staring at the splendid crests that seemed to go on forever. "It took my breath away the first time I saw it."

There was no reference for knowing how high up they were. They were above the peaks of a chain of mountains. Everything was white. "I understand why it's been so hard to breathe; I thought it was anxiety. Mary Lynn . . ." he began but she interrupted him.

"I was just as overwhelmed when I looked out this window for the first time." She wrapped her arms around his waist and put her head against his chest. "Your heart is strong and soothing to my soul."

"Having you in my arms is all that matters." Harry closed his eyes. Nothing could interrupt his happiness right now; not even Christine who was still trying to convince James that her plan could work.

"I know what it took for you to find me," she sighed.

"Is my heart telling you that?" he asked and kissed the top of her head. They held each other close while staring at the mesmerizing snowy crests until they realized that Christine and James were no longer arguing. They both turned around; Christine was kneeling on the floor wiping tears from her cheeks with the backs of her hands. James was gone.

"He doesn't understand!" she sobbed. "The Nephilim could have a place in the world."

Mary Lynn broke from Harry's arms to go to her mother but stopped short when something outside caught her eyes. "Look, an avalanche!"

"And over there too!" Harry pointed to another crest that looked like it was separating in slow motion. "Beautiful, and yet so destructive."

Mary Lynn knelt down beside Christine. "Mother, we should go to the tunnels now." She looked up at Harry when the mountain shook so hard that she had to brace herself against the floor.

"Ms. Christine," Harry pleaded. "Please, we have to go now."

"That's just Kokabiel implementing tactical moves." She stood and dusted off the skirt of her robes. "It's a diversion they use to discourage climbers and other intruders. The army must be getting closer."

"Mother, forget about the book." Mary Lynn took her mother's arm. "Let's get out of here. Let's go home."

The walls shook again. Snow piled against the window, sending two long vein-like cracks across the thick panes.

"I'll go with you as far as the mezzanine and point you in the right direction from there." She took Mary Lynn's hand. "I'm sorry sweetheart, but I must stay and talk to Kokabiel. He must allow you to have a copy of the Bible. You can't tell people about us without it. Besides, I can't . . . I won't leave without your father's blessing. He's always been supportive of my genetics methods. And there's more work to be done. Al never understood how much I loved the research I was doing in the lab at Woodlands. He didn't . . . we weren't . . ." She couldn't find the right words to describe what was wrong with the marriage. "Saying we weren't compatible just sounds cliché. The effort here to integrate the Nephilim DNA into the world population was something I couldn't resist. In fact, the whole Nephilim colony fascinated me beyond my wildest dreams."

"Genetics methods," Harry said as they rushed to the door when the walls vibrated again. "Does that have anything to do with the orphans; the ones that live at the monastery?"

"I was introduced to genetic manipulation while at the fish hatchery," Christine said as Harry pulled on the door that seemed to be jammed, perhaps misaligned because of the avalanches. "Kokabiel had been observing my work long before he showed himself to me. Instead of plucking me up in the middle of the night like so many of the others with the Rh factor, he took the time to discuss the nominal success midwives were having harvesting and implanting eggs. I offered my help."

"James and I were created by using IVF?" Mary Lynn asked. Her mother silently nodded *yes*.

Harry finally freed the door and they rushed into the hallway.

"I don't belong here, Mother. Neither do you, but if you insist on staying, please get word to Kunchen. Thank him for me. I'll try and use what he taught me to the best of my ability."

"We need you, Prana," Christine said with urgency as if trying to convince her to stay. "You are a most gifted healer. Perhaps the best. The way you healed that boy's burns was like nothing I've ever seen."

"You have other healers. I'd rather not be part of what you're doing here," she said, looking at Harry. "Although, I suppose I already am," she added.

***

Greenfield turned on the battery-powered lamp hanging from a snap hook over Harry's cot. He found the power cord he was looking for on the floor after shaking out his sleeping bag. He sat on the edge of the canvas bed and watched the charging bars in the upper right corner float up and down. Two months ago, he would have been ecstatic about being this close to concluding the team's mission. The project was into its fifth year and was scoffed by everyone as a lost cause from the first day of its inception. Claims it was a waste of taxpayer's money crossed everyone's minds and lips at one time or another. He only took the job because he was jaded by three failed relationships, tired of hunting down psychos and lowlife's and saw too many fellow officers die in the field or crumble to alcoholism or drugs under the weight of PTSD. He supposed he was trying to salvage a piece of himself when he agreed to make the lateral move to the low-key, seemingly non-essential taskforce. Decades of information, collected from implausible witnesses, unauthenticated photographs, and fragments of problematic physical evidence had been compared, collated, and analyzed in a database run by a quartet of unkempt nerds. His duties seemed easy enough; re-interview witnesses and analyze their accounts from a seasoned detective's perspective. Hunting down the dog's blood sample had inadvertently put him at the scene of a kidnapping that got more interesting when hair samples collected turned out to be that of a takin. The detective in him suddenly sparked to life. The disrespected assignment had suddenly taken on legs. The mastiff and the goat were both native to Bhutan. It was the first substantial evidence produced in all of his five years with the team.

He picked up the Surface to check the charge. It was at forty-percent. Two more emails from Harry with photo attachments were in the queue waiting to be opened. The giant's full physique was visible in the next batch, along with another woman walking beside Mary Lynn just ahead of Harry. They appeared to be walking through excavated stone hallways. There was a shot where he was looking down on a room where women were milling around a fireplace . . . giant women. Photos of giant creatures on file at the FBI, that most people referred to as Sasquatch, were taken so far away that no one knew for certain if the objects were real or a photo-shopped rendering. He had a decision to make: what to do with the images. Cdr. Hanna would consider the creatures a threat and bypass any protocol regarding peaceful first contact. The monk's holy buildings would be invaded. He would push anyone who got in his way to one side, whether it be monks or the faithful of Bhutan. The sight of them would blow his mind; he'd lose all reasoning, interpret them as extremists, and hunt them with everything at his disposal. Until someone came along that could take charge of the situation with diplomacy, the only way to protect the creatures, the people of Bhutan and the monks for now, was to delete the emails and their attachments and not breathe a word of what he knew to anyone.

"There," he whispered to himself after completing the deletion process. As he sat there on the cot staring at the thin silent curser, he thought of one person who deserved to be told the truth. After taking a deep breath and expelling a long lamenting sigh, he pressed Al's contact number.

"What time is it there, Al?" he asked when the old man answered.

"Afternoon." The old man thought the agent's voice sounded uncharacteristically wounded, defeated. Al tried to prepare himself for the words he feared from the first day he was told his daughter was missing, that she was dead. He sat down on one of the bar-stools in the kitchen, leaned his head against his fist and closed his eyes. "Please, just tell me. I don't want to hear no small talk."

"Well. . ." there were a few seconds of hesitation that seemed to take hours. "I know where she is; she's alive. Harry's with her; he sent me a picture of her. They're in the mountains. I haven't quite figured out how I'm going to get them out of there yet. An order of monks controls whoever comes and goes up there and . . . well . . . all I can say for now is I'm working on it."

"Sounds like there's somethin' you ain't wantin' to say. Was it the monks that took her?"

"Before I pressed your number, I was thinking about a couple of guys I met up in Washington State. That's where I was when I got the email to check out the blood sample from a dog in Louisiana. It's the looks on their faces that I've never been able to get out of my head when I told them the hair samples we collected were of a brown bear. They took me out to their favorite place to hunt and cut firewood, the place where they claimed to see something, a Sasquatch. They said they could communicate with it. The three of us went up there and they took me to this stand of large redwoods. One of them picked up a piece of split wood. He hit it against one of the trees three times. Nothing happened, so he hit it against the tree two more times, and then we heard a sound in the distance. Do you know what a pile driver sounds like when it hits the ground?" He didn't wait for Al to answer. "Well, that's what it sounded like . . . two pounding noises. He asked me to try; I did. I hit the tree three times. The pile driver sound answered with three strokes. I couldn't explain it, no one could. They didn't believe me when I told them the results. Immediately, without hesitation, they both shook their heads and said it didn't matter. They knew what they saw."

"Why are you telling me this story?" Al whispered.

"Because Harry sent more than the one picture of your daughter. Some were of giant humanoid-looking creatures that wear clothes made of animal hide and fur. The look on their faces was the first thing that flashed in my head when I realized what I was looking at; it was their Sasquatch. I don't know who to trust with this. The post commander is squirrelly. He'll send a detail up there with rockets blazing. I deleted the pictures."

"Good choice; he'd kill my daughter and Harry. Damn! Wish I could be there to help you. Guess I need to do some prayin'. I say that cuz I been spendin' a little time readin' one of Christine's Bibles I found on a shelf in our closet. Thanks for bein' honest with me. I know you didn't have to tell me anything and probably ain't s'posed to."

"Praying might be a good idea, Al. Might be the reason I called. This is a delicate situation and I'm in need of some extraordinary help." He heard hammering in the background on Al's end. "Is someone there with you?"

"Oh, you hear that?" Al tried to sound testy, but a bit of pride slipped through. "Dale's here helpin' me do some fixin' up on the house. It's givin' us both somethin' to do while we wait. We're tryin' to get it finished by Christmas. My daughter-in-law and two grandkids are comin' in a couple weeks. I ain't never met them before."

"That sounds great, Al. I hope . . . I wish . . . I'd like to make it an even better Christmas for you . . . I just can't promise. . ."

"I know." He paused for a second. "Hey, listen, I was wonderin', do you think I could have Mary Lynn's pink tennis shoes? They were her favorite and, well, I'd like to have them . . . to give back to her when, if she comes home."

"I'll have someone bring them to you."

Chapter 19

"Sir, sir!" Lt. Fisher joggled Greenfield awake by repeatedly poking his shoulder.

"Wha-what? Stop!" he moaned, squinting into the light of her LED flashlight while swatting at her hand. He quickly sat up and swung his legs over the side of Harry's cot. Something serious must have happened for her to be so unrelenting. She was dressed in full combat gear with her helmet tucked under her arm.

"What is it?"

"I've been looking for you everywhere; thought you should know. Cdr. Hanna is conducting more strikes."

"Where?" he moaned.

"At higher altitudes than before; it's been going on since 0400." She saw him pick up the blue notebook from the floor underneath Harry's bunk when she tried to hand him a cup of coffee she had picked up for him in the mess tent. "What's that?"

"Nothing," he grunted. "What are your orders?"

I'm part of a drop team assigned to go in after each assault to look for . . . um . . . remains." She punched her vest with her knuckles. It made a knocking sound. "The shield is in case we run into hostile survivors."

"I hope the hell you don't find the bodies of innocent monks and shepherds." *Or Harry and the Bennett girl.*

"Me too, sir."

Smoke that looked like tornado funnels trailed upward in the sky behind Greenfield as he raced through the tent rows headed to the command center. The hub was bustling with movement. A few uniformed personnel were standing at white-boards drawing lines from one point to another. Most were talking back and forth over headsets. One got up quickly from his chair and rushed over to place a note in front of Hanna who was standing in front of a map pinned to the wall. The commander had a Combat Net Radio in one hand and headphones cocked to cover only one ear. ISR video was running on a laptop on a table just below the map. Greenfield paused at the sand box. All the sand-colored markers were on their sides, meaning Hanna had accomplished his search and destroy mission throughout the lower levels. The two fuzzy black markers set in the foam block mountains were still upright.

"Is the operation over?" Greenfield asked.

"You know it's not," Hanna replied without turning around. "Not until I take care of what attacked you and my men."

"You're not sending airships?"

Hanna turned his head. His eyes followed the agent's arm down to the standing markers. "Something on that ledge attacked you," he snarled. "*If* you remember. We're scanning the landscape now to see what turns up."

"ISIS militants can't be up that high." It was obvious the post commander was anxious to get back to the map. "Nothing can live up there this time of year except for mountain goats."

"You told me you thought Foster and the missing girl were up there."

"That's the best reason not to go up there with guns blazing," the agent said, stepping closer.

"Stop right there." Hanna took a few steps toward the agent and planted his fists on his hips. "Save your breath FBI. We never stopped accessing the boy's emails. Yeah, that's right; we have the images Foster sent. DOD has priority over your little team at Quantico and the authority to do whatever it feels necessary when a threat to national security is imminent."

"Who's national security? Bhutan is the only nation at risk here, from you."

"Everybody's security asshole . . . the whole world."

"I'm sure you had a hand in convincing DOD that killing this race of people was the only way to save the world."

"Don't tell me those images didn't scare the hell out of you."

"The locals call them Nephilim. They're an ancient race of people that have brought no harm to the Bhutanese. The locals consider them deities. You came here to remove ISIS sympathizers from Bhutan, not their gods."

"Those monsters aren't gods. What's wrong with you FBI? You've been drinking the native Kool-Aid?"

"You made your case to the King about ISIS. You need to present him with one about the Nephilim and see what he says."

"Humph!" he grunted. "I leave negotiating to the generals." He turned his attention to a laptop to see what he's missed during their discussion.

"Drop me and Lt. Fisher on that ledge. I'll take those damn pills if I have to. Just get us up there. I made a promise to Al that I'd do everything I could to bring his daughter home. I think his wife Christine was in one of Foster's photos. Other missing civilians could be there . . . US citizens."

"Do you hear yourself, FBI?" the commander howled, not taking his attention off the video. "You just got through saying these *things* are responsible for kidnapping the girl, her mother, and who knows how many others. Maybe I'll get lucky and capture one of them, and then you can ask it yourself why it abducts innocent civilians."

"You'll never find them," Greenfield said. "They'll leave, go somewhere else, and I'll have to start over. They will defend themselves if forced to; I don't think you're not prepared for them." He turned and left the tent to seek out Lt. Fisher.

***

Kokabiel's size and stance exemplified the elder's worthiness of respect and fear. The trio had made it halfway down the hallway to the lift when the fearsome-looking Nephilim appeared, blocking their way. The man was a substantial blockade, with broad shoulders and a mighty girth. James resembled his father, except for the white hair and aged face creased with lines, etching him as permanently annoyed. Forged armor covered his hide clothing and creaked when he stepped forward. He had armored forearms and held a wide pointed shaft of hardened wood in one hand that was nearly as long as he was tall. He pounded it on the ground with each step, making Harry's nerve endings spark. "Where do you think you're going?" His plangent voice caused something to vibrate loose from the ceiling somewhere behind them and crash to the floor. No one looked to see what it was. Harry cautiously grabbed Mary Lynn's arm, while they stood frozen in place.

"Kokabiel, you know who this is," Christine said, breaking the silence.

Harry moved in front of Mary Lynn to shield her from the giant when he lowered his head to focus his dark orbs on her.

"I do." His voice was gut-wrenching. The demands of hierarchy had made it coarse and deep. "I'm sorry this did not work out the way you had hoped, Christine," he said, straightening his back and raising his chin. "But I warned you this would happen."

Christine anxiously grabbed hold of Kokabiel's staff and pulled on it. "Kunchen bestowed her with the name Prana. She's already proven worthy of the name. I witnessed it for myself. And this young man," she looked at Harry and then back up at Kokabiel, "he loves her deeply, he will help her deal with the responsibility she carries. You know what I'm saying is true." Christine and Kokabiel stared at each other for a whole thirty-seconds that seemed much longer. Their expressions flexed as if they were carrying on a silent conversation. Maybe he was considering her words and would let them go. Harry slowly stepped backward a fraction of an inch at a time herding Mary Lynn along with him towards the doorway leading to the stairwell.

Kokabiel suddenly addressed Mary Lynn, startling them to a standstill. "What do you have to say, Prana?"

"I didn't ask to be brought here," she replied quickly.

Harry's throat was too dry to speak. Mary Lynn's first instinct to be defiant broke through this time but it was minus the typical emotional outburst. She didn't take her eyes off the giant who looked perturbed over her brashness.

"I've always been different, restless, reluctant to commit to anything because of my oddities," she continued. "I came to realize my calling to be a nurse on my own. That's what humans do." She looked at her mother. "I don't want to lose the things I learned from Kunchen, nor do I want to forget my heritage. I want to remember seeing my mother again and meeting James and . . ." she looked up at Kokabiel. ". . . you, Father. Part of me wants to stay and get to know you. However, my roots are in the place where I grew up, where my values were formed. I can only hope to make a small difference there."

Kokabiel remained judgingly silent.

Christine pulled on the staff. "Isn't she beautiful? She's going to make us proud, Kokabiel."

"You may go," he finally said. "I will know if you so much as whisper our name, or compromise our safety." His voice was calm but his brow was deeply trenched.

Harry pulled Mary Lynn by the arm through the doorway.

They stopped and looked at each other when they reached the landing and then looked up and down the carved-out hollow stone shaft.

"I suppose down would be the way out," Harry said.

"Why in God's name didn't you take them to safety?" Christine scolded.

"She made her choice," Kokabiel replied harshly. "I must warn you in advance, the outcome does not look good for them. It is between her and the gods now."

Christine turned toward the door to follow them, to warn them that the odds of survival were against them. Kokabiel went down on one knee, grabbed her up and they vanished.

"I can't believe he just let us go." Harry's voice echoed throughout the vertical tubular well. "And I remember everything," he said, referring to how he, John, and the crew of the Augusta were cast out of the sky and their struggle afterward to remember how the plane ended up on the ground or the reason for the mission. He noticed Mary Lynn looking back at the doorway behind them. "I know you don't want to leave her," he said, trying to be sympathetic.

"They're already gone; Kokabiel has taken her to the tunnels," she sighed. "He let us go because . . . well, I'm being tested; to see if I can get us out of here safely."

"Some father," he said, shaking his head. "I'm still trying to wrap my mind around how he can possibly be your father. They know about artificial insemination?"

"Apparently. And it sounds like my mother is helping the other healers do it."

Harry closed his arms around her. "Healers. It sounds impossible, but I saw what you can do."

Mary Lynn looked back toward the door again. If only her mother would appear on the landing, if only she would choose to come with them.

"Listen, I have a feeling you're going to see her again someday."

"She left us for this place a long time ago and didn't come back. She wasn't kidnapped, this is where she wants to be."

"But she did come back," Harry said. "Remember the night you destroyed the china cabinet? Remember the blanket I found you holding the next morning on the back porch? John had it analyzed; its weave is from goat hair. You were brought here from Louisiana by some incredible means, so it's obvious there's a way to travel back and forth; there's no telling how many times she visited without you even knowing."

She squeezed her eyes closed. "If I could only find the right prayer to make this end well."

"Let's find our way out of here and go home," Harry said.

They proceeded down the stairs, checking the hallways at each landing, finding nothing to make them think it was a way out.

"I don't guess the monks taught you how to blink your eyes, nod, and then, *whoosh* we'd be home. We could use a little help about now." Harry made a long exhale when they sat down after descending twenty flights. He cushioned his body against the backpack and leaned his head against the wall. The altitude and vigorous movement were affecting his breathing and equilibrium.

"I guess Kunchen didn't have enough time to teach me how to be a genie," she said with a grin.

Harry smiled as he watched her play with her hair, twist it into a knot, and make a ponytail. He'd seen her do this a thousand times; now he was savoring the moment. "You can work on your 'Jeannie' skills after we get home."

"I have visions, Harry," she said wrapping her hands around her knees. "Like the ones I had of you. And I can hear what people are thinking sometimes. Empathy always came naturally, and it's mostly why I became a nurse. Seeing things in colors was just an indicator of what I'm capable of. Kunchen taught me exercises, mental exercises that have enabled me to unlock more of what I was born with."

They felt a jolt. Mary Lynn reached for the edge of the step to keep from sliding to one side but she missed and fell against the wall. Harry tried to stand but was forced to his knees when the mountain suddenly felt like a wave and rolled up and down. Rocks rained all around them, including large pieces that fell with a whoosh down the middle of the stairwell, dragging sections of railing down with them. They scrambled through the next doorway. The situation wasn't much better in the great room they found themselves in. Film-like dust hung in the air making it difficult to see. A boulder fell from somewhere above, smashing to the ground in front of them, sending shards in every direction. They managed to duck out of the way of the rock fragments and ran along the edge of the wall until the quaking stopped.

"I wonder if this is more of your father's tactics, or . . .?" Harry was huffing, gasping from the silt and thin air. He looked back; Mary Lynn was on her knees. "What's wrong, are you hurt?"

Her arms extended as if she was reaching for something; her eyes were closed. "That way," she said and pointed ahead. "There's an opening; it will not free us, but it will let in air."

"We can use your scarf to make a signal." Harry helped her to her feet and watched her move slowly ahead of him. "John will have the army use their intelligence surveillance to find us."

"It should be right here," she said, after creeping along for about fifty yards.

"Here?" he asked, looking at the solid wall. He pounded the hard rock with the heel of his hand.

"It's here," she said. "I'm sure of it." She placed her palms on the stone. "I can feel the ice on the other side."

The mountain started to shake again. Harry pulled her under a rock shelf where they hunkered with their arms over their heads while rocks poured down outside the small shelter. It was even harder to breathe now. Harry covered both their faces with the skirt of Mary Lynn's robe to keep from choking on the debris that was slowly sealing them in. The rumbling and shuddering went on for five minutes. When the quaking finally stopped, they pushed and shoved against the packed rubble with their hands and feet until they were able to make an opening big enough to squeeze through. Harry made bandanas to cover their faces with ripped strips from her robe.

"Look, daylight!" Harry shouted; his voice muffled by the bandana. They stumbled through mounds of litter to get to the slither of light in the tall vertical crack.

"Let me go first." Harry scaled a number of large rocks to get closer to the slit. "The fresh air feels great," he said, pulling down the kerchief.

Mary Lynn carefully followed him to the three-foot-wide passageway. "Harry, we're alone," she whispered after pulling down her mask. "I mean, they've gone."

"Everyone?" he asked. "James, your father, Christine?"

"Yes, everyone."

"How could so many leave so fast?" He reminded himself that James had carried them to the mountains instantaneously from the Dzong without so much as a flutter. He retrieved the boy with the burned leg just as promptly. "You'd think they could have taken a minute to deposit us down the mountain somewhere. How many Nephilim are there? Do you know where they went?"

She shook her head. "A couple of thousand. They went somewhere like this . . . uninhabitable."

"Thousands!" he sighed. "That's quite a feat, to move that many people in so short a time. Stay here." The space was narrow so he slid the backpack off his shoulders and lay it beside her. "I'm gonna take a look."

"Don't go out there!" she shouted, but he was already inside the crevasse and couldn't hear because of the blaring snowstorm raging outside. She sat down on a nearby rock, folded her legs, and closed her eyes. The broken mountain became silent around her; the sifting walls ceased sprinkling its powder. *Holy God, my father,* she prayed silently, *Kokabiel is testing me to see if I can survive on my own. I am not afraid of transitioning from this life to the next. But, please, please spare Harry.* When Harry touched her shoulder, it was as if he had awakened her from a long nap.

"Where were you?" he asked. "You looked a million miles away."

Without answering, she got up and stepped into the passageway.

"Wait, didn't you hear me? The wind is blowing fifty miles an hour out there," he shouted while climbing after her. "There's no way down. We're still too high." He was doing his best to yell over the wind but she continued to walk all the way to the edge. Was she walking in her sleep? Should he risk startling her? The tips of her sandals extended over the icy edge. "The face is a straight drop. We have to find another . . ." His voice was drowned out by a roaring sound . . . a helicopter, and then he heard *rat-a-tat*, like automatic gunfire. "Get back!" He reached out to her with his hand, but she paid no attention; she was staring, concentrating in the direction of the noise. A yellow hue formed twenty feet from the edge out in front of her. It conjoined with the moist white wind creating a swath of icy daggers. The blustering gale picked up the nebula and carried it away. The helicopter's motor and the rat-a-tat ceased. "What did you do?"

"I sent the storm in their direction," she said eerily as she slowly turned around. "But more are coming."

"That means we'll be rescued . . . right? We should put out the signal." They were standing in sub-zero temperature. Mary Lynn's expression morphed to distress. Tears trickled down her face and froze to her cheeks.

"They're coming to kill us," she whimpered.

"Come on." Harry pulled her away from the edge. "Let's go back inside. You're in shock. God knows I'm doing everything I can to hold it together."

"Harry, you understand what Kokabiel being my father means?" she said when they were back inside and sitting under the rock shelf trying to warm themselves.

"I do. Well, trying to, it's all pretty incredible." He huddled close to her and rubbed her arms and legs.

"And James is my step-brother. He's the baby that Mother lost two years before I was born; everyone thought she miscarried. She had an option with me, because I was more like her. I saw it all in her eyes when we were walking together to the lift. Children from every part of the world have been born here. The boys are educated by monks; girls like me are home-schooled by Mother and the other women. Many are sent to live in the villages; some have migrated to other countries. She convinced Kokabiel to let me grow up at home. Harry, I'm never going to be normal."

"Normal," Harry sighed. He smiled and pulled her closer. "You have found your normal, Mary Lynn. The colors, the weird feelings were your normal. Whatever you're feeling now, that's your normal, and it's okay."

"Thank you, Harry," she whispered. "For understanding, for being my only true friend." She couldn't take her eyes off his. Her mind's eye could see that his words, his feelings were pure. She lifted her hand and touched the side of his face. He put his hand behind her neck. Their lips were almost touching, and then they kissed.

"Harry," she whispered. "What took you so long? I don't mean to rescue me." She meant why it took him so long to let his feelings show.

"I was afraid of losing you. I couldn't admit it, even to myself. If you didn't feel the same, then things would be awkward; you would've avoided me. I couldn't take that. But when I thought I lost you, or worse, that someone might be hurting you, there was no more denying how important you are to me."

"What about now, after everything you've seen?"

"You're seeing colors never scared me away. This only proves how amazing you are; something I've always known."

As they embraced, she sensed his feelings were indeed greater than his words could describe. She squeezed her eyes closed, but couldn't erase the vision that came to her when she was standing on the edge of the icy cliff that felt like the edge of the world. Death was coming. The vision brought her to tears. She saw Harry being pummeled underneath hundreds of boulders, buried, bleeding from internal wounds, suffocating.

The roar of another Augusta interrupted the disturbing scene in her head. "They're back . . . to kill us."

"Let's find that lift," Harry said. "If we go deep enough, they can't track us with their infrared. Just pray the mountain doesn't fall down on us."

His words astounded her. Had he read her thoughts? How could she lose him before they had a chance to start their new journey together? Her heart felt heavy; she couldn't budge. Harry had to pull her along by the hand.

"Why are they shooting at us?" she asked, looking back over her shoulder.

"They think we're ISIS terrorists. The post commander is hell-bent on snuffing out every one he finds."

The lift door was lying on the ground outside the shaft opening. The wood plank floor was still intact, as well as one wall. A rope was tied to the slat ceiling and dangled over the edge. When Harry yanked on it, the lift swayed.

"Harry, stop," Mary Lynn gasped. "The rope is all that's keeping the lift from falling."

"Yeah, that's not good," he sighed.

"We should look for another way," she moaned.

"Let me try something." He pulled as hard as he could on the rope; it swung free. "Hop in; I'll get in at the same time and hold onto the rope to control the descent."

"I absolutely don't know who you are," she sighed. "I never saw you consider anything so risky before."

"I'll be right behind you," he said, loosening the knot and grinning at her. "Let's see how far down this thing will take us." He wrapped the rope around his right arm.

Harry felt the weight of her body affect the rope's tension as soon as she stepped inside. The lift immediately began to drop. Harry pulled as hard as he could, but the weight of the battered cage was too great and slammed him against the rickety ceiling. He pushed flat footed against the top, straightening his legs. The lift slowed. "I think I've got it," he

said, looking down at Mary Lynn who had been thrown to the
floor and was now braced against the one wall. "Now, I just
need to let go a little at a time."

"I hope the rope is long enough," Mary Lynn said,
crawling to her knees.

Harry unwound the rope from his arm and gripped it with
both hands. He was still upside-down with his feet against the
ceiling. He released the rope an inch at a time until he felt
confident enough to allow more.

"Is there something I can do," Mary Lynn asked.

"Pray," he said with a half-smile.

She could hear the strain in his voice from trying to
control the full weight of the lift plus the two of them.

Harry suddenly flipped upright when the lift jerked to a
stop, and then it abruptly started to plunge. The lifeline slipped
off his arm but a knot at the end of the rope caught between
two of the slats, holding the crate suspended. He welcomed
the relief to his arm, but then the slats pulled apart and the
rope flew up whipping past him. Just as the lift began to
plummet into a free fall, a large pulley came crashing through
what was left of the splintered ceiling. There was nothing to
be said; they knew what was about to happen. They sat in one
corner of the lift wrapped in each other's arms. Mary Lynn
buried her head in Harry's chest and began a prayer. Harry
squeezed her tight and closed his eyes. Of all things, one of
Al's sayings came to his mind . . . *It's not the fall that kills
you; it's the sudden stop.*

Harry opened his eyes to look at his love for the last time.
He felt euphoric, like he was floating instead of falling. They
were turning as if on a slow-motion Lazy Susan. Mary Lynn
was chanting lowly to herself with her eyes closed. She
loosened her arms from around him and they each floated
freely facing each other. A pale-yellow hue surrounded them
like a bubble. He tried to reason what was happening but
somehow it didn't matter. Maybe they were already in heaven.
He remembered hearing a near-death expert on TV say that

souls held on to pleasant memories in order to make the transition easier. He would certainly love to arrive in heaven with her in his arms. He felt his boots touch the ground, his knees jutted up and his butt thump on the stone floor. He lifted his head after rolling over on his side. The lift and pulley were lying in six inches of soot. Their touchdown created a plume of dust around them at the bottom of the dark shaft. Broken pieces of the lift were scattered everywhere in the sediment.

"Mary Lynn," he choked. He pulled the bandana up over his nose and mouth. "Mary Lynn, are you alright?" He spotted her silhouette through the haze. "There you are," his voice graveled. He crawled through the rubble to where she was sitting upright with her eyes closed. She was covered in dust, her legs folded in front of her with her arms out, palms up. He wasn't sure she could hear him. "Mary Lynn," he whispered. "Let's go." He could see a light shining down from around the corner of a crude spiral staircase. He helped her to her feet. She looked dazed and didn't have the strength to walk. He picked her up and carried her up the stairs toward the light. "We have to find air," he said while navigating the uneven steps with her in his arms. After a couple of turns, he found a small crack in the wall that was filled with ice. "Ice: damn, we're still up too high." He sat her down on a step. He felt for the straps to the backpack, but it was gone. "I'm going back down to look for the backpack or try and find something sharp to break the ice with." He was relieved to see her look up at him with a little more clarity.

"Don't go." She gripped his camo sleeve with her fist. "I'm beginning to doubt that I can save us, Harry. Maybe Kokabiel is right. Maybe I'm not strong enough."

"Of course, you are. We're gonna be okay. Sit tight, I'll be right back."

Chapter 20

"We're approaching the coordinates, sir," Lt. Fisher's voice reported to Agent Greenfield over the headset inside his helmet. Cdr. Hanna had approved her request to take Greenfield along on the search for signs of life. "Should be right down there on your right."

"I don't see a thing," his voice came back after scanning the wall of snow below them. "Where's the ledge? We must be in the wrong place; I'll bet Hanna gave you the wrong coordinates on purpose."

"I checked it myself; we're over the exact longitude and latitude where the incident took place," she shouted, competing with the roar of the engine turning the rotors above their heads. "There's been a lot of seismic activity here in the past few days."

"What does that mean?" the agent grumbled.

"Avalanches," she came back through the headset. "Our operations could likely be the cause. Huge layers of snow and ice have been breaking free all over up here. Whatever was there before has probably been covered by ice and snow. I'm not getting anything on infrared."

"How are we supposed to find them?" he shouted.

"We can do a visual search." They looked at each other through their face shields, knowing it was most likely going to be a fruitless attempt. "Until we get low on fuel, that is. Then we'll have to return to the post," she added.

***

Harry returned with the rope looped over his shoulder, the pulley on one arm and holding a piece of wood with a sharp end. "I thought maybe I could use this to . . ." Mary Lynn wasn't where he left her. She was standing in front of the icy cleft in the wall. "You okay?" he asked and carefully put down the materials he'd gathered.

"I feel helpless," she sighed. "Kunchen never told me how to change the future."

Harry rushed to her and grabbed her arms, turning her away from the crack in the wall. "You don't have to do anything," he whispered. "I found some stuff to help me punch through the ice."

"Harry, when we were falling, I felt like I was sitting with Kunchen in the temple. Everything slowed down and I felt calm and light." Her eyes suddenly found his. "If I could just get to that place again, maybe I could save . . . save us. But I can't seem to find it . . . oh Harry," she sobbed, "I can't find it. I have failed us . . . you."

Harry pulled her in close and held her while she cried. He looked down at her. Her eyes were even more luminous through the tears. "I know it was you that slowed our fall." He brushed her tears away with his hand. "It must have taken everything you had to do that. You're exhausted. You should sit; rest and regain your strength." He nodded to the large step behind her. "Don't think about anything; I'll try and get some air in here."

After twenty-minutes of determined chipping with the board, Harry managed to trowel through four foot of ice but still hadn't broken through. He sat down on the step next to Mary Lynn to catch his breath. "This is harder than I thought."

"Sit here next to me for a while," she said and put her head on his shoulder.

"Okay, but I'm gonna breach that baby," he said, nodding at the gouges he'd made in the icy wall. "There's my girl," he said when he saw her smile. He gently kissed her lips.

"You always could make me smile when things seemed the darkest," she said, after kissing him back. "You look like you could use some water. No point in wasting all that ice; it should be safe to drink. I think I saw something that resembled a bowl back there." She looked down at the dark curved steps. "I feel better now," she assured him when she sensed his concern. "Here, take this." She slipped the yellow rachu from her shoulders and handed it to him. You can tie this to the end of the board and flag someone down after you break through." She handed him the scarf and carefully walked down the bulky steps to look for something suitable for collecting ice.

***

"I'm sorry, sir." Lt. Fisher's voice was loud and clear inside his flight helmet. "The gauge says it's time to turn back." He ignored her and continued looking through the door's wide paneled window. They had been searching the frozen slopes for forty-five minutes and hadn't seen so much as a goat. Along the way, they witnessed firsthand the peaks letting go of their picturesque pillows and taking everything with them. "We could try checking the monastery," her voice continued, "it was their last known whereabouts. It's on the way back. Worth a try?" He turned to her and reluctantly nodded. When she looked at the infrared one last time before turning back, she noticed something on the GPS that made her look outside the windshield in front of her. "We're not alone up here," she said. "Look at the screen."

Greenfield looked at the grid map on the instrument panel and then through the glass in front of him. A green dot indicated there was an aircraft a hundred yards in front of them. "I see it," he said.

"It's a Blackhawk," Lt. Fisher said curiously. "I thought everyone was called back to post." She radioed the pilot using the aircraft's call numbers that appeared on the radar/GPS map. "Blackhawk 2312, you have company up here. This is Augusta 116, Lt. Fisher; we have visual on you."

The pilot came back. "Fish, get clear of this area ASAP. My guns are locked on a target one mile to your port side."

"What target?" she came back loudly. "We're up here looking for a couple of lost civilians. How do you know for sure you have a target? White, is that you?" she asked, thinking the voice sounded familiar.

"Commander's orders Fish. I saw something yellow hanging on the side of the mountain to your left. Commander determined it belongs to an ISIS sympathizer and ordered me to fire on it."

"White, we're up here looking for Harrison Foster and Mary Lynn Bennett," she said slowly and clearly. "You remember Foster from the monastery school detail? You need to stand down."

"Affirmative," he responded. "Weapon is off-line. Good thing you were up here. I kind of thought it looked like one of those scarves the local people wear."

Greenfield gave her the "wrap-up-the-conversation" sign by circling his hand around and around.

"Send me the coordinates for the yellow garment."

"Here you go," he said and the two sets of numbers appeared on the Augusta's GPS screen. "Follow me, I'll take you there."

Greenfield searched both sides of the mountain for the garment as the two lieutenants conversed over their headsets. "I see it," he gasped and smacked Lt. Fisher on the arm. "Lower, on the right."

"Yes," Lt. White replied. "That's it. What do you think? Wait! Someone else is up here. Fish, you see something on your radar?"

"It's another Blackhawk," Lt. Fisher replied. "Whose is it?"

Lt. White initiated a call out to the pilot of the second Blackhawk. "Whoever it is, they've got their weapons on. Blackhawk 2020, stand down. Target has been determined to be civilians."

"I gave you an order Lt. White; you failed to follow it!" The angry voice of Cdr. Hanna blasted over everyone's headsets.

"Communication has been sketchy, sir. I intended to make contact as soon as I descended," Lt. White responded. "We believe the piece of clothing might belong to Mary Lynn Bennett."

Lt. White's words weren't heard by Cdr. Hanna because an explosion of snow had already erupted below them and was spewing ice and rock. The sudden blast of energy rocked both their crafts. It was only because of their assiduous training that they were able to right themselves and maintain control.

"Why did you do that?" Lt. Fisher screamed into the microphone.

"Settle down, Lt. Fisher," Cdr. Hanna's calm voice came over the headset. "This is above your intel level. Terrorists aren't the only things that have invaded these mountains."

"You're a murderer!" Greenfield interrupted. "You had nothing to fear from those two kids."

"You know what I'm looking for, FBI," his voice crackled over the radio.

"You have nothing to fear from them either." The agent wiped a hand over his face, wondering how he was going to explain this to Al.

"Oh my God!" Lt. Fisher gasped. "What's that?"

Greenfield looked out the windshield, seeing the fear in her eyes. "Reverse course!" he yelled when he saw the all too familiar cloud rounding a distant pinnacle; it was headed straight for them. "Get us out of here!"

"White!" she shouted into the mic.

"Already in about-face mode, Fish."

She did the same, turning on the radar-assist system to guide them around objects on either side and in front of the aircraft, so she could concentrate on boosting speed. Lt. White's green marker shown ahead of them on the radar map as they navigated handily through the network of mountains. Cdr. Hanna's remained fixed.

"Best to get down low as quick as you can," Greenfield said. "They just want us out of their mountains."

"Who, sir?" she asked. She looked over at him when he didn't answer; he silently stared back at her through his shield. She looked down at the green spot representing Hanna's position. "The intel he was referring to?"

"Just get us out of here." No way in hell was he going to tell her about the giants.

Cdr. Hanna's indicator flickered and then went out as if someone had turned off a switch. "Sir, are you there?" Lt. Fisher looked at Greenfield.

"Damn stupid fool," he grumbled; you can't do battle with the gods and expect to win."

"Sir?" Lt. Fisher asked.

***

Mary Lynn found a wooden bowl within the remains of the lift. It had a two-inch chip on one side at the rim but otherwise looked suitable for melting ice in. She sat on a boulder to wipe it clean with her robe. When she looked up, Harry was standing at the foot of the steps smiling at her. The dim light from the spiral stairs behind him gave him the appearance of an angel. His silhouette seemingly sifted away when the steps crumbled under his feet and rocks rained down on him until his image faded away into a dust cloud.

"Hey," he said, interrupting the apparition. "I see you found something, great. Did you see my backpack? Lt. White might have a nutrition bar in there or something to sustain us until someone finds us."

"Harry, stay with me, right here." She patted the boulder she was sitting on and scooted to one side making a space for him. "Don't go back up yet."

"Here it is," he said, lifting the backpack from out of the rubble by its straps. "If James hadn't destroyed my phone, I could've used this to . . ." he took John's crumpled and torn solar panel from out of the bag. "Oh well, never mind." He grinned at her, bent over, and gave her a kiss on the cheek and then swung the pack over his shoulder.

She reached for him with both hands as he walked away. "Harry, stay . . ." When he put his foot on the bottom step, it was as if he'd stepped on a land mine. The mountain exploded violently above them. The force slammed Mary Lynn up against a wall, knocking her unconscious. Rocks and boulders dropped down freely filling the stairwell and the bottom of the shaft, burying Harry. When Mary Lynn awoke, she was lying in a shallow grave of rubble. Dazed, and with an aching head, she let out a moan as she tried to move. Rocks fell off her arms when she forcibly lifted them. She shoved the debris off her body and legs and sluggishly sat up. She looked like a ghost; dirt and soot were impaled into her clothes and skin. The air was foul with dust and the smell of burnt metal. "Harry?" she coughed. More light was coming in from the stairwell than before. "Harry!" she tried to call out. The blast created a large cavity in the side of the mountain. She crawled toward the place where the stairs used to be. She found a large boulder with protruding edges, grabbed hold, and stood upright. "Harry! Where are you?" she screamed, looking in all directions. She bent over the large spiny rock and squeezed her eyes closed. Instead of blackness, she saw nothing but white and a figure of Kunchen sitting on a large red cushion, as he often did during meditation sessions. He addressed her as Prana. His monotone instructional voice was telling her to appeal to the gods for help. "Please let Harry be okay," she screamed at the vision. "That's all I want," she sobbed. "Please, please, please," she said repeatedly until she heard a popping noise. A rock above her head separated and broke off. It missed her by mere inches when it fell into the endless whiteness. She staggered backward into the cavity as more sections of the wall repelled away one by one until a twenty-foot opening in the mountainside had hollowed out. She pressed her back flat against the newly formed mountain face. She expected to be plucked away any second and flattened her fingers against the wall. The deadly tomb of ashes had been replaced by thrashing wind gales. The fierce gusts snatched at the toga around her shoulders. Her rope belt fretted in the tempest and her ponytail unraveled and became electric. "Stop!" she screamed at the gusts. She closed her eyes trying to distil her thoughts, to find calm. *I must control my fear, my sorrow.* It was hard to maintain control when everything around her was literally blustering with uncertainty and Harry's body was somewhere buried in a pile of rock that used to be the stairwell. She struggled to put her emotions in check by slowing her breathing. "Oh Lord, God," she cried, "help me with this awful pain. Please! Don't let me lose Harry. Give me strength; prepare me for whatever is next." The usual barrage of reasons to give up contended for recognition. *Help me, even though everyone thinks I'm a freak; Help me, even though no one understands me.* The path of least resistance was always easier, always there, ready to push her strengths aside. A memory came to her. She was sitting next to her mother on the front steps of the house on Hartwood. Her mother was telling her how special she was, *born of greatness;* she never knew what it meant before now. She said it often, always with a serious tone, sometimes sitting her rambunctious daughter down to make sure she listened. She heard Harry's words; *this proves how amazing you are.* Harry, forever my cheerleader.

Ice and dust spat in her eyes and clung to her eyelashes; she could barely see. The inundation was weakening her grip; she could feel herself being peeled away from the rock. From out of the torrent, three large figures appeared hanging in the air; their heavy fur cloaks bellowed in the updraft. Was this another apparition? There was nothing vague about their helmets and thick animal hide and tightly strapped leather boots. They seemed unaffected by the raging wind. Their menacing dark faces made their intentions unclear until the one on point spoke.

"We have been dispatched to take you to safety." His voice was deep and commanding.

"Not without Harry," she countered, screaming to be heard over the wind.

"He has not survived," he replied conclusively.

"I'm not going anywhere without him, alive or dead."

"The elders have decided; you are to come with us."

"No!" she shouted back louder. She locked eyes with the giant's as he floated in closer to grab her. "Are you going to defy the wishes of the daughter of Kokabiel?" she demanded.

The giant raised his chin and then turned his head to the right and the left and nodded to his companions. Another flood of rocks fell away from the side of the mountain. The giant enclosed her within his cloak before she had a chance to see if they found Harry. When the veil pulled away, she was alone in the familiar outer great room of the Dzong. The giant must have deposited her on the ground and left in one motion. Plywood was nailed to the wall where the large door used to be. A partially built doorframe lay on the floor. A heavy smell of weather protectant permeated from the new door propped against a wall. The window Harry dropped down from was also boarded with plywood. She heard a noise in the hallway. Two monks, most likely the carpenters, were rushing away to alert the others. She followed them. Monks from other parts of the complex joined in behind the two as they trotted through the labyrinth. Distant melodious chants became louder as she neared the main temple. It was the familiar call to prayer chorus. The double doors to the temple were wide open and she entered behind the cluster she had followed. The temple had never been packed with so many worshipers at one time. She worked her way through the horde of monks who were slowly settling down on their prayer mats. Kunchen stood at the edge of the inner circle of holy men, talking to the two monks who were obviously reporting the intrusion. Everyone else was facing the revered golden statue of Buddha. Harry's body was lying on a blue pallet on the floor beneath it. His uniform was removed and replaced by a tan robe. Two monks were kneeling beside the pallet wiping dirt from his face and arms with rags. Bruises and whelps covered his distorted arms. Broken bones pierced the skin, tracks of coagulated blood trickled from his ears and nose.

"Your friend's spirit is between worlds." Somehow, Kunchen's voice prevailed over the chanting voices. "The unrelenting military," he nodded toward Harry, "has driven our protectors from the mountains. This has been their home for thousands of years. Kokabiel will be here shortly to collect you."

"I'm not leaving without Harry," she whispered. "He risked his life for me."

"You are welcome to pray with us in the meantime. We are asking the gods to make his journey to the spiritual world an effortless one."

She rushed to Harry's side, knelt down beside him on the pallet, and leaned over, pressing her ear to his chest. She closed her eyes and envisioned the array of blues she used to see around him. Sometimes they were so pale they seemed silver and at other times were as blue as the deepest ocean. She tried to conjure every memory she ever had. "He has life," she whispered. "I can hear his heart." She waved her arms, gesturing at the circle of monks. "Tell them to move back. They're taking up all the air."

"He is far too broken," she heard Kunchen's voice say but ignored him and turned back to Harry. She gently wrapped her hands around his feet and thought about the skeletal system the cranky professor from LSUA insisted she memorize. She began to rearrange the small, displaced bones that connected his toes and ankles. Nerves and vessels needed to be reattached and muscles repaired. The tibia, fibula, and patella were crushed, as was his femur, pelvis, and rib cage. Internal organs, liver, stomach, spleen, lungs, intestines, were all bruised, torn, and bleeding. She prayed as she moved her hands under and around his broken back, damaged kidneys, and then his arms. She lingered at his neck and longer around his skull. "Prana . . ." It was Kunchen's voice again. "You must recall, as a child when you ran to the aid of the small dog after being hit by a vehicle."

She remembered how badly she wanted the little black dog to live. It wasn't breathing; its tongue was white and hanging out one side of its mouth. Its side was scraped and bleeding. Her mother taught her to pray, so she did. One of its legs jerked and a few seconds later, it scrambled out of her arms and ran away.

"And the bird you found on the ground when you were five?"

"Yes," she said to herself, remembering how she had picked it up, ever so gently, in her cupped hands. Then it suddenly fluttered its wings and flew away. "His injuries are far greater." Kunchen's voice and was letting doubt creep into her mind, making her think that even the newly acquired sense of healing might not be enough. She leaned her body over his again, capped her hands around his head, and whispered in his ear. "I will fix you, Harry. With everything I have; I will fix you."

Chapter 21

The two pilots rushed through their shut down procedures, flicking switches and pushing sliding levers. It seemed they couldn't remove their harnesses and unbuckle their safety straps fast enough. They exited their respective aircraft in a full run toward one another and grabbed each other at arm's length when they met.

"What just happened?" Lt. White blurted out, staring wildly into Fisher's eyes. "This is the second time I've had to buzz villagers after being run out of those mountains by whatever the hell that was," he ranted. "I don't think I can classify that as a storm this time."

"It's like it was locked onto us somehow!" Lt. Fisher was just as rattled.

"What did he have to say?" Lt. White asked while looking at Agent Greenfield, who was just exiting the Augusta and watching a large truck approach from an adjacent landing strip. It was pulling a flatbed with a damaged helicopter cabin strapped down to its bed along with a tail rudder, rotors, and other parts that had been ripped from the hull.

Lt. Fisher shook her head. "Not much. You piloted him that first time, right?"

"Right. The first time, this very same thing happened."

"I escorted him while he interviewed villagers. They believe their gods reside in the mountains. It's ridiculous but I- I certainly have no earthly explanation for what just happened."

Greenfield walked past them without speaking. "Wait, where are you going?" Lt. White shouted. "We need to talk about what just happened up there."

"That's Hanna's Blackhawk," Greenfield growled, slowing but not stopping. "I'm on my way to check on him."

"I'm coming with you, sir." Lt. Fisher hurried to walk alongside. "Is he in the hospital or the morgue?"

"Medics said he's still alive," Greenfield replied. He looked at her, wanting to add *they don't kill people,* but thought better of it.

Lt. White followed the truck to the hanger where the downed Blackhawk was being off-loaded and where two other wrecked airships were housed.

The agent entered the med tent where he and Foster had been taken after having experienced the same type of rapid descent and landing, and where Adam Reeves had died. Thirty-five of its fifty beds were occupied with soldiers who had crashed their respective aircrafts while patrolling the snowy mountainous terrain. All were in different stages of consciousness. Dr. Rush walked over after spotting the agent and Lt. Fisher.

"They all seem to be suffering from shock," Dr. Rush sighed. "And, like you and Mr. Foster, have nothing more than bumps and bruises. The few that have woke up are experiencing memory loss. They can't remember anything that happened to them. Sound familiar?"

"Is Cdr. Hanna in here, doc?" Lt. Fisher asked.

"He's just back from getting an EEG," he said, nodding to somewhere in the rear of the facility. "We're getting him settled in."

"You look a bit more concerned than when me and Foster were brought here after being swatted out of the sky."

"Agent, could it be possible that you and the others were exposed to some sort of chemical agent? Some are talking in their sleep, rambling about an angry-looking cloud."

Greenfield shook his head. "That's for you to figure out Doc. Did you hear back from Landstuhl Med about the two airmen that were with me and Foster?"

"Nothing conclusive. A general is landing in two hours from Baumholder, Germany. I'm hoping he'll have something to share."

Dr. Rush led the agent to Cdr. Hanna's shrouded bay where his clothes had been removed, bagged, and sent to Landstuhl to be tested for chemical exposure. He was dressed in hospital grays; his face and hands were smudged with dirt and sand but he had sustained no injuries; not even a bruise. His breathing was slow and deep, a sign that he wouldn't be waking up soon.

"A nurse is coming with IV fluids," Dr. Rush said as they watched his chest slowly rise and fall. "The EEG shows he's looping in continuous NREM sleep. That's when a patient only has delta waves, or slow waves, and the heart and blood pressure slow down. It's the most difficult stage to awaken from. Every one of these pilots are going through the same cycle. Some are experiencing night terrors, which is also symptomatic. On the positive side, it's a restorative stage. I'll send someone to find you when he wakes up if you'd like to get some rest."

"I'll be in the command tent," Greenfield replied, waiting on the general."

***

Many of the monks had excused themselves for dinner. The remainder continued to pray in the shadows on their knees, bent over, their arms and hands flat on the floor as if reaching for the golden Buddha behind Harry. Mary Lynn lay her hands on him for five hours and was now lying beside him with an arm over his chest while the monks chanted their homage. He had been breathing for four hours, his pulse strong for two. The color of his skin was now pink instead of ash gray. It had been a slow and arduous process, reconstructing every broken and crushed bone, mending ribs, reattaching muscle tissue, veins, and capillaries, repairing organs, and restoring life into his lungs. She was exhausted.

Kunchen approached out of the darkness and offered his hand. "I sent one of the brothers to the village with a note," he said after waking her and carefully helping her to her feet. "It gives the army post permission to come and get him. Their doctors will see to his complete recovery. A plate of food is waiting for you in your room."

"I'm not leaving him." She had nothing left to give except to be by his side.

"He's not alone," he said and pointed out the monks scattered in the shadows with the sweep of his arm.

"Can you just have someone bring my food here?" She felt dizzy and almost fell forward but Kunchen steadied her.

"I'll let you know if there is any change." She put her hand in his and allowed him to lead the way to her room.

***

Greenfield stood as if it was expected of him, as any infantryman would when a lieutenant general touting three stars on each shoulder and a chest full of medals entered the room.

"You're the FBI agent Col. Jackson interviewed a few weeks back about the incident that sent three of our men to the hospital?"

"Yes, sir." Agent Greenfield had been sifting through one of the bulky operational laptops trying to make sense of Hanna's reports while waiting for Lt. General Charles Huffman to arrive. The decorated officer had an entourage of two warrant officers, a staff sergeant and three first lieutenants. The matured officer's body language and the way he turned his head and moved his arms showed a genuine concern for the infirmed men. He was sizeable with an imposing voice, but his eyes told the story. He wasn't out to prove anything, just follow orders and get the job done. "How are they doing?" Greenfield asked.

"They're back in the states now undergoing psychiatric treatment; still not cleared for duty. And now it seems there are thirty-six men in the infirmary suffering from some sort of chemical exposure."

"Please, you must put a stop to the maneuvers Hanna's been conducting," Greenfield implored, swinging the laptop around that he'd been studying. "These reports are lies. They were written by a crazy misguided man with an agenda. ISIS militants are not in the high elevations he's been rocketing. His attacks have caused avalanches, putting innocent monks that live in the monasteries in danger. Pilots have been flying perilously close to villages. He may have killed my friend, the other man Col. Jackson interviewed when he was here. Hanna fired a rocket at a yellow scarf, a signal Harry most likely put out to help us find him and his friend. I was up there. Lt. Fisher tried to stop him but he wouldn't listen. The FBI sent me here to look for three missing civilians. I found two of them. All he wanted to do was shoot and ask questions later."

"Save your breath, agent. I'm here to coordinate the dismantling of this place. We've been asked to leave the country. The Indian Armed Forces are taking over the safeguarding of Bhutan."

"Thank God!" Greenfield sighed, pressing his fingers against his forehead. "Our military has been this country's biggest threat."

Lt. General Huffman dropped a thick suitcase on the counter where Hanna usually stood observing the real time action. The entourage set about disconnecting laptops and terminals. Two privates rolled in a couple of large fiberglass containers, unlocked them, and spread them open. Huffman looked at Greenfield as if wondering why he was still standing in front of him. "You can start packing whatever gear you brought with you. Someone will advise you of your departure time."

"Sir, I'd like to look for Harrison Foster, or his remains, just one more time."

"I'm not risking another pilot or billion-dollar aircraft in those mountains."

"Then let Lt. Fisher take me to this one particular monastery. It's the last place Foster was seen by one of Hanna's men."

"No one's going anywhere," the robust officer bellowed.

A corporal entered the tent carrying a small piece of paper and gave it to the general. He read the note and then looked at Greenfield. "There's a woman at the gate. She wants to talk to you . . . only you. She claims to know where to find your friend."

Karma recognized John's shadowy gait when he appeared from the first row of tents. A first lieutenant holding a rifle across his chest stood between her and the chain-link gate. No one was getting past him, particularly someone with flowing garments capable of hiding almost any type of contraband. He stood to one side when Greenfield pushed the gate open. Karma saw that another man had followed him, a uniformed man with rows of medals across the top of his jacket. She panicked, turned, and ran toward the road.

"Karma, wait!" The sound of John's voice made her slow down. "I was hoping it was you. Did you walk all this way? Where are you going?"

"Someone has followed you. My note stated I only wanted to speak with you."

John looked back; the lieutenant general was standing next to the guard, holding the gate open with one hand. He directed her away from the lighted entrance to the shadowy side of the guard shed. When they were between the building and a large truck, he grabbed her up in his arms. She was trembling. "What are you doing out here so far away from the village? Wait, is Bassui okay?" He felt her head nod against his chest.

"I did not want to come to the devil's door, but I felt I had to."

"The note said you know where Harry is?" Her head nodded again.

She looked up at him. "One of the monks came to my door and gave me the message. He's at the monastery; the one you went to before. He's injured. The monks have given the military permission to collect him."

"And the girl, Mary Lynn?"

"There was no mention of her. I'm sorry."

"Wait here," he said. "I'll go tell the general. And then I'm driving you home."

***

Mary Lynn awoke looking at the blurred figure of Kunchen standing over her with his hands cupped together under his chin. "How long . . . how long was I asleep?" she asked, unaware she'd been asleep for nearly twelve hours. She sat up quickly. "Is Harry okay?"

"He is fine. The army picked him up only moments ago. Thanks to you Prana, and the homage of our brothers to the teachings of Buddha, the gods' have given us favor. Your friend will heal nicely under the army's care. He will not remember his time here and the army will assume you perished when the mountain was hit by their rocket. That should put an end to the military intrusions."

"What?" Mary Lynn leaped out of the bed. Kunchen turned his eyes away because she was wearing only a single thin robe and was bare-footed. The country's general culture disallowed looking at bare skin.

"Kokabiel has decided," he said, raising his chin and staring at the plastered wall, "you will join your mother and the Nephilim colony in their new home where you are needed."

"No," she argued and pulled a maroon robe around her that was draped over the chair. "I'm supposed to go home. You told me I would go home. Everyone told me I was going home."

"You are not ready to be left to your own devices Prana; you need further training. You will come with me." When he turned around, Mary Lynn was dressed, sitting in the chair, and putting on her sandals.

"No, I'm not," she said. "You can't keep me here against my will." Her voice was defiant.

"Your friend survived because of the gifts you inherited; gifts we helped you hone. Some of the Nephilim's most talented healers were lost in the attacks. Your Nephilim family is in desperate need of your skills."

"Tell me where it's written that Buddha says it's okay to hold someone against their will. She picked up the rest of her ensemble, a yellow tunic and rachu, and draped them over her shoulders.

"There is so much more you must learn, Prana."

"No!" she grunted. "I don't want to learn more."

She rushed from the room. She could feel him watching her as she fumbled her way through the maze of corridors, bumping into walls and turning into false pathways that led to nowhere. She thought she saw him turning corners just behind her as she ran from one long chamber to another. When she found the great room, rhythmic flashes of light were pulsing through the windows along the ceiling and she could hear the airship's rotors buzzing outside.

"He is gone, Prana." Kunchen was standing at the entrance to the hallway, holding out his hand and beckoning her to take it. "Come, we should join the others for evening prayer."

"You can't make me stay here." The replacement door had been installed. One of the monks was bolting the lock after seeing Harry off. The monks were once again safe and secure from the outside elements, whether it be wild animals, weather, or the military. Now, the door was keeping her from escaping with their secrets. "Please, let me go."

"I will not keep you here against your will, Prana."

Kunchen was standing behind her now. It was startling how quickly he had crossed the room, given his normal snail's pace. It only reaffirmed a slow realization she had been coming to for the past weeks: the man had great powers.

"Fear is your nemesis, Prana. Don't let it block your way." He nodded to the brother standing by the door with the key in his hand; he returned the nod and unlocked the deadbolt. "It would be wise to wait until morning. As you can see, it is dusk. Predators will be out hunting shortly."

"You can stop trying to scare me; I'm not afraid of the woods." Hiking was a given when camping. Her father . . . her real father, schooled both his children in the sounds and signs of the woods. Even without the colors she normally relied on to showcase the warm-blooded creatures hiding in the weeds, wiry vines and brush and sometimes crouching in the trees, she was taught to follow the stars and listen to the surroundings.

Kunchen reached for her head with both hands but stopped within six-inches. "We only touched the surface, Prana." He spread his fingers apart. "You have a lifetime of misinformation to weed out in order to find that perfect state of happiness. It's there," he said and touched the crown of her head. "Spend as much time as you can in meditation. It will help clear the way to find your center."

"I will, Kunchen," she whispered. "Thank, you."

"Animals come down from the mountains to hunt at night," he continued after resuming his original position and folding his hands in front of him. "They roam the forests and valleys and are not like anything you are familiar with. If you will not listen to reason, Prana," he added, because he could sense her desire to leave was far greater than the danger he was trying to convey, "then I will immediately go to the temple and urge my brothers to join me in prayer so the gods

will give you favor and guide you safely to your destination."
He bid her good-bye with an abbreviated bow.

Chapter 22

Eight hours of sitting, walking the floor, and drinking coffee while waiting for Harry to stir gave Greenfield time to wonder what his future with the FBI might look like. The Quantico team in DC had gone silent. There had been no reports in twenty-four hours and no one was responding to his messages. The dynamic of the mission had clearly changed since Cdr. Hanna went down, along with thirty-five of his men. Harry was now in the infirmary with them. Lt. Fisher had volunteered to pilot the mission to retrieve him after Greenfield's request to let him go along was denied. She promised to report to him whatever first-hand observations she made. However, she was ordered to remain with the helicopter, to stand guard and keep the motor running. Dr. Rush immediately ordered a litany of tests upon his arrival. An EEG and CT scan revealed evidence of recent brain trauma. Healing bruises of blended yellow, black, and purple splotches covered his body. X-rays presented an inconceivable amount of mended bones. Vitals were remarkably stable considering what his patient must have gone through. An IV bag of saline fluids hung above his head along with a piggyback of preventive antibiotics; a thin oxygen tube was hooked under his nose. John slid into a metal folding chair next to the narrow military hospital bed. He looked at Harry and felt the burden of guilt, like an elephant sitting on his chest, for allowing him along on the search. He thought about the monks that surely knew more than the vague tail they provided Dr. Rush as to how Harry ended up in their care. Kunchen, the monk he dealt with before, had given the doctor few details. *Someone* had found him and brought him to their compound.

If he'd only been allowed to go along. He would have challenged him using every interrogation technique in the FBI arsenal to get the truth out of him, no matter who or what he claimed to be. He bent forward, rotating his neck back and forth and trying to get the kinks out. *Be patient,* he told himself as his eyes fell on Cdr. Hanna's shrouded cubical. Seeing the pig-headed man's shadowy outline only constricted the nerve he was trying to subdue. Part of him was glad to see the man paying the price for taking it upon himself to obliterate an entire species. Granted, he was one of the brave and fearless, having operated in some of the most dangerous tactical arenas in the world. He skeptically wondered just how many times the military found it necessary to clean up his messes. There was a certain commonality between them; he put the same demands on himself when an investigation required it. After two hundred and sixty-seven murder investigations and three failed relationships, the special division searching for Bigfoot looked inviting. Easy work, he thought. No more grisly homicides, no more beatings and rapes, no more bomb threats. Just an endless search for something that everyone considered a fairy tale.

Lt. Gen. Huffman came around during the third hour of the agent's reckoning to assure him they both would have seats on a flight to Germany when Harry was stable enough to fly. He added, "Good luck with your next assignment."

"Thanks," was all John could think of to say. *Next assignment,* just when he was on the verge of cracking the mystery, he was being reassigned? There was no Bigfoot. There was a species of giants clever enough to taint witnesses' memories and leave behind false evidence in the form of hair or blood indigenous to local wildlife. Giant people that only wanted to be left alone, yet curious about the world and the humans who occupied it. They traveled everywhere, observing our habits and convincing witnesses who caught a glimpse of them, they'd seen the infamous creature known as Migou, Almasti, Tengmo, Sasquatch, Yeti, and Bigfoot. They made their own clothing out of hides and woven animal hair; they had sustained themselves for who knows how long, maybe hundreds of thousands of years. Now, the plug was suddenly pulled on the project or, most likely, moved up the ladder to DHS. The next step in disclaiming the project's existence would be to assign him to the furthest point from ground zero. The worst part, of course, was his failure to bring Mary Lynn home and having to face Al after coming so close. This was harder than facing the vilest of criminals. Prior to five years ago, it was part of the job…giving families bad news; he had become good at it. He squirmed in the hard chair that was too uncomfortable to doze in so the thoughts kept coming. Why did the giants bring women to the mountains of Bhutan? Who were the lighter-skinned, redheaded orphans that lived in the monasteries and villages? He needed more time. He needed someone to brainstorm with over the conundrum. He thought about Karma and then looked at the time on his phone. It was 3:00 a.m. He wondered if Lt. Fisher was still awake.

"I might have known you weren't here to thank me for flying Dr. Rush to the monastery," Lt. Fisher complained when the agent woke her and insisted that she drive him to Mondar. "You know, you still haven't thanked me for saving your ass from crashing." She pulled an army jacket on over her grey sweat suit sleepwear. "And isn't it weird how everyone seems to want you out of here ASAP. My superiors are keeping a close eye on me too."

"Very observant, Lieutenant. You should come work for the FBI."

"I don't like it when someone tries to flatter me either, Greenfield."

"I'd like to hear your take on what happened up there, how Hanna crashed, and the conditions of the soldiers in the infirmary."

"Well, sir," she began, "I think if I want a future in the military, I'll just keep certain things to myself. Otherwise, I could be shipped off to Antarctica or some other nonessential place guaranteed to stunt my career."

"Okay, I can respect that. Did you hear about any remains being found; or did anyone bother to go back and look?"

"Yes, sir, of course they did. A search was conducted using GPR that reaches depths anywhere from ten to a hundred meters, depending on the soil. We came up with nothing. I'm sorry, sir," she added seeing the disappointment on his face. "Listen, keys to the Humvees are kept in the glove boxes. I guess you have nothing to lose by borrowing one."

"You're right about that," he grunted, "since the lt. general is shipping us off to Germany. I'd like to update Karma and Bassui before I leave."

Lt. Fisher shifted her weight to one hip and tilted her head to one side.

"What?" he grumbled when he saw the dubious look on her face.

"Karma...really? You shouldn't be discussing anything that pertains to this post, or its operations with these civilians." Her suspicious frown changed into a grin. "Okay, go on, it's dark, no one's gonna see you. Just like that other time I saw you sneaking off post. Don't look so surprised; I could work for the FBI, remember?"

"I could have saved myself some time before if I'd thought to look in the glove box."

"Some detective you are," she quipped.

Greenfield crouched as he moved from truck to jeep through the motor pool. He chose a vehicle parked in the shadow of a large tent. Portions of the barricaded grounds were already dismantled. Humvees are built for far more difficult terrain than the rocky desert area that surrounded the post and crossing the perimeter through a torn down opening was relatively easy. Once he reached the scant road to the village, driving was easier, smoother with only the occasional washout. He parked well outside the settlement and walked in carrying Bassui's blue Surface under his zipped black FBI hoodie. Returning it was a perfect excuse for showing up at the mud and mortar house. He picked up a small rock and tapped it against the windowsill in the rear of the house. The hide curtain suddenly flipped to one side. Karma's shrouded face appeared in the window.

"Please, I'd like to talk to you and Bassui, if it's all right," he whispered.

The stiff pelt quickly fell back into place. Greenfield waited for her in the group of trees behind the house where they talked before. A few minutes passed before he saw her cloaked, bundled figure round the front of the house.

"Thank you for seeing me," he whispered. She removed the blanket from around the two of them. She had broken tradition by allowing the rachu to drape around her shoulders instead of securing it across her face. Maybe she was thinking the same thing he was, that this might be the last time they'd see each other.

"I'm glad to see you're still alive," she said lowly. "We heard the explosions."

"I'm fine." He got down on one knee in front of Bassui. "Harry wasn't so lucky; he's pretty bruised up. The doctor believes he was buried under some rocks during one of the blasts. He suffered a head injury and he hasn't woken up yet. He's at the post infirmary. He found the girl we were looking for, the one in the picture you sent him. That was a very important picture, Bassui. It gave us proof that she was still alive. Thank you so much."

Bassui nodded. "But, how do you know she wasn't injured, like Harry?"

"They were together in the pictures he sent you. We won't know what happened to her until Harry wakes up. That is, if he can remember. Sometimes people can't recall things for a while after a head injury. I can tell you that someone worked a miracle on him. So, I have no doubt that the same would have been done for her."

Bassui looked up at Karma and then back at John. "It was the gods, they answered our prayers," he whispered.

John unzipped his jacket and slipped the boy's blue notepad from inside. "I'm sorry, but I had to delete Harry's pictures and the ones you took. I suppose I was trying to protect . . ." he looked up at Karma. "I was trying to protect all of you. Your gods, you, the monks."

"So, you saw them," Bassui said, prying open the Surface.

"You have nothing to fear from them." John placed a reassuring hand on the boy's shoulder.

"Of course, we have nothing to fear from them," Karma said contentiously. "That's what I've been trying to tell you. They were born of the gods. Now they're gone. Because your soldiers went looking for them and tried to kill them."

John stood and turned his attention to Karma. "The army is afraid of them. Because they're big and strong and have done things to their soldiers that can't be explained."

Bassui found the very first photo he and Harry took together; their smiling faces pressed against one another's cheeks. "Will I ever see him again, Agent Greenfield?"

"I'll see to it that he contacts you when he wakes up."

"He will not be corresponding with anyone from America ever again." Karma's voice gushed with starch conviction. "American's put their own selfish needs over anyone else. I don't want Bassui to turn into a person like that."

"I know," he said. "Believe me, I understand." She wasn't the only one feeling frustrated. "I'm disappointed because I really wanted to bring Mary Lynn home to her father. There are good people in the United States, Karma. You're going to have to teach him to be able to tell the difference. He's going to meet a lot of them on that thing right there." He nodded at the Surface in Bassui's hands and then realized something. "Bassui, I thought I deleted all the photos. Did I miss the one you just showed me?"

"No sir, Agent Greenfield." Bassui proudly held up the notepad. "They are all in the cloud."

"The cloud," the agent sighed. He deleted everything of the kid's he could find from the military's hard drive while he was waiting for the new lieutenant general to arrive and hadn't thought about the cloud. "You need to delete your cloud account. Do you know anyone with an external drive?"

"I know someone," Karma said. "Bidhan, the butcher sells them."

John bent down to watch the boy scroll through the photos in a folder titled *Harry*. "Wait, go back one. See that woman with Mary Lynn?" He pointed to a second woman wearing brown robes. "Her picture is on file with the FBI. Her hair is grayer now."

"They are related," Karma noted. "They have the same eyes."

He grabbed the notebook, pulled it close and then pressed his fingers apart to enlarge the picture. "Her name is Christine. She's Mary Lynn's mother." He straightened, to look at Karma face to face. "She's been missing for seven years." Karma's eyes were darting, a classic indication that she was holding back. Why was she afraid? What was on her mind . . . the truth? The reason why people are being abducted by these giants.

Bassui said it for her. "She has red hair, like the orphans, the children of the gods."

"Bassui!" Karma fretted.

"Tell me about the orphans, Bassui," John asked.

"It is forbidden to talk about them."

"That's okay. I'm sorry, you don't have to." He looked back at Karma. Her eyes expressed relief. "As strange as this is, it's actually starting to make sense to me now."

Karma pulled on John's arm, turning his attention away from Bassui. "Our gods, the Nephilim have lived in the mountains for as long as anyone can remember. They found Harry and left him with the monks and then took the girl with them when they fled."

"How do you know this?"

"The monk that came to my door said as much."

"Al suspected he wasn't Mary Lynn's father."

"Her father must be . . ." Bassui began but was cut off by Karma.

"Hush, Bassui," Karma hissed and then gave John one of her sternest frowns. An expression that made her all the more attractive. "Don't you understand?" she added prophetically. "She is one of them."

"A child of the Nephilim?" he whispered. He rubbed his fingers against his forehead as if trying to organize his thoughts. "Theoretically," John said, thinking out loud, "the Nephilim could fear their days are numbered. I've seen mountaineers heading for base camps. More tourists are visiting the villages. Wars across the borders have brought the military and people like Hanna here. Inevitably, someone was going to find them. It's possible they're attempting to integrate with us."

"Think of it another way," Karma whispered. "They're giving us a part of themselves. That way, they can live on after your people have killed them off."

"I can't imagine Quantico buying this theory."

"John, you're still not a true believer. Maybe, after you've had time to think about what you witnessed here, you will become one. But you can tell no one what you have seen here."

"Listen," he said, lifting her chin with his hand. "I came here tonight because you're the only person I can talk to about this. You're the only one I can trust to help me figure this out. The army is breaking camp, packing up for Germany. I'll be leaving as soon as Harry's cleared to travel. I came here to tell you both good-bye, and to thank you and to tell you . . ." All that would come out of his mouth was air. What good would come of telling her how he felt about her? How could he expect her to feel the same about him? Being American made it impossible.

"What, John?" Karma asked.

"I would have never got so close to finding the answers if it weren't for you and Bassui. I understand now why you didn't want to disturb your gods and I'm so sorry they left."

"I thought you came here tonight to return Bassui's notepad." A half-smile appeared in one corner of her mouth.

He grinned in response. His attraction to her was real, overwhelming. "I appreciate your feelings for the monks, too, even though I'm pretty perturbed at them right now. I'm going to miss you. I had myself convinced this was an easy assignment. There was never going to be proof of alien abductions that correlated with Almasti sightings. And, I never dreamed I'd become so attached to a place and its people."

"We will miss you too, Agent John Greenfield," she said. He cupped his hands around her arms and pulled her close to him. He moved them to her waist and gently hugged her. They stared at one other for a moment. Their faces gravitated closer until they kissed.

"I've been craving another one of those ever since the first one," he said when they separated.

"I'm glad I got to know you, John," she whispered. "The real you. You are a good man after all."

He bent down and hugged Bassui. With a heart that felt as heavy as the mountains behind him, he walked back to the Humvee. He stopped to look back at them several times along the way and before pulling on the door handle. On the drive back to the post, the reality of never seeing Karma again hit him even harder. His chest ached. It was a different kind of pain than a panic attack. *Is this what heartache feels like?* None of his marriage breakups left him feeling like this.

***

Greenfield pushed an empty bed up next to Harry. It was a thousand times more comfortable than the folding chair and it allowed him to nap off and on for the next six hours, at which time he noticed Harry's eyes blink. John raised his bed and helped him sip some water from a straw. He patiently gave him the short version, as he understood it, of why he was in the post infirmary. Harry looked at his bruised arms and then around the room as he listened. "Some of them made it back to post; some landed near Mondar," Greenfield said noticing Harry fixating on the sleeping patients. "Those guys haven't come out of it yet. You're lucky to be alive, you know. Dr. Rush seems to think. . .well. . ."

"What? Why are you hesitating? What happened to me?"

"He said you apparently received life-threatening injuries, but he doesn't know exactly how or when; the healing process doesn't sync with how long you've been missing. Maybe we should talk about this some other time when you've regained your strength and your memory."

"Frankly, John . . ." his voice was raspy as if it hurt to talk, "I can't remember how I got here or what happened to give me all these bruises. I was with Mary Lynn; the military was shooting rockets at the mountain. I suppose they were trying to flush out ISIS militants?" he said, trying to pry the memories from his brain. "Mary Lynn and I were trying to find our way down through an elevator shaft hoping to get out of radar range. The elevator fell," he paused as the memory formed, "but we floated." He nodded his head. "Yeah, I remember that very clearly, we floated all the way to the bottom." His face knotted up as if tasting something bitter. "Oh God," he sighed, "I drew their fire when I shoved her scarf through the hole I made in the ice. It was meant to be a signal for help."

"Lt. Fisher and I saw it. We were up there looking for you. But Hanna was up there too and, well. . ."

"I was talking to her and . . . wait, where is she?"

Greenfield bowed his head, "The monks summoned the military to come get you. She wasn't there, at least not in sight. I think that monk, Kunchen, knows something, but he just talks in riddles. I've been waiting to hear what you had to say. If the lt. colonel would've let me go along, I'd have given that monk a proper interrogation."

"John." Harry's voice sounded weak. "I have a lot to tell you, but it can't go in any report and Hanna can't know."

"Hanna doesn't know anything right now," he said and nodded to the closed curtain surrounding a bed across the room. "He was blown out of the sky just like we were. You remember that? He hasn't uttered a sound since they brought him in," he said when Harry nodded. "Lt. Fisher and I saw the whole thing. The blast of air, or whatever it was, almost took us down, too. Bhutan's prime minister sent word from King Wangluck. He's given the army thirty days to dismantle the post and leave the country. Hanna's airstrikes toppled three mountains. As far as I know, you're the only one retrieved from up there. And that was a miracle," he sighed. "I want to hear everything you remember when you feel up to it; it won't go any further than these ears." Greenfield frowned, feeling tremendous regret over the missed opportunity. "I'm so sorry, Harry," he whispered. "I can't-I don't know what I'm going to say to Al."

"We have to go back there," Harry said, leaning forward. "To the monastery. I saw them, John, the giants." He grabbed the agent by the forearm and pulled himself up. "I want that monk to look me in the eyes and deny they exist and tell me they don't know where she is."

"That's impossible. The Bhutanese government has forbidden it."

"We could go," he said, clamping down harder on John's arm, "on our own. We know the way. We could disguise . . . oh . . ." His eyes closed; his head dipped forward.

Calm down before you pass out." Harry opened his eyes. He was wild-eyed and taking short frantic breaths. Greenfield helped him lay back against the incline and offered him another sip of water.

"A colony of giants was living in carved-out caverns inside the mountains." The water seemed to give Harry a short burst of strength, although his voice was no louder than a whisper. He was afraid he might die before telling the agent what he knew. "The walls were decorated with tapestries and hieroglyphics. Men, women, and children with human features, ten to fifteen feet tall lived there. Mary Lynn is the daughter of one of the hierarchies. Kokabiel, his name is Kokabiel." He swallowed hard, took a breath, and continued. "Christine's with them. She and Kokabiel also have a son named James; he's Mary Lynn's half-brother."

"Hey, maybe you should rest for a bit." Harry had turned pale, as if all his strength had been drained.

"I saw Mary Lynn heal a boy that was badly burned." He looked at his bruised arms. "I took pictures, but James destroyed my phone." He tried to clench his fist to mimic how James crushed it but the pain in his hand prevented him from closing it. "The colony evacuated because of the air strikes. There was a tunnel somewhere."

"Your pictures reached the boy. I'm still trying to process them in my mind."

"But there was no signal; I don't know how they went anywhere." He was silent for a moment, weak with fatigue, then lifted the sheet and looked at his rainbow-colored legs. "John, I dreamed she was praying over me," he said solemnly. "Just like the boy." He went silent again and sank his head into the pillow. "John." His voice sounded dry and hoarse so Greenfield picked up the cup with the straw again. "The giants took her with them," he said in a whisper. "Wherever they went; they took her with them."

"I'm sorry, Harry." John didn't know how to comfort Harry, because he, too, was struggling. Checking all the blocks on the white board just wasn't enough. "I'm gonna find Dr. Rush and tell him you're awake."

The doctor agreed that his patient could use a light sedative when John told him Harry was grieving over the loss of his friend. After that, he took a walk through the camp hoping the cold night air would clear his head, calm his temper, and help him put things in perspective. He found himself outside Lt. Fisher's tent again and considered going inside to ask for her help but decided against it. Her supervisors were probably watching and there was no point in jeopardizing her future. Moving on, as if following an instinct, he weaved through what remained of the tents until he reached the motor pool that was shrunk to a half-dozen vehicles. He tucked himself in between two Humvees. If the keys were in the glove box, he could sneak off post like before and take the narrow road up the mountain to the monastery school. He'd have to be especially careful of the loose rocks along the edge at night. From there he could walk across the valley floor to the Dzong. It would be daylight by the time he reached the wall and the wooden door, but he would find a way to force his way inside like Harry did, find Kunchen, and squeeze the truth out of him. He slowly and quietly pulled on the passenger door of one of the vehicles. To his disappointment, the glove box was empty. He quietly clicked it closed and felt behind each visor. While patting the floor under the mat he heard a clicking noise and instinctively glanced over his shoulder. He didn't expect to see the MP standing behind him with an M16 pointed at him.

***

The bitter night air was exceptionally exhilarating to Mary Lynn as she made her way down the quarter-mile rocky hillside path, her first steps toward home. The departure was bittersweet. She was a different person now thanks to Kunchen. She knew things about herself that she never would have known had he not brought them to the surface. There was no emotional display of affection when he bowed and wished her well. He would never have accepted a hug. The clunk of the lock bolting the door had sealed the departure. Now, if she could just avoid the dangers he cautioned her about. The helicopter's running lights were mere specks in the sky by the time she stepped outside, but it gave her a bearing to follow. The night was cloudy with no moon or stars to guide her. She would have to rely on the tree line just below the tiny blinking lights. Maybe the wildlife Kunchen spoke of would be inclined to hunker down without the moon's natural light to hunt by. There was a wide stand of trees below the boulders and beyond that an open valley. She wasted no time making the downward climb. Everything was much darker when she reached the woods. She kept bumping into stumps of fallen trees and getting tangled in underbrush. She heard her father's voice like an echo, reminding her she was making entirely too much noise. The anticipation of going home heightened the memories of his ardent lectures. *Moss mostly grows on the south side of trees in the south. It's the opposite in the north.* She paused to take a breath and say a prayer. It gave her eyes a chance to adapt to the dark and she noticed a small clear patch in front of her. Its leaves and straw were pressed to the ground. A sign something had bedded down there. *What is it? Where is it, out hunting?* She stepped across it and found a defined animal trail leading away from the den. Her daddy's voice was telling her not to follow it. The well-worn animal trail was too tempting; it would likely lead her directly to the valley and she forged ahead . . . toward home. The forest thinned with open patches of grass as she approached the valley. *What's that?* A noise. *My own footsteps, my own breathing?* She stood still, took a deep breath, and held it. She heard it again. *A whine? A growl, what?* The trees were tall and thin around her. One of them might hold her weight if she found it necessary to shimmy up. She hadn't done anything like that since high school and if she remembered correctly, it was much easier sliding down the pipe or gutter when she was sneaking out than climbing back up the next morning. She peeled off her sandals and placed a foot against the tree. She flexed her toes and pressed them firmly against the textured bark. *Monkey toes*: the name her daddy used to describe her tree-climbing skills to friends, relatives, embarrassingly to just about anyone. The robes were going to be a problem, but . . . *uh, there it is. What is that?* She peeked around the tree just enough to see a black object trotting toward her. *Oh!* She could hear it panting, huffing, as if it had been running. It barked. *A dog?* She peered around the tree again. This time she heard a whine and was able to see that is was a dog with a long hairy wagging tail. "It's okay," she whispered in a soft high-pitched voice. "Come on, boy." She bent down to pet it. "Let's get out from under these trees so I can look at you." The dog followed her as she led it to the tall grass at the edge of the valley floor. The large black canine came closer, beating its tail even harder as if happy to see her. She squatted down and stroked his head and neck. "You have the same markings as . . . Mutt! It's you?" He licked her face and placed a paw on her shoulder, knocking her to the ground. They both sat in the grass looking at each other. "How did you find me?" The dog sat down and looked at her in silence. "Well okay, then, let's go." She slipped her sandals back on and they made their way through the knee-high grass until they came to the valley of shorter grass that stretched for miles. She rubbed Mutt on the head every few minutes, amazed that it was really him. There was a herd of takin bedded down about a half-mile to the west. Mutt knew they were there too; he had his nose in the air as if smelling them. Mary Lynn ignored the persistent warning in the back of her mind that kept telling her to be cautious and hurried toward the herd anyway, all the while talking to Mutt as they trotted. "Daddy's going to be so happy to see you," she said, perhaps a little too loud.

A shepherd cloaked warmly under a fur-hooded garment sat stoking a fire he built to roast a rabbit he killed earlier with a crossbow. He was too far away to hear the one-sided conversation, but he turned his head in their direction across the grassland. He stood and reached for the crossbow and quiver that lay on the ground behind him.

Mountain lions are instinctively patient when it comes to stalking prey before gracefully attacking. Hunting in groups almost always guarantees a meal. Mary Lynn stopped when Mutt suddenly glided to a standstill. He made a low guttural growl that quickly turned into a louder more serious snarl. She scanned the valley. The clouds had thinned, allowing the dim light of the crescent moon to cast its light over the verdant valley. She turned in circles; her eyes opened wide to take in as much as possible at one time. Mutt's teeth were showing now, his hair standing on end. His warnings quickly graduated to bellows. "Oh, God Mutt, what's happening?" she cried out. Then she saw it, a large beige cat. It was at least seven feet long and 300 lbs. It was galloping straight toward them. She spotted another one approaching somewhat slower from the left. A gurgling growl came from behind her. A third mountain lion was airborne; its paws stretched wide; his claws fully extended. She fell to the ground next to Mutt, put her arms over her head, and braced for the impact. The three cats would waste no time on her, no matter how hard Mutt tried to interfere. One would go for the neck while the other two held her down and systematically tore away her flesh with their large, gnashing incisors. She felt a gush of wind rush past her arms as she cowered. Another short whoosh followed. She looked up between her crossed arms and then slowly lowered them. Behind her was a hooded shepherd, holding the bulky stock of a cross bow to his chin. Four arrow-like projectiles lay handy across the prod. He was already reloaded and taking aim. Mary Lynn quickly looked around for the mountain lions and saw two of them laying on the ground with bolts protruding from their upper bodies. The bowman had shot them both through the heart. The third was timidly tiptoeing away with its head lowered. Mary Lynn put her arms around Mutt as if to shelter him while staring up at the hooded archer.

"Prana, you are safe. Come with me." The shepherd hung the bow over his shoulder and extended a hand.

Mary Lynn stood, refusing assistance. She backed away, wondering why he addressed her as if he knew her, until he pushed back the hood. "Neal!"

They studied each other for a split-second. The entirety of their short relationship rushed through her mind, including the feelings they had for each other once upon a time. He only nodded and walked past her. He made sure the big cats were dead and collected his bolts.

"What are you doing out here alone?" he asked as if reprimanding her. "Didn't anyone tell you how dangerous it is at night? Have you learned nothing?"

"Kunchen let me go. Do I really have to explain? Can't you read me the way I'm reading you right now?"

"I was looking for the dog. He's one of mine."

She looked down at Mutt. "No, you weren't! You can't lie to me, Neal."

"You were in trouble," he replied bluntly.

"That's better. Besides, he belongs to my daddy. I'm taking him home with me."

"You should stay in my camp tonight," he conceded. "It's not my place to argue with the daughter of Kokabiel. Gods willing, I'll take you to the monastery school when the sun rises. That's where you were headed, right?"

"Where did you learn to shoot a crossbow?" she asked as they started toward the camp.

"Archery is popular in Bhutan. I was asked to train for the Olympics when I was at Cornell. We aren't allowed to call attention to ourselves. Sorry I never told you."

"I guess we both had our secrets," she sighed.

"I live in seclusion now to be one with the gods," he said. "In hopes of hastening my healing."

"How far is your camp?" She realized Neal's attention had been drawn to something behind her, something over her head apparently. He suddenly went down on one knee and bowed his head.

She turned, looked up and saw Kokabiel's mighty figure standing behind her. "Oh, no, please no." She fell to the ground beside Mutt, wrapping her arms around him. The reason the elder was there was very clear. He was there for her.

"Thank you, Jeped." Kokabiel's deep raspy voice was soft, kind, filled with stately gratitude. "Your flawless skills were invaluable to this intervention. Please, take these blessed animals to your brothers."

"Yes, my lord. I will see to them," Neal replied, still on his knees, resisting the urge to look up at him.

Kokabiel leaned down to pick up Mary Lynn; her arms were wrapped determinedly around Mutt. "Something has happened and we need your help."

Japed rose when the silence of the night returned. He removed the long rope karo wrapped around his waist and proceeded to tie the legs of the mountain lions together. He would drag them back to his camp one at a time, field dress them and take them to the monks for processing. He would sleep peacefully knowing he had responded in a timely fashion to the intuitive notice of danger. He had pleased the gods by doing so, and saved the love of his life.

Chapter 23

Harry and John were among the fourth wave to transfer out of the Yangphula post. Harry was slated for Landstuhl Med Center in Germany, John, to a refurbished barracks nearby that were remodeled to accommodate families of the infirmed. A week and a half in, Harry was enduring painful physical therapy every day from a truly regimented physical therapist who slapped him on the shoulder after every session, assuring him that he was showing signs of improvement. Results from various doctor's scans, X-rays, and ensanguining syringes seemed to concur. Projections indicated that one more week of rehab would merit him a plane ticket to the states. He made use of down-time between workouts to visit the various pilots and crew from the post who, like himself, would never fully recover from an ordeal they may never wholly remember. Similar to John, some were experiencing severe nausea and bouts of anxiety whenever thinking about returning to the specialized aircraft they were proficient in flying. All were suffering from post-traumatic nightmares and were undergoing some form of psychiatric care. He had tabled visiting the man that pulled the trigger on him and Mary Lynn, but he recognized that his festering hatred was also making him ill- tempered. When he was told his flight out was in twenty-four hours, he hobbled over to Hanna's ward on a recently acquired single crutch.

"I know you," Hanna whispered when he woke from in-and-out consciousness and saw Harry sitting in a wooden folding chair next to his bed. His eyes seem to fix on the pillows Harry was sitting on that he'd confiscated from nearby unoccupied beds to cushion his knitting hip fractures.

Hanna looked beaten down, like there was no fight left in him. His cheeks were sunken; his eyes looked like burnt sockets; his lips were dry and cracked. It looked like justice served as far as Harry was concerned; being that he was the one that fired the shot that destroyed his life, physically and mentally. He could hear Mary Lynn's voice in his head: *treat this man with empathy, give him respect. He has fought valiantly for his country in the past.* His mental response to her: *don't mistake valiance for a man with no heart.*

"How do I know you?" Hanna surrendered, giving up on trying to remember.

"My name is Harrison Foster." Harry stood, propping himself on the crutch to make it easier for the commander to see his face. "FBI agent John Greenfield and I spent some time with you at Yangphula. We were. . ." He shook his head, not wanting to make it sound as if they'd given up . . . "We are searching for a missing woman from Louisiana."

"FBI," he sighed. "hum . . . vaguely familiar." His eyebrows knitted together as he grasped for the memory.

"Do you know where you are, sir?"

He nodded, just barely; but his eyes expressed uncertainty.

"Do you know your name?"

"Um, yeah . . . Hanna," he whispered and then, as if in a daze, said, "I saw three angels," and then he asked, "why am I here?" He gawked around the ward, wild-eyed as if lost. "Why can't I remember?" his voice quivered.

"Relax, everything will come back to you, sir. It'll just take a while." Harry couldn't believe such compassionate words for this ass had crossed his lips. He was sure it was Mary Lynn's influence. "The overall consensus is that you're having an adverse reaction to extreme altitude changes. You were at 20,000 ft. when your helicopter malfunctioned and plunged," he said, repeating the familiar story he heard every day in the post infirmary regarding the patients around him. The same rhetoric was going around at Landstuhl. The confused commander nodded, seeming to accept the explanation, but he doubted Hanna would ever know the true reason he was forced out of the sky.

Greenfield mostly kept to himself except for the lunch he had with Foster every day. They went over what they should and should not say to FBI interrogators once they arrived in DC. Since he had never mentioned Karma or Bassui specifically in his interview notes, their names would never be uttered. The monks would go on record as being uncooperative. As far as Cdr. Hanna was concerned . . . well, he hadn't kicked someone when he was down in a long time, but it needed to be on record that the single-minded man had failed to listen when one of his own lieutenants warned him civilians were in his line of fire. They would be debriefed separately. What he was not sure of was his future with the FBI. He was actually enjoying the sense of freedom the uncertainty gave him.

The eight-and-a-half-hour first-class flight to DC was a thousand times more comfortable than the hastily put together excursion Greenfield had hitched them a ride on from Louisiana. The comfortable wide seat felt better than anything Harry had sat in since leaving home. Their first stop was Quantico to tie up loose ends and finalize the dismantling of the team that, up till now, had been a mere enigma, a group of mysterious eggheads within Greenfield's notebook. They spent two days debriefing and six hours repeating and re-repeating their rehearsed accounts to a trio of military generals. Judging by the long silences between answers, it seemed no one was prepared for their testimonies. The unique team romanticized over several outlandish theories throughout their brainstorming sessions to explain the reported sightings and abductions. *Sasquatch* was only one in the mix of several exciting possibilities because of witness accounts and always noted in italics. The objective was to find a scientific reason for the puzzling testimonies and bazaar experiences . . . a mental explanation that involved drugs, hysteria, or bad dreams. They were not prepared for Harry's statement detailing his first-hand encounter or for the seasoned FBI agent to verify it. It certainly gave everyone pause. They were warned not to leave Virginia before their testimonies could be evaluated. In the end, the CIA took over the project and established a protocol that did not include them. Since all videos and photos that supported their testimonies were "inadvertently lost," any leak or rumbling on the subject was to be refuted and their reputations smeared, similar to how they treated the witnesses who claimed they saw strange Area 51 activity, and Roswell aliens, and UFOs. They were provided a commercial ticket to Louisiana and a dialogue to recite when engaging family, friends, and co-workers or anyone that questioned their whereabouts for the past five months.

"So, are you going to follow the CIA's directive and tell Mr. Bennett that bull-shit 'Doctors without Borders' story?" Harry leaned forward, bracing himself against his cane. It was hard to find a comfortable position in the vinyl cushioned chairs in the boarding area at Ronald Reagan Washington National. They were both dressed as civilians, wearing sports shirts and Docker jeans with no hint of military sand or FBI insignias. Their Delta flight to Hartsfield-Jackson Atlanta was on time.

The agent leaned forward, propped his elbows on his knees, and spoke as quietly as possible. "I already spoke to him."

"We were warned against doing that, you know." Harry watched the agent fretfully rub his hands together.

"I know," he whispered. "I bought a burner and had him call me from a neighbor's phone. He's hurt and disappointed. I could hear him crying; he was trying to keep it quiet, but I could hear him. He just ended the conversation with, 'I understand.' The only comfort I could give him was to tell him the whole story."

"So, he knows I was rescued and she wasn't?" Harry asked.

Greenfield nodded. "He also knows the shape you're in."

"Thank you for that. I can't tell you what a huge load of guilt this is . . . I still don't know what I'm going to say to him. Did you tell him about Christine?"

"He already suspected there was something off about her disappearance from the get-go. He was a deputy sheriff, remember; he determined right away that the evidence was planted. He deserved to know the truth about her, too."

"Well, I'm glad you deleted Bassui's photos from Hanna's hard drive. Hanna doesn't remember anything and I think we convinced the CIA he was fixed on chasing ISIS ghosts when he ordered the attacks in the mountains."

"I'm almost sure they'll send someone else," John groaned; "probably posing as a climber or some ridiculous rouse to check the mountains. I'd like to see whomever they send try and talk their way past that monk, Kunchen. Or get any information from Bidhan, the butcher, or Karma," he paused at the thought of her. "No one's gonna talk; just like they did with us. If you recall, they never really offered us anything to amount to much. Cordial and kind . . . always, but they keep their secrets well."

Harry leaned his forehead against his hands that were cupped across the rubber- cushioned cane handle grip. "I had her . . . I had her in my arms, John," he moaned. "We kissed; we were developing a new relationship, falling in love. It's killing me to go home, to leave her with them."

Greenfield laid his arm across Harry's shoulders. "I don't know how or when Harry, but I'm going back there. First, I'm going to re-interview some of the witnesses I met. The ones my gut told me were telling the truth. It'll mean a lot of traveling. You're welcome to come with me."

"You can't tell anyone what you know; we were warned against doing that."

"I want them to know that I took them seriously. I think I can do that without, you know, spilling all the beans. I'd rather they spend the rest of their lives feeling some kind of justification for coming forward instead of embarrassment."

Harry picked up the new backpack next to his chair. "It's time to board."

"What?" John looked toward the boarding counter. The tarmac door suddenly opened. He helped Harry to his feet, wondering how he knew the female attendant was about to open the door. He looked around for some kind of warning light that the door was about to open; there was none. She took her position behind the counter and started calling out rows over a hand-held microphone. She waved them to the head of the line when she saw Harry hobbling awkwardly.

For the first time since Harry met the agent in the lab at RRMC, there was no sign of a notebook within his reach. The team no longer existed; the mystery had been solved and filed away in some top-secret X-file never to be spoken of again. As for himself, he didn't know how to deal with so many truths. He was in no physical or mental condition to follow John around the world on his journey of redemption. There would be no one to confide in, no redemption for him. A physiatrist would never believe his story. He had found Bigfoot, but it's actually a race called the Nephilim who dress themselves up to make people think they are Bigfoot. And by the way, the Nephilim are descendants of the gods that were cast out of heaven. Yes, he would be categorized as delusional. How could he concentrate on work while wondering where the Nephilim had taken Mary Lynn and if he would ever see her again? Al would grow to hate him over time for letting his daughter slip through his fingers. An image appeared to him as they slowly made their way through the boarding bridge. It was Mary Lynn. Her eyes were closed. The image panned out; she was praying with her hands pressed together in front of her.

"You okay?" he heard John say through the fog in his head. The former agent had his arms around his chest, holding him up. "Think you can make it just a few more steps? We're almost to the door."

It took twenty-five minutes for a medic to okay him to fly and for the crew to complete the boarding process. Harry's head ached while everyone went about their routine settling in. The cabin was noisy with passenger chatter. John was staring out the window. Another memory appeared in Harry's head. It was of the day he was sitting on the ground next to Bassui, getting to know him. John was sitting beside Karma on a wooden bench and Harry sensed more was happening between them than just conversation.

"What?" John said when he turned and saw Harry staring at him.

"Nothing, I was just thinking about you and Karma and Bassui."

"So was I," John said smiling and nodding as if eager to talk about them. "Remember our second trip to the village?" John said. "You were connecting with Bassui and I was talking to Karma. I was just thinking about how easy it was for her to make me spill my guts about anything, my career, my past marriages. I'm going to miss her. I'm really gonna miss her," he repeated with a long sigh.

"You were thinking about them, just now?" Harry asked.

"Yeah, what about it?" John quizzed, shrugging one shoulder.

"No reason," Harry sighed. Something had felt different when he woke up in the infirmary on the army post. Granted, his body was weak because of the trauma it went through and his head was woozy from medications. He tired easily and his thoughts drifted all over the place. A normal occurrence for shock victims, he knew that. He'd seen changes in patients with head injuries before, had verified their hormonal and chemical production changes from under the microscope. Patients forgot where they were or where they were going and admitted to having one-sided conversations with loved ones, even dead ones. Sporadic memories of his experiences in Bhutan were inadvertently materializing in his head, like just now. Except that, John was having the same memory at the same time. Was it a coincidence? What about the attendant he saw come through the door to announce the boarding order before she actually opened it? He even saw her waving them to the head of the line before she actually raised her hand. "I think I'll try and get some rest," he said when a flight attendant handed them a set of headphones. He tuned it to noise cancelling. He didn't want to hear music; he wanted silence. He closed his eyes and tried to turn his mind off and think of nothing.

Chapter 24

It was the week before Easter. Dale's wife, Aria, had bought two egg-dying kits and two dozen eggs. There would be egg hunting in the back yard for days if tradition was followed, and rotten eggs found in the foliage around their rental home for months. Aria was from a large Georgia family and used to preparing hearty holiday meals. Easter's would be equally as the grand as the first two holiday meals she prepared in Louisiana, Thanksgiving and Christmas. Harry had skipped the two previous holiday gatherings. Maybe guilt kept him away, or memories; whatever the case, he wasn't ready to fake happiness. Easter welcomed spring and lifted spirits in anticipation of the long-awaited warm weather. Aria was eager to start landscaping the yard around their rental home and plant a garden. Of course, everyone in Louisiana knew better than to put plants in the ground until that last cold snap that according to tradition, came one week after Easter. Louisianans would never know what freezing temperatures really were unless they'd spent a winter in the Himalayas. Harry had nothing to look forward to; life was boring without his best friend to share it with. She was the reason he got up every morning. As a kid he looked forward to school every day so he could sit beside her on the bus, carry her backpack, make sure she did her homework. They joined the same clubs in middle school, met at every high school function, carpooled together to college, made sure they were placed at the same hospital. He met her for lunch and after work at Red's, listening to her every exploit. He was living in his apartment again, working in the lab, but felt detached from everything and everyone. He got around without assistance now, although sometimes, there was a slight limp that was more pronounced when he was in a hurry. Al had given him a welcoming bear hug the first day he and John walked through his front door. Harry held on to him just as hard, trying to hold back tears that leaked through anyway. They sat in the living room for hours, giving him as full an accounting as they could.

"So, I was right about her," Al grunted, staring at John. The two had become friends over the past five months, emotionally attached, even though their interactions were over the phone. "She elected to leave and then seven years later took our daughter." His voice tinged with bitterness.

"I don't know what to say; Christine seemed happy." Harry found it harder to relay the story than he anticipated, periodically having to take a breath to center his thoughts. "As for Mary Lynn, maybe she chose to stay because . . . because . . ." His eyes were fixed on nothing, as if his mind were somewhere else . . . back in Bhutan; with her, in the mountain. "I get this feeling . . . like she's trying to tell me something. I think her decision involved my well-being or someone else's. I can't explain it; it's as if I woke up in the med tent with some sort of insight . . . her insight. Al, I saw her do things no normal human can do."

At times, he wished he'd gone with John on his trip around the world, but the former agent's journey was to end in Bhutan. There was nothing in Bhutan for him. He had heard nothing from Bassui, no emails, no texts. Their gods were gone and the Americans were to blame. John had thicker skin, was better trained to face that kind of disdain.

Work was mundane, but it helped pass the time. The newly acquired ability told him when someone was about to come through the lab door, which made work more interesting. He spent time in the hospital gym going through a regimen of exercises one of the trainers recommended. His general physique had benefited. Girls were starting to notice him, flirt, and ask to sit with him at Reds. Their endless chatter about nothing of substance bored him to tears. He tried to pretend they were Mary Lynn, but their irritating squirming, hair twirling, and eyelash batting defined nonsense. Sammy always brought him at least one beer on the house, sometimes more. One evening after a late shift, Sammy sat down beside him at the dark end of the bar where he'd begun sitting to discourage company. He knew something was up . . . *bad news*, he sensed. Sammy started out talking about the weather and then politics, nervously pausing between subjects before finally coming out with it. He was retiring. He had sold the restaurant to a young couple who promised to keep everything the same: same menu, same employees, same atmosphere. Harry properly congratulated him and told him how much he would be missed. Everything around him was changing. He found himself mindlessly driving out to Camp Livingston from time to time to reminisce about the old days when life was simple and fun. Fun because they were kids, fun because of *her*. The main gate was padlocked after six p.m. because campers and trail riders were having parties and becoming a general nuisance. "Imagine that!" He would chuckle to himself as if talking to Mary Lynn. "At least we didn't destroy stuff and knew when it was time to bounce. Everybody knew not to stay in one place long enough to get caught.

***

John looked forward to re-visiting the area near the Olympic National Forest in Washington State. The woods were abundant with hemlock, Douglas fir, ponderosa pine, and the distinctive smell of the western red cedar. Seeing nothing but the different varieties of Lodgepole, White Bark, and Ponderosa gave him a sense of peace, something he didn't feel before, simply because he wasn't paying attention. Karma would appreciate the essence of the forest. "I wish I could bring you here so you could see this for yourself," he whispered. He arrived unannounced, same as in every location he re-visited the past month. The current point of interest was near Quinault Rain Forest. An off-road vehicle was required to reach the spot where two hunters had walked up on the creature people in the northwest call Sasquatch while searching for a place to cut wood. Theirs was the last names on his "most believable" list to "check in on. To see how they were doing. There was nothing to report; just wanted to let them know they weren't forgotten." That was his intro to the start of every conversation. He parked the Tundra four-wheel-drive behind a faded blue, mud-spattered Dodge truck that belonged to one of the hunters. It was parked off to the side of the trail in the grass. He checked his notes to verify their names, *Josh and Chuck, blue Dodge Ram registered to Josh Chambers*. He strode through the knee-high grass hoping to see something familiar to guide him to the spot where they had pounded on trees with pieces of split wood. A man wearing a blue flannel shirt was sitting on a tree stump petting a large black dog with a yellow reflective collar. When he stepped closer, he recognized him as one of the men he interviewed. "Josh, or is it Chuck?" he asked politely. "Sorry, I don't remember . . ."

The man's head was bent down; one hand was resting across the dog's back. "I'm Josh," he said, staring sadly at the dog. "This is Chuck." His face was solemn when he finally looked up at John. "I'm sorry," he said, seeing the confusion on John's face. "My friend Chuck died in a car wreck a few months ago. Found this guy here waiting for me when I finally got up the nerve to come back out here." He rubbed the dog's head. "I named this guy after him. He's been by my side ever since."

John went down on one knee. The pieces of wood they used to knock on the sides of the trees to signal their Sasquatch lay undisturbed under a couple inches of leaves next to the tree trunks. "Josh, I'm so sorry; I didn't know." He rubbed the dog behind one of its ears. The dog was very large, at least 150 lbs., black with long hair like Mutt. "You know this is a Bhutan mastiff?"

"No, I haven't given it much thought, actually," he sighed.

"I've been to Bhutan looking for . . . well, you know. These dogs are very smart and valued for their herding skills. They're rarely found in the US The Bhutanese say that when one picks you, it means you will have good luck always."

"Is that so," Josh whispered. The dog hadn't taken his eyes off Josh the whole time.

"I have a friend that knows a lot about these things. Her beliefs are a little different from ours, but if she were here, she would tell you the gods sent this special animal to you."

Josh began to cry uncontrollably. He covered his face with one hand; the other he used to grab a fistful of the dog's hair and pull him closer.

"I came here looking for you," John said, "you and Chuck, to tell you that you were partially right about what you saw out here. But," he looked at the dog and shook his head as if he still found it hard to believe what he knew to be true, "there is more to the phenomenon than I'm allowed to say. The people I used to work for would have my head if they knew I traveled the world talking to witnesses like this. You should change his name though. Chuck wouldn't want you to wallow in sorrow every time you talked to this fellow. He'd want you to enjoy your new life with your new companion."

"Sometimes, I can't help but think it was Chuck that sent him."

"Something else my friend would tell you is the gods must think highly of you or they would never have shown themselves to you."

"I thought you weren't supposed to talk about it." Josh looked up at him. His eyes were red and swollen.

"I was just telling you what my friend would say."

"So, what we saw was really Sasquatch?"

"I can tell you that it wasn't Sasquatch. But that's what they would like everyone to believe."

"They? That's all you can tell me?"

"I'm afraid so. Except, you're gonna be okay, Josh," the former agent said while petting Chuck on the top of the head. "This fella right here is going to see to it."

***

Temperatures in the new homesite were comparable to that of the Himalayas, but the landscape was remarkably different. Four mountains with monumental peaks, surrounded by rolling hills of snow and ice amassed the new residence. One could see for miles before a distant set of prominent twin buttes rose in the east to meet the feathery sky. Judging by the extensive work done within, the excavation process must have gone on for decades prior to the exodus. The colony was supplied extensively with food, clothing, and every essential. An unexpected complication had emerged, however . . . a serious one that required they boil the water that streamed throughout the inner grottos. Half the population became ill within a week of their arrival. Mary Lynn's medical training and newly heightened sensibilities told her an aggressive foreign bacterium was in the ground-water. Boiling water was the only recourse since there was no natural remedy on hand and healing prayers weren't having the desired effect. They had already buried four Nephilim and two of the human children.

Mary Lynn's awareness prompted her when Kokabiel was near. It was always late, when the colony was settling down for the night. He presented himself in her quarters, holding the large staff that seemed to be permanently attached to his hand. He enjoyed pounding it on the stone floor like a gavel. It made their conversations feel more like an inquisition than a getting to know you visit. He wasn't as agile as the younger and middle-aged Nephilim she was getting to know. Wisdom and old age came with stiff joints and rigid muscles.

Their first conversation started with Kokabiel complimenting her on making it as far as the valley. But it quickly turned to belittlement: "Before facing your death."

"So, you were testing me," she countered. "I thought so. Sorry to disappoint you."

"You will never be what we are," he continued. "Your mother has faith in you, as a mother should, but she's wrong. You have talent, but your insolence hinders you from becoming one with the gods."

"Sorry you feel that way," she replied. "But, I'm not ready to give up on myself and I don't think the gods are either."

He continued the disparagement on a subsequent visit. She was sitting on the floor, sharing bits of bread with Mutt when he burst in from out of nowhere. "Why did you conduct yourself so poorly when you were young?" he asked, again pounding the staff. "Why didn't you venerate the gifts you were born with and devote time to your calling?" He was dressed more casually this time, wearing similar robe-like garments that she'd seen others wear in their work places.

She refuted the mighty man's analytics as respectfully as she could. Calm had returned to her psyche as a result of daily meditation. "My mother coached me to keep the knowledge of my oddities to myself to avoid harassment." She winked at Mutt, the new keeper of her secrets, and let a cynicism slip. "Surely she explained this to you in the many conversations you had before she left us?"

His face remained stoic as if unmoved. His reply was a simple resounding yes.

"It's not right, using people from all over the world, my mother being one of them," she coolly challenged, leaving the bread for Mutt to finish while she pushed herself up from the floor. "I don't know how you justify it. Is it your way of getting back at humanity for abusing your ancestors thousands of years ago? You're not in charge of how life evolves; you should trust the wisdom of your gods and mine. Kunchen taught me to let these things go. You wanted me to learn from him, but you seem to have forgotten the basics. You cannot successfully spread your bloodline by deception and force. Someone or something will always resist and come looking for you." A moment passed; she could feel his concession and then his response: "Your perspective has been noted."

Mary Lynn stepped into a chair and then onto a table to get closer to him. "Tell me, do you know where the other colonies are?"

Kokabiel frowned. "Japed has a loose tongue when he's around you!" he grumbled and prodded the spear on the stone floor.

"Yes, Neal was trying to help me understand the history and the plight of the Nephilim."

"Thousands of years ago, it was agreed and sworn, that no one would speak of this!" he shouted. "You shall never speak of it again!"

The volume and vibration of his voice nearly shook her off the table. She fell to her knees and steadied herself with her hands. When she looked up, he was gone.

The Nephilim people weren't that much different than other societies of the world. They had nearly the same since of humor and the same family situations. Workers came to her with minor wounds and injuries, an easy task for Prana, as everyone called her. Medicine or special instruments for cuts and scrapes the diligent carvers suffered while chiseling out closets and cabinets to accommodate the needs of each household weren't necessary. The Nephilim physique and organ structure were equivalent to humans, with the exception of being broad, tall, and hard to reach. Platforms of graduating levels were built that allowed her to examine and tend any affliction. The Nephilim tolerance for pain was remarkable. Lacerations were comparable to a bee sting to the mighty giants. Nothing in her purview, however, told her what to do about the bacterial illness spreading rapidly throughout the colony. With each meditation, she prayed for Harry's counsel.

She needed his keen analytical eye to isolate the pathogen. But how could that happen without access to a lab and pharmaceuticals? Without a diagnosis and proper treatment, their Prana could only ease their fever, achiness, and diarrhea, not cure them.

Mary Lynn sensed her mother walking behind her late one afternoon as she made her way through a mountain doorway. It had been a demanding day in the area now called *The Clinic*. She kicked her way through a small snowdrift buildup with Mutt by her side. She rarely went anywhere without him. He sat close to her in the clinic and curled up beside her when she meditated. He was her touchstone, her reminder of home, her father, and Harry. Once outside the cave opening, she took a moment to fill her lungs with fresh air while she waited for her mother to catch up. Only hunters ventured outside the four mountains, as it had been in the Himalayas. Most were afraid to go out into the open. Meditation was significantly more uplifting in the fresh air, as she learned from her time spent in the courtyard at the Dzong.

"Mother," she greeted, when Christine finally cleared the cave opening. "The air has the same bite doesn't it? But, look at all the trees. There were no trees in the Himalayas. Mutt and I have seen white foxes and caribou out here. I'm concerned about what to do when the food supplies run out. We no longer have the monks to help supply us." She turned to face her. "Do you know where we are?"

Like her daughter, she was dressed in a thick white hooded robe to blend into the surroundings. She stopped to brush the snow from her arms that had fallen when she passed under the jagged opening.

"Did Kokabiel confide our location to you?" Mary Lynn asked, sensing that she didn't know. "He's very good at hiding what's on his mind."

"Don't be angry with your father, Prana," she said, catching her breath and expelling a warm vapor that quickly turned to ice. "He is the highest-ranking elder. He's trained to keep certain things to himself; he carries a ton of responsibly on his shoulders."

"He's obstinate, set in his ways. He won't listen when I tell him the sick need antibiotics and IV fluids."

They looked at one another through the opening of their hoods. "You must be patient, sweetheart. We will make it through this."

Mary Lynn turned back to the landscape. "Mutt and I have been out here at night. We can see the magical light show of the Aurora Borealis. That should give you a general idea of where we are."

Christine cast her eyes down. "We are in northern Russia."

"Russia!" Mary Lynn gasped. "Russia is the last place we should be! People are dying; we could all die. Do you think anyone in Russia will care?"

"We must rely on the wisdom of the elders," Christine replied.

"James and I could sneak into a hospital pharmacy and get supplies and the medicine we need. Security may not be as good as in the US. I'd never try to escape under those circumstances; at least, not until I knew everyone was cured."

"At least your talent outweighs your sharp tongue Prana. When was the last time you stopped long enough to meditate? Kunchen taught you that answers come only when you let them."

"Believe me, Mother, I am meditating. Twice a day when I'm able. The Clinic is overwhelmingly busy."

Christine moved closer. "I've been watching you with the daughters."

"Is that what you call the orphan girls, *the daughters?*" Mary Lynn gasped. "Those little girls should've been left behind with the villagers, or taken to the monasteries with the boys. The wing I stayed in was empty. There's no reason to isolate them like this."

"Prana," Christine said, placing a hand on her daughters' shoulder. "Monks choose to remain celibate. It's forbidden to have women living in the Dzongs. Tradition states that only boys are allowed to become monks. You were allowed to study there only because you are the daughter of Kokabiel. The daughters look up to you; they are desperate to learn from your example. Surely you are aware."

They stared at each other for another moment. Mary Lynn sensed her mother's agenda. She always had one; there was no point in arguing with her. She squatted down next to Mutt, remembering how no one, not her Daddy, not Dale, not her best friend from the neighborhood, Ms. Lilly, was able to dissuade her from something she was passionate about. "Who cares about genetically engineered frogs and fish?" Al would argue. "James says you have our father's ear," Mary Lynn finally said.

"Kokabiel and the elders decide what's best for the Nephilim," Christine replied.

"But they're going to die. You must convince him we need medical supplies."

"If only you had married Neal," Christine sighed wearily.

"Really?" she gasped. "So, this is my fault? My purpose in life is not to be a Nephilim or have their children, Mother. Even Neal understands that. Truth be told, so does Kokabiel. Why can't you?"

"I'm sorry, sweetheart, I didn't mean that. I'm just frustrated. Evil steps in when anxiety plays on people's weaknesses. I suppose I could use more meditation myself. You should stop relying on modern medicine; we never had to use it before. The cure will come to you."

"Is there something else, Mother?" Mary Lynn sensed there was.

"Yes, I've been wanting to tell you . . ." The look on her daughter's face told her she already knew the words she was groping for.

"James already told me that he has a daughter like me," Mary Lynn said in response to her mother's unspoken words.

"Yes. She's been shadowing you in the clinic. You must have singled her out by now."

"There is this one girl," Mary Lynn said, "she's unusually curious about where I came from. She sits next to Mutt and watches me."

"Alisha; her name means 'protected by the gods.' She's curious about the western world, like James was as a child. After all, it's where his mother and her grandmother came from."

"I remember James telling me he had a daughter."

"I convinced Kokabiel to let you grow up in America. I read American history to him. It tells of how people in the west handled *different* with little compassion. But times are changing; attitudes are evolving. It would help to have someone that looks and acts as they do to follow. I don't mean by standing behind a pulpit or preaching," she said when Mary Lynn frowned. "You're smart, Prana; you'll figure a way to balance your talent with bringing people into the gods' fold."

"My father's not going to let me go anywhere." She looked toward the distant trees, wondering how far she might get if she made a run for it. She noticed her mother smiling; her eyes were glistening. "What?"

"I love your spirit, Prana. It's always been your best quality. I'm so very proud of you."

A minute passed before either spoke again. Mary Lynn watched a rabbit jump through the snow about ten yards away. Mutt saw it too and chased after it. It disappeared, along with Mutt below the crust and then they suddenly leaped in the air, landed, and disappeared again. It was hard for the dog to keep up as he labored to pull himself out of the deep snow. It would be just as difficult for anyone to make good time under these conditions. "This place is not safe. It's too easily accessible." She pointed to the sloping hills, a clear contrast from the steep mountain drop-offs of the Himalayas.

"Kokabiel said it looked very different thirty-years ago when he and the other elders first picked it," Christine said. "The snow banks were a mile high."

"The Nephilim will never be able to tolerate the water. Kokabiel should find another place to live. Someplace with fresh air. When I asked him about the other two colonies, he nearly knocked me off the table I was standing on with his answer."

"No one is allowed to talk about . . . them," Christine said in a whisper.

"You know where they are, don't you? Oh my God! They didn't survive!" Her mother's thoughts were easier to read than her father's, the highest-ranking elder. "Neither colony?"

"That is what the elders believe," Christine replied, bowing her head. "Those who travel have found no sense or sign of them. It is believed that the only reason this colony survived is because of the monks," Christine whispered.

"Then we must go back to Bhutan. Everyone is acclimated to the minerals there."

Christine frowned curiously.

"Here's a crazy idea . . ." Mary Lynn began.

"It makes sense, but Kokabiel won't like it," Christine replied, reading her daughter's thoughts.

"Kunchen can help by interceding with the King to guarantee their protection," Mary Lynn continued, staring off into the cotton-like hilly snow. "Wouldn't it be amazing if the Nephilim introduced themselves to the world?" she whispered as if in a daydream. "They could go outside without fear." She envisioned the men building shelter's outside, the children romping in the valleys and women tending large vegetable gardens nourished by the sun. "The Bhutanese already believe their gods live in the mountains. They would be honored to know them in person."

"It's too big of a risk," Christine said, considering the proposal. "Not everyone is sick; you're not, I'm not. I suppose

320

those not affected could stay. You can use it as a compromise when proposing this to Kokabiel."

"Me?" Mary Lynn gasped.

Christine hooked her arm through Mary Lynn's and steered her toward the cave opening. Mutt raised his head from the trench he was rooting in and dashed after them. "He considers what you say more than you know. The resistance will come from the other elders, and it will be fierce."

"It will take a lot of courage to present such a risky idea to them, assuming he agrees," Mary Lynn added.

"It could be perilous; they might vote him off the council for going against tradition. Your father is a brave man. I will do what I can to help convince him."

"Why would you?" Mary Lynn asked.

"Because I pray every day that they be accepted by the world, despite their stark differences. The Nephilim have been taught from birth that they must remain hidden in order to survive. Sometimes clinging to tradition is the easier path; more comfortable than the mayhem that comes with change, even if it means a better life."

***

The guilt pangs grew stronger every time Harry drove past Oakland Nursing Home where Ms. Lilly Morrison, Christine's best friend from the old neighborhood was staying now. The need to visit Camp Livingston had Harry ignoring the responsibility to update her on Mary Lynn's whereabouts at first. It seemed impossible to stay away from the army camp that held so many memories of the carefree days from a lifetime ago. His need to walk the ground, sit under the moonlight. His desire to be with her, even if it was in a memory, steered him past the lighted sign pointing to the turn into Oakland. The improved roads and the turns to the old haunt were burned in his brain. The path through the thicket was overgrown. If it hadn't been for the thin piece of weathered one-by-four that someone hastily nailed to a tree ten years ago, he might never have found it. The scribed arrow in magic marker pointing the way to the sacred circle was weathered down to invisible but the small plank assured him he was in the right spot. He carried a blanket, often staying too long and finding the gate chained and padlocked. That would summon Sgt. Dan Prestridge, the MP with three E5 sergeant stripes, in a Range Rover to unlock the padlock and chain after seeing him on the security camera above the gate. Sgt. Dan reminded him each time of the 6 p.m. closing time. The remembrances were addicting but lately had morphed into something more. Not only did he imagine seeing her dancing on top of a car or toasting marshmallows with a grill lighter when he closed his eyes, but he could picture her face, looking at him with those amazing blue eyes, smiling. Sometimes she was praying over a sickbed, or showing him a snowy landscape. Dreams, he supposed. Sgt. Dan always gave him the same warning: "Don't let it happen again, Harry." The sergeant was familiar with the Christine Bennett kidnapping and he had been working in the FBI field office that occupied a building in the adjacent Camp Beauregard at the time of Mary Lynn's disappeared.

Lilly Morrison, longtime neighbor, babysitter and good friend of the Bennett's was in failing health. Her husband Hank had been gone for ten years. Gatherings at the Bennett and the Morrisons were a regular thing before Hank died. Harry had been home nearly a month and had yet made himself go see her. Lilly was that wise older woman mentor to Christine. Hank was the calming presence that took the edge off Al's bad moods after a troublesome day in the line of duty. Lilly filled the void for Mary Lynn after Christine disappeared. Hank died two years before the tragedy, so Al had no one to lean on. It was heartbreaking, confessing his failure to bring Mary Lynn home to Al. It was time to come clean with Ms. Lilly.

A nurse's aide led him through the fragrant social rooms and formal areas where tables were set with dishes, cutlery, and napkins. Cushioned sofas and chairs were stationed around coffee tables and two wide-screen TVs and a cozy fireplace. Aides were taking down Easter decorations and putting them away in large plastic tubs. As she guided him deeper into the facility where the private rooms were located, he began to pick up the familiar smell of sterilization that was abundant throughout every health care facility including RRMC. He lightly knocked on the door, entered, and pulled a visitor's chair up close to the bed. Lilly's head was turned away toward the window where cards, bouquets, and knickknacks were lined along the ledge. Her mind was definitely somewhere else and she didn't hear him drag the chair across the floor. Her blue nightgown was loose around her pale thin body. An oxygen tube wound through her uncombed gray hair and connected under her nose with a nasal cannula. He unfolded a blanket at the foot of the bed and covered her. Her hand felt like an icicle when he picked it up. "Ms. Lilly," he whispered.

"Harrison?" Her voice sounded distant and raspy as if she were returning from somewhere far away. She strained to raise her head. "How are you, sweetheart?" She said, clearing the phlegm in her throat.

"I wasn't sure you'd recognize me. I hardly know myself these days."

"Oh, honey," she said, leaning her body toward him. "I remember now, you went off with that FBI agent to find Mary Lynn. How did it go?"

"That's why I'm here." He lowered his eyes. "I found her, but . . ." he breathed in slowly and then exhaled. "There was an accident; I was hurt, and I'm not sure what happened to her. I think she's still alive, but . . ."

"Where did you find her?" Her voice was curiously insistent for a woman in such a deteriorating condition. "Was she with Christine?" she asked as if she was expecting a yes.

"What?" He asked, confused by the question. "How did you know?"

"I always suspected she was still alive. I was the only person she trusted enough to confide in about certain things. Like her relationship with Al, her frustration over Mary Lynn's struggles, Dale's rebellious teenage years, the research she was doing, the child she lost. Al never understood her dedication to the work they were doing at the fish hatchery. She was curious about those sorts of things because of her own genomic differences."

"And Mary Lynn's," Harry said with a long exhale.

"The colors," she sighed nodding and nearly out of breath. "Christine taught her how to deal with them."

"It's more than just colors," Harry said. "Much more."

"Yes, I know," she sighed and cupped a shaky hand over his. "Christine was so excited when the giant sought her out," Lilly said. "You know, she was never afraid of him; I would have been petrified. In fact, she loved everything about him. Oh, what was his name? Koca . . . something?"

"Kokabiel," Harry said just above a whisper as if someone might be listening.

"She told you about him?" she likewise whispered.

"I met him," Harry replied as quietly and clearly as he remembered Lt. White's voice being in the wilds of Bhutan.

"Ohh, that's amazing," she gushed. "What's he like?"

"Very tall, human-like, and ferocious-looking. Pretty awesome actually."

"As excited as Christine was about the insemination, she was equally devastated when Kokabiel told her she couldn't possibly carry their baby. She wouldn't let him have Mary Lynn though."

"You knew about all this?" Harry whispered.

"Yes, she was desperate to be with her son. I knew something was up the last time I saw her; there was something different about her goodbye. But I always suspected she might come back for Mary Lynn because she was special."

"You knew about the colors," Harry sighed. "Why didn't you tell the sheriff or the FBI any of this?"

"They wouldn't have believed an old woman with such a crazy story. They wouldn't have bothered to even write it down."

John would have written it down, he thought to himself. *He wrote everything down no matter how insignificant.*

"Now, tell me everything," she said, squeezing his hands. Hers felt much warmer now.

"Alright, but you have to promise me, like you did Christine, that what I tell you goes no further than this room." He tried to give her as much detail as he could in the one sitting. She never flinched. Her eyes were wide as if she had been anxiously waiting for someone to tell her the rest of a story that had begun much longer than seven years ago. It took him thirty-five minutes, starting with the mysterious dog that brought the FBI agent, John Greenfield to his lab, their search in Bhutan, the near-crashes, and the friendships they made with Bassui and Karma. He described the rocky countryside, the beautiful lush valleys, and snow-covered icy mountains and the hard-nosed commander Hanna, the monks, the Dzong, the monastery, and the orphans. "Christine's living quarters were in a huge carved-out room inside one of the mountains. There were family photos on a table; there was one of you and Hank. Over two thousand giants were living within the catacomb of passageways. James, Christine's son is at least twelve feet tall and Kokabiel, fourteen, if not more. They looked as human as you and I, but have Tibetan features or maybe Indian, dark-skinned but not black."

"You're talking about them in the past tense," she interrupted.

"The giants left the Himalayas, evacuated. Kokabiel let Mary Lynn and I go; we were working our way down, inside a mountain because the post commander was most likely using infrared to hunt for what he thought were ISIS militants and shooting at everything that moved. I stupidly put out a yellow scarf as a signal. Hanna fired a rocket at it. I should have died. I can't help but think that Mary Lynn somehow played a part in me being alive."

Ms. Lilly gently placed her hand to the side of his face. "You could be right, Harrison," she whispered. "I wouldn't be in this place if she were still here."

"I saw her heal a boy that was badly burned. I'm so glad I came to see you, Ms. Lilly. Sorry it took me so long." He was red-faced, trying to hold back a gush of tears the storm of emotions had built up. "I have no one to talk to about this. My friend John left shortly after we talked to Al. And Al's not the discussing type. Once Al understands the facts, that's it, no more need to talk about it."

"Yes, I remember how Hank used to start out doing most of the talking where those two were concerned. It would take about twenty minutes for Al to finally start chiming in."

Lilly suddenly started picking at her blanket, lifting it as if looking for something. She came up with the TV remote and pointed it at the television on the wall near the ceiling, unmuting it. "What the hell? Harrison, do you know what this is about? Fox's *Special Report* is about Bhutan."

Harry was sitting with his back to the TV. He turned in the chair and then stood to see the screen. One-half of the divided screens had a photo of King Wangluck. Next to that was an artist's comic book-like rendering of a Sasquatch. The reporter was reading a statement issued by His Highness, that Bhutan had given asylum to 1100 Nephilim giants. The supreme council, in an emergency meeting, had passed laws giving them a territory of their own to govern in the Himalayas. No one would ever be allowed to enter its borders or airspace without permission from the supreme council. *"These are intelligent self-sufficient human beings that wish to be left alone,"* the reporter read from the digital notebook in his hand. *"I realize this public announcement will produce curiosity seekers,"* the reporter read, *"so be warned. Bhutan is a monarchy and as long as I am King, no one will be allowed*

*to enter the newly designated territory. Intruders will be
prosecuted in accordance with the severity of the breach of the
Nephilim's borders."*

Harry looked back at Ms. Lilly. Her expression had
changed from surprise to joy. Her eyes glistened like stars; her
cheeks bulged from behind the aged hands covering her mouth
that repressed the emotional outcry.

"Does this mean?" she gasped.

"I don't know what it means. Let me think." Harry looked
around the room, not really focusing on anything, waiting for
an answer to come.

"Do you think Christine and Mary Lynn could possibly be
with them?" She was trying to whisper but she was so eager it
came out as a high-pitched cry. "Harrison!" She grabbed his
arm and shook it trying to get his attention. "Do you think they
are with them?"

"Uh-I suppose it's possible . . . I need to talk to . . . John,
he could be in Bhutan by now. If he is . . ."

"I wonder if Al has seen this?" she interrupted. "Harrison,
where are you going?" she yelled as best she could, her voice
cracking with excitement, but he was already out the door,
hobbling with the telltale limp through the hallways to the
exit.

Sweat beaded up around his neck and face as he sat
quietly, his head against the steering wheel, trying to compose
himself. He looked up into the rear-view mirror. It was hard to
distinguish the sweat from tears. He turned on the ignition and
aimed the AC vents toward his face. *Is this what a mental
breakdown feels like?* He rolled out of the parking lot
intending to turn on the familiar Camp Livingston Road only a
short half-mile ahead. He reminded himself it was late; the
gate would be chained and padlocked. He had been given so
many warnings by Sgt. Dan who found him more than once
standing outside the gate. Sometimes he would find him
sitting in his truck, staring. He contemplated using a bolt

cutter on the floor behind the seat under the blanket. He needed time to think, somewhere to sort out what the newscast meant. He kept repeating to himself, *I should have gone with John*. He pressed the accelerator hard, passed the camp road, and continued north. *He must be in Bhutan by now, I would be there now if I had just gone with him.* He turned into a convenience store parking lot, pulled out his phone, and hit the contact number for the former agent. It went directly to a "no longer in-service" notice so he threw the phone on the seat and pulled back out onto the highway. His mind was reeling, yet he continued to drive north on 165, following his unconscious mind. Tiny specks of sleet started to stick to the windshield. He turned on the wipers when it accumulated to the point where he could no longer see and almost missed the turn on Hwy. 8 while fiddling with the switch. After blowing through the Hwy. 84 east/west stop sign, the sleet turned to flurries. Harry couldn't remember an after-Easter cold snap that included snow. A question he'd save for Al or Ms. Lilly. He felt numb, detached, stymied in a place where determination reigned. He gripped the steering wheel, almost afraid to let go. Something outside of himself seemed to demand he keep driving north in the direction of Al's camp. "Nothing is there anymore," he argued. Dale pulled the camper out and sold it after posting it to a Facebook garage sale site. The tents were stored in the rafters of the garage on Hartwood where Al was living now. The camp's provisions had been donated to the Food Bank. Al was threatening to burn the cabin to the ground. He had certainly picked a long way to go if he was looking for a new place to wallow in self-pity. *I should have gone with John*, echoed in his head. He picked up the cell phone laying on the seat and tried to call Al. Maybe he had heard from John, but the call went to voice mail.

"Damn!" he blurted out when he scarcely missed an object in the road. He had crossed the double yellow centerlines and almost hit it. "What was that?" he gasped. *A deer*, he thought, *a shadow? Are my eyes playing tricks on me?* He looked in the side mirror and thought he saw a dog walking alongside someone in a gray hoodie. He touched the brakes; the Tacoma spun around on the icy road. Blacktop, white and yellow lines, trees all whirled before his eyes in one big blur. *Turn into the spin,* a familiar voice shouted. *How many times do I have to tell ya?*

"Tommy?" Why was he hearing Mary Lynn's old boyfriend's voice in his head, the one that cheated on her? He was giving him driving instructions? Tommy died in a car wreck ten years ago drag racing in Baton Rouge. His voice was as clear as a bell. He turned the wheel into the slide as instructed, the truck slowed but not before spinning twice. It came to a stop in the gravel on the opposite side of the road facing south. He stumbled out, leaving the door open. The headlights glanced off the falling snow, hindering a clear view. He saw something that at first, he thought was just another fantasy, another false specter. Pink tennis shoes, ripped jeans, hair too long to be contained by the hoodie. The phone on the seat alerted and lit up *unknown caller,* but he was too far away from the truck by now to hear it. It fruitlessly rang again, this time displaying Dale's name on the screen.

Mary Lynn couldn't see the face of the man hobbling toward her. The headlights blacked out his features, but she knew who it was. She'd been praying he'd be the one to find her. The flurries started while she and James were saying their goodbyes in the woods, standing in the same place where her feet left ruts in the ground, where they departed over six months ago. It wasn't an outwardly emotional goodbye but she was sure the precipitation signified her half-brother's feelings.

Harry grabbed her up in his arms, almost toppling them over. Mutt was beside them, barking his hello while prancing and wagging his tail. "Tell me I'm not dreaming," he said, placing his hands on either side of her face to make sure it was her.

She shook her head. Her face was blushing and wet from tears and melting flurries. "No, you're not dreaming." They threw their arms around each other again and held each other close. Then they knelt down together next to Mutt and rubbed their hands through his hair. "He's a gift to Daddy from Kokabiel."

"And Christine?" he sighed, although glad she didn't return with Mary Lynn.

"Mother chose to stay in Bhutan with Kokabiel," she replied. "It's okay; I'm okay with it. She's trying to help the Nephilim rebuild and settle back into their Himalayan home."

"I was visiting with Ms. Lilly," Harry said. "She lives in Oakland Nursing Home now. The breaking news came over the TV in her room. So, it's true, the Nephilim have come out to the world. Who decided this . . . surely not Kokabiel?"

"Ms. Lilly?" she asked. She assumed her friend had gone home and was doing well. "Ms. Lilly's at Oakland? How long has she been there? I feel so bad. I haven't thought about her in so long."

"You're gonna want to sit down with her soon. She knew all about Kokabiel. I think she can fill in the missing gaps for you where your mother is concerned. One thing for sure, after today," he continued, "the Nephilim are going to be part of everyone's daily conversation, as well as their speculation. I can't help but think you had something to do with this."

"It was a bold and brave move my father made," she said, glancing around, thinking that from now on, flurries, sleet, or snow will be a permanent reminder of the people she left behind. "Many contracted a bacterial infection. They had to return to Bhutan. If this proves to be a safe decision, the rest might follow. Kokabiel is aware of how dangerous human nature can be; what humans don't understand they fear, try to control, or destroy if there is resistance. They're writing a new chapter for themselves."

"In their Bible. Yes, this will go down in everyone's history book. Hey, they'll be okay," he said, putting an arm around her when she turned up a flat palm to catch the unexpected snow. "We're getting soaked; let's get in the truck." Mutt staked his place next to Harry in the front seat. "Sorry buddy, you get to sit by the window. My girl sits next to me."

"There's something else I want to tell you that you won't be hearing about on the news."

"Is your mother okay? Kokabiel? James?"

"Yes, they're fine. For only the second time, the monks have allowed a female to live and study at one of their Dzongs."

"You being the first," Harry said, proudly caressing her shoulder.

"Her name is Alisha. She's James' daughter. Mother is living there too as a chaperone."

Harry raised his eyebrows. "Wow, tradition has really gone out the window."

"It's a start," she shrugged. "Only the 'daughters' will be allowed for now; the 'daughters' is what they call the orphan girls. Kokabiel has suspended the insemination project."

Harry nodded his approval. They gave each other a long look before he shifted into drive. He thought about Bassui and the burden he carried knowing the orphan boys were "of the gods" and the giants, who he was never allowed to talk about.

"Yes, their world is changing," she said, acknowledging his thoughts. "This is where I chose to be; this is what feels right to me, Harry." She rubbed his arm and then laid her head on his shoulder. "I prayed every day that you'd be okay, because the last time I saw you . . ."

"I know," he whispered and kissed her on the forehead. "I've been aware."

Dale left his phone on the desk next to the back door while helping Aria carry in groceries and fill the pantry. He didn't think about it while helping prepare dinner or playing three games of *Sorry* with the kids before putting them to bed.

He didn't see the trail cam motion detection notification on the top banner until 7:30. It was normal for the sensors to activate; creatures strolled by all six of the strategically placed cameras continuously every day, all day long. It became his routine to wait until the evening routine was over before checking the wildlife videos. It recorded to a hard drive set up in Al's living room that was connected to his TV. Dale drove up to the camp every month to replace the batteries. Al always refused to go with him. But after months of watching deer forage for acorns on the ground, squirrels scamper in and out of view, birds land and peck for bugs, and turkeys wander around in their normal meandering style across the lenses, he was determined to talk his dad into keeping the lease so they could go hunting together next fall. An error indicator displayed for Camera 1, the designated name for the first cam they set out, and the one Al always reminded him to check first. They mounted it to a tree and pointed it at the spot where investigators found the scrape marks on the ground and Mary Lynn's shoes; where the forensic team determined she had been abducted from. Al put the shoes in a plastic container, along with her favorite pair of ripped jeans and hoodie, wrapped a bungee cord around it and staked it to the ground between the impressions. Camera 1 recorded a flutter, then twenty seconds of pixelization before it returned to normal . . . well, almost normal. The house he and Aria rented was one block north and parallel to Hartwood. He cut through two yards, crossed the street, and knocked on the newly painted red door. When his father didn't answer, he went around back and found him sitting on a refurbished iron patio bench, staring into the stone fire pit of lumpy white and red coals.

"What's wrong?" Al asked when he looked up and saw the frown on his son's face. Dale took his phone from his back pocket and sat down beside him and then pulled up the video and handed it to him.

"It's gone!" he sneered. "No animal coulda dragged it off, not the way I had it staked." He thought for a second. "Poachers!"

"Maybe," Dale said, still frowning. "Except, the container was there and then there was that weird interruption and now it's gone. I'll show you." He sat down next to Al and backed the video up two minutes prior to the distortion.

"Same thing happened when the FBI bugged Harrison's apartment," Al said after they checked the hard drive and found the same decidedly edited video. "I put one of my traps in his freezer; it went missin' and the video was messed up just like this. I need to talk to the kid."

"He's not answering his phone."

"You've been trying to call him? Why?"

Dale pursed his lips, hesitating. "To ask him if he's heard . . . well," he paused.

"Come on, spit it out!" Al growled.

"Aria was watching the news in the bedroom while I was checking the cams. When was the last time you heard from your FBI friend?"

Al answered by shaking his head and asked, "What's on the news?"

"Where's your phone?"

"In the bedroom, I think. Somewhere, I don't know, I never use it anyway. What happened?"

Dale found Al's phone next to the coffee pot. "You missed a call from John." Dale made four failed attempts to return the calls while Al looked for the TV remote and finding between the cushions in the sofa. "The whole world must be calling Bhutan."

"What's happnin' in Bhutan?" Al asked and pointed the remote at the TV.

"Tell me something," Mary Lynn said to Harry when the Tacoma's headlights lit up the reflective *Alexandria City Limits* sign. The flurries had stopped. Mutt saw the sign, too, and turned his head as if reading it and then looked back at her. "Is there such a thing as driverless electric cars?"

"Prototypes maybe, but there's not likely to be any around here anytime soon. Louisiana is always last on the list. Most think us coonasses incapable of understandin' such technology," he said, with a conspicuous southern accent. Her smile came quickly, which was what he was after. "What made you think about driverless cars?"

"Is Red's still . . . Red's?" she asked quickly.

"Sure. But Sammy's . . . retiring," he said slowly, suspecting there was a reason for the query since she was holding her breath waiting for the answer. "He told me he sold the restaurant to a couple but they're supposed to keep everything just as it is, even the menu."

"What about RRMC, does it still look the same? Has it been remodeled? Does it have the same lighted red letters?"

"Well, yes . . . but there's talk about adding a new ER across the front on the west side. Why are you asking these specific questions?"

"Because I think I saw the future."

"Is that something you can do . . . see the future?"

"It happened the night I was taken, long before my enlightenment. I thought I was dreaming. I think I was being given a glimpse into my future. After being grabbed in the woods on my way to Daddy's camp, I woke up on the ground; it was just starting to snow, like tonight. I made my way to the road; a girl stopped and gave me a ride into town." She looked up at him smiling slightly. "You're taking me to the house on Hartwood, right? I saw it too."

Harry nodded.

"It was full of people, full of life, like it used to be before mother . . ." She looked at him and took in a breath . . . "disappeared, and life got so complicated. A very tall cab driver drove me there. James told me later that it was him that allowed me to see these things."

He smiled at her. "So, guess what?" he nodded. "The part about Hartwood has already come true. Dale and his family moved back home. Hand me my phone; they'll want to be at the house when we get there."

"Wouldn't it be fun to surprise them?"

It was good to hear the playfulness in Mary Lynn's voice again and the gleam of mischief in her eyes.

"As long as it doesn't give Daddy a heart attack." She retrieved the phone on the seat and handed it to him.

"Look, three missed calls from Dale, and two unknowns, probably John," Harry said, after pressing *recent calls.* "They're all hoping the same thing as me after seeing the story about the Nephilim on the news." He looked up from the phone. Harry could tell there was something else on her mind. Another reason why she wasn't ready to go home.

"You're right, there is something else," she said. "I had Diana, the girl that picked me up, drop me off at RRMC. It looked very different and Red's was a Pizza Hut. Harry, I'm absolutely sure this girl's going to be a part of our lives someday." She took his hand. "She had red hair and blue eyes and was very tall. She was majoring in mathematics at ULM."

"Wow, our daughter's going to be a genius." He smiled at her as he turned onto North Third Street and pulled up in front of RRMC. The hospital's bold red lettering was still there, and Red's looked the same. He put an arm around her shoulders and pulled her in close. Mutt stretched out filling the vacant part of the seat and lay his head against her leg. "We're gonna watch the changes you saw together. It must have been hard, leaving your mother and James and your father." She picked up his hand and then kissed it. "You know, it's kind of strange, but since I woke up in the med tent at Yangphula, I keep getting these weird thoughts. It's like, sometimes I know what's going to happen before it does."

"I was there when you were brought to the monks," she sighed, "I spent hours praying for you. Not only for your broken body to heal, but that you'd wake up with a better understanding of what I'm about, what the Nephilim are about." She reached up and placed her hands on each side of his head, just as she did when he was laying on the blue pallet in front of the statue of Buddha. "I feared my prayers weren't good enough because they weren't enough to cure the bacterial infection. I was so disappointed," she said and turned away as if not wanting him to see her sadness. "The Nephilim worked so hard to prepare the place in the upmost northern region of Russia that was supposed to save them and they couldn't even tolerate the water. They wouldn't have survived. They had to leave or die."

Harry tickled the side of her cheek with his fingers and then turned her face toward his. "Hey, the monks will protect them, as well as the King."

"I know it's hard to imagine," she said, wiping her eyes, "but my mother and Kokabiel have a strong relationship. I actually got a kick out of watching them argue. It wasn't at all like the arguments she and Daddy had. You remember them; they were desperate arguments with sounds of futility in their voices. With Kokabiel, I could hear the respect they have for each other. He's got a real soft spot when it comes to her," she said, smiling. "I'm glad I was able to witness it. I might have never understood what was missing in our house. She reached over and stroked Mutt on the top of his head. Mutt reciprocated by raising his head and licking her wrist.

"I want to make another stop before taking you home." Harry straightened in the seat and started the engine. "You're gonna like it, I promise."

When Harry parked the Tacoma in front of the house on Hartwood, there was an additional passenger in the back seat with Mutt.

"It's just how it looked in my dream," Mary Lynn sighed. "All the lights on and full of life. The yard landscaped; the door repainted." She turned to look at the passenger sitting behind Harry. "Did you ever think you'd see the house look like this again, Ms. Lilly?"

"No, honey . . . not ever." Lilly leaned forward and patted the back of Mary Lynn's seat. "What are you waiting for, let's go inside. I can't wait to see the look on Al's face when he sees the both of us," she giggled. Harry opened the back door and held out his hand. Mary Lynn hurried around the truck to help, but Lilly was already halfway up the walk with Harry and Mutt on either side of her, and much stronger than the frail woman that could barely hold herself upright twenty minutes earlier. Mary Lynn smiled, grateful to her God for not limiting her with Ms. Lilly tonight. But it suddenly occurred to her, that perhaps God had purposely constrained her, limited her healing ability in order to give Kokabiel time to think. Time to realize what had to be done. By revealing themselves to the world, it was no longer necessary to hide. They could live openly and free. They could grow their crops in the lush valleys where sunlight was plentiful and clean rivers flow freely. Orphans would be a thing of the past. She looked down at the brilliant brick and white concrete porch as Harry reached for the bronze door handle with Lilly standing beside him, her arm wrapped around his and Mutt prancing with anticipation. Memories of playing with dolls on the porch flooded back when she saw the rebuilt trellis and the small pink-flowered vines on their way, climbing to the top. It had been a good place to escape while learning how to live in a world of colors. Very soon, it would be a place to meditate; perhaps even pray with her daddy. Harry opened the door when there was no answer. Mutt leaped inside ahead of them. Music resonated from Dale's old bedroom; roux emanated from the kitchen. Al was standing inside the open back door, his hand still on the doorknob. Smoke from a crackling fire in the yard trickled in with him. Dale was standing behind a newly built island in the kitchen; Aria was in front of the stove holding a large wooden spoon. They looked frozen in time while watching her rush past them headed to her father's open arms. The kids came running out of the bedroom when they heard the uproar. Everyone talked at once, asking questions.

Harry didn't feel the phone in his hip pocket vibrate, notifying him of yet another call from the *unknown caller*.

Chapter 25

Karma stood in the shade under the roof of the porch John added onto her modest hut. Her arms were folded; her head and face covered except for her eyes that searched every face in the busy market that was as crowded as a national holiday. Prayer flags were draped from every building, even crossing the streets. Prayer wheels whirled in every window. Other flags with designs of sacred animals were displayed everywhere. Windows and doorways were retouched to their original brilliant colors. John had gone to the square where the boys played soccer. The prominent men in the village had gathered there to listen to a foreign journalist interviewing a man from a village five miles west of the Dzong. The reporter pressed the unnerved man dressed in a long red and orange shirt, covered with a green gho. He used all the trickery of a seasoned correspondent, rewording his queries in order to ask the same questions in reverse; like John would have done in an interrogation when determined to make someone slip up and tell him what he wanted to hear. Network trucks and vans had been scurrying around the narrow streets since King Wangluck's message to the world. Bidhan the butcher and other merchants in Mondar were forced to lay out traffic restrictions to keep their markets navigable to the walking patrons. Interviews were to be held in the village square only. Bassui and the rest of the boys from the village were spending the week at the monastery to shelter them from the frenzy. The King had recently provided every schoolgirl with home-schooling materials.

"What did the man from Saram have to say?" Karma anxiously asked John when he stepped onto the porch.

"Nothing," John replied. "He doesn't know anything."
John Greenfield had taken on the look of the locals that

included a mix of long bright and dark colored layered shirts and baggy pants, as well as a knit hat that men were covering with a wool scarf these days. He was also sporting a full beard.

"Or he is merely protecting his gods," she sighed from behind her orange rachu. She was sporting a more colorful look herself since John surprised her, standing in the market three weeks ago in full Bhutanese attire. "It is only fair that we do this for them since they protected us for as long as anyone can remember."

"Well, in any case, he was very convincing. The reporter looked very disappointed. Bidhan said the Royal Army has officially confined the media to the outskirts of every village and has forbidden them to detain traffic."

"Let's sit out here for a bit. I have five girls today; they are taking a test and still have five more minutes." They smiled at each other when they heard the wooden bench squeak when they sat down. They both knew John would be tightening the braces soon. She found him to be quite the handyman. "You've been a welcome addition in Mondar."

"I'm thinking about becoming a citizen," he said with an eager smile. "It would make it easier for us to get married, you know."

"I'm afraid there's more to it than that, former Agent Greenfield. Even though I am adopted, my adoptive parents will still have a say-so as to whether or not there will be a marriage. And there are many religious rituals that must be performed by the lamas."

"Well, at least intercultural or interethnic relationships aren't forbidden anymore," he said. "One of the benefits of modern times."

"Have you been able to reach your friend Harry?"

"Not yet," he sighed. "The satellite trucks must be interfering with the signal."

"It's time to check on the girls," she said. "Until ten years ago, when our young King was abdicated, girls were never

340

treated with such equality. Our young King and his royal
family are determined to revolutionize our country."
"And wise enough to respect its traditions."
"Thank the gods."

***

Sgt. Prestridge was in a deep sleep, leaned back
comfortably in a contoured flexible armchair with his mouth
gaped open. An incredible rattling came from the back of his
throat with every breath. Two feet from the thick rubber heels
of his black military boots that were propped on the desk in
the guard shed, was a sixty-inch monitor displaying images of
various points within the camp. It was naptime according to
his circadian clock. Four a.m. was the perfect time to sneak
one in. Who would be rambling around the camp at this hour
other than deer, a family of raccoons, or a few armadillos?

The celebration at the Bennett house quieted after Dale
and Aria took the kids home and Al, with Mutt at his heels,
called it a night. "Where are we going?" Mary Lynn asked
Harry when he turned right when leaving Oakland's parking
lot after returning Ms. Lilly to her room. They tucked her in
and prayed while holding hands until she fell asleep.

"Where are we going?" Harry repeated with a
mischievous grin. "It's a surprise."

Sgt. Prestridge didn't see Harry waving his arms at the
camera lens outside the gate and calling his name or Mary
Lynn standing beside him. It wasn't until he started choking
on his tongue that he awoke and saw the small red light
blinking on two screens, indicating the Gate and Rifle Range
Rd. cams had recorded something.

"Jesus Christ!" he grumbled after viewing the replay of
the Gate Cam. He watched the couple walk back to the truck,
Harry returned with a bolt cutter and then drove his Tacoma
through the gate. The Rifle Rage Rd. cam caught three
seconds of the truck as it passed. The sergeant stomped out of

the security office and jerked open the door to the Range Rover parked outside. "I've been far too easy on that kid," he thought as he turned the key. "Now he's brought a girl in here with him. I'm putting an end to this, right now!"

"Okay," Mary Lynn said playfully, "fold your legs like this. No silly, tuck your feet under a little," she laughed. They were sitting, facing one another on the ground on what Harry called his "blanket of memories."

"This isn't very relaxing," he complained. "My calf muscles are cramping. I thought meditation was supposed to be calming, peaceful."

"It is, once you focus. Now put your shoulders back and rest your hands on your knees."

Mary Lynn couldn't believe he'd found their old party spot. The army had torn up nearly all the streets back then to keep people from driving around the abandoned army post except for this one. It led to a deteriorated swimming pool that people used for target practice and sighting-in their guns.

"Palms up or down?"

"Doesn't matter, however you're most comfortable." She had already assumed the meditation position; her eyes were closed.

"Your fingers are up. I'll put mine up," Harry whispered.

"Close your eyes, take a deep breath in, hold it five seconds, and then let it out very slowly."

"This actually does feel . . ." It felt as if he had taken a breath of the purest air. The rejuvenating kind that makes you light and refreshed.

"Now, listen: "Om Mani Padme Hum." She repeated the chant three times.

"What does it mean?"

"Hail to the jewel of the lotus. This mantra calms fears, soothes concerns, and heals broken hearts. I know another one that's specifically for success. It also helps eliminate problems and suffering. It's called the Medicine Buddha Mantra."

"Yes, I want to do that one."

Sgt. Prestridge slowly rolled to a stop on the right-hand side of the road next to Harry's Tacoma that was in the grass pointed down the slope of the ditch. He got out, leaving the door open and the headlights on; a fair warning to someone hiding in the woods that they were about to be caught. The MP only intended to give them a good scare, to make them think twice about coming back again after hours. He never gave his gun belt a thought and left it on the hook in the guard shack. Harry didn't seem to be the dangerous type, just a heartbroken kid. He crept through the sporadic sprouts of spring grass breaking through the damp decomposing pin oak leaves. The moon projected a large yellow backdrop for the tall pines and oaks. He caught sight of the couple through the thicket. They were about twenty feet away and facing each other, staring into one another's eyes as if they were under some hypnotic spell. She was singing something in a low voice. He inched closer, then saw something unbelievable. He squeezed his eyelids closed and opened them again. They were elevated two feet above the blanket, as if sitting on something invisible. "What the hell?" he mumbled. His mind tried to reason they were sitting on hover-boards, even though he'd never seen one that far off the ground. He heard a noise in the brush to his right that sounded like a branch breaking under someone's foot. The moonlight caught something very large moving between the trees . . . toward him. He put his hand to his hip; there was no gun. He took a step backward, intending to run to his vehicle where he had left his phone. The sergeant only managed to take one short step before being whisked away. When his relief reported for the 7 a.m. shift, he found him asleep in the back seat of the Range Rover. Prestridge had no memory of how he got there or why. Every breaker in the guard shack's electrical panel had been thrown because of an apparent power surge, but not before frying the security system's digital video recorder.

Harry and Mary Lynn passed through the gate, making sure to wrap the chain around it and the steel frame to give it the appearance of being locked, as they did after Harry cut the chain to get in. It would be discovered, of course, and perhaps someone from Camp Beauregard would investigate. As they continued down Camp Livingston Rd. toward the highway that would eventually take them to Harry's apartment, they both knew their actions would be resolved without incident.

Harry had experienced some remarkable things on his journey to find Mary Lynn. Tonight's was indescribable. The word tranquility didn't come close to how the ten-minute meditation felt, when time and gravity didn't exist. He fully appreciated Kokabiel's concerns. Great responsibly comes with such abilities; and many of them could be misunderstood. Could he protect her the way Christine assured Kokabiel he could? He was lying next to her now, watching her sleep. She breathed in and breathed out slowly, rhythmically, like when she meditated. They had made love as soon as they got home. She was everything he ever wanted in this world.

He went to the kitchen for a glass of water. The white refrigerator stood out in the dark because of a dusk-to-dawn light shining through the window over the sink. He thought about the ice cream that was tossed on the floor by Greenfield's men. Blue Bell, Pecan Pralines 'n Cream, Mary Lynn's favorite. As he felt the cool water refresh his dry throat, he thought about how difficult the Nephilim gene was going to make their journey together. She was born to make a difference in this world; the challenge would be keeping it subtle. They were going to have a daughter. He saw Diana, imagined her, the moment Mary Lynn spoke her name. It was the same when she told him about her niece Alisha, who he knew would join them sometime in the future. There would be up-hill battles, trials, and hardships ahead, but it would be balanced with laughter and joy. Not an easy life, but certainly a rewarding one.

Mary Lynn opened her eyes when he slipped back into bed. She smiled and reached out to him. "I can't wait for all of those things to happen," she whispered, as if she knew exactly what he'd been thinking.

He leaned in and kissed her. "Me too."

"Do you suppose that twenty-hour Walmart we passed on the way here has Blue Bell, Pecan Pralines 'n Cream?" she sighed playfully. "Something's got me craving a big old bowl."

THE END

Made in the USA
Middletown, DE
19 July 2020